THE
STONE FLOWER

Novels by
Alan Scholefield

A VIEW OF VULTURES
GREAT ELEPHANT
THE EAGLES OF MALICE
WILD DOG RUNNING
THE YOUNG MASTERS
THE HAMMER OF GOD
LION IN THE EVENING
THE ALPHA RAID
VENOM
POINT OF HONOUR
BERLIN BLIND
THE STONE FLOWER

History
THE DARK KINGDOMS

THE
STONE FLOWER

Alan Scholefield

WILLIAM MORROW AND COMPANY, INC.

New York 1982

Library of Congress Cataloging in Publication Data

Scholefield, Alan.
   The stone flower.

   I. Title.
PR9369.3.S3S8   1982   823   81-22397
ISBN 0-688-00981-6   AACR2

Printed in the United States of America

First Edition

1 2 3 4 5 6 7 8 9 10

BOOK DESIGN BY MICHAEL MAUCERI

For John and Thelma Bloch

PROLOGUE

On 12 February, 1578, the Portuguese galleon *Nossa Senhora da Coimbra* was helplessly adrift off the southwestern coast of Africa. She had left Goa three months before with rotten sails and a defective rudder—"at the mercy of God to save four crusadoes," as the saying was among the sailors. Off the Cape of Good Hope she had been struck by a southeasterly gale and had run before it. The rudder lost three pintles and was swept away. A new rudder was made and with this she limped up the coast for seventeen days, until another gale smashed it to pieces and ripped out her foremast. In heavy seas and thick fog she was set remorselessly towards the shore.

The littoral of southern Africa at this point is a strange and ghostly place: a cold desert, beset by dank fog and icy seas. Great white dunes and massive black rocks give way to harsh scrub desert and it is only after one has penetrated fifty miles into the interior that the fog dissipates and the heat is felt.

Nossa Senhora da Coimbra was a vessel of one hundred and eighty tons carrying a cargo of silks, cloth of gold, spices, carpets from Cambay and Odiaz and mats from the Maldives; also ambergris, tortoiseshell, mother-of-pearl, coral, diamonds from Golconda, and pearls from Ceylon as well as caskets inlaid with ivory and filled with incense. Her passengers, all Portuguese who had embarked at Cochin and Goa, numbered with her crew one hundred and fifty-three. There were also one hundred and ninety-four black slaves, making a total of three hundred and forty-seven souls in all. Her captain was a tough seaman born in Sagres in Southern Portugal who had been brought up on stories of Prince Henry the Navigator. His name was Manuel da Sa and as a youth he had often sailed in the rough seas off Cape St. Vincent. He had made the voyage between Lisbon and India twice before, yet even he was frightened as he had never been.

Had there only been some letup in the wind or the fog, or both, something might have been done to help the ship, but when the wind slackened the fog increased, and when the fog lifted the wind blew a gale.

At one point when the wind had lessened and the fog had returned, most of the passengers were either below or kneeling on the afterdeck where they were being led in prayers by a Dominican monk. The crew, as well as many of the black slaves, strained their eyes into the fogbanks, trying to penetrate the gray walls. Manuel da Sa had had little rest for more than three weeks but he also stared into the fog. His tired eyes saw visions of angels in a golden light and he knew that he was going to die.

At noon one of the sailors reported hearing surf. An attempt was made to veer the ship, but without a rudder and a foremast this proved impossible, so instead the ship's boat was made ready. At 1:22 P.M. the vessel struck a reef of low black rocks and began to make water. Soon afterwards the pumps broke down, choked with pepper from the holds.

The Dominican monk, Father John of the Rosary, wrote an account of what happened next and this forms what has become known as *The Chronicle of the Wreck of Nossa Senhora da Coimbra*, one of several chronicles which exist telling of wrecks on the African coast such as those of the *São Thome*, the *São João*, *Nossa Senhora da Belem* and the *Santo Alberto*.

"Within the ship nothing was heard but sighs, groans, wailing, moans and prayers to God for mercy," wrote Father John. "In

the 'tween decks it seemed as if all the evil spirits were busy, so great a noise was made by the things that were floating about, striking each other and washing from side to side in such a way that those who went below fancied they beheld the likeness of the Last Judgment."

The ship's boat was launched and a hundred and four people, including sailors, scrambled into it. The number was such that there was almost no freeboard. One of the survivors in the boat was a woman, Leonor de Mendoca, a widow on her way home who had already lost her two-year-old daughter in the rough seas. She was hysterical and could not be made to sit, but stood up, screaming and tearing her clothes until she threatened the lives of the others. A sailor caught her by the hair and threw her into the sea.

As the ship's boat made for the shore the cries of those on the doomed galleon and of those drowning in the swell were pitiful to hear, but when anyone tried to clamber aboard, the sailors smashed their fingers and pushed them away with oars. One man, Bernardhim de Carvalho, formerly captain of His Majesty's Dockyard in Goa, offered ten thousand crusadoes for a place in the boat. His offer was accepted by the sailors and he was hauled aboard. He was very fat and should have floated but he wore a magnificent brocade coat patterned with gold and silver thread and decorated with glass buttons, which had become waterlogged and threatened to pull him under. Once he was in the boat two black slaves were thrown into the sea to make the weight equal to what it had been.

The sailor in charge was named Bartolomeu Barreto and he had been born and bred like a rat in the Tagus docks. He was a heavy man with a knife scar running down one side of his head. It was he who had thrown the woman and the slaves into the sea. He stood at the steering oar as the boat moved into the Atlantic surf. The waves were curling and booming and the fog made the task even more hazardous. But Barreto had seawater in his veins and he held hard and called the stroke to the oarsmen. They came in on the back of a wave, slid forward before it broke and sped down the hill of green water ahead of the creaming foam. Women screamed and men prayed but Barreto held on and soon the impetus slackened and the boat was carried onto a shore of clean white sand.

Of the original three hundred and forty-seven passengers and

crew, one hundred and thirty-eight survived the wreck. Of these, twenty were to die of their injuries within a day or two. The water was stained red with blood and of the bodies that were washed ashore some had been smashed against the rocks so badly that they were no longer recognizable; others reached the beach with their injuries. One man, a factor from Cochin, had splintered his right leg and marrow dripped onto the sand. He died soon afterwards.

Late in the day a westering sun burned away the fog and the survivors could see where they were. It was a bleak prospect. A steep white beach broken by tongues and outcrops of black rock stretched away on either side as far as the eye could see. The ship, her masts, sails and rigging hanging over her sides, made a melancholy picture. Waves battered her and her planking snapped with the sound of pistol shots.

The survivors held a service of thanksgiving on the beach and a crucifix was tied to a lance which was pushed into the sand; the sight of it calmed many people. Father John led them in prayer and when the service was over the fit collected what had washed ashore from the wreck. Soon a little village grew on the beach of tents made from carpets and mats and silk hangings and cloth of gold.

A strong current which ran parallel with the beach had swept many people southwards. Most perished but some survived and these came into the camp in ones and twos during the next few days.

The captain had not been seen since the ship had run on the rocks and in his absence and in the absence of any other officer, leadership had been assumed by Barreto, who had a following among the sailors. With great skill and courage he took the ship's boat back to the wreck before she broke up completely and brought to the beach some casks of flour and pickled beef. He and a dozen seamen made four visits to *Nossa Senhora da Coimbra* before she was finally smashed to pieces. Each time they landed on the beach the survivors cheered. Barreto placed two sailors with muskets to guard the stores. They found a spring of sweet water and this, too, was guarded. It was only then that the survivors learned that the food and water were not to be rationed among them but were for sale only. A cup of water cost ten crusadoes, a kettle holding six quarts a hundred, half a pound of meat fifteen, a mug of flour ten. A dead shark was washed ashore

on the third day and Barreto and his men cut it up and sold slices two inches thick for fifteen crusadoes each. Half its head fetched twenty thousand reis. The whole shark brought in as much as a good farm cost in Portugal.

Some of the survivors had been wealthy merchants in Cochin and Goa and had brought with them their money and jewels in body belts and so were able to pay these prices; others had lost everything in the wreck and would have died of thirst had they not received water from those more fortunate. For food they scavenged along the beach, cutting black mussels from the rocks. Once they saw a pile of empty shells in a small rock cave and Father John said that bears had feasted there. But there are no bears in Africa. What they had seen were signs of other human beings, a small group of Strandlooper ("Beach Walker") Hottentots who had wandered along this shore eight years before on a journey southwards.

On the afternoon of the eighth day the captain walked into the camp. He had been washed down the coast in the strong current and was on the point of drowning when a wave cast him ashore. He lay at the tide line for a day before regaining consciousness and was so disoriented that he wandered south along the beach instead of north. But by doing so he came upon the mouth of a river. He walked inland for a time surveying the country and then set off to search for other survivors.

It did not take him long to discover how things were with Barreto and the dozen surviving sailors. Manuel da Sa was a short, tough man with bandy legs and a strong wiry body and was afraid of no one. But one does not become captain of a galleon without brains and he knew that the passengers, who might support him, would be no match for armed sailors, so he bided his time until he could speak quietly with Barreto and ask what he planned. The sailor had no plans. He was, for the first time in his life, wealthy beyond dreaming. He could not think further than that. Having heard him out, the captain asked Father John to hold a service and when prayers were over he addressed the survivors.

He told them that on the east coast of Africa, the opposite side from where they were now, there was the Portuguese settlement of Lourenço Marques and if they crossed Africa almost due east they would come to it. He thought the distance was less than two thousand leagues. He went on to say that ships called occasionally

at Lourenço Marques but that here on the west coast nothing was ever seen of a vessel unless it was a wreck like theirs.

Barreto and the sailors stood to one side, listening. Then Barreto said, "How would we get there?"

"Walk."

"Two thousand leagues?"

"It can be done." He told them of other wrecks, the *São João* and the *São Bento,* which had foundered on the east coast of Africa and whose survivors had walked to safety. He did not tell them how few had reached their destination.

Those who were strong enough to contemplate so great a journey cheered the captain but Barreto looked on with hostility. There was still a great deal of money and jewels to be won from them and he was content where he was.

But the mood was against him. Anything was better than dying on this bleak and foggy beach.

"What about water?" Barreto said. "I have been inland. It is nothing but desert."

The captain told them of the river which flowed east-west.

On 22 February, 1578, the survivors began the long journey, leaving behind only an elderly man with a broken leg who had no money and a black slave boy whose right foot had been smashed. All the women could pay and were carried in litters made from planking which had been washed ashore; the former captain of Goa dockyard, Bernardhim de Carvalho, had bought the help of four men for twenty thousand crusadoes. They had made a hammock out of the ship's rigging and fastened it to four carrying poles, in which he lay back in his glass-buttoned coat and closed his eyes. The river along which they made their way is now called the Orange. It winds into the heart of southern Africa. Then, no one had named it, but to the few bands of wandering Hottentots and Bushmen it was known as the G'riep. It flows through some of the most hostile terrain in the world: gorges of great rocks, burning hot to the touch, are followed by mile upon mile of stony, desiccated country where the scorpion and the snake are king. The heat is immense and February is often the worst month, with temperatures reaching 112 degrees during the day and dropping only to the middle 90's at night.

In the sixteenth century it was empty land, still to wake from its long sleep. Although Portuguese navigators had rounded the Cape of Good Hope a hundred years before in their search for

India, they had not colonized it. The Dutch, who would, were not due for more than sixty years. Little bands of Bushmen and Hottentots, the original people of the country, occasionally wandered through it but their permanent homes were hundreds of miles to the south and they had yet to be driven north by invading colonists. The black Bantu were a thousand miles away.

Progress was slow. In the first month the party covered less than a hundred miles and lost more than half its number. People died of a variety of causes, some in accidents on the steep sides of gorges, some of heatstroke, some of sunstroke, some of scurvy, some of the bloody flux and some of starvation. Many died of simple misery. Because some were stronger than others and traveled more quickly the party soon strung out over a distance of more than three miles. At its head walked Father John, holding the crucifix on its lance. Those at the back dropped farther and farther behind until at last they gave up and were seen no more.

The blinding heat affected the women in their heavy dresses. There were fifteen of them. As their money ran out or their husbands died they were forced to walk. It was thought that they would die almost immediately. But they stripped themselves to their shifts and made padded foot coverings from their dresses and kept up as strongly as the men. Six weeks from the coast, Dom Bernardhim de Carvalho, who had weighed more than three hundred pounds at the time of the wreck but who now weighed considerably less, was asked for more money by the men who were carrying him.

"We agreed on the price," he said, wiping the sweat from his face, where it immediately re-formed.

"You are too heavy," one said.

"I grow lighter."

"We grow weaker. Give me your coat."

"Nothing more."

They left him. He did not beg but sat in the heat of the sun as they trailed past him. "Good-bye. Go with God," he said to each of them. That night Barreto was missing. When he returned to the campfire Dom Manuel saw he was wearing the brocade coat with the glass buttons.

Each day someone died; most now of starvation or scurvy or both. Their main diet was yellow-fish and barbel which they caught in the river, but Barreto had made this his monopoly and

he sold his catch to the highest bidder. Others looked for snakes or berries or roots. Sometimes they found melons and wild onions and once they found the half-eaten body of a baboon. All along their road they had company. It was possible to estimate where the rear of the column was by the circling vultures. Leopards had been wary at first, coming only to dead bodies, but later as they grew bolder they began to kill off the stragglers. By the end of the winter all the women were dead and only a handful of the strongest men survived. Even the sailors who had had the pick of the food were diminished in number because of disease. Of those now remaining the strongest were Dom Manuel da Sa, Bartolomeu Barreto and Father John of the Rosary, who still carried the crucifix high on the lance and kept his Bible in its leather pouch slung over his shoulder. He had not been parted from either since they left the beach.

"What do you write?" Barreto had asked him one evening soon after they had begun the march.

"Our chronicle," he had replied. He was a tall man with sunken cheeks and burning eyes and a brown habit, stained and torn from the journey, which reached down to thin but unyielding calves. The Bible and the crucifix were the only things he had saved from the sea. The Bible had been wrapped first in oiled cloth and then buttoned into the leather satchel, so seawater had been unable to get into it, and he wrote his chronicle on the blank top and bottom of each page, using a mixture of wood ash and water as his ink and the wing feather of an osprey for his pen.

"Everything?" Barreto asked, drawing the brocade coat around him against the cold.

"Everything."

The monk and the captain had become friends during the past months, each finding in the other a different strength. They watched Barreto as he turned away. He carried his money in leather body belts which, even in the hottest weather, he had never taken off.

"Be careful, Father," Dom Manuel said to the monk. "He is dangerous."

"So are the leopards and the snakes. We must put our trust in God."

Winter was over and the first burning-hot days of spring had come. No rain had fallen in the desert for nearly a year. Occasionally the sky would darken but instead of rain, wind-

storms would come, blowing dust in great eddies. Now only three survivors followed the almost dry river: Father John, Dom Manuel and Barreto.

One day Father John picked up a shiny stone in the riverbed, about the size of a child's fist and roughly oblong in shape. It appeared to be some kind of quartz or dull glass. He showed it to Dom Manuel.

"God has been kind to you," the captain said, holding the stone in his trembling hand. "I have seen such stones in India straight from the mine but never a tenth of this size. This is a diamond, father, but such a diamond!"

Barreto moved closer to hear.

"What will you do with it, father?" Dom Manuel asked.

"What should I do? It is only a stone. It is man's vanity that makes such things wanted."

"Father, it is worth millions! I know the trade."

Father John thought for a while and then said, "I shall build a shrine to Our Lady if what you say is true."

Father John and Dom Manuel shared a cooking fire at night but Barreto kept to his own about forty paces away. It was a strange interdependence. He did not wish to be one with them but could not strike out on his own. He would sit at his fire staring at them through the darkness as the monk used the firelight to write in his Bible. Sometimes when Dom Manuel or Father John woke in the night they would see him hunched over the embers, his face turned towards them.

Food became more difficult to obtain. In their weakened state the trapping of fish was almost too much for them. Instead they would look for snakes or frogs or eggs. All were suffering from scurvy. Their teeth had loosened and their gums were purple.

Late one afternoon Dom Manuel returned from a foraging expedition. In his absence Father John had collected wood and built a fire. They shared the tasks though Dom Manuel did the harder work to make up for the effort which the monk put into his chronicle. It had become a vital document for both men but especially for Dom Manuel, who wished to see Barreto hanged.

That afternoon Dom Manuel had found three duck's eggs. They would bury them in the sand, rake the embers over them and cook them in their shells. As he came along the riverbed in the dusk he saw Father John kneeling at prayer before the upright lance. But the crucifix was missing. The captain hurried.

The monk had been killed at his prayers. He had been stabbed in the back and his head had fallen forwards against the shaft of the lance so that he had remained in a kneeling position.

Before animals could mutilate the body Dom Manuel buried it in the sandy bed of the river and covered it with stones. He took the lance, for he had no other weapon, moved half a league away and kept watch all night.

In the morning he found Barreto's footprints in the sand and began to follow them. One thing only remained in his mind: to kill Barreto and somehow save the chronicle; it was all there was to show that more than three hundred people had come to this country and died. Of the diamond he thought very little; he was too far gone for fantasies of wealth. All that day and all the next he followed the footprints. Because of the drought there was more sand in the riverbed than water.

Barreto moved heavily, each step an effort. He knew that Dom Manuel was following him and for the first time in his life he was afraid. He had killed Father John on impulse because of the diamond—the chronicle had no meaning for him since he could not read or write and therefore valued words as nothing. He had taken the crucifix and flung it into the deepest pool of the river. Then he had become afraid and was unable to destroy the Bible because he was conscious of having attacked what was God's. He carried the book with him and it weighed him down. He was wearied as well by the weight of all his belts of money, the heavy coat, the cutlass, the musket and the pistol. The diamond also helped to weigh him down. He had put it in his pocket and there forgotten it. He did not recognize his own weariness for his thoughts were on the man who was following him.

If he could kill the captain he could make a plan. He would not go to Lourenço Marques. He had heard sailors' tales of black kingdoms where, if one had riches, one could live like a king oneself with a dozen black wives and herds of cattle.

He decided to circle back and come into the river behind Dom Manuel: the hunter would be the hunted.

He moved away from the river into a landscape broken by low hills and black rocks. The heat was terrible. He lay up during the day on the far side of a hill, thinking to reenter the riverbed by night. But in the afternoon the sky turned gray and a violent wind began to blow clouds of sand. He could not see ten paces ahead of him. He returned to his hiding place among the black

rocks and waited for the sandstorm to blow over. But in the morning it raged as fiercely as ever. He had made a water sack from the intestine of an antelope whose newly killed carcass he had found some weeks before, but there was not much left in it. He decided he would have to go back to the river.

He pushed out into the wind, the brocade coat flapping like a sail, the sand lashing his face and eyes. He had to use his hands to save them. The sand grains swarmed about him like gnats, driving him mad. He whirled this way and that but there was no escape. He flung down the musket, covered his face and staggered on towards the river. But soon he came to the slope of another hill and knew this could not be the way. He turned, looking through the chinks he made in his fingers. Black rocks loomed up, so did bushes and trees, but he could not see the outline of the hill he had left. He wandered on and soon he was lost. He would have to stop and take shelter and try again later. Perhaps the wind would die at evening and he could reach water.

He plowed on, looking for an outcrop of rock, picking his way between camel thorn trees that were lashing their branches in the wind. On the edge of his vision something moved laterally, in a solid sideways movement, upright, a rock moving in the driven sand. Suddenly he was face to face with Dom Manuel.

The captain had followed his tracks out of the riverbed and into the broken hills. But then he, too, had been overwhelmed by the storm. Now, with a cry that sounded above the roaring of the wind, he raised the lance and ran forwards. Barreto had no time to draw his pistol and prime it. He grabbed for his cutlass but the coat flapped and covered the handle and by the time he had grasped it Dom Manuel was upon him and the lance had gone through his shoulder. He swung the cutlass at Dom Manuel's neck, severing the great artery, and the captain fell, spouting blood like a sow.

Barreto pulled the lance from his shoulder and tried to staunch the wound, but the blood dripped down steadily. The captain was dead; Barreto was alive but he would only stay alive if he reached the river. He caught up the lance and plunged into the driving wall of sand.

He never knew how far he walked. That day passed and then a night and half of the following day and still he went on. The wind had dropped, the sand was still, the only thing that moved in the burning landscape was Barreto himself.

He staggered, stopping sometimes to lean on the lance. The wound had become poisoned and the poison was affecting his mind. He thought he was being followed, but when he turned there was no one. Later, as coherent thought died, he began to have hallucinations. Figures loomed towards him, becoming bigger and bigger until they grew up into the heavens and disappeared. They were the figures of Dom Manuel and Father John of the Rosary. He stumbled on muttering and shouting to himself. He aimed his pistol towards the figures and fired. He dropped the gun and went on. Later he flung his lance at Father John, only to see it strike a black rock. He left it. Then, in his madness, he flung away his body belts. He clung only to the Bible, as though his life depended on it.

Above him a pair of white-backed vultures slowly circled, waiting for him to die. Behind him came a leopard waiting for him to grow weak enough to kill. Behind the leopard came a silver-backed jackal and behind the jackal a pair of bat-eared foxes.

Barreto's great strength gave way. He stumbled and fell, pulling himself up, went on, fell again. He came to a mudhole containing water. He slithered forwards into the mud to drink and the leopard attacked. He saw it only as a shadow. He rose on his knees. It sprang from his left side, knocking him into the mud. It stood for a moment watching him. In one last desperate act his fingers closed on Father John's diamond and he threw it at the leopard's face. The leopard jerked away and the stone fell into the mud. Then the animal came at him again and disemboweled him, ripping away his clothing to get at his flesh.

When it had eaten its fill it drank and moved off. The jackal and the bat-eared foxes fed; so did the vultures. By evening the ants were moving in to devour what was left of Barreto.

Almost three hundred years were to pass before the stone came into human contact again. During that time North America was colonized and Australia discovered, Marie Antoinette lost her head and Charles Darwin sailed in the *Beagle*. The world was a very different place, and so was southern Africa.

BOOK ONE

In the misfortunes of our best friends, we find something that is not unpleasing.

—Duc de La Rochefoucauld

1

The north bank of the Orange River—still not named the Orange, but now called the Great River—12 November, 1857. Dusk.

An ox wagon stood by a camel thorn tree, the bullocks having been taken to water at the river. The wagon was the only sign of life in the huge expanse of dun-colored desert, its white canvas hood marking the position for miles around. Along the river the green of mimosa trees softened the harshness of the scene. There were five people around the wagon: three Hottentot servants, a white man and a white woman. A fourth Hottentot youth was in charge of the oxen. A total of six people, then, accompanying the wagon on its journey north.

The white man was the Reverend Matthew Parker. He was a man of middle height, with heavy side-whiskers turning white, and a broad, solemn face. His eyes were blue and watered from

the constant glare. His wife, Susan, was in her thirties, with a plain, scrubbed face and a sturdy, full-breasted body underneath a long black dress. Both were formally clad for the time and place. Like his wife, Mr. Parker wore black, a tailcoat and trousers—covered in dust—a white clerical collar and a black hat. The servants wore castoffs, multicolored and much patched.

"Are you ready, Susan?" he said. "It's time."

"Couldn't we have the service out here, Matthew?" It was hot even though it was dusk, and she was dabbing at her face with a towel. The heat reminded her of Georgia, where she had been born.

"You know how I feel about that."

"But it's so hot in the wagon." She spoke with only a slight Southern accent, for she had been educated in Boston.

"No one said our mission would be comfortable. I am sorry if I gave that impression."

"No, Matthew, you didn't."

"Are you ready?"

She put down the towel and took up a shiny black straw hat decorated with artificial roses. While she put on her hat, sticking the pin into her bun, he was taking off his. He unfurled a Union Jack and ran it up a small flagpole at the back of the wagon.

"Come along."

The servants stood to one side and watched as their master and mistress clambered into the wagon. "Let us pray," said Mr. Parker, and he and his wife knelt a few feet apart. "O God, our heavenly Father, listen to our prayers as we journey on thy behalf in this wild land. . . ."

She watched him as he prayed. Like his whiskers, his hair was going white and the lines on his face gave it a humorless and often harsh look. Sometimes when she watched him like this something inside her quailed at what she had let herself in for. But then she told herself: "He's a good man. I'm lucky."

She *was* lucky. She had known she did not have the looks to attract men, and if she had not guessed this herself she would have eventually come to it through the ordinary but brutal frankness of family life. She was the oldest of seven children, three brothers and four sisters, and it was impossible to live in such close contact with people her own age without recognizing their opinion of her: she could see that while they loved her, there was an element of pity in that love. She remembered her

father once saying, "You may have to make your own way in the world, Susan. That is why I am giving you the most precious gift I can—an education."

Her family owned a small cotton plantation in Georgia near the town of Centerville. It sounded grand in the mouth but it was too small to be an economic unit, too small to fight against the big landowners who brought in slaves through Charleston, reequipping themselves as fast as they could, knowing that the end of slavery was coming but not envisaging its end as war.

Her mother was of Puritan stock from Boston: plain and scrubbed and unadorned like Susan herself. Her father was an Episcopalian and a sometime lay preacher who, like many a Southern slave owner, found himself torn between his wife and his conscience on the one hand and the facts of economic life on the other. Without slaves—even the few he kept—the plantation would fall into ruin. With them, he found it increasingly difficult to face his God. These dichotomies contrasted abruptly in Susan's life: the cool Puritanism of Boston where she was educated, with its elegant architecture and homes on Beacon Hill, its civilized living, its closeness to its European roots, and the heat and color and violence of life in Georgia, where existence depended uneasily on keeping others in servitude.

The family was in economic decline when, at a neighbor's home, she met the Reverend Parker. She listened to him preach there and again at the meeting house in Centerville. He spoke about slavery from a viewpoint she had never heard expressed before, which helped to ease her own mind as she watched her father struggle to make ends meet. At the time the South Carolina Committee on Colored Persons had recommended that the moratorium on the trade be lifted. "What shall we do?" the Reverend Parker asked his congregation rhetorically. "Free all the blacks? How will that help them? Will it help them to starve? To wander the land homeless? Will it help them to watch their children die? To go without religion? Shelter? Succor? For that, my friends, is what will happen. No! I say to you that if this be an evil, then it will wither on its own accord. It will die away. It will change gradually. That, above all, is what must happen: gradual change."

For an Englishman, whose country had outlawed slavery years before, to be saying such things came as a tonic to the proslavery lobby of Centerville and helped people like her father, who

invited Mr. Parker to preach at his own plantation the following week. He and Susan struck up an acquaintanceship which ripened into friendship. Her family watched with approval. When he asked her to marry him, it would have seemed churlish and ungrateful to them—after all they had done for her—to refuse.

Now, in the midst of this vast African desert, Mr. Parker was in touch with his God. ". . . We ask not that the way be easy, but that Thou should grant us the health and strength to journey along it. Above all, O Lord, we ask that we be in time."

When the short service was over, they descended to the stony ground and in the warm gray dusk he held a second service for the servants. He did this every evening. She thought of her father and her own family in the big decaying drawing room at home. There, for evening prayers, and also on Sunday mornings, the slaves would gather, kneeling around the walls, singing, praying. True, the family did not kneel beside them, but they were in the same room, there was no real feeling of separation; one God did for both colors. But with Mr. Parker, things seemed different. Months before, soon after leaving Cape Town, she had asked him if they could not have one service for all and he had replied, "It would not be seemly, my dear. God in his wisdom has seen fit to make us different."

Later, as they sat by the wagon eating their supper he came back to the theme of his prayer. It was one to which he often returned: would they be in time? For Mr. Parker this meant, would he, as representative of the Royal Missionary Society of London, be in time to gather a harvest of souls for the Lord?

"We're late in the field," he said. "The London Missionary Society has its people with the Griquas. The Germans are at Bethanie. The Paris Evangelicals with the Basuto. The Boston Lutherans have moved into Zululand. That's why we've had to come so far." When he spoke of his mission his eyes burned.

She only half listened. She sat with her back to the wagon wheel chewing hard ship's biscuit and drinking weak tea made with river water. Matthew was obsessed by his mission; she supposed the reason was that he had such high ambitions; no less than to finish his career as inspector general of the Royal Missionary Society. That was why he had taken on so difficult an area—the fringes of the Kalahari Desert hundreds of miles to the north of their present position.

Night came quickly, a black sky blazing with stars and an orange moon. She lit the lamp in the tented wagon—they always slept inside for fear of snakes—and she began to brush her hair. It was long auburn hair and her best feature. She heard Matthew undressing outside. Soon he would slide under the mosquito net and say his prayers, then he would wish her good night, blow out the lamp and leave her staring into the dark, unhappy and unfulfilled. She brushed her hair and stared at the reflection in the mirror propped up on the clothes chest. In her nightdress and softened by the lamplight she saw a sturdy young woman with a round face and a short nose. Her heavy breasts pushed the nightdress out in two mounds. "I may not be beautiful," she thought. "But I'm still young. Why, then? Why?"

After a week of marriage in which nothing had taken place between them she had thought it might be because of shyness on his part, and one night in bed she had put her arms around him and tried to draw him to her. She had felt him stiffen. "I did not marry you for that," he had said.

"Why did you?" She held back anger and disappointment.

"If my mission is to be successful I need a wife. No single man has been appointed to high office in the Royal."

The brushing became more vigorous. She heard Mr. Parker at the other end of the wagon. He was ready for bed. She lay beside him and he blew out the lamp. "Good night, my dear," he said.

The heat of the night descended on her like a blanket of warm black velvet. Her eyes stared, unseeing, at the roof of the wagon and a feeling, almost of panic, came over her as she thought of her future with her husband.

She awoke to an unfamiliar mixture of sounds: shouts, the jingling of bridles, the sound of horses' shoes on the hard desert floor. Mr. Parker lit the lamp.

"What is it?" she said.

"I'll see." He pulled on his trousers.

"Take the gun."

"There's no need for that."

She looked through the laced-up opening at the rear of the wagon. Three horsemen were between the wagon and the servants' fire. The horses were lathered and frightened and difficult to control.

"What's the meaning of this?" Mr. Parker said.

They swung round to face him. She saw they were carrying

long-barreled guns and swords. Their bodies were crisscrossed with bandoliers, and powder horns hung at the saddles.

"Who are you?" he said.

One moved forwards. He was about thirty and dressed in a motley collection of clothing, including the high-collared mess jacket of a British regiment, which still showed remnants of its original braid and frogging. On his head he wore a kerchief tied at the back of his neck and there were gold rings in his ears. The other riders joined him. They were similarly dressed but when Mr. Parker held up the lamp Susan saw that their skins were brown while his was almost white and their noses were flattened while his was straight.

"What do you want?" Mr. Parker said, raising his voice. He turned to the servants. "What do they want?" The servants stood in a frightened clutch near their fire. The horses swung this way and that, backwards and forwards, sawing at the bridles, unwilling to be still.

Suddenly the leader spoke in a language Susan did not know. She thought it might be German or Dutch.

"Can't you speak English?" Mr. Parker said.

The man pointed to his chest. *"Kaptein,"* he said.

"Captain? You, a captain?"

"Kaptein." He gave emphasis to the last syllable, pronouncing the word "cup*tain*."

"Your name?"

"Kaptein." The man nodded. Then he said, "Meat."

"We have no meat but we have food." He turned to the servants. "Give them food."

Kaptein said something to the other two and they dismounted and ate biscuits which they dipped in tea. When they had finished he said, *"Brandwein."*

"I have no brandy."

"Pipe."

"There's no brandy or tobacco."

Both, as Susan knew, were stowed in one of the chests. They had been brought as trade goods for food.

Kaptein suddenly caught Mr. Parker by the arm and began to shake him. "You give."

Susan had been watching with growing apprehension and now took up the shotgun which hung from hooks under the canopy and which was their only protection. Her brothers had taught her

how to handle guns. The gun was kept loaded and she pulled back one of the hammers. It made a loud click which was heard by Kaptein. He turned, saw her for the first time and took several paces towards her. She drew back the second hammer. They looked into each other's eyes and something he saw in hers stopped him. Suddenly he laughed, flung down the mug of tea, gave an order to the others and in a moment they mounted up and were gone.

Mr. Parker watched them go, then he turned to her. "I don't think we needed the gun. I was handling it reasonably but firmly."

One of the servants said, "They can kill you, master."

"I can't accept that at all."

"They can kill us all. They are Korannas."

Susan felt a chill. She had heard about the Korannas, a tribe of Hottentots who had become border raiders, giving sanctuary to criminals on the run from justice farther south. They were feared all along the river and into the country of the Basuto on whose cattle they had preyed for years.

"We must go back," one of the servants said.

"Back? What new nonsense is this? Just because three men rode into camp in the dark! Would you have me turn them away as Christ was turned away? May I remind you that we are on the Lord's business. Place your trust in Him."

Susan slept very little for the rest of that night and when she and Mr. Parker got up at dawn they found the servants had gone.

Nothing in her life had prepared her for this moment, nor was she helped by her husband, who walked about in circles, saying, "But it's not possible! They cannot have gone."

They searched along the river, calling the servants' names. They found no trace of them, but they did find the oxen. They had been knee-haltered to keep them from straying and between the two of them the Parkers managed to drive them to the wagon. The oxen, fourteen in the span, were well trained, and Susan, familiar with working animals at home, managed with her husband's help to yoke them. When they had finished it was almost midmorning and the sun blazed down.

"Well, now," Mr. Parker said. She glanced at him and was shocked to see how much older he suddenly seemed. "Well, now," he said again. It was as though he were waiting for someone, her perhaps, to give him a lead.

She was by nature an optimist and her earlier despair had disappeared. They had food, a wagon, oxen, and were near a river. They would, at any rate, survive. "Won't you thank God for what we have?" she said, knowing that prayer would ease him.

"What? Of course. There is always something to be thankful for. And we have each other."

For the first time in their married life he had said something which touched her. "Thank you, Matthew," she said. They prayed together and both felt better.

"The question is, which way do we go?" he said.

Southern Africa had changed greatly since Father John, Dom Manuel and Barreto had come this way. The most important change was that people had come from Europe and had moved across the land searching for places to farm; land itself, after the crowded slums of Europe and the religious oppression, had become the eldorado. The Dutch had founded a colony at the Cape of Good Hope in the mid-seventeenth century. It had been taken by the British, returned to the Dutch and retaken by the British who had now held it for fifty years. The descendants of the early Dutch and French Huguenot settlers found the rule from London irksome and many took their wagons and trekked into the interior looking for unoccupied land where they would be free from the laws of a foreign power. This had a ripple effect on the indigenous people of the country, the Hottentots and the Bushmen. As the whites moved north they pushed these tribes ahead of them into ever more desolate wastes. The largest single movement of whites was the Great Trek of the 1830's and by 1857 white farmers occupied land mainly in the center and in the east of the country. The deserts of the northwest, where the Parkers had been abandoned, were still empty except for the occasional white hunter, Hottentot settlement or band of Bushmen roaming the land in search of game.

"I'll not turn back," Mr. Parker said in a firmer voice.

"We cannot go north without servants who speak the language of the country."

They could not go west, for it was uninhabited desert. Therefore it had to be east along the river until they came to an area of settlement, two hundred or more miles away, where they might be able to recruit servants willing to help them continue the journey to Mr. Parker's mission. They followed the course of the river as best they could and when, because of the terrain, this

proved impractical, they swung inland. They were helped by the fact that good rains had fallen earlier in the year and some of the shallow pans on the desert floor still held water.

Days turned to weeks as they struggled eastwards. Once they came across two Griqua Hottentots with a herd of goats and bartered a bottle of brandy and tobacco for milk and one of the goats. On another occasion a small band of Bushmen brought them melons in exchange for tobacco. They saw this group of fifteen several times. They would disappear for a few days, then return with more melons or ostrich eggs or part of an antelope which they had shot with poisoned arrows. The Parkers managed to survive in this fashion for nearly three weeks, then one day the Korannas came back.

It was their practice to start the day early, stop early—about three o'clock—and lead the oxen down to the river to water them. This could take two or three hours depending on how far away they had camped. On this day they watered the oxen as usual and about six o'clock, just as the cooling evening breeze stole over the desert, they made their way back to the wagon. They had left it in a patch of shady camel thorn and as it was hidden from view they had no warning of what had happened.

The first thing Susan saw was their belongings strewn over the ground. The clothes chests and the food chests had been opened and emptied. Then she saw the three Korannas. Kaptein was sitting on the tailboard of the wagon, the other two were standing beside it. Each had the remains of a bottle of brandy in his hand.

"In the name of God, what have you done!" Mr. Parker said, going forwards, his face flushing a deep red.

"Matthew, stop!"

But it was too late. Mr. Parker had reached Kaptein. "Give that back to me at once!" He held his hand out like a schoolmaster, waiting for the Koranna to give him the bottle. Instead, Kaptein put his bare foot against Mr. Parker's chest and pushed. The missionary staggered backwards and fell. Kaptein reached for his gun. Mr. Parker was getting to his feet when he was struck by a lead ball big enough to bring down an elephant. He died instantly, a look of enormous surprise on his face.

Susan had screamed when she saw the gun. She ran to her husband, calling his name. Kaptein caught her by the shoulder and flung her aside. He said something to the others, who dragged Mr. Parker's body behind the trees and began undress-

ing it. When they returned, one was wearing his black coat, the other his trousers and shoes. His feet were too big for the shoes so he had cut off the toe caps.

The Korannas stood in a circle around Susan. For the first time she could look at them closely. The two brown-skinned men had flattened noses and tight-curled hair, but Kaptein, she realized, must be an octoroon, for his skin was light and his features European. He was also bigger than the other two. She felt that the end of her own life was near but what she feared most was the interim period.

Kaptein took a thin leather thong from around his neck and tied her hands together behind her back. He then tied her to one wheel of the wagon. The three men took the last of the goat which the Parkers had bought and grilled it over a small fire.

It was still daylight when they finished and Kaptein untied her hands. He took off the kerchief that he wore on his head and his long black hair fell about his face. Then he took off his British mess jacket. He had a smooth, well-muscled body, light yellow in color. He indicated her dress. She knew what he meant, but her strength drained from her. He put his hand into her bodice and ripped the fabric away. She fell forwards and he picked her up by the hair. She stood, dressed only to her waist, covering her breasts with her hands. The other Hottentots stared at her; breasts were of no interest to them. She knew that if Kaptein grabbed at her again he would hurt her.

"I will do it," she said.

He seemed to understand, for he allowed her to remove the remainder of her clothing. She no longer tried to cover herself. It was the first time that a man had seen her adult naked body. The two dark-skinned Hottentots laughed and pointed to her pubic hair which was almost black compared to the auburn of her head, and very bushy compared to the sparsely covered pudenda of their own women.

Kaptein used her several times that night. He had tied her hands and feet to stanchions in the wagon, although she had no idea of struggling. She bled badly from the first perforation and when he saw the amount of blood he appeared to be puzzled. Perhaps it was because of this he did not kill her, perhaps he thought she was already dying. But later when she thought about it she wondered if there was not another reason. Twice during the night the other Korannas had wanted their turn with her but

Kaptein had driven them off. The second time, crouching over her and about to take her again, he had said: "They Hottentots. But I and you white people."

In the dawn they left, driving the oxen with them and leaving her tied as she had been all night. She was only semiconscious for he had been rough with her, bruising her internally and mauling her breasts. She lay in the wagon as the sun rose, turning it into a bake oven. Sometimes she came to and struggled with the thongs but they were the sinews of a kudu and immensely strong. In the early afternoon, when she was already suffering from heatstroke and within an hour or two of death by dehydration, the little clan of Bushmen arrived to barter for tobacco. She was aware of their small heart-shaped faces at the rear of the wagon and heard their strong clicking speech. They took her down to the river in the shade of the mimosa trees and bathed her. The women boiled the leaves of the wild olive plant and made a tampon which they inserted into her vagina, then they pounded the root of the latifolium and placed it on the scratches and bites on her breasts. The root is red and when she first saw herself she thought she had been flayed. It was a day before she could walk.

The Bushmen were small people and even the men came only to her shoulder though she was not above middle height. They wore cloaks of animals' skins and the men carried bows and quivers of arrows, the heads of which were daubed with poison. The women wore almost no clothing and their only adornments were necklaces made from small pieces of ostrich-egg shell. Constant exposure to the withering sun gave their skins, all but those of the youngest, the look of crushed leather.

Two women took her by the hand and led her past the wagon, past the trees, and pointed at something. It was a dusty heap and she realized it was all that the animals had left of her husband. One woman made a scratching motion on the hard desert surface, and Susan knew she was being asked if she wanted him buried. She nodded and they understood.

They used horn-tipped digging sticks and made a hole in the riverbed and placed in it what remained of Matthew Parker. They were about to push sand on it when Susan saw that something had been uncovered. She pulled it from the sand. It appeared to be a cross, a kind of crucifix. She could not think where it might have come from, unless a missionary had lost it miles upstream and it had washed down. It was eighteen inches

high and made of wood badly scarred by the action of the river stones. Once there had been an inscription on it but that was illegible now. It seemed so wonderful to her that she had found it there, so direct a sign from the Lord to mark Matthew's death that she placed a cairn of stones on the top of the bank close to where his grave was and wedged the crucifix into it.

She stayed with the Bushmen that day and the following one and then she returned to the wagon. The clan came with her. She gave them what she could. That night she slept in the wagon. The next morning the Bushmen had gone but outside was a small pile of melons, roots, berries and bulbs. She realized that, knowing there was no tobacco remaining, they had gone for good and that this was a final gift to her. What she did not realize was that it was their custom, so hard were their lives, to leave behind the old and the sick in exactly the same way, expecting them to die.

She went through her stock of food. The servants had taken some when they left and the Korannas had looted the remains. But they had missed a small bag of flour and another containing three pieces of dried beef weighing about a pound. The gun had vanished, but she found a sharp cutting knife and more cutlery and cooking utensils than she could use. She sat in the shade of the wagon and tried to think things out. There was only one inescapable conclusion: if she was to reach the white settlements she would have to walk.

She cut the wagon sail and made a bag in which to sleep, then she made another to carry the food, matches, her knife and a cake of soap. She found a pair of Matthew's trousers and one of his shirts and put them on: among the naked Bushmen she had felt no shame, but when she had returned to the wagon convention had returned with her.

At dawn the following day she began to walk east. She had no idea how long her food would last but anything was better than doing nothing and she placed her trust in the Lord, who had given her so strong a sign. After three days her food was finished and she began to learn how to survive. She collected frogs and she found that the finches' nests which hung from the trees could be robbed at night. She took the tiny birds and cooked them over coals and ate them. But at the end of ten days she was starving. Walking became a greater effort and she had to rest more frequently. She became light-headed. On the twelfth day as she knelt by the edge of a pool to drink she heard a noise in front of

her and looked up and thought she saw a great animal in several parts.

It stood in the dappled shade and when she concentrated, its sections coalesced. It was an ox, but like none she had seen before. It was much bigger than those that had drawn their wagon, of a reddish color, with long curving horns. There was a movement to her right and she saw a second and a third. Then she saw a black man with a gun and the gun was pointed at her. She had been wearing Matthew's hat against the sun and now she took it off, allowing her hair to fall onto her shoulders. The black man, seeing she was a woman, relaxed, and she crossed the river to him. She wondered what language he spoke. Just then a voice shouted, "Mopedi!"

The black man indicated that Susan should follow him up the bank. At the top was a wagon not unlike their own, but in a state of dereliction. The canvas hood had been burned and some of the wood was splintered. A white man lay on a blanket on the wagon bed. He said something to her in what she thought was Dutch and she shook her head. "I can't understand."

"I said, 'Who the devil are you?'" He did not rise and she saw that his leg was hurt.

The black man, Mopedi, who she later learnt was a Basuto from a country far to the east, made strong black coffee and gave her hard bread rusks which she dipped into it.

The man in the wagon was named Frans Delport. He was a hunter and had wandered west from his normal hunting grounds looking for new areas in which the game had not been destroyed. He was anxious to know her story and she told him everything except of the night she had spent with Kaptein. Something, apart from natural modesty, caused her to keep that hidden.

"Three Korannas?" Delport was a big man with light brown hair streaked by the sun and wind. He had an open, frank face with brown eyes and a sunburned skin.

"Was one of them not a half-caste?"

"Yes."

He lifted a gun from his side. "Have you seen this before?"

"It was my husband's shotgun."

"And this?"

"A brooch of mine."

"The half-caste was wearing it in his coat."

"Do you know them?"

"Don't be afraid. They gave me this." He tapped his leg. "And I gave them this." He picked up an elephant gun.

The Korannas had come on his camp two days before. They were driving oxen on which he could see the marks of yokes and they wanted to barter one for brandy. He became suspicious. He gave them a meal from a springbok he had shot, and opened a bottle or two. Later in the night they attacked him and shot him in the leg. They burned the wagon's canvas hood, but Delport was prepared. He had shot one dead and, he thought, wounded another. By sunrise they had gone, driving their oxen with them.

"Which one did you kill?" she said.

"The half-caste."

She felt her spirit lighten.

She cleaned up his wound, which had become infected. "What have you put on it?" she asked.

"Dung. From the oxen. Goat dung would have been better."

She searched for the leaves of the wild olive, the same leaves which the Bushmen women had used to heal her, made a poultice of them and tied it onto the wound. In three days the infection had gone and it was healing, although she thought he would never be able to walk without a limp.

That is how Susan Parker met Frans Delport, who was to become her second husband. She cared for him there at the river and when his leg was healed they trekked back to fetch her wagon because it was the better of the two. At first the plan was that he should take her to the white settlements, but that was before they began to live together as man and wife. In later years when she thought of her behavior she was amazed she could have done what she did. Yet she knew the reason: she wanted his sperm inside her. She knew there was a chance she would have Kaptein's child, but if she slept with Frans she could erase Kaptein from her mind. It would *never* be his child. Two weeks after she had met Delport she began to share his bed and just under nine months later a daughter was born whom they named Marie. It was a difficult birth and she was helped by two Griqua women, who told her she would never have another child. They were right.

During those nine months, while they drifted across the pristine African desert (once they had become lovers the journey to the settlements was abandoned), they came to know each other more intensely than either had known anyone before. They

camped where there was water, they trekked where they wished, as long as they had food they were content. Frans, she discovered, was a descendant of the family Delporte which had fled French religious oppression in 1699 and had come to the Cape of Good Hope. They had founded a grape farm in the Cape, then the family had grown and generation after generation had extended it inland. Frans was a remote cousin of the original landed family, who were the largest wine producers in the Cape. His own family had trekked north in the 1830's when he was a child and had farmed land in Natal. Frans, restless and footloose, had become a hunter.

The nine months of wandering before Marie was born made both Susan and Frans look at the desert with new eyes. They were aware that a family would eventually cause them to become less nomadic and they began to see possibilities in the land they had missed before. The local Hottentots were able to maintain large flocks of goats which thrived on the barren ground. They based their future on this when Marie was born.

At first they lived in the wagon but then they decided to build a house and searched for a suitable site. It had to be near water, so they chose a south-facing hillside, for the shade, near a tributary of the Great River. But they needed mud to make the bricks and the river bottom was sand. Frans knew of a waterhole two days' trek away which contained all the mud they would need. They decided to camp at the waterhole. It took them more than three months to make the bricks and cart them to their hillside. They made them by shoveling mud into molds and allowing the sun to bake it hard. One day Frans dug up a leather satchel. He brought it to Susan and they opened it. The outside was sodden and quickly broke up once the sun dried it. But inside was a piece of oiled cloth and inside that a book.

"Why, it's a Bible," she said. "But what language is it?"

Frans had hunted elephant in Mozambique and recognized it. "Portuguese," he said.

"Look, someone has been writing in it. I wonder what it says." They finished making the bricks and took the last loads to their farm. It was a place more remote than any Susan could have imagined, and yet she was happy. Sometimes in the evening they would walk down to the river and watch the sandgrouse fly in to drink. Although the landscape was different there was something about the soft quality of the warm evening air that reminded her

of Centerville and her childhood. "If only we could get the water up from the river we could grow things," she said.

"One day we will."

Sometimes they would talk about the Bible and wonder about it. They thought that finding it was a kind of miracle. Susan remembered the crucifix and told Frans about it and they decided to call their farm Portuguese Place. The Bible became their first family treasure.

2

After living for so long in the wagon, the small mud hut was like a palace. Susan had not been able to visualize the kind of house they would eventually build, but when it was completed it sat against its slope as though it had grown naturally from the desert. Frans had built it with the help of a few Hottentots who had come to live nearby, hoping for a share in the white man's riches. For all the additions that were to be made in later years and the greater comforts achieved, this was the heart of the house. It comprised only a living room and a bedroom. It had no bathroom nor kitchen. Washing was done in the bedroom with a basin and jug that sat on a washstand; the needs of the body were catered for in the early days by the wide-open veld, later by a wooden privy built over a deep hole. A wooden seat was made with openings of two sizes, one for adults and a smaller one for children because it was feared that a child might fall through.

The adult side was covered by a heavy wooden lid that sometimes held spiders, which Susan hated. Snakes and scorpions invaded the privy from time to time and it was common practice to open the door with a kick, then stand back to let the wildlife escape.

As in many early homesteads the kitchen was built separately, for cooking had to be done on an open fire or in a mud oven.

The most important part of the house was the veranda, which was called the *stoep*. It was raised from the desert floor on mud bricks and ran along the front of the house. It was ten feet wide and shaded by reeds cut from the river. Much time was spent on the stoep; this was where they ate their breakfast and where they sat as the evening breeze stole over the veld and cooled the air.

"One day we will have a grapevine growing here," Frans said, as he put up the trellis in the heat.

She brought him a pitcher of water and he drank deeply.

"You always say 'one day,'" she said, smiling. "One day we'll do this, one day we'll have that."

"It's true. 'One day' will come."

"We don't need 'one day.' We have everything."

From the veranda the eye was taken down the hillside of low scrub and reddish earth, to the vivid green of the trees growing along the banks of the river. As far as either knew this river had not been named, and so they called it the Green River. The trees were not big in the way Susan knew trees but they were fibrous and tough, and grew to a height of twenty or thirty feet. They were unsuitable for planking but Frans was able to make simple furniture from them.

It was during these early months, when they were settling into their house, that Susan began to realize his quality. Physically he was big: strong and enduring. His hair and beard were brown streaked with lighter bands where the sun had bleached them. He looked what he was, a man who could cope with the empty land. She had early realized that she was better educated and cleverer in bookish things than Frans. His learning had come from his parents, themselves barely literate, and he could read and write with difficulty and was only able to add and subtract. These deficiencies did not bother either of them for he had little time to read and, in the beginning at least, few animals to count. What he lacked in education he made up for in practical ability. He had built the house without drawing a line on paper and it had come out square, straight and strong. It was the same with furniture.

40

He used the planking from his wagon to fashion them a table and the base of a bed. The remainder of the furniture, which comprised only a few chairs and two benches for the stoep, he made from acacia wood, and antelope-hide thongs for seats.

While he made the furniture Susan wove rushes to make window blinds—there was no glass—and mats for the floor. She used some of the canvas of the wagon hood to make a mattress cover and stuffed it with sweet-smelling leaves. She helped Frans when he needed her and she looked after Marie.

Her short square body was as enduring in its way as Frans's bigger frame. She had been endowed with large, heavy breasts and had ample milk for Marie. Food was not the problem she had once envisaged. Living for most of his life in a hostile environment Frans had learned how to survive from the tribes through which he had passed, and taught her what he knew. The main items of their diet were antelope he killed along the river or in the hills behind the house, guinea fowl, partridge and wild duck. There were ostrich eggs to be had from wandering Bushmen— Susan never saw her band again—and a kind of coarse-haired, long-tailed sheep which the Hottentots bred. What they missed above all was any kind of fat, for the meat was stringy and lean. Occasionally they were able to make up for this by buying a sheep and letting it fatten on the grass and shrubs by the river. The fat was held in the tails and when these weighed six or seven pounds Frans would slaughter the animal and they would gorge themselves on the fried fat, eating it in lumps until their hands and faces shone with grease. They also missed vegetables and Susan learned to collect wild garlic and wild onions, melons, the cores of aloes and various berries of which she never knew the names.

A diet such as this might have had a deleterious effect on health except for one thing: sour milk or, as Susan learned to call it, sack milk. This they got from their goats and it was kept in a large leather bag which hung inside the house. As the milk went sour it thickened like buttermilk. Each day more milk was added to what was left and so the souring process was continuous.

These early years were the happiest Susan could remember. They were alone in a vast, unexplored land. At first, trekking through it with the Reverend Parker, she had feared it; now, learning how to live in harmony with it from Frans, she grew to love it. The heat in summer was intense, but she was used to the sticky heat of Georgia. This dry heat was bearable. Sometimes on

hot afternoons she would take Marie down to the river and Frans would join them there and they would immerse themselves in a long pool with a sandy bottom which had become known as the Breakfast Pool because when they were building the house they would go there to sit and have their coffee. Before servants came to Portuguese Place they would take off their clothes and be naked together as naturally as children.

It was in the crushing heat of midsummer that she realized why Frans had built the house on the slope above the river and not, as she might have expected, down by the water's edge in the shade of the trees. Each evening a small breeze would begin to blow across the veld, rustling the reeds on the stoep and cooling the air. But down in the river bottom the heat remained, suffocating and claustrophobic.

Winters were best. The nights were cold and frosty but the days were blue and golden and warm at noon. Sometimes the milk in the sack would be frozen, sometimes a light powdery snow would fall, sometimes there would be a bitter wind and she and Frans would build a huge fire in the living room and sit over it. On these evenings they would use a little of their precious lamp oil and Frans would talk and plan—"one-day talk" as she called it—and Marie would sit in her cot and watch and listen. He spoke always of goats and sheep and crops—the latter only if they could somehow manage to irrigate the land near the river.

Sometimes she was infected by his one-day talk. "If we could only get the water we could grow cotton," she said, remembering the fields of her childhood.

"I've never seen it," he said. "But there must be some way."

"My father had a pump."

"One day when we are rich, we will buy one."

"I don't want to be rich," she said.

She meant it. There was nothing which money could buy; there was no shop, no bank, no lawyer, no doctor, no government taxes; only the semidesert, the river, the trees, the group of Hottentots who lived behind the hills, and Mopedi, Frans's "boy" who had hunted with him and who had now taken a wife from among the Hottentots and was living in a hut near the house. None of these people wanted money. Currency was anything that could be bartered. The Hottentots had sheep and goats and scrub cattle; Frans had rifles, shotguns, powder, lead, bullet molds, bandoliers, brass buttons, beads, copper and brass wire,

nails, pots, pans, mugs. He bartered for what he needed. As the house grew, so did their farm stock. Soon they had a small flock of sheep, a few goats, and one or two cows that gave milk.

But even if money had been of some value, wealth itself had little meaning for Susan. Each day she thanked God for being alive, thanked Him for her man and her child. Each day she prayed and put aside some minutes to sit with the Bible on her lap. She could not read it, of course, but she guessed at many of the phrases. It was a talisman that became more and more important to her as time passed. Sometimes she would wonder who had owned the Bible, who had come this way before her. Then she would remember Mr. Parker and the Koranna, Kaptein. After what had happened to her just to be alive was enough.

The fact that she was more than just alive was a bonus. She had been willing to make Mr. Parker a dutiful wife—more than dutiful—for she knew that under her plain and practical exterior there were depths of affection, of passion, he had never touched, never even tried to reach. Then had come her brutal awakening with the Hottentot. Had she not slept with Frans within the first weeks of their meeting for a specific reason she might never have taken to a man's bed again.

It was Frans who awakened her in a different way. His masculinity was tempered with kindness and much of their lovemaking had a tenderness seemingly out of place in the wilderness, and within a few months of their being together she was giving herself, opening herself to him, in a way she could never have thought possible.

Sometimes when she lay with him in the big lumpy bed in Portuguese Place, as the early morning sun stole into the room, and as she planned the day to come, she felt a contentment unknown during her marriage to the Reverend Parker. Her days then had been times to be endured; now each was to be lived fully from dawn until darkness sent them to bed. "Hold this moment," she would say to herself. "This is happiness. Remember it." And then Marie, as she grew older, would run into the room from her bed in the sitting room and would climb into the big bed and snuggle up and Frans would wake and Susan's day would begin.

They lived as simply as three people could possibly live. Twice a year they would take the wagon and journey north to the small mission station of Griqua Town where they had been married

There was no shop but supplies of food were held there and they would barter for flour and rice and the occasional simple household item. For the rest they made do with what they had; it was a way of life at once attractive and fraught with problems.

One morning in autumn, seven years after they had first come to Portuguese Place, they were having their morning meal on the stoep. Frans had been building a new sheep kraal of river stones, replacing the original one which had been made of cut thorn brush, and he was ravenously hungry. But when he came to eat the boiled venison reheated from the night before, he put down his spoon and said, "Lord, but I'm tired of meat!"

"I know."

"I would give my right hand for a pot of coffee."

"And a bar of soap. I'd make some but we have no tallow or caustic. And bread! Oh, for a loaf of sourdough!"

Their supplies had dwindled to almost nothing. The lamp oil, the soap, the coffee, and the rice, had all given out and they were reduced to a diet of meat and whatever *veldkos*—the wild food which Frans had taught her was edible—she could gather. Their stock of medicines was also dangerously low. They knew that a visit to Griqua Town would not suffice and they would have to go farther afield. Frans had spoken of the mission village of Galilee, six days' trek to the southeast, but had shown no willingness to leave the farm. Susan knew why. Although he did not often speak of it, his one-day talk sometimes touched on the fact that he did not know whether or not they owned the farm. He was even uncertain whether in this wild and far-off place he was still under the rule of the British Government at the Cape of Good Hope. The second worrying factor was the possibility that one day others would come to live and farm near them. Susan tried to reassure him. "There's enough land for everyone, surely," she would say. But the wilderness had an almost mystical value for Frans and he wished to have it to himself.

"We'll have to go to Galilee," he said, picking at the unpalatable food, but again no plans were made.

Then two things occurred which precipitated action. The first concerned Marie. Susan had been teaching her numbers and the alphabet and had thought to barter for some simple reading books at Griqua Town. But there were none. She began to worry about her daughter and to realize that isolation brought as many problems as benefits.

44

Lack of the self-discipline inherent in the learning process was having an effect on Marie. She ran wild with the children of the Hottentot servants and soon was fluent in the Low Dutch which was the lingua franca of the country and which Frans also spoke. While Susan could see no fault in this association she realized that the child would grow up as the Hottentots were growing up, backward and only semicivilized. It was hard enough to get her to her lessons now; she would grow gradually more willful.

"Why?" Marie would say, her dark brown eyes under the black hair glinting up at her mother. "Why must I learn writing?"

"Because you won't grow up to be a lady otherwise."

"But Father can't write."

"Of course he can."

"He can't! He can't! He can't!"

The other factor was news of a large herd of elephants that were feeding some miles upstream. Susan knew what that meant from the early months when she had lived with Frans as a hunter's wife: it meant ivory. They yoked the oxen and trekked upstream.

They stayed with the herd for five days. Frans had no horse and had to keep up with the elephants on foot. With his bad leg this meant he was taxing his strength to the limit, for most of each day was spent in running after the herd, trying to keep up with the animals as they moved along the river. Susan followed as best she could in the wagon so that at nightfall she could have a hot meal ready for him. She watched him limp about the camp, drained, smelling of blood and gunpowder, red to the shoulders from cutting out the tusks; she watched the Hottentots descend on the great black bodies that lay near the water; whole villages were on the move, brought by the chance of meat. Bushmen arrived. The smell was dreadful, for the paunches were carelessly opened allowing the gall to pour out. She hated it; hated the killing, the smell and the barbarism. It was the dark side of Africa which she herself had experienced in the wagon with Kaptein.

But when it was all over Frans had killed fifteen elephants and there was a great pile of tusks on the ground next to the wagon.

The mission station of Galilee was so called because it had been built at the edge of a shallow pan which held water in the rains and even in the worst droughts never quite dried up. It had been founded by the Caledonian Missionary Society of Edinburgh in

the 1840's and now, more than twenty years later, had developed into a small village. At first there had only been the house which had served both as a dwelling and a church. Then the church itself, a small mud building, had been constructed, and later had come other buildings and small houses until now there were more than a hundred souls living in and around Galilee. It was in softer country than Susan and Frans Delport were used to. Here there was grass, and a number of small farms had been started in the surrounding hills, growing maize and wheat and rearing cattle and horses.

The people were a mixture of races and nationalities. At the center was the Reverend McNab and his wife, representatives of the Edinburgh mission. Then there was an Englishman, Mr. Harper, who had opened a store and who sold or bartered everything and anything. Over the door was the motto "Nothing too big, nothing too small." Mr. Harper had a Hottentot wife and four half-caste children; the McNabs were childless. There were also true Hottentots who lived in mud huts and who had been wooed to the Christian Church by Mr. McNab, but who stayed in the area because Mr. Harper also sold brandy brought up in barrels from the Cape and they had developed a taste for it.

The village normally wore a sunstricken, abandoned air, lost in the hugeness of the dusty plains, but on the day Susan and Frans arrived in their wagon it was bustling. The reason was obvious: a train of a dozen wagons traveling north had stopped to revictual and were parked in a circle behind the church. Frans had bought supplies in Galilee twice before but he had never seen it like this.

"Where can they be going?" Susan said.

"I don't know," he said, with a worried frown.

They parked their own wagon beside Mr. McNab's house.

"Why, it's Mr. Delport!" said Mrs. McNab. She was a short woman with gray hair caught severely in a bun. Her husband joined her. He, too, was short, but his hair was unkempt and hung in gray skeins almost to his shoulders. "And a bairn!" said Mrs. McNab, seeing Marie. "You must be Mrs. Delport. Come away. Come away in."

The house was larger than but as simply furnished as Portuguese Place. The McNabs gave them tea. Frans held the small cup in his large hunter's hands and when he thought no one was looking swallowed its contents at a gulp. Susan watched him out of the corner of her eye and smiled to herself as she saw a look of

satisfaction, almost of wonder come over his face. It was the first cup of tea they had had for more than a year.

They talked about the weather and the persistent drought and then when Frans asked about the wagons parked by the church, Mrs. McNab said, "It's been like this for weeks."

"We've never seen the likes," Mr. McNab said. "It's turned us upside down." He poured his tea into his saucer and blew at it before drinking, his lank gray locks falling forward.

"Where are they heading for?" Frans asked.

"Where? Haven't you heard then?"

"We've not spoken to anyone for a long time," Susan said. Marie was leaning against her knees and Mrs. McNab said, "Come and have another biscuit." She put her arm about Marie's waist to hold her but the child twisted away and returned to her mother. She chewed the biscuit, looking at Mrs. McNab with hostile eyes.

"It's all this talk about finding precious stones up on the Vaal River that's done it," McNab said. "They canna wait to get there. Some don't even stop here, just push on and on till the bullocks drop. We've never seen the likes and we've been here fifteen years this Christmas."

"Precious stones?" Frans said.

"Aye. Diamonds, would you believe? It'll be a year ago now. Some children found a pretty stone and showed it to their father and I'm blessed if it didn't turn out to be a diamond. That started it. We've had scores of wagons going through here since then. It's changed this place so you'd not know it."

"I can see that," Frans said.

"Aye, but you wait," Mrs. McNab said severely. "You'll see things you shouldna see anywhere, let alone at a mission. You take care, Mrs. Delport."

They had supper with the McNabs and turned in early. As Susan drifted off to sleep she heard shouting and laughing at the other end of the village but she was too tired to wonder what it was.

The following day they sold the ivory to Mr. Harper and then spent most of the money he had paid them in his shop. "It's a good way of doing business," Frans said sourly to Susan.

Mr. Harper was a big bald-headed man with a forbidding manner. He stood by the door of his shop, and watched as his half-caste daughters did the serving. Susan thought them an

attractive but sulky trio. At supper Mr. McNab had expatiated at some length on the place the half-castes had found for themselves or in his opinion had *not* found. "Mark my words," he had said. "One day there'll be trouble with them. They hate the Hottentots because they're ashamed to have them as forebears and they hate the whites because they'll never be accepted as whites. There's no place for them at all."

The store was full of people, both white and Hottentot, and the Harper daughters served the whites first, making the Hottentots wait. Susan and Frans had spent days making a list of all the things they needed, the purchase of which was made possible by the ivory, and now they spent nearly forty minutes amassing a pile of goods on the boardwalk in front of the store. Apart from such household necessities as flour, rice, coffee, tea, caustic soda, yellow soap and scented soap, candles, matches and lamp oil, Susan bought reading and writing books and bolts of printed cotton for dresses and curtains as well as for barter. She bought yards of elastic, needles and thread, underwear for herself and Marie and made Frans buy underwear which he was too shy to order from the half-caste girl. It was as though they were equipping themselves anew and in effect this was true, for not only had their household supplies dwindled to nothing but their clothes were in the last stages and could not be repaired. She bought shoes, a dress for herself and one for Marie and saw that Frans bought corduroy trousers, a jacket, work shirts and boots. Then they stocked up on their medicine chest.

All of them, like the Hottentots, were susceptible to veld sores, ulcers that affected the legs and arms; for this they bought Martin's bandages and zinc ointment. Their diet, with almost no roughage, meant that they needed extract of senna and Glauber's salts. They bought wine of ipecac in case of colds and coughs, Fowler's solution of arsenic to improve the constitution, alum for use as an astringent, calomel, belladonna, Dover's powder, paregoric and tansy oil, as well as spirits of 'niter' to break a fever.

The half-caste girl paid little heed when Susan asked for goods but it was different when Frans presented his list of window glass, tools and farm inplements. She displayed a coquettishness which caused Susan to smile and Frans to become awkward with embarrassment.

Most of the morning was spent loading the supplies into the wagon and in the afternoon Frans bought two horses—a stallion

and a mare in foal—from one of the nearby farms. They rode them back in the late afternoon, Marie sitting in front of her father on the stallion, her eyes shining, her face alight. "Make him go faster!" she said.

But Frans only held her more tightly with his left arm. "First you must learn to walk before you can run," he said.

"I don't want to walk!"

That evening Susan said, "Have we spent everything?"

"Very nearly."

"That was me, I'm afraid. But we were down to bedrock. I'll get us something to eat."

"No. Not tonight. Put on your new dress. We're eating out."

"Out? Where? There isn't anywhere to go."

But he had seen an eating house beyond the church.

She put on a white cotton dress patterned with small red roses and did her hair and Marie wore a new dress and Frans put on his new corduroy coat. Susan and Marie walked barefooted to the eating house and when they reached it they put on their new shoes. Susan had not eaten in a restaurant for nearly ten years.

The eating house was primitive, a room in a dwelling house with a few tables, but to her it had an air of enchantment. There was a white cloth on the table and they were given proper napkins of linen. They ate bean soup and followed it with boiled mutton and cabbage (of which Frans had three helpings) and then an orange for pudding. Marie had never seen an orange before and again Susan felt a twinge as she thought of the deprivation which must inevitably become a problem for her daughter.

"How do I eat it?" Marie said.

"I'll show you," Susan said.

"I want Father to."

It was dark when they had finished eating and they had to pass Harper's store. The lamps were lit and the place was crowded. Half a dozen Hottentots stood on the steps outside. There was laughter and loud voices from inside. Frans looked through the window and saw that one section of the store was a canteen. More than a dozen white and half-caste girls were drinking brandy. One of the Hottentots outside came up to them and said something to Frans, who shook his head and took Susan and Marie along the dusty road to the wagon. "What did he want?" Susan said.

"He was begging," Frans said.

"He wanted money to drink," Marie said, for she had understood perfectly.

Frans went to check the oxen and the horses while Susan took Marie into the McNabs' house where they had been invited to have a bath. Unlike the small zinc bath which they used at Portuguese Place in front of the winter fire, this was a large enamel bath with a wood-burning water heater. Susan used some of the new scented soap she had bought and put on her new underwear.

They said good night to the McNabs and returned to the wagon. Frans had lit the lanterns and Susan could see two people standing in the glow. One was Frans but she could not make out the other. As they got nearer Marie said, "It is the girl from the store."

She had her hand on Delport's arm. Susan saw that she had changed her clothing and was wearing a dress that displayed much of her well-developed bosom. Frans said something in Dutch and shook off her hand as Susan and Marie reached them. The girl turned and looked angrily at the two women and said something to Frans, then laughed. Susan was dumbfounded at what happened next. Frans hit the girl across her face with the flat of his hand. It was a heavy blow and it knocked her to the ground. She sprang to her feet and ran twenty yards, stopped, turned and shouted something more, then she vanished into the night.

"What happened?"

Frans shook his head.

"What did she say? What did she want?"

"Money . . . She wanted money. . . ."

"But why did you strike her?"

He opened his mouth and closed it.

"It was something she said!"

"She was rude. She said something rude to me. Come, we have an early start."

Susan turned to Marie. The child's face was drawn and still. There was anger in her eyes. Whatever had been said, Marie had not liked it, nor had Frans, but there was nothing Susan could do without nagging further and even then she sensed she would not get the truth. Troubled, she tucked Marie into her blankets.

Frans was sitting on the wagon. "Can't you tell me?" she said.

He shook his head. "It was nothing, forget it."

Later, when Frans was asleep, she heard Marie crying. "What is it?" she said, lifting the blankets and taking the child in her arms.

But Marie, like her father, shook her head. Susan noticed that she was sucking her thumb, something she had not done since she was a baby.

Frans drove the bullocks hard on the way back to Portuguese Place. They should have been happy to be going home but they journeyed in silence most of the way. Even when they reached the Green River and trekked along the bank towards the farm Frans's spirits seemed to lift only marginally. Ten miles from home they came upon a sight which he had feared all the years they had lived at Portuguese Place: a group of five white-tented wagons was drawn up near the river and smoke from their fires rose straight up in the still autumn air.

"Perhaps they have lost their way," Susan said.

But she knew and Frans knew that this was not likely; the track to the north was far to the east of Portuguese Place. No one could lose his way by such a margin.

3

Settlers had come to the valley of the Green River and they became the Delports' first neighbors. The word "neighbor" in its normal usage has a friendly ring to it, but not as used by Frans Delport. In his mouth, at least at first, it sounded like an expletive and even in the years to come when the land gradually filled with farmers, he never totally accepted white people—the Hottentots and Bushmen he regarded as part of the land itself—living where he had for so long existed alone. In the sense that the rest of the world used the word these newcomers to the valley were hardly neighbors at all. Those nearest to Portuguese Place were a German family called Lessing who had built their dwelling ten miles upstream, while a second family, the Jordaans, lived ten miles beyond that. For several years no one came to live on the western edge of Portuguese Place—much to Frans's relief—because the land was drier and harsher there.

At first his way of dealing with the intrusion was to ignore it; as

far as he was concerned the newcomers did not exist and it was only due to Susan that relationships were forged at all. She, too, felt a sense of loss at having to share the untouched land, but she was more flexible than Frans and in any case life was changing and things were happening which caused her to welcome the new neighbors.

In the months that followed their return from Galilee she noticed a change in Marie. The child no longer seemed so wild, no longer wanted to play continually with the Hottentot children, indeed she no longer played with them at all, and she was less intransigent about coming to her lessons. Susan found that she kept much more to the house and when she was making curtains or doing needlework Marie would often come and join her. Normally Susan would have been delighted with her company, but she sensed that Marie was not acting naturally and that her behavior sprang from reasons which Susan did not understand. She seemed to be much on the defensive, and while she remained silent for long periods, her temper, when it erupted, was worse than before. Susan noticed another change: Marie became self-absorbed to the extent of constantly examining herself physically and Susan had twice seen her standing in front of the looking glass in the bedroom examining the nipples and areolas of her as yet unformed breasts. Susan knew this to be normal in puberty and she herself had examined her own body minutely, especially when she had gone through the stage of having pimples. But Marie had not reached that point yet. There was clearly something worrying the child but try as she might Susan could not penetrate her reserve. What made it worse was that often she would catch Frans staring at Marie with a brooding, unfamiliar expression on his face.

Susan was a straightforward woman and found it difficult to endure the air of mystery and so she spoke to Frans about it, not stressing it, but simply wondering aloud, coming at the subject tangentially, why Marie had changed.

"Changed?"

"You've seen yourself how much time she spends in the house with me. She no longer plays with the Hottentot children."

"It would have stopped sooner or later."

"But she's still a child. It's not natural."

They were sitting on the stoep in the dusk and now he stood up and went down the steps.

"Frans?"

"You're imagining things. All girls go through times like this. My sisters did."

But Susan was not satisfied. She watched her daughter become more and more isolated. There was not much she could do in terms of education that she was not already doing with the books brought back from Galilee, but this did not solve the problem. The Lessings had children of Marie's age and she resolved to get them together. But how was she to manage it? She knew that Frans would never consent.

Then, two years after the Lessings had come to the valley, an opportunity arose. One wild night, when Frans was away with Mopedi on a trip to Griqua Town to barter for flour, Susan was wakened by the noise of galloping hooves and then a banging on the door. She lit a candle and opened the door to see a young white boy standing outside in the pouring rain, his hair plastered to his skull. He was tall and gangling and a few years older than Marie. It was such a strange and unexpected sight that she was nonplussed for a moment. "Who are you?" she said.

It took him a moment to catch his breath. "Hans."

"Hans?" He pointed upstream.

"Oh, Hans Lessing." She had only seen him once or twice and had failed to recognize him. "What is it, Hans? Come in."

"My mother," he said. "She's sick."

"What's wrong?"

"She was bitten by a snake."

"I'll come. Marie! Wake up!" They saddled up the mare and the foal which was now fully grown and Hans Lessing got up on his small Basuto pony. The river was a torrent. The boy had nearly come to grief on his way to Portuguese Place trying to force his horse across, but Susan knew a ford where the water was less turbulent and managed to get across without incident.

It was past midnight when they reached Saxony, the Lessings' farm. The rain was still lashing down and she could make out very little but she had been there once before and knew that the house was much like their own. There was a pattern to these lonely, primitive mud-built houses. As she went through the front door she noticed how clean everything was. There was a dresser and on it stood blue plates from Delft and burnished copper pans. The furniture itself, apart from the dresser, was much like their own. In the shadows on the far side of the room

she could make out three servants sitting against the wall, their eyes large with apprehension.

Mrs. Lessing was lying on a big brass bedstead in the larger of the two bedrooms, and Susan realized that it must have come, like the dresser and the plates and pots, all the way from Germany.

The Lessing family was crowded into the room. Helmut Lessing, the husband, was cradling his youngest child in his arms and there were two other children, a girl somewhat younger than Marie and a boy about five years old. Lessing rose as she came in and gave the baby to his daughter whom Susan knew as Ilsa. "When did it happen?" she asked.

"We have our food," Lessing said. "She goes to call the servants. The snake was maybe by the door at the back."

He was a man of medium height but looked shorter because of enormous shoulders. He was heavily bearded and gave an impression of massive solidity. He spoke with a thick guttural accent but his face was gentle and his eyes were the light blue of Saxony skies. His wife was a big woman with flaxen hair done in two plaits. Her face was lined, prematurely old, and her hands were big and hard like a man's. She tried to smile. "Such a fuss!" she said. Susan saw that she was sweating. She had been bitten in the left foot just above the instep. Like everyone else, she had been walking barefooted, both to save on shoes and to be more comfortable. Her feet had developed soles of hard skin like those of the Hottentot women. The area around the punctures was mottled in shades of blue, orange and black.

"Have you got the snake?" Susan said.

"*Ja*, but I do not know it," Lessing said.

Hans brought it in. Lessing held the lamp so she could see. It was about two feet long and she could not make out all its coloring but it seemed to be mainly brown with zigzag markings. It had been killed by a blow which broke its back, so its head remained recognizable.

"It's a night adder," she said.

"That's bad?" Lessing asked.

"Better than a puff adder."

"Ja, I think better."

She had watched Frans deal with several cases of snakebite and he had taught her which snakes were dangerous. He killed them on sight as a matter of principle and so she had had opportunities

to study them and learn their names. Night adders were quite common in this part of the country and their venom was often fatal. She knew that by now much of the poison would have already worked into Mrs. Lessing's body but she did what she could. First she tied a bandage above the wound which would cut off the blood supply. She told Lessing to release the ligature every few minutes or so before retightening it. Next she asked for the sharpest knife in the house and made three deep incisions horizontally across the wound. She sucked the area as hard as she could, spitting out mouthfuls of blood. She asked Lessing to heat a piece of wire in the flame of the lamp until it was red-hot, then she cauterized the wound. Mrs. Lessing twisted and moaned but her husband held her by the shoulders, leaning his bulk onto her and murmuring in German all the while. Lastly she rubbed Condy's crystals into the wound and tied a piece of flannel loosely over it.

Mrs. Lessing had lapsed into unconsciousness by the time she was finished and the children had been put out of the room so as not to witness the cauterization, except for Hans, who watched with anxious eyes the pain his mother was enduring. Susan washed the sweat from her face and neck and loosened her clothing. The woman floated into consciousness. "Thank you," she whispered.

"Now we wait," Susan said.

She told the servants to make coffee and she gave a mug to Helmut Lessing. He took it in silence, deep lines of anxiety between his eyes. She put the children to bed and then sat by the bedside.

Mrs. Lessing seemed worse in the morning and there was a bright red line up her leg showing the course of the poison. Susan sat with her all that day, sleeping only when Lessing took his turn in the hard chair by the bed.

Sometimes they held watch together. Mrs. Lessing was unconscious for most of the time and often in severe pain.

"Is she to die?" he asked.

"Are you a Christian?"

"Of course."

"Then we could pray for her."

They prayed in silence, one on each side of the bed, and Susan fell asleep on her knees and woke suddenly, ashamed of herself.

But it could only have been for a moment, for Lessing was still bent over his folded hands.

By the following night the crisis was over.

"She's strong," Susan said.

"Ja. She need to be."

They talked more easily now and he told her how they had emigrated to the Cape of Good Hope four years earlier and had spent some time trying to farm, but they had been raided often by the Korannas—Susan's mouth tightened at the word—and had given up when they had lost all their stock. They had gone on to the Vaal River diamond diggings, where he had practiced his trade as a blacksmith before trekking on to his present farm.

"Are there many people at the diggings?" she asked, remembering the wagons coming through Galilee.

"T'ousands *und* t'ousands! God help us!"

They slept, he on the floor, Susan in the chair. She woke at dawn and saw that Mrs. Lessing was recovering quickly. Her color had returned to normal and she was no longer sweating. The house was quiet. The world was still. Susan had not been outside for more than forty-eight hours. The rain had cleared away and the river had gone down. Everything was fresh and sparkling.

The Lessings had built their house where the valley floor was flatter than at Portuguese Place and they had done something which she and Frans had never done: they had planted crops, and now in midsummer there was a belt of green on the flatlands by the side of the river. It was an amazing sight, for the scrub desert simply ended and the green began, finally merging with the trees along the river.

She walked down and looked at the growing crop; it was maize. She realized the amount of work that the Lessings had put in and she knew why Mrs. Lessing's hands looked as they did. It was always said that the Germans were the hardest workers of all.

"Good morning," a voice said.

Lessing was coming towards her.

"She's better this morning," Susan said.

"Ja. I think so."

"She'll be all right now." She indicated the maize. "You've done well. How do you irrigate it?"

"Irrigate? What is that?"

"Bring water."

"I show you."

He took her a little way upstream and showed her the dam he had built across the river. It was a primitive wall but it raised a head of water and enabled him to lead it through his fields.

She had coffee and zwieback which Mrs. Lessing had made and then prepared to leave. Marie was still asleep and Susan said, "Let her stay. If you need me, send her." She knew perfectly well that Hans could ride as he had done before, but it was a way of helping Marie to get to know the Lessing children.

"Good," Lessing said. "Hans and Ilsa speak too little English. What can I give you?"

"Give me?"

"I must something give. You have come to help us."

"Neighbors help each other, that's enough. Anyway you have already given me something—an idea. I might try to grow some crops myself. . . ."

"Then I will give you maize." And he went into the house and brought out a small bag filled with precious seed.

But Frans was not impressed. "If this country is good for anything then it is animals." And he seemed to be right, for his flocks thrived on the harsh feeding. Often she would catch him staring out over land on which sheep were moving and she would sense an almost mystical feeling of ownership in him. More than once he said, referring to the stock, "A man can never have too many."

Marie spent a week at the Lessings' and when Susan went back to fetch her she found all the children getting on well together. Marie and Ilsa seemed particularly close. The young German girl whose fair skin and blond hair showed her north European ancestry followed Marie everywhere and she was already speaking English more fluently. Hans, although he was only thirteen, put in a full day on the farm and when Susan arrived he was working in the fields with his parents. Mrs. Lessing had recovered fully and seemed shy in Susan's presence.

"I t'ank you a t'ousand times," she said, putting her hand on Susan's arm.

"We were lucky that you were so strong, and lucky that the bite was so far from the heart."

The person who had worried Susan was Frans, because he had

said very little when he and Mopedi returned from Griqua Town to find Marie absent. When Susan brought her back she was so happy and natural and bubbling over with what she had done and with plans for more visits that his eyes seemed to lose the frowning, worried look.

Susan found only one aspect disquieting and that was Marie's treatment of the Hottentot children. Before she had stayed at the Lessings', she had broken the pattern of her friendship with them and had seemed indifferent; now she was actively hostile. There was one particular Hottentot child, a girl of Marie's own age, with whom she had played endlessly, called Nonna. She still occasionally came to the rear of the house to call for Marie, as a dog comes to search out its master.

On the first two occasions Marie told the servants to tell the child she was busy. On the third, a few days later, Susan was nearby when Nonna arrived. She was dressed as usual in ragged castoffs and her pale brown skin was dusty. But she had a bright, attractive face and Susan had always liked her.

"Get away!" Marie had shouted in English, for she rarely spoke Low Dutch now. "Get away from me!"

The Hottentot child had not understood the words, but had certainly understood their meaning, and had turned and walked disconsolately back to the huts in the hills behind the house.

"That was a cruel thing to do!" Susan said.

The anger in the child's face drained away and was replaced by her former tight-lipped expression. "I don't want to play with her," she said.

"She was your friend."

"I don't care."

"Don't you ever do that again. Don't make me ashamed of you."

That night Susan told Frans. He shrugged. "It is always the same. White children play with the Hottentots and then there comes a time when they stop."

"It wasn't that," Susan said. "It was the way she did it. Like kicking a dog."

She was remembering her own childhood in Georgia, playing with the children of slaves. When she was little her great friend had been Jim, the son of Selina, their cook. She could remember Selina so clearly. Unlike the conventional picture of an ample, contented cook, Selina had been rail-thin, with a pair of half-lens

spectacles on the end of her nose. These were often misted up by steam. On cold winter days Susan and Jim would spend most of their time in the kitchen "helping" Selina. "Helping!" Selina would say while the two of them sat at the big table, cutting or peeling, "Lord, Lord! If that's helping!" and she would go about her business muttering to herself and trying to see through her misted spectacles, and leave the black boy and the white girl, like a little island, to themselves. She was brusque, but love was there. In summer she would give them sandwiches or a slice of pie or a handful of cookies each and send them out to play. They would have "grown-up" picnics down by the river. It seemed to Susan that this was what her childhood had been: Selina and Jim and herself and her family, all warm and loving in the old house.

Then she went off to school in Boston and when she came back for her first vacation things changed abruptly. She returned to her place at the big kitchen table, but Jim was no longer there and when she asked where he was Selina said, "He ain't coming no more, Miss Susan."

Selina had never called her Miss Susan before and when Susan had gone to her father to find out what was happening, he had said, "You're becoming a big girl now. Things change."

Susan had never rejected Jim, nor anyone else for that matter, as Marie had rejected Nonna, but she knew what Frans meant now: there came a time when the mixing had to stop.

But that was the only small cloud on her horizon. A different sort of life had begun, one that she had almost forgotten. Visits between the two families became regular occurrences, especially by the children. Marie was forever nagging to be allowed to go to Saxony and, from what Susan could gather, the same was taking place there and it was Ilsa who was putting on pressure to come to Portuguese Place. Sometimes when the work was light Hans would be allowed to come, too. He was a rather grave boy, serious-minded in the German way, taking after his father. He was overjoyed when Frans offered to teach him to hunt. The two would go off together, sometimes camping miles away down-river. They would come back tired and dusty, but happy with the success of the hunt. Sometimes as Susan watched their growing friendship she felt a touch of sadness and regret that she had never been able to give him a son.

The two families began to spend Christmas together. Until then the day had passed almost unnoticed at Portuguese Place,

but the Lessings kept it in the German fashion and would trek to Galilee in November to lay in supplies for the great day. Saxony would be decorated with mimosa in place of fir and they would eat lamb and goat instead of carp and goose; the spirit of the time was kept intact, and soon it became a tradition that they spent Christmas alternately in each other's houses.

More and more Susan was reminded of her own youth as she watched the children opening their presents and being happy together and it was borne in on her that this was what had been missing, this friendship, this relationship with others. She had needed it, so had Marie and so, in spite of his own defenses, had Frans. The two families, with the Jordaans farther upsteam, formed a small community. There was enough variety of personality to give interest and both the Lessings and the Jordaans felt the same way as Frans did about strangers. The one farm had become three, but in a sense their lives at Portuguese Place had been improved by the change, for now in sickness there were others to turn to. Frans found that if he needed an implement made he could go to Helmut Lessing. And Lessing knew that if his family was short of meat he could come to Frans. Jordaan's specialty was horses and he had a way with them. When they were sick he knew what to do.

Frans had been building up his flock of sheep and cattle and he now employed three shepherds who did nothing else but see that the depredations of hyenas, wild dogs and jackals were kept to the minimum. There was not much they could do to control lions.

Susan still had her bag of maize seed and she and Frans had several times discussed the possibility of plowing the land near the river and growing maize as Lessing had done. But there was always the problem of water. The river was narrower and deeper at Portuguese Place and there was no natural position to build a weir. Lessing had been consulted and he had gone up and down the stream and examined the fall and had finally shaken his head and said, "You need a pomp!"

Frans looked relieved and Susan thought she knew why. His life had been nomadic and like a nomad his interest had been in stock: he saw his wealth in terms of the numbers of his cattle, sheep and goats. Susan's memories were of things growing and she missed them at Portuguese Place.

Several months later, on a blue and gold winter's day, Susan

was teaching Marie how to hem a handkerchief. Although the night's frost still lay on the ground in the shadow of the house, on the stoep the morning sun was warm.

"Your stitches are too big," Susan said. "Here, let me show you."

They worked in silence for a while, both absorbed in what they were doing, then Marie raised her head. "Listen. Someone is coming."

A figure on horseback rode through the trees, having crossed the ford at the river.

"It's Uncle Helmut," Marie said, throwing down her sewing and running to meet him.

The children called all adults "Uncle" and "Aunt" indiscriminately; to the Lessing children the Delports were Uncle Frans and Aunt Susan. To Marie, it was Uncle Helmut and Aunt Greta.

Lessing got down from his horse but stood at the bottom of the steps. "You're in time for coffee," Susan said.

"Ja. Ja. But later, I think."

There was a worried expression on his face and he said, "Where is Frans?"

"Is something wrong?"

"Maybe."

"Marie, get Father. Sit down, Helmut." She went in and told the servants to bring coffee. By the time she returned Frans was limping hurriedly round the side of the house.

Lessing had brought them disquieting news. His own concern was obvious in the way he spoke for sometimes he lost his English altogether and substituted German words so that when he finally paused Frans had only taken in half of what he said and now had to go back and ask him questions.

"You say that there has been another diamond strike? Not at the Vaal River? Is that right?"

"That is so. Much closer to here."

"But not on a river?"

"No."

"I thought all diamonds were found in rivers."

"Ja. I, too. But this is a new strike. A different kind of strike. Just in the middle of the desert. No river. No water."

"Who told you?"

"There was a man on my farm. He came to look for diamonds.

I spoke to him and he told me of the discoveries. Everyone is rushing there from the river diggings on the Vaal. T'ousands *und* t'ousands."

They sat back and looked at each other in silence, contemplating the implications of what had happened. Susan could hardly recall a time now when the massive solidity of Helmut Lessing had not been just over the horizon. The days when she and Frans and Marie and the few Hottentots had had the entire world to themselves seemed far away and unregretted, for the friendship of Helmut and Greta had given a new meaning to their lives. This latest intrusion was different. The world was coming to their front gate with a vengeance. It was not necessary for any one of the three to bring up the possibility of taking part in such a scramble and they would have answered on oath for Pieter Jordaan as well. They were farmers, they wished to be left alone.

"What happened to the man?" Frans said.

"I say good-bye."

"And he went?"

Helmut picked up the coffee cup, which almost disappeared in his large hands, and nodded slowly. "Ja. I said it would be better if he went."

Susan, in spite of the tension she felt, smiled to herself as she imagined the scene: the stranger facing this wild-looking man with the black beard and great shoulders, who might have been quarried from the ironstone of the desert outcrops.

That night she and Frans talked it over sitting in front of a blazing fire of camel thorn wood. "What does it mean, Father?" Marie said.

"It means the end," Frans said. "The end of all this." He waved his hands, encompassing the farm.

"Frans, it's not as bad as that," Susan said.

"A man cannot live in his own country anymore without being crowded. Half of these people are foreigners, Helmut tells me. They come from all over the world."

"But Helmut is a foreigner," Susan said mildly.

"Won't it mean people?" Marie said. "And houses and shops?" Her eyes had brightened at the very thought.

"Why should you want that?" Frans said.

"We don't know yet," Susan said. She had wondered herself what it would be like, and had envisioned something on the lines of Centerville, a small, quiet, rural town with a grid of streets

lined with oaks trailing Spanish moss. It had not seemed so bad an image and there might be opportunities for Marie to go to school. Then she had to remind herself that this was not Georgia, but harsh scrub desert where any town would be like Galilee, a sunstricken conglomeration of corrugated iron and clapboard.

Marie had her own room by now—again Frans had trekked to the mudhole and made the bricks and built it at the back where they were planning a bathroom and even a kitchen—and once she was in bed Susan said, to try and cheer him up, "We're safe here. No one can come onto our land unless we let him."

"That's the trouble," Frans said. "We don't know if it *is* our land. I am going to drink a brandy."

It was not often he took alcohol and it gave her an indication of his anxiety. When he sat down again he said angrily, "And Marie! What is the matter with her?"

"Any young girl would be interested in something new," Susan said.

"But why? We have our life here."

"We have *our* life. It's the life *we* want. That doesn't mean Marie will want it too."

Frans looked up in surprise. "You mean she wants to leave here?"

"Frans, she's only a child. She doesn't think like that yet. But one day she might."

"She cannot," he said fiercely. "She must stay here. She cannot leave."

"You can't make her a prisoner. You can't keep her here against her will."

"Prisoner? What sort of talk is that?"

It was not often they argued, but now that the subject had arisen, Susan decided to take it one step farther. "You traveled the whole of this land before you settled down. I saw much of America and London and parts of England. What has Marie seen and done?"

"She has us. She has all this."

"It's not the same. I was going to leave this until the time was right, but I may as well say it now: I think she should go to Cape Town for her education."

"Cape Town!" It was as though she had said Gomorrah.

"Two or three years will make all the difference."

"Never!"

"Think about it, Frans. Don't reject it out of hand."

He took another brandy. Then he said, "Where do you think we'll get the money?"

"We'll get money somehow; you always do when you need it."

She lay awake a long time going over the conversation in her mind. She was glad that they had spoken, glad the seeds had been sown. Frans always took a long time to get used to a new idea, but once he did he was amenable. The Lessings were an example. At first he had treated them as though they were lepers; now they were the greatest of friends and he would have been embarrassed if she had reminded him how he had originally felt about them. He would eventually see that Marie's future would be more secure with a good education. There was only one thing that bothered Susan: he seemed to feel a need to protect her—but from what?

The next few weeks were tense ones at Portuguese Place. Frans seemed to spend most of the time watching the river crossing and the hills behind the house as though he were expecting an invading army, and Susan watched Frans. Things were not made easier by Marie's constant questioning about what was likely to happen, and finally Frans became irritable with her, which Susan had never seen before. When she could stand it no longer she said, "If it's God's will that other people come to live in this country then it will happen, and there's nothing we can do about it. But let's not anticipate things."

"God does not have to look after my sheep and cattle."

One day she saw him packing blankets in his saddlebags and cleaning his rifle and checking his bandolier and she said, "What's happening?"

"I'm going to ride the boundaries."

"How long will you be gone?"

"A week maybe."

They had marked the boundaries during the first year they had lived on Portuguese Place. They had taken the river as one line and Frans had ridden upstream and downstream, built cairns at both stopping places and then ridden into the desert, building cairns wherever he thought necessary. In this way he had marked out a huge, rough rectangle, one side of which was the river. They had no idea how big the farm was. They had never seen it all and the area encompassed several ranges of hills, a salt pan, various other pans which filled with water when it

rained, the mudhole from which the bricks had been made and two Hottentot villages. It was immense but so dry and arid that one sheep needed five *morgen*—more than ten acres—to keep itself alive, and he was now running hundreds of sheep, some goats and scores of scrub cattle.

"Let me come with you," she said.

His eyes lit up, and then he frowned. "What about Marie?"

"She can stay at Saxony. Just the two of us. Like it used to be."

Marie needed no urging and the following day Frans and Susan set off. They each rode a horse and took a third as a pack animal. Susan was to remember this week always as one of the best she had ever spent for there was a poignancy about it in hindsight that gave it an added dimension; it was a watershed in their lives and nothing was ever to be the same again.

For the first few days they rode into the high country, camping at night over a huge fire and sleeping as closely together as they could, for it was cold in the hills. They rode through a tawny landscape under the great blue dome of the sky and a warm yellow sun. On the hilltops in the early morning the air stung their ears and burnt their nostrils. "I had no idea it was so big," she said.

"Look around you" he said. "Everything you see is ours."

Then they came down lazily to the river and felt the first warm wind of spring. They camped on a sandspit and Frans caught yellow-fish and they sat in the sun and ate them. Susan remembered how she had walked along the Great River until she had nearly died of starvation and all the time it had been full of fish and she had not tried to catch them.

The noons were hot now in the confines of the river and one day, towards the end of the week, as they were making their way home, they came through a gorge and felt the heat from the rocks and Susan said, "Summer will be here soon."

Frans said, "There's a pool. Let's swim."

"You go in."

"I mean together."

They had not done this for many years, not since Marie was a baby, and Susan felt suddenly embarrassed at the thought of exposing her short square body, now misshapen by childbearing and hard work.

"Come," he said.

She put her hand into the water. "It's too cold."

"We'll swim together," he said.

She had tried to make a joke of it but there was an underlying tension in his voice.

She took his hand and brought it to her lips. "Things don't stay the same," she said. "Everything changes. You have your swim and I'll start a fire."

He seemed about to say something more but she moved away and he said, "You're right. It's too cold."

The following day, within a few hours of home, they saw a stranger at the water's edge. They came upon him suddenly without warning. He was crouched on the bank with an enamel basin in his hands. It contained gravel and water. He swirled the pan in a circular motion allowing the water to escape and then turned it upside down on a rock and sifted through the gravel. Frans and Susan sat like statues watching him. Then one of the horses whickered at the smell of water and the man looked up. He took in the situation instantly and glanced towards his bedroll where his shotgun lay. Frans saw the movement and urged his horse forwards. "Who are you?" he said in Low Dutch.

The man straightened up. He was poorly dressed and appeared to be about forty years old.

"Who are you?" Frans repeated this time in English. "What are you doing here?"

"Who's asking?" the man said. He was thin, with a somewhat ratlike appearance.

"You're on my land," Frans said. "What do you want?"

"The name's Miller."

"I don't care what your name is. What are you doing on my land?"

"I ain't done nothing wrong. I got a piece of paper that says I can prospect for diamonds and other minerals along this stretch of river."

"It's my river."

"What? You own the bleedin' water as well as the land?"

"Yes."

"You ain't God! Look!" He'd been fumbling in his shirt pocket and now took out a piece of printed paper and handed it to Frans. As he took it Susan saw that his hand was shaking with anger. He did not even look at it, but slowly tore it into small pieces.

"Here! You can't do that!"

"Now you have no paper."

"That cost money!"

Miller had been circling slowly towards his bedroll and the shotgun but Frans pressed the horse a few steps forwards and forced Miller along the riverbank. Each time the man tried to move away from the water's edge Frans herded him back with the horse. He had to either swim or keep moving away along the bank.

"For Christ's sake, mister!" he began, as Frans pulled his rifle from the saddle holster.

"Frans!" Susan's voice was shrill.

Frans paid no attention. "If you come back onto my land I will shoot you," he said.

"All right! All right!" Miller moved fifty yards upstream and stopped to watch.

Frans dismounted, picked up the shotgun and smashed the stock on a rock, then threw the basin into the river. He lifted the bedroll and tossed it in Miller's direction. "One hour," he said.

It was a bleak homecoming. Susan had been frightened by what she had seen, not so much by the action itself, but what it meant for the future. Frans was angry and depressed. They had not been home for more than an hour when he said, "I'm sending for Helmut and Pieter."

The meeting took place the following day. Jordaan was tall and thin and wore side-whiskers. An accident with a horse had hurt his back when he was younger and he walked with a slight stoop. He was a loose-jointed man with high cheekbones and a sandy look to him.

They came with their wives. It was the first time Hendrina Jordaan had been to Portuguese Place. She was short, fat and cheerful and was longing to take Susan aside and talk about household affairs, but things were too serious for that. The six of them sat in the living room and drank coffee and the men each had a brandy because the situation was grave.

Lessing had had two more prospectors on his land and Jordaan three. Frans had been lucky to have had only one.

"They have papers," Lessing said. "I cannot read the papers."

"We must have papers, too," Jordaan said, sipping his brandy.

That was the nub of the discussion. They talked for hours, the womenfolk sitting in silence, and always, although they went off

at tangents, they were gradually pulled back by one simple question: did they own the land?

"If we are here then we are here," Lessing said. "The land is ours."

"But can we prove it?" Jordaan said. "Have we a piece of paper which says so?" He paused, then said, "We can chase these people away when they come in ones and twos but later . . ."

They sat digesting this. They knew that people would bring government and government meant pieces of paper.

"Where I lived before," Lessing said, "we registered our land."

"But first it must be surveyed," Jordaan said. "I know that much."

"Then we will *have* it surveyed," Frans said. "But we must get a surveyor."

"In a diamond rush you will find t'ousands of surveyors," Lessing said. "That's where they make their money."

"All right," Frans said. "We'll go and get one."

"Who?" Jordaan asked.

"What about you?" Frans said to Lessing.

"I hate such places."

"All right, I will go myself."

The wagon stopped at the top of a rise and Frans and Susan looked out on one of the most amazing sights they had ever seen. The whole plain in front of them was dotted with tents and wooden shanties. Everywhere men were digging, black men and white, digging feverishly in spite of the heat of the noon sun and every now and then the point of a pick glinted in the sunshine as it fell. On the far side of the plain they could see wagons and carts hurrying to join the roiling ant heap of men already there: everything spoke of rush and hurry as men ran from one place to another searching for vacant ground on which to dig.

"My God," Frans said. "I have never seen anything like this."

They had left Portuguese Place two days before, taking with them two servants and two sheep for slaughter because they did not know how long they would be away. Susan saw a look almost of fear in Frans's eyes. He was right, she thought, things would never be the same, and a kind of panic swept over her. "Let's go back," she said. "Let's turn round."

A voice said, "Good day to you."

A man was standing by the wagon. He was dressed in a dark city suit with a brown bowler on his head and a watch chain looped on his waistcoat. He was a plump, fair-skinned man and was covered in dust.

"Is this the Dry Diggings?" Frans said.

"The same, sir."

"It's like the end of the world."

"Or the beginning, depending on whether you're finding anything or not and, believe me, sir, they're finding stones by the score. I take it you haven't come to dig yourself?"

"No," Susan said.

"Are these yours?" He pointed to the two sheep grazing on the dry bush near the wagon.

"Yes," Frans said.

"What'll you take for them?"

"Take?"

"I'll give you a fiver each."

Frans and Susan sat like bumpkins, hardly able to believe what they were hearing. "Six then," the man said. "Six pounds a-piece."

Suddenly Susan laughed. "It's more money than we've seen in a year," she said. "But we haven't much use for money. So I'll make a bargain with you, Mr. . . . ?"

"Levinson. Levinson of Lewisham in dear old London town."

"We're searching for a land surveyor. You find us a surveyor and we'll *give* you the sheep."

For a moment Mr. Levinson looked at them in disbelief. "That's all I have to do?"

"That's all."

"Done and done," he said, and he hurried off down the road, his coattails flapping, one hand on the crown of his brown bowler.

He found them a young man called Richards, another Londoner, who jumped at the opportunity of surveying three farms. They left immediately. As they turned the bullock wagon and began to move away through the Dry Diggings they saw a large crowd gathering under an acacia tree.

On a trestle table there were mounds of freshly butchered meat. A hand-lettered sign was pinned to a tree. It said:

As the wagon passed by, Levinson came from behind the table. He wore a white apron, but his head was still covered by the dusty bowler. His forearms were red and he held a large butcher's knife in his hand. "Got any more?" he said to Frans.

"Yes."

"Where can I find you?" Mr. Levinson looked over his shoulder, making sure no one heard.

There was a moment of silence. Susan realized what was going though Frans's mind. But the panic she had felt earlier had been replaced by realism: they could not put their heads in the sand like ostriches.

"These people won't go away," she said to Frans. "We've got to be strong enough to live with them. If that means trading, then so be it."

Frans sat stiffly. He was too confused to reply, so she spoke for him. "The farm is called Portuguese Place."

"Thank you, ma'am. We'll make our fortunes. Shake on it." The three of them shook hands.

4

At five o'clock on a hot midsummer's afternoon in 1875 the S.S. *Northbrook,* twenty-one days out of Southampton, berthed in Table Bay Docks, Cape Town. In the captain's cabin, Jack Farson stood in front of the desk at which Captain Woods was seated. Both men were sweating freely.

"You're a fool, Farson," the captain said. "The place is rotten with people like you, who've come to dig diamonds and failed."

Above the creaking of the ship's timbers Jack could hear the cries of seabirds and shouts from the bumboats. Captain Woods was a short, florid man in the white tropicals of the Castle Line, with a wing collar and a black tie. He had a ledger on the desk in front of him. "Ninety percent of the passengers in the ship will be penniless in a month. Half of them will die on the diggings. Still, it's your business. I make it twelve pounds thirteen and six."

"Sir, it should be nearer forty!"

The captain looked down at the book. "Hammer and scraper lost overboard before we left port. Then you had tobacco three times . . . and you were drunk twice . . . a shop window broken in Madeira . . ."

"Sir, that wasn't me."

"The mate says it was."

"Sir . . ."

"That's all, Farson. If you're unhappy, take it up with the company."

Jack pocketed the money, slung his seabag on his shoulder and turned to go. "When you've found your diamonds you won't worry about a sum like that," Captain Woods said, shutting the ledger with a snap.

Jack went to the gangway. The crush of passengers trying to disembark was five deep. Most had come to dig for diamonds at Kimberley, which the Dry Diggings were now called. The S.S. *Northbrook*—the "Diggers' Special": from England fifteen pounds bought you a bunk in the hold, ten square feet for your baggage, and as much tea, bread and tough beef as you could manage— was one of dozens of ships from all parts of Europe and America bringing men to the scene of the greatest diamond rush the world had known. There was a feeling among the passengers of haste, almost of panic, to get on with what they had come to do, to reach the mines, to start digging, to get rich quick. The object was to get there before the next man, before he dug up the wealth and left you with nothing. But Cape Town was more than six hundred miles south of the diggings and there was still a long way to go, a long way to hurry, a long way to race your neighbor. Speed . . . speed . . .

Jack Farson, too, was caught by the feeling of urgency. He was in his early twenties, a big man, craggy, ginger-haired and freckled, with a square bony frame that looked as though it had been cast in a foundry. His hands were large and as hard as boot soles from pulling on a thousand ropes. He had been to North and South America, to most of the ports of Europe and twice to Australia, but no matter where he had journeyed his goal had been the country that now lay before him. Sometimes he had thought he would never reach Africa or that all the diamonds would be dug up before he got there, and his frustration would boil up into a helpless anger. But then he would hear of new and richer strikes and ambition would burn again.

Now the excitement and aggression of the crowd round the gangplank infected him. The diggers came from every country and walk of life, some in city suits, some in checked shirts and knee britches, carrying picks and shovels from the gold rushes in Bendigo and Kalgoorlie, chronic diggers, caught by the panic to get on, to get there first, to snatch their wealth from the hard, stony soil.

Jack's mood was heightened by a sullen anger at what he thought was sharp practice on the part of Captain Woods, and he pushed his way to the top of the gangway with scant regard for his fellows. Some turned in irritation as they felt his elbows, but when they saw the big, gaunt man with the face like a sandstone cliff, they edged away and let him through.

The press on the gangway was uncomfortable, but the dockside was worse for here, mixed with the disembarking diggers, were porters touting for customers, servants from city hotels singing the praises of their establishments, Cape carts—the equivalent of the London hansom cabs—picking up and dropping fares; there were pickpockets and whores and fishermen returning from the day's work; everyone was shouting and pushing. In the midst of this, not surprisingly, an altercation had broken out between two of the passengers. Jack tried to ignore it and push through but people on the quay rushed to see what was happening and those on the gangway were unable to go forwards or back. Jack, who was on the lower step, recognized the two men involved in the quarrel. He had seen them frequently, although never together. One was of medium height and wore a dark city suit and a white panama hat. Jack had noticed him during the voyage because he read books and kept to himself and never was seen without his hat. The other man was a big bearded Welshman called Williams. Jack knew his name because he and a stocky Scot called Mackay were two of the troublemakers of the voyage. Both men had been frequently drunk and once Williams had vomited on B deck outside the main saloon and the first officer had ordered Jack to clean it up.

The quarrel had broken out because the young man in the suit had accidentally knocked into the water a package belonging to Willliams which contained two spades.

"It was an accident," he was saying. "I'll be glad to pay you for them."

'You bloody Jew-boys think you can buy anything and anybody with your money!"

"They were only spades. I mean . . ."

"They weren't *your* spades, Jew-boy." Williams began prodding him on the right shoulder: short, sharp jabs that sent him backwards.

"Give them room," someone shouted.

"Make a ring!"

"Gi'e him a lesson, Taff!" a voice shouted, and Jack recognized that it belonged to the Scot, Mackay.

Williams and his victim were at the bottom of the gangway. Jack was crushed as the young man backed into him. The anger that had arisen in the captain's cabin, combined with the memory of cleaning up Williams's vomit, caused him to say, "Give over!"

"I'm going to teach him a lesson."

"Give over!"

"You mind your own bloody business."

Jack hit him. People who saw it said at first they thought he had hit him with a leg of mutton or a shoulder of pork, so big did his right fist seem. Williams went down like a felled tree. But instead of a cheer there was a hush. Men looked at Jack, muttered to each other and then began to disperse. Soon he was standing by himself as Williams was helped away on rubbery legs.

"Thank you," someone said.

Jack shook himself. For several minutes he had been unconscious of his surroundings. Rage had transported him onto a different level. Had Williams not fallen instantly, he would have been on him like an animal. His vision cleared and he looked at the young man.

"My name's David Kade."

They shook hands.

"Jack Farson."

"Are you going to the diggings?"

Jack swung his seabag over his shoulder. "Yes."

"Perhaps we'll meet there. Perhaps I can repay you."

Jack turned towards the city that lay under Table Mountain. He had not gone more than a few yards when he felt a hand on his arm. "Excuse me. . . ."

He turned angrily. He did not want more thanks, he had not done it for Kade's sake. But this was a different face, lined,

sunburnt, a face of the country.

He looked at a man who had once been his own size but who now, in middle age, had shrunk inside his skin. "I saw what happened," the man said. "I heard what you said. I can take you to the diggings."

"Why?"

"I've come to fetch a water pump. It's in the ship. I need a strong fellow to help me get it to my farm."

"Where's that?"

"Near the diggings."

"How long will it take?"

"Two months, a bit more, perhaps."

Jack shook his head. "The coaches take ten days."

He began walking away. The man walked with him and Jack noticed that he limped.

"They cost money."

"I've got money."

"If you change your mind, ask for Delport. Frans Delport. I'll be in the wagon park on the Grand Parade for two more days."

At the bottom of Adderley Street, the main street of the town, Jack paused. Rearing up ahead of him was the great, slab-sided block of granite called Table Mountain. A southeasterly wind was blowing and a tablecloth of white cloud obscured its top. The town was compressed between the mountain and the sea. It was geometrically patterned, the streets at right angles, the buildings formal and of the same height. He walked up into its center. Cape carts clip-clopped up the unpaved streets, fishermen in conical Malay hats blew fish horns to announce their catch, flower sellers lined the pavements, the shop windows were filled with goods that had been brought from Europe.

The Cape at this point in the nineteenth century was a British colony and Cape Town itself a bustling seaport, busier than it had ever been because diamonds had been discovered in the hinterland and it was the main port of entry. It was an entrepôt of half a dozen cultures, black, white and mixed. Jack knew none of this and could not have cared less. Cape Town for him was an irrelevancy on his journey to the diggings.

He found the office of Messrs. Arnholz and Company, who ran the coaches between the Cape and the diamond diggings, and stopped in amazement at the crowd around the doorway. It appeared that everyone in the city was trying to jump the queues

that stretched halfway round the block. He pushed with the rest but it was half an hour before, sweating, dusty and hot, he stood in front of one of the small brass grilles. The ticket clerk was just as hot and his once stiff collar was limp.

"Single or return?" the clerk said.

"Single."

"First date in three weeks."

"Ain't you got nothing sooner?"

"Not a blessed thing."

"How much?"

"Fifty."

"Quid?"

"Pounds. Sterling."

Jack was stunned. With the twelve pounds he had been paid that morning he had a total of just over twenty-seven pounds. He had thought that ten or, at the most, fifteen pounds would do the journey.

"That's bloody robbery!"

"You want it?"

"Fifty quid!"

"Next!"

He turned away angrily. At the next window he saw a familiar face. It was the man from the docks. His white panama was on his head and he was shoveling five-pound notes over the counter. Jack watched bitterly. They were all getting ahead of him.

He had a meal at the London Hotel in Greenmarket Square and then walked down to the docks. He had no alternative now but to take up the farmer's offer. He had heard of men walking to the diggings but the wagon, slow as it was, would be better than that. But Frans Delport was not to be found. Then he recalled he had spoken of a wagon park on the Grand Parade, and was directed there by the first man he asked. It was an open space about the size of three city blocks. Trees bordered one end while at the other there were flower sellers, fruit sellers, farmers selling mounds of yellow pumpkins and old Hottentot women selling scrawny hens. Dusk was falling and lights were being lit. Photographers were packing up their booths and the snake charmers were unpacking their mats and setting out their round baskets to be ready for the evening's entertainment. He was reminded of the New Cut in Lambeth.

The main difference was the heat. Here people's faces shone

with sweat as they strolled through the hot, dusty darkness. Over the heads of the crowd Jack saw, at the far end of the Parade, twenty or thirty white-tented wagons. He was walking towards them when he was stopped by a sound of clapping. To his right he saw a wooden platform on which a small man in a garish checked suit was doing a balancing act; he held a walking stick on his forehead and was balancing a plate on its other end. On one side of the platform was the sign MEECHAM'S MARVELOUS MAGIC SHOW, and underneath, in smaller lettering: "Amazing and Mysterious Feats of the Past and Present."

The man finished his act, placed a straw boater on his head and said in a gravelly showman's voice, "And now, ladies and gentlemen, what you've all been waiting for! The sweetest voice in three continents: the Surrey Nightingale!" He gave two loud introductory chords on a battered upright piano and a young woman came onto the platform.

Jack had little ear for music and began to turn away. Then she started to sing. There was a sweetness in her voice so ineffable that it touched something in him he had not known existed. He felt a great sadness come over him, yet he had nothing to be sad about.

He pushed forwards. She was about his own age and beautiful in a way he had never seen before. Her skin in the light of the torches that blazed at the corners of the platform was alabaster. At the end of each song the crowd shouted and stamped their approval but Jack stood silent, transfixed by her voice and her looks. He was still standing there when she finished and left the platform to the barker.

"After Beauty comes the Beast!" he shouted. "A big hand now for the champion of Singapore and Macao! Bare-knuckle champion of Adelaide! Famous in Europe and the Americas! World-renowned with or without the mufflers! Ladies and gentlemen, the Batavian Giant!"

The new arrival was one of the biggest men Jack had seen. He was dressed only in a pair of Turkish trousers that were caught in at the ankles. His body was covered in tattoos: snakes wound from his chest to his back and down his arms, fish swam on his stomach and even his sides were decorated. His head was shaven and, like his body, had been oiled. He had a broad flat face that gazed contemptuously at the crowd.

"Stay three rounds with the Giant, and it's twenty-five quid for

you. Knock 'im down and it's fifty. Now, who's first?"

A challenger was already in the corner, a young farmer whose body, except for his neck, hands and forearms, was as white as snow. He had little knowledge of boxing and the Batavian Giant sent him to his knees inside half a minute. The next man was a digger, by the look of his clothes, and he lasted into the second round before being knocked into the crowd. There was something coldly savage about the way the tattooed man dealt with them and Jack was reminded of a cat playing with a wounded bird. He had done his share of fighting as a sailor and, inspecting the Giant, he realized that he was overweight as well as being older than he looked. If Jack could stay three rounds he would have enough money for a ticket on the coach. If he could knock the Giant down, he would have money over.

The third challenger was being picked off the floor by the barker when Jack pushed forwards. "I'll have a go!" he shouted.

The barker looked down at him and shook his head. "Three's the limit."

"Give us a chance!"

"No more than three."

"What about tomorrow, then?"

"We won't be here tomorrow."

Jack saw his chance slipping away. He looked up at the glistening face of the Batavian Giant. "You afraid of me?"

The crowd liked that. But the Giant was not to be outfaced. "We meet one day," he said in a heavy accent. "Then we see who is afraid."

He draped his shoulders with a green silk dressing gown and jumped down from the platform. Alongside the ring were the closed wagons of the troupe—they reminded Jack of gypsy caravans—and the tattooed man pushed open the door of one and went in. Jack caught a glimpse of the girl who had sung so beautifully before the door closed again.

"You should have had your chance," a voice said, and Jack turned to see David Kade. He was holding his hat in his hand. His hair was short and fitted closely to his skull like a cap. He gave an impression of composure and neatness and Jack suspected that under his dark suit there was a sinewy strength. "I saw what happened at the coach office," he continued. "I could lend you a tenner if that would help."

Jack opened his mouth to say he didn't want his money, but the

Jew seemed a decent enough person, so instead he said, "It's all right, thanks, I can manage."

It took him some time to find Frans Delport, who was standing at the rear of his wagon smoking a meerschaum pipe. A small fire burned nearby and on it stood a coffee pot. He looked at Jack and smiled.

"I told you it was costly," he said.

"When do you leave?"

"Tomorrow morning, early. You can sleep there." He indicated the area under the wagon where his own mattress was already laid. The wagon suddenly shook and the tent flap was pulled to one side. A girl's head emerged. "Father, aren't you going to offer him a cup of coffee?"

Frans introduced Marie. She clambered down from the wagon and Jack saw a girl of about sixteen with raven-black hair, black eyes and a smooth olive skin. There was almost a gypsy look about her.

"Won't you be seated?" she said, indicating a bale of hay as though it were a grand, silk-covered chair. "Do you take milk? Sugar?" Her eyes sparkled and Jack saw her father smile behind his hand. Were they laughing at him? He took the mug of coffee, feeling clumsy and ill at ease.

"What's the news from London?" she asked.

"What news?" Jack said, in a surly voice.

"Pay no attention to her, Mr. Farson." Frans Delport was smiling again. "It's this Cape Town school she's been to, Miss Menzies's . . ."

"It is pronounced 'Mingies's.' Miss Harriet *Mingies's* Academy for Young Ladies. You will have heard of it, Mr. Farson. It is very well known." Abruptly, she got to her feet and clambered back into the tented wagon. Again her face appeared through the flaps. "Good night, Mr. Farson. I hope you do not snore."

Frans Delport employed two Hottentot servants to look after the oxen and to gather firewood and make the cooking fires. Jack's main function was to help Delport with the wagon itself: to manhandle it up slopes where the bullocks needed assistance, to act as an anchor on the down-gradients when it might have run away with the oxen, to float it across streams or to go ahead and see that the fords were not too deep and that there was a good stony bottom, for the pump was heavy and the wagon wheels bit

into the surface of the ground more deeply than usual.

The pump itself was in several parts, each boxed and labeled "The Invincible, G. A. Gwynne, Hammersmith, London," and had come out in the cargo of the S.S. *Northbrook.* Delport would check the boxes two or three times a day and once he patted one of them and said, "Where we come from, water is worth more than diamonds."

"It's a present for my mother," Marie told Jack.

"Mr. Farson will think we're strange people giving presents like this," her father said. "But she wants to grow crops and the land is too dry. If we can pump water up and irrigate the fields, then we can grow many things, especially maize, what you in England call corn on the cob."

"It's a surprise," Marie said. "Don't you think it's a lovely surprise? Perhaps we'll keep it for her Christmas stocking." Her eyes flashed at him and he saw Frans Delport's slow smile; again he wondered if he was the butt of some joke he did not understand.

At first he minded his own business. Around the evening fire he was silent, recognizing his own roughness when he was in their company, especially Marie's; even her father, who had lived a life far removed from civilizing influences, seemed polished by comparison with himself.

Marie treated him much as she treated Frans, as though they were overgrown boys who had to be watched and bullied so she could have her way. He had no idea at first how to react to such behavior. His only experience of women had been his mother, his half sister and the brothel women he had used in a score of ports around the world. Marie was something new. Slowly his irritation changed to a kind of heavy-handed banter and he found himself enjoying the unfamiliar relationship.

They would often find themselves in each other's company as they walked alongside the wagon through the heat of the day and he learned from her about the farm in the desert of the northwest and about how her mother and father had met and built their house and started keeping sheep and goats. When she spoke of it her face would sometimes tighten and her mouth would turn down. He had the impression that she did not want to go back and once when he asked her she said angrily, "I'm only a girl. I have to do what I'm told."

He discovered she had a passion for England, and she tried to

use him like an encyclopedia. Miss Harriet Menzies, it seemed, had installed into her girls a fascination for the British social scene and Marie would press him about such beings as dukes and earls and viscounts. Had he met any? Did he know a real lord? Did the aristocrats eat off gold plate? More than once, she professed an ambition to spend Christmas in a grand country house with thick snow all around. Jack, she said, might come with her, if he liked. Her father, listening, wondered out loud what nonsense Miss Harriet had stuffed into her head.

Often, when Jack was alone with Frans he would ask about the diggings. He learnt that diamonds had orginally been found on the Vaal River, but then the big discoveries had been made at what was now called Kimberley, after a British politician. A town had already grown up.

"Have you ever worked on the diggings?" he asked.

Delport shook his head in distaste. "I keep as far away as I can."

"Without the diggings we would have no money," Marie said waspishly.

"We were better off without it," Frans said.

"You would never have been able to send me to school."

"Maybe that would have been better, too."

"Tell us about Kimberley," she said. "Tell us about the shops and the music halls." She turned to Jack. "Some people say it's the most exciting place in Africa."

The journey was a slow one, taken at the pace of the oxen, and it was a good day when they managed ten or twelve miles. But it was a journey on which Marie, Frans and Jack came to know each other well and it did not take long for Jack to realize that there was another side to Marie: superficially she was a vital, energetic girl with an ebullience that was very attractive. But there was a darker area: sometimes, for no apparent reason, or at least none that he could divine, she would become morose, withdrawn and angry. Her rages came out of the blue, violent and irrational. She seemed to reserve the worst side of her nature for the Hottentot servants, and it only took a minor miscalculation on their part to bring down her wrath on their heads.

This naturally had an effect on Frans, and Jack would see him staring at his daughter with a brooding and sometimes unhappy expression. Jack thought there must be some intimate family problem affecting the two of them which would explain the

circumstances, but which was not to be revealed to him. He was content that this should be so.

He found he was enjoying himself. At first he envied the family bond, then found he was becoming part of it. Some of his rough edges were smoothed away and he began to change. Instead of having to deal with a man whose tight-lipped and morose presence made the evenings difficult to endure, the Delports found him becoming more human, more relaxed. And with this change in attitude they felt they could ask him about himself. At first he parried their questions. He was unused to revealing himself and in the fo'c'sle a man's past was never volunteered and never inquired into. But when he saw the puzzled looks that greeted his circumlocutions he knew he would have to say something, however little. He told them just as much as would satisfy them.

The truth was that Jack Farson was the son of a whore and a Norwegian seaman. No one knew much about his father. Down at the East India Docks and the Port of London they remembered him as a big man, with a shock of red hair and fists the size of hams. He was lost at sea when black ice struck his ship off the Faroes. More was known about Jack's mother. Her name was Emma Cook; she was the daughter of a curate in Gloucestershire and was educated at home by her mother. Her brother entered the Church and she became governess to two girls in a wealthy family in Salisbury. She did then what many young governesses have done: she fell in love with her charges' brother, Herbert, who was twenty-four. He was the first young man with whom she had been in close contact. She became his mistress on the understanding that they would marry, but after taking her on a tour of the Continent, he married someone else.

She took up with a cavalry officer who, when he was tired of her, passed her on to a colleague who handed her on to a sergeant (by whom she had a daughter named Mary) until finally she was anyone's woman.

She met her Norwegian sailor in the Earl of Effingham, a theater in the Whitechapel Road, and took him back to her lodgings in Bluegate Fields. They liked each other. Whenever he was in London she would keep herself for him. Of this union John was born and took his father's name of Farson. No one in

Bluegate Fields ever used his mother's real name. She was called China Emma because someone once said she looked like a china doll.

They moved from Bluegate Fields to rooms in Dean Street near the West End. Jack was twelve when his father was killed. At that time China Emma was in her late thirties and was taken over by a bully called Truman Rutter. She turned her tricks in Perkin's Rents, a warren of rooms in Westminster. But she kept her rooms in Dean Street: this was the family home and she wanted it separate from her business. It was this vestigial remnant of respectability that cost her her life, for she kept back money from Rutter to pay the rent and save for her children.

At first she hid the money about the apartment but when Rutter became suspicious she began to deposit it with a money-lender in the New Cut in Lambeth, using Jack and his half sister, Mary, as go-betweens.

One day when Jack was fourteen and Mary two years older, they were taking money and one or two items of which China Emma had relieved her clients—a watch, a silk handkerchief and a silver cigar-cutter—when Jack noticed Rutter following them on the opposite side of Regent Street.

It was coming on evening of a bitterly cold winter's day and there was already fog in the streets, heavy with the acrid smell of smoke from a hundred thousand coal fires. The gas lamps were lit and the West End began to gather pace for the evening's entertainment. Jack saw Rutter's reflection in a shop window, and paused.

"Stop gawping," Mary said. "We've things to do." She was a pretty girl with the same soft coloring as their mother.

"It's Rutter. He's followed us."

"Well, you know what to do."

They had talked this possibility over with China Emma and had a plan ready.

They walked on. Rutter, on the opposite side, kept station with them and all Jack could see in the evening crowd was a figure wrapped in an ulster and a scarf, with a tall hat, battered and dented, on his head. Jack was frightened of him. Recently Rutter had caught him alone and said, "Come on now, Jack. You and me's old friends. Where's she hid it then? Where's the rest of the money?" One of his women had smashed Rutter's nose and he had a permanent drip.

"There ain't no rest of it."

"Let's have the truth, Jack. You know what I can do. . . ."

That had been two weeks ago and Jack knew it would not be the end of the matter. He had warned his mother, but she was so far gone on a mixture of gin and laudanum called Mother's Blessing that she hardly paid heed.

They crossed Shaftesbury Avenue, dodging past horses' heads, sliding in the dung. Then Mary said, "Now!" and she went one way and Jack the other, both losing themselves in the evening crowd before Rutter knew what was happening. After crisscrossing a dozen alleys and going back on his own tracks until he was certain that Rutter was not following him, Jack continued his journey to Lambeth.

At seven o'clock at night, under fog-haloed lamps, the New Cut was at its busiest. It was a market of sorts, kept free of horse-drawn traffic. The gin shops were roaring, the market was bustling, the place was full of working people out for an hour or two. On each side were stalls selling meat, fish, fruit, and over everything was the harsh smell of roasting chestnuts. Mary was waiting for him in a doorway opposite a tailor's shop.

They went up the stairs and she knocked at the door at the top. A voice, curiously light and high like a child's, said, "Who is it?"

"It's Mary, Mr. Berkis."

"Mary who?"

"Mary from Dean Street." It was always the same.

Jack heard a step on the far side of the door, the sound of a bolt being drawn, then the turning of a key in the lock, and he smelled the familiar smell of incense. The room was hot from a coal stove in one corner. There was a deal of brassware and bamboo tables—it was said that Mr. Berkis had been a clerk in a Malayan godown when he was a young man—and a pair of long joss sticks burning in a tall Chinese vase.

Mr. Berkis was short. He looked like an elderly baby, with chubby hands and rolls of flesh under his chin. He wore an old silk dressing gown and a Turkish smoking cap of blue velvet decorated with a tassel of gold thread. His face was pink and round and he had no eyebrows. "Come in, my dears."

Jack placed the watch, the silk handkerchief and the silver cigar-cutter on the red leather desk top in front of him. Mr. Berkis moved the objects about for a moment with his small, chubby fingers, and said, "Four pounds the lot."

"Why, the watch is worth that alone!" Mary said.

"Look." A fat finger went out and pointed to the inscription on the back. "Can't do good business with inscriptions. The police 'ave been sniffing about already."

"All right," Mary said. "Mam says you're to add this." She pulled out a purse and counted out a handful of florins.

Mr. Berkis thumbed through the pages of a small book, added a new set of numbers to the column of figures, drew a line underneath and wrote in the total. "Twenty-two pounds, seventeen and sixpence ha'penny," he said. It seemed an immense sum to Jack.

The rooms in Dean Street were dark and cold and empty when they got back. They ate slices of bread and meat dripping, then crawled into the bed they shared. Jack was shaken awake by Mary in the small hours of the following morning.

"Mam's not home," she said.

He tried to clear the sleep from his brain. She was always home by nine or ten, for she worked mostly by day, picking up customers in the streets and taking them to her room. She tried to keep the evenings for her children.

"What do you think?" he said.

But the same thought was in both their minds. "We'd best go to Perkin's Rents."

"D'you think he . . ."

"I don't know, do I? But just in case, we'd best go and tell her he was following us."

It was freezing cold and nearly five in the morning and the first carts were already rumbling into the metropolis with the day's supply of vegetables. Perkin's Rents loomed against the night sky, a large building complete in itself. Arched passageways led into the central courtyard around which the three floors were built. They climbed the stairs to the cheapest rooms, under the roof. Halfway up a woman stepped out of the shadows. Jack knew her as Beauty, a friend of his mother's. Her dyed hair hung to her shoulders.

"You'd best not go up," she said. "They're arguing something awful."

But Mary pushed past. "Come on, Jack."

Then Jack heard shouting, the high-pitched voice of a woman and the roar of a man. There was a smashing of glass and an oath, then a moment of silence and a scream that was cut short.

They ran up the stairs and threw open the door. The first thing he saw was blood.

It came from his mother's head. She was sprawled across the bed and her dress was soaked in blood. She had been cut about the face and neck but most of it was coming from her skull. On the far side of the room Mary was struggling with Rutter, clinging on to his right hand, in which he held an iron bar.

Beyond them burned the coal fire and in front of it was a poker. Jack grabbed it and with all his strength hit Rutter on the left knee. He gave a great cry of pain and let Mary go. She fell backwards as Jack struck again. This time Rutter went down. Jack raised the poker and hit him on the back of the neck. There was the sound of a stick breaking, and Rutter's limbs began to twitch.

The room was lit by an orange glare. Mary's dress was alight. Jack beat at the flames with his hands and finally grabbed a blanket and covered her in it. She stood with smoke tendrils rising from her body, whimpering in agony.

"It's all right," Jack said. "It's all right."

He led her to the stairs. She walked like an automaton and for the first time he smelled the odor of burnt flesh. Beauty stood in her doorway and watched. "You'd best get to the hospital," she said.

He took her to Westminster Hospital just around the corner. The place reeked of suppuration and decay. They drugged her with laudanum, washed her with a solution of carbolic acid, then covered the burns with grease-soaked cotton. They let him sit with her in the ward. Two hours later she died.

When he came out into the corridor Beauty was there. "The police are round at Perkin's Rents," she said. "Won't be long before they come looking for you."

She took him to Wapping where he was lodged in a brothel for nearly two weeks, then she found him a place on a Whitby collier sailing for Newcastle. He was not to see London again for many years.

The road from Cape Town to the diggings was nearly six hundred miles long, a single track that wound up from the coast through the forbidding Hex River Mountains, to the semidesert called the Karoo which stretched to Kimberley and beyond. After life at sea Jack found the journey not too taxing and he might even have enjoyed the slow metamorphosis which his life was

undergoing had it not been that he chafed to get on. This mode of traveling was too slow. The feeling of being left behind was made worse by the coaches that daily thundered past them carrying their loads of diggers to Kimberley. He would watch angrily, eating the dust, as the mule or horse teams galloped past, whips cracking, hooves pounding.

"Can't we go faster?" he said once to Delport.

"We'd kill the bullocks. Don't worry, there are more diamonds in the ground than ever came out. If the Lord wills it you'll get your share."

But Jack was not content and his feeling of frustration was made worse when one of the iron tire bands came off a wheel and a new one had to be sweated on. As he and Delport were working a coach came crashing along the stony track. Jack looked up and saw that David Kade was one of the passengers. His face was covered by a scarf to keep the dust from his mouth but the panama hat was like a beacon. Their eyes met for a second and David half raised his hat, then Jack was left in a cloud of choking dust.

5

Dust was affecting David Kade as he rode the coach to the diggings. Dust and heat and a blazing sun that hung in the sky like a great burnished disk, its rays beating down on a dry wilderness of low scrub, baked earth and rocky outcrops. This was the semidesert and through it the coach carrying David and eleven other passengers pitched and swayed as the driver, a Cape Colored man with a tall ostrich feather in his hat, lashed at the eight-horse team with a long stock whip. It was the fourth day of David's journey but he had lost count. He, like the other passengers, existed in a private world of pain and discomfort and all were on the verge of heatstroke.

"I've seen people's legs swell up in these coaches," his neighbor, a Mr. Levinson, had said to him on the second day. "I've seen people have fits because of the conditions. I've seen people go half mad, you know, and try to jump out."

"Don't, Father," Levinson's daughter had said. "Please don't go on about it. It's bad enough."

"I'm just telling this young man," her father had said, pitching and heaving and trying to hold on as the coach hit a deep hole. "I'm just warning him what's in store. That way he can adapt."

It had been worse than he had said. So far David's ankles and feet had not swollen up and he had not yet had a fit, but his eyes were red and filled with dust. He could feel the dust between his teeth and in his hair. Dust devils spun across plains that glittered balefully in the sun.

The coach had been converted from a large Cape bullock wagon and weighed, with luggage, nearly four tons. Four benches were placed across the body and on each bench sat three passengers. They were squashed up tight without room to move. It was impossible to read, impossible to do anything except exist.

There was substantial two-way traffic on the track; wagons and carts drawn by bullocks, horses or mules were traveling north or south and so were men on foot, some with hope in their hearts going north, others, destitute, traveling south. Their coach stopped for nothing, swerved for nothing, everything got out of their way as they plunged on through the heat of the day.

The sides of the coach were covered by canvas blinds but some had torn away and the sun beat in directly on the passengers. Levinson and his daughter wore smoked glasses and David kept his panama hat pulled down over his eyes so that the glare would not become too great.

"You want to have smoked glasses," Levinson had said. He was a plump man in his fifties with a bald head and long traceries of hair combed sideways over it. He wore a dark suit and a fob watch and was very respectable. "I've seen people get ophthalmia. One man went blind."

"Please, Father, don't," Miss Levinson said. She was sitting on the far side of her father and now she leant forwards and smiled at David. "He is always saying things like that."

"It's the truth," Levinson said. "So I mustn't tell the truth?"

Miss Levinson was about twenty, plump and ripe, with dark hair taken back into a bun. She wore a long traveling gown and a veil to keep the dust from her face, but occasionally when the coach stopped, she would lift the veil. She had a broad face with high cheekbones which reminded David of the Slav faces of his childhood.

But even her attractive presence could not ameliorate the misery he felt. He wished now with all his heart that he had not

come. The cheerlessness of his cousin's house in North London and the emptiness of his life there suddenly seemed enviable by comparison. His mind dwelt on streets and shops, taverns, music halls, great buildings, elegant terraces and grassy parks where people strolled on summer Sundays. Here, there was nothing but rock and scrub, dust and heat.

He even thought longingly of Cape Town; its sticky heat was preferable to this furnace. He thought of the girl singing on the Grand Parade. He had never heard a voice so beautiful. Then other memories. The incident at the docks. Jew-boy. Well, he was used to it, though that didn't make it any easier to bear. Many a day he had fought the gangs of boys in London who waylaid Jewish children on their way to and from school. And the big red-haired man with the fists. There was something about him. In spite of his curtness, David felt drawn to him, yet apprehensive of him at the same time. There was danger there, but also a rocklike quality. He was someone you wanted on your side. It was strange seeing him on the road mending the wagon wheel. It made David feel slightly less alone, though he wished the man had taken the loan he had offered and that he were sitting in the coach right now. He reached under the seat for his bag and brought out one of a dozen books that lay under his shirts. It was called *In Search of Diamonds.* He tried to read, but the pages jerked before his eyes.

"Ever been to Lewisham?" Mr. Levinson said.

"Just through it."

"I was born and bred there. Levinson from Lewisham. My father was a tailor." He held up his hand and seemed to draw a sign in the air. "'Levinson's Bespoke Tailoring for Gentlemen. Best Quality.' You know anything about tailoring?"

"No."

"It's not a bad life. Not a good life, but not a bad life. First the back goes, then the legs go, then the eyes. You can do well as a tailor. But with eight children, who can do well? Eight children. Eight mouths to feed. Sixteen feet for shoes. I came out to this country as a young man, like you. I took a job in Messrs. Stuttaford's. Do you know them?"

"No."

"The best. Respectable, good-quality merchandise. I worked there for ten years. Haberdashery. Household goods. Gloves. Ten years. And during that time they found diamonds up in the

desert. I said to myself, 'You're still young, you've still got your strength.' I was married. Hilda was only a child. But I said to Mrs. Levinson, 'Now is the time. If we are to make our fortunes, we must go.' So we went. And now I no longer work for others, I have my own place. Levinson's." Again the hand came out and drew the sign in the air above them. But this time it seemed, in both men's imaginations, that it was much larger than the sign of Levinson's Bespoke Tailoring. This was Levinson's Emporium, an altogether more exciting concept.

"I and Mrs. Levinson own that place. We have a house with a wooden floor. We are able to send Hilda to England on a visit. Do you know how I got all this?"

"Father! Mr. Kade doesn't want . . ."

"Hard work, Mr. Kade. I worked like a kaffir—a black man. I went round the diggings with a sack on my back selling things. Anything: candles, shoes, soap, razors, combs. Anything. Then I began to sell meat. Me, Levinson, who had never cut up anything before. I bought sheep and I killed them and I cut them up and sold the meat. Blood to here . . ." He indicated his shoulders.

"For goodness' sake, Father!"

David felt slightly queasy.

". . . like a kaffir. Every day and half the night. That's how I started up there. Now . . . well, now it's different. Levinson's Emporium . . . Yes, it's different now. . . ."

To reach the diggings in ten days from the Cape and to make a profit for the owners, the drivers were changed with almost the same regularity as the horses and no attention was paid to the passengers' comfort. The coach would stop at a farmhouse in the middle of nowhere at ten o'clock in the morning or four o'clock in the afternoon and it would be luncheon, always the same, fried mutton chops and fried eggs. Or it might pull into a small village at nine o'clock at night and the passengers would be given their supper and then shown to rooms where they could spend a few hours on a bed before leaving at two or three or four in the morning, charging through the dark starlit night.

Everyone was exhausted and spent much of the time on the coach trying to sleep away the hours. David closed his eyes against the glare and fell into a waking doze. His mind was on coolness, the coolness of shade and water; harsh cold, the cold of the River Dnieper at Kiev with the ice floes snarling and growling as they split and his grandfather holding his hand and walking in the bitter wind.

Sometimes such memories would come flashing into his mind, pictures of his grandfather and grandmother, the house in the Podol, the smoke and the flames. But if he *tried* to remember, the pictures faded, faces became elusive. He had been only eight years old when he had been sent out of Russia to his cousin's home in London, and that was more than twelve years ago.

His clearest memories were of Kiev itself, Mother City of all the Russias, perched on the high bluffs overlooking the river, with its parks, trees and churches. Being a Jew and living in the ghetto of the Podol, which was on the low ground of the opposite bank, he always had to look up towards the city. On crisp sunny autumn days when the sun struck the golden domes of the Lavra, the Byzantine monastery, the light seemed to splinter and the larches were golden, the poplars and the birches were golden; in the cold autumn air everything was a blaze of golden light.

Then his name was David Kadeshinsky and he lived in his grandparents' house because his own parents had died of cholera. He had a tutor, a young Englishman named Mr. Hemlow, whom he remembered well: blond, with a wispy moustache and a weak chin. He loved poetry and communicated this love to David, but knew little about mathematics and even at eight years old David was able to tie him up in a maze of angles, sines and cosines.

His grandfather's house, in the Street of the Martyrs, gave the impression on the outside of being small and poor as did all Jewish houses, so that they would draw less attention to themselves, but inside it was richly furnished, for Moshe Kadeshinsky was a jeweler and a wealthy man. David could remember the wolfskin rugs on the floors, the huge painted porcelain stoves and the rich wall hangings.

At the back of the house was a room which his grandfather called the factory and here he employed four men to cut and polish rough gemstones, and two others to make the gold and silver settings. At the front of the house was the office where he did most of his business and spent most of his time. It was an elegant room furnished in leather and velvet with two tall rosewood cabinets in which he kept his jewels. You did not come to Moshe Kadeshinsky to buy a cheap diamond ring for an acquaintance of the night, you came to buy something special, a brooch, perhaps, of diamonds and emeralds once owned by the emperor of Abyssinia, a necklace worn by Madame du Barry, a ring said to have come from the regalia of the House of

Braganza; or else you came to choose a rough stone and have it cut and set to your own desire. There was nothing as vulgar as a counter in this room; no jewels were on display; you made your wishes known and Moshe Kadeshinsky went to his cabinets and pulled out drawers lined with black velvet and brought out stones or pieces of jewelry for your delectation. Most of his customers came from the city above the river.

David did not often go into this room but when he did it was with an air of breathless expectation. His grandfather would send for cups of hot chocolate, whisked in the French manner, and David would sit in one of the big leather chairs, his feet not quite touching the floor, sipping at the steaming liquid while his grandfather told him stories about jewels, sometimes going to the cabinets and returning with a diamond, saying, "Look into it, *dushka*, deep, deep, into the center. What do you see?"

And David would put his grandfather's loupe to his eye and look deeply into the stone and the light would splinter into red and yellow and blue and orange and indigo and violet; sometimes it would burn with the white-hot fire of the kiln, sometimes with the blue, searing cold of an ice cave.

"What do you see?"

"Fire and ice," David said.

"You're a good boy."

But the times he liked best, the times he was to remember all his life were those moments when, secure in the big chair, the steam of the chocolate rising before his eyes, his grandfather would tell him stories of the great diamonds which had disappeared over the centuries, the "lost diamonds," he called them: the "Great Mogul" found in Golconda in India, which had been set into the Peacock Throne of Persia and had disappeared in l747; the "Mirror of Portugal" smuggled out of Lisbon by a nobleman fleeing for his life; the "Sancy;" the "Côte de Bretagne"; the "Blue Tavernier." The names alone held romance for David.

Then all at once this security was shattered: his grandfather was arrested and taken to prison to wait trial on a charge of having sexually assaulted and killed a boy whose body was found in an alley near the rear of the house. No one in the Podol believed this. Years later in the drab house in North London his cousin, Miss Joseph, had read him his grandmother's letters to her, describing what was happening, but at the time he had been

too young to understand. The letters reconstituted memories and brought shape to events, so that later he could not tell whether his memories were real or a mixture of what his cousin had told him and what he had experienced himself.

One memory was sharply in focus; it was his visit to the jail to see his grandfather. Although the sun shone and the autumn air was dry, bright and crisp with frost, the prison seemed to have a different climate. There everything was dark. Warders carried lanterns with them wherever they went, the air was heavy with damp and there was a smell which David had never smelled before: a mixture of unwashed bodies, sewage and mold. The walls were wet to the touch and in the light of the prison officer's lantern he could see patches of growing fungus. These were the dungeons of fairytales and he shivered with cold and unhappiness.

He wished Mr. Hemlow had been allowed to come in, too, but the warder had shaken his head and said, "Only the *barin* can visit." He had said it mockingly, calling David his lord, his master, but no one was fooled. He was a short man with a twisted back and hurried crabwise down passageways that had been cut into living rock. "Don't lose sight of the lamp or you will wander here forever," he said with a laugh. David kept close behind him and at last, in the coldest, dampest and darkest part of the prison, they came to a small wooden door. Behind it David could hear someone coughing. The warder undid a chain and unlocked two locks. "You would think we had a tiger in here," he said. He pushed the door and for the first time in two years David saw his grandfather.

He seemed only half the size of the man he remembered. He had shrunk by several inches and was emaciated. He sat at a table on the far side of the cell, which was lit by a single tallow candle. He wore a dirty gray blouse torn under the arms, gray trousers and peasant's boots on his feet. On the floor was a horsehair mattress and he had taken a blanket from it and wrapped it around his shoulders. His head was shaved because of lice and he reminded David of a *muzhik* they had once found lying in an alleyway in the Podol who was within a few hours of death by starvation. The immediate impression was of grayness: gray clothes, gray skin, gray skull, sunken eyes, facial bones jutting out of the skin. The nose, which had seemed to fit Moshe Kadeshinsky's large fleshy face, was now almost a caricature of a

Jewish nose: big, hooked, high-bridged, out of proportion to the thin features.

"David!" he said. "Is it really you?"

"Yes, Grandfather."

"You can go in," the warder said.

The smell in the cell was very bad and much of it emanated from the bucket in the corner which was all the prisoner had for his bodily functions.

The old man rose shakily to his feet and held out his hands. David moved slowly towards him. He knew he was supposed to love this old man but everything was unfamiliar and frightening. He could not relate his memories to this cell, to this strange, bent, emaciated figure. Moshe Kadeshinsky took his grandson's hands in his and brought them to his lips. "You have grown up," he said. He coughed, then turned to the warder. "If it please your honor, may we have more light?"

David was startled. Was this his grandfather? Factory owner, wealthy jeweler, householder, master of servants? *Your honor?*

"It will cost you," the warder said.

"I know."

The warder placed a second candle on the table and lit it. The door clanged shut behind him. A grille opened and his face reappeared. "The *barin* has one hour. That was the agreement."

The extra light penetrated to the shadowy corners of the cell and David saw that more fungus grew there. It was bitterly cold. His grandfather had another coughing spell. The light also brought out the graffiti on the walls and David noticed a drawing that looked fresher than the rest. It was of the *menorah*, the many-branched candlestick. He realized that his grandfather must have scratched it on the rock.

"Sit," the old man said. "Sit on the chair. I wish to walk. Unless I walk each day I cannot get up off the floor." He began to shuffle up and down the small cell. For some minutes there was silence and then he said, "How is your grandmother?"

"She sends her love. She says she is well."

"Good. Today I go for the verdict. When they have executed me . . . no, no, don't look startled. Prepare for it. I have. Your grandmother has. You must, too. When I am gone she will have no one. Then *you're* the head of the house. You must look after her. You must be me." He broke off and began to cough again. "It's the damp. It attacks one here." He tapped his chest.

"But *why*, Grandfather?"

"Why?"

"Why are you here? Why are they going to execute you?"

"Your grandmother never told you?"

"She said you wished to speak to me about it."

He drew the blanket more tightly around his shoulders and shuffled backwards and forwards across the bare stone floor. David could feel the cold creep up his legs even though he was wearing fur-lined boots. "And the servants? Masha? Have they not spoken?"

"They said a boy was found behind the house. That he had been . . . been murdered. They said that's why the police had taken you."

"That is true."

"But *you* didn't kill him."

The old man touched him on the shoulder and this time he did not mind the contact so much. "No, *dushka*. Of course not."

"Well, *why* then?" Anger spurted and he felt tears come to his eyes.

Phrasing it as carefully as he could, with little emotion in his tone, Moshe Kadeshinsky explained how the Kiev police had begun searching for a tramp who had been seen in the area the previous day. Then, within forty-eight hours, an article had appeared in a Moscow newspaper alleging that the Jews of the Podol had murdered the boy.

The old man tried to explain the Blood Libel—the allegation over the centuries that Jews killed young children to use their blood at the Passover—but David began to cry and held his hands to his ears and a little later the warder came to fetch him.

The other memories of that day were blurred, but some moments stood out, like the return, that afternoon, of his grandfather. After a trial lasting nearly a year, the old man had been found not guilty. He was carried home from the courthouse in triumph. The alleys were choked with Jews all cheering and shouting. It was the greatest day in many of their lives: a Jew found not guilty by a jury of peasants.

It was towards evening when the pogrom began. It had started earlier with an attack on one of the two synagogues in Kiev and had then moved to the Podol. Many of the Jews there had recently come from other parts of the Pale of Settlement—the enormous strip of territory stretching from the Baltic to the

Black Sea in which all Russian Jews were confined—and had no residence permits for Kiev. They were hunted down by police and those who were not killed ended up in jail.

Events happened so quickly after that, that in David's memory they overlapped and became a jumbled mass. He remembered the money belts being strapped around his waist, he remembered the servants crying, he remembered running with Mr. Hemlow through the alleys filled with flames and smoke, he remembered being taken to a house where he lived in a room not much bigger than a cupboard for what seemed like weeks but in reality could not have been more than a few days, while passage on a barge was found for Mr. Hemlow and himself. Then the long, long journey to England—by barge, coach, train and finally ship from Flushing—which ended in the prim house in Highbury.

The desert country began to change, wide plains giving way to a broken landscape of rocky outcrops. Hills collided, making a jumble of ravines and valleys with great dark red rocks piled one on top of another, radiating heat they could feel in the coach as it wound in and out between them.

Just when the passengers were starting to feel desperate, the horses turned off the road, wound through a valley for a mile or two and pulled up at a lonely house.

They ate their unvarying meal of mutton and eggs at small tables in the main room. The house was a derelict farm which had been bought by the transport company as a way station. A man and a woman lived there to prepare the meals. Rooms in the back contained mattresses on which travelers could stretch out for a few hours.

"What do you know of diamonds, may I ask you?" Mr. Levinson said.

"I beg your pardon?"

"Diamonds. You know nothing."

"I hope to learn."

"He hopes to learn! You've seen these men walking the road? They hoped to learn, too. They spent all their money and still they didn't learn. Before we left the Cape I said to Mrs. Levinson, 'What do we know about digging for diamonds? Nothing. But people who dig must eat, they must wear clothes, they must keep warm.' Do you know what she said?"

"Yes, Father, we can guess what she said," Hilda said.

"Is this how you speak to your father?" He turned to David. "Have you ever thought of the mercantile life?" He used the word grandly, giving the impression of a merchant venturer, which was perhaps how he saw himself. David shook his head. "Well, you should think. Use your head, not your hands." He cut a fried egg in half and filled his mouth. "Listen, I could do with a good boy like you. One with brains, a head on his shoulders, someone who can deal with figures."

David was aware of a sudden look of interest on Miss Levinson's face.

"Do you know figures?" Levinson said.

"I worked in a bank."

"There you are then, it's fate."

David smiled and shook his head.

Later Mr. Levinson smoked a cigar on the stoep and David and Miss Levinson strolled in the cool of the evening. "Father means it about the shop," she said. "Good people are difficult to find."

"It's kind of him."

"It's not *kind*," she said, with a touch of irritability. "It's practical. But you don't want to. You want to dig in the ground and trust to luck."

"I've come a long way," he said. How could he make her understand how he had felt in London, in the grim, prim house where there had been no love and no warmth?

"You said you came from Russia," she said, mistaking his meaning.

"That was a long time ago."

"You don't sound Russian. I mean, you have no accent."

"I had an English tutor. Anyway, I was only eight when I left."

"A tutor? Your family must have been rich."

"Yes."

"What happened to them?"

He did not want to talk about the pogrom. Instead he said, "They were old; they died."

"And then you went to London?"

"To my grandmother's cousin."

If there was anything that might have put him off the "mercantile life," as Levinson phrased it, it was his cousin's constant reiteration of the words "the family business" or "the family firm." This, it turned out, had been a tobacconist's in the High Street, Islington, which had been sold when her father died

and on the small proceeds of which she now lived a life of gentility steeped in poverty.

David had grown up in an ambience of prudishness and primness and snobbery. He had gone to the local board school but had easily outstripped his classmates and had taken a scholarship to Highbury Grammar, where he had changed his name to Kade. "Too outlandish," his headmaster had said of Kadeshinsky. "Too much of a mouthful. Anyway, it's not English." He found out later that there were several boys of Polish and Russian immigrant parents who had also changed their names or shortened them. At first his English, though fluent, was heavily accented and this, with his size, which was on the small side, made him the target of casual bullying. Because he was much on his own, he read a lot and began to live in his imagination. When he was fourteen he started to grow again. He never became tall, but his shoulders and arms strengthened and he found he could fight as well as, and in many cases better than, the boys who had dominated him for years. Soon he was left alone.

"You should go on to the university," his headmaster said more than once after he had written an unusually good essay, but there was not the money. Instead, one of Miss Joseph's acquaintances— an old man who had known her father from his tobacconist days—found David a job in a city bank.

This was much worse than school. Each day he took the omnibus into the City, worked at his ledgers, and then caught another omnibus home. He paid his cousin for his board and lodging and what little money he had left over he saved to buy books or sometimes blew on a boat trip to Hampton Court where he would eat his sandwiches along the towpath.

It was in the bank that he began to come across names like Du Toit's Pan, Bultfontein, De Beers and New Rush; names which involved large financial transactions based on diamonds. In gray London winters these names had a romantic ring. He started buying books about the diamond fields of southern Africa. He read everything he could find—which was not much. Some of them told the personal experiences of diggers who had made their fortunes. He became obsessed by diamonds. He spent hours at diamond exhibitions, haunted the windows of jewelers' shops and pored over newspaper reports of fluctuations in the diamond market.

But there was never the slightest chance of his making the journey to the diggings, for he had come to learn—from the same old gentleman who had found him his position—that his cousin was practically penniless. The house was all she owned and that was mortgaged. She had slowly gone through her capital—much of it spent on his upbringing—and now she depended upon what David could earn. He felt trapped. He could see no way ahead except year upon year of his high stool and his ledgers.

And then one day he came back from the bank and opened the front door and saw Miss Joseph lying in a huddle at the bottom of the stairs. She was dead. The doctor said she must have had a seizure at the top and fallen to her death. The house was sold, her debts were paid and there was left over the sum of one hundred and sixty pounds. He bought a ticket on the first ship sailing to Cape Town, outfitted himself as best he could, packed his favorite books and left London, as he thought, for good.

Of that money he kept some on him for day-to-day expenses, but the bulk of his capital—eighty pounds—was sewn into the lining of his traveling bag. Now, as he said good night to Miss Levinson—for they were to rest for several hours before resuming the journey—he went to the coach and checked to see that the money was still there. It was. He took out a box of paper and replaced the bag under his seat.

Bodily functions and the schedule of the coach did not often coincide and the watchword, as far as he was concerned, was do it while you can. Whenever he could he chose the wide-open veld and the privacy of darkness. He walked round the house and struck off into the low hills. It was easy to see his way for the stars were bright and the desert was bathed in silvery light. He walked on until he had put a decent distance between himself and the house, then he lowered his trousers and squatted. When he had finished and adjusted his dress he started back, but after a few steps he stopped. The landscape looked unfamiliar from the new angle. Was this the right way?

He started off again. This time he walked for several hundred yards. Again he stopped. He felt sure this was not the right direction. But which way *was* right? He thought of all the books he had read: what would the old "Africa hands" have done in these circumstances? Followed their tracks back to the farmhouse. But he could not make out his tracks. Take a direction

from the moon. But there was no moon. The Southern Cross then. But he had not looked up to find the constellation of stars when he had set out so it could not give him a bearing now. He decided to climb a low hill to see if he could see a light from the way station. He could see nothing and when he came down, stumbling and bruising himself, he knew he was well and truly lost. He began to hurry, first one way, then another. Sometimes he ran, so great was his panic. Dawn, a gray dawn that gave way to lavender and gold, found him stumbling about like a drunken man, clothes torn, skin scratched from a dozen falls, and his mouth dry as tinder from lack of water.

On and on he went, as the sun began to heat the air. About midmorning, when what little strength he had left was running out, he came across the track from Cape Town to the diggings. It stretched away on either side of him like a scar on the surface of the moon. He lay down in the shade of a bush and lost consciousness.

He woke late in the afternoon and found two diggers staring down at him. He tried to say something, but his lips were cracked and his tongue was swollen.

"Don't try to speak, son," the older man said. He had a water bag and moistened a handkerchief and placed it in David's mouth. He sucked it. The man wet it again and returned it. After a few minutes David was able to take the water in small amounts and in an hour he was talking.

The older man's name was Joseph Malone and David put his age at about sixty-one or -two. He was scrawny and lined, his blue eyes were faded by tropical suns and he appeared to be generally weather-beaten like an old desert shack. When he spoke the loose skin on his neck quivered and his prominent Adam's apple bobbed up and down.

Dusk was falling. They made David comfortable and then searched for firewood. He saw a strange contraption—a large, two-seater tricycle—at the side of the track. When they returned he asked about it.

"Daniel made it," Malone said with pride. "He can do anything with his hands. Show him the sail, Dan." Daniel Halkett was in his early twenties, a short, quiet man. At first he appeared shy and self-effacing, but later David was to discover that he only spoke when he had something to say.

"Go on, Daniel, show him."

Halkett went to the tricycle and raised a canvas sail on a simple wooden frame. "He invented it," Malone said. "Calls it a sail-cycle. When the wind's behind us I guess you could say we was sail-cycling." He chuckled and his Adam's apple bobbed.

They sat around the fire, shared what little food they had, and talked. Malone was an American whose life had been spent in the search for valuable metals and stones. He had prospected for gold in California, for silver in Colorado and for diamonds in Brazil. Now, with Daniel as his companion, he was on his way once more to where the action was. Halkett's background emerged slowly over the next few days. He was the son of a yeoman farmer in Hampshire and had left the farm to try his luck. He and Malone had met in another "Diggers' Special," this time sailing from Liverpool. On board Dan had developed scarlet fever and Malone, whose life had forced him to learn the basics of doctoring, had nursed him through it in a cabin specially isolated. He had then waited in Cape Town while Daniel's strength returned, spending his own money on a good boarding house. Penniless, they had set out to walk to the diggings and had now reached almost halfway.

"Easy to get lost in these parts," Malone said. "Same with most scrub deserts. This place reminds me of the Mojave. Got lost there myself once. You're lucky to be alive."

They had been on the road for more than two months and David was to find out the following day how they existed without money. Since he was still weak they gave him the rear seat on the tricycle and took it in turns to pedal. There were few farms in this dry part of the country but they existed and at each farmhouse Halkett and Malone would offer to do jobs for food and lodging.

Halkett, as Malone had said, was a genius with his hands. Nothing seemed beyond him. David saw him take the innards out of a fob watch and put it right; he saw him with his short, stubby fingers mend a delicate ivory fan so you would never know it had been broken. He reset a cameo brooch, made a picture frame, tinned pots, soldered pans and put a shaft on a windmill that had broken down. While he worked Joe Malone set up an easel and made quick but accurate sketches of the members of the family in charcoal, the old fingers flying back and forth as he sought for a likeness. The children would crowd round as he drew their mother and father—stolid, serious-minded farming folk whose lives were hard and whose expressions were grim—and they

would laugh. David realized that for the children this was an unexpected break in their dreary lives. Normal children, as he knew them, would have been at school, but here there were no schools. The farmers told him that education was their biggest problem.

He was struck by the simple brilliance of the Malone-Halkett partnership. They were utilizing their skills in the only way they knew how and not only were they made welcome, in many cases they were begged to stay on.

They were together for nearly three weeks before they reached the village of Victoria, the halfway stage on the road to the diggings. During that time he had revised his opinion of his two companions. In his quiet way it was Halkett who appeared to be the older and wiser of the two. Malone was a dreamer: the gold was always over the next hill, the diamonds round the next corner. Halkett would listen to his tales of prospecting in California and Brazil and David would wonder how often he had heard the same stories, for even David was now hearing some for the second time, yet Halkett never gave any indication of boredom.

One curious incident gave him a clue to their relationship. A farmer offered them each a glass of his homemade peach brandy after their evening meal. Malone had stretched out his hand to take it when he must have caught a look in Halkett's eyes, for he dropped his hand and, embarrassed, said, "Thanks, I never use it."

They reached the village of Victoria in midafternoon. It was an oasis comprising a single short street on which stood the Lord Somerset Hotel, a post office, a bank—both the latter were one-roomed affairs—a boarding house with a tin roof, a general store and a few private houses. The street was lined with pepper trees, and a stream, marked by wild willows and mimosa, wound its way past the village. David first saw Victoria from a low hill two miles away and his impression was of a square of green in a huge brown plain.

Instead of spending the night there, Halkett and Malone decided to push on. "We don't trust villages," Halkett said in a surprising rush of words. They asked David to continue with them but when he refused they did not press him, for it was clear that three men were not as efficient as two. He stood in the dusty

street and watched them cycle precariously out onto the hot dusty plain and felt a pang of loneliness he had not felt for a long time.

He went to the Lord Somerset Hotel. It was painted white and was turreted, a cross between an English castle and a desert fort, with the Union Jack flying at the masthead. The place was full of diggers going to Kimberley or coming south. Meals were served around the clock, for coaches were apt to arrive at any time of the day or night. The hotel owner was a thin-faced, sweaty Englishman who spent most of his time shouting at the servants in the boiling kitchen. He was also the agent for the coach line.

"You're breaking my heart, friend," he said when he heard David's story, "but if you ain't got money and you ain't got a ticket, then that's all there is to it."

David stood in the street and counted his money. He had less than four pounds. He went into the general store and bought himself a cheap blanket, a dozen lined exercise books, six lead pencils, a billycan, coffee and two simple reading books. He asked for, and was given, a sack to carry his things. Now he had less than ten shillings. He was thirsty and he crossed to the bar of the hotel, which was beginning to fill up at this time in the afternoon. He bought himself a glass of beer and took it to a table in a quiet corner at which a man was sitting.

"Do you mind?" David said, indicating a vacant chair.

"Please yourself."

The man looked up and David found himself staring at Jack Farson. They were equally surprised.

"I thought you'd be at the diggings by now," Jack said.

"I thought so too."

David saw a big, rawboned man who had taken on a slight sunburn and had also put on weight since he had last seen him. Jack saw a man travel-stained and weary, whose clothing was dusty and torn and who did not look the same person who had shoveled five-pound notes across the ticket counter in Cape Town.

David noticed that Jack's glass was empty and he put his own down in front of him. "I'll get another for myself."

They drank the beers and Jack bought a round and they each told the other briefly what had happened.

Jack said, "How will you get on then, if you ain't got your money?"

David pointed to the sack on the floor and described what he had bought and with what idea.

"Teach? At the farms?"

"Why not? I had a good education. I worked in a bank. I can read and write and work with numbers. That's all that's needed."

"It'll take a time, won't it?"

"No longer than that wagon of yours. Let's have another."

He bought two more beers and brought them back to the table. "Well, that's that," he said, pulling his trouser pockets inside out.

"That's what?"

"I mean, that's every penny." The beers had gone to his head and he laughed.

Jack laughed, too, but in a puzzled way. "You ain't got a penny left? Is that what you mean?"

"Not a penny."

Jack stared at him in amazement. No one had ever spent his last penny on him; in fact, not many people had ever spent anything on him. What amazed him even more was that this generosity should come from a Jew.

They drank up and he said, "What are you going to do? It's dark."

"Can't help that," David said, feeling slightly light-headed. "Can't stop the sun."

"You'd better come with me and get some food inside you."

He took him to the wagon park on the outskirts of the village and introduced him to Frans Delport and Marie.

It was a friendly supper and afterwards Delport showed David his pump. All he could see were wooden boxes but to the farmer even these had a kind of magic. "All the way from Hammersmith in London," he said, patting the wood. "'The Invincible'! That's a name, isn't it?" Later they showed him a place to sleep under the wagon.

The following morning he was washing at the stream when Jack came up.

"When are you moving?"

"The sooner the better."

"You say that the other man . . . Halkett? . . . You say he did odd jobs?"

"Not odd jobs. He's a genius with his hands. I've seen him take a clock to pieces and put it back together and not one piece was missing."

Jack looked down at his own huge hands and flexed his fingers.

"Mr. Delport says we've got to lay over here a fortnight to give the oxen a rest. I was thinking . . ."

"Yes?"

It came out in a rush. "I ain't a genius with my hands but I learned the sailmaker's craft and I can mend the canvas tops of wagons. And I was helper to a ship's carpenter and I can work with wood. And Mr. Delport says he don't mind as we're over the biggest mountains . . . and I've got a few quid, just in case . . ."

At first David was not sure what he was talking about, then it came to him. "You want us to join up? Is that it?"

"If it's all right."

David could see the sweat on his forehead, brought out by the effort it had cost him to ask.

"Of course it is! I'll teach them school and you'll mend their wagons. Why, it's the best thing I can think of!"

Two months later they came to the diggings. They were different men by then; toughened to the ways of the country and the desert sun. As they made their way north they had stopped at farms and villages. At each place David had given lessons in return for food and lodging and Jack had spliced ropes and cut new sailcloths and mended wagons. They had slept hard and eaten short and sometimes they had starved and often been dry as old bones; they had come to expect little and get little; they had grown close in the sense of closeness brought on by hardship.

As was natural in two men of much the same age and ambition, removed in time and space from backgrounds which would have militated against their ever meeting one another, let alone becoming friendly, a bond formed between them. They were very different: David realized that Jack, basically ignorant of anything academic, knew how to work with his hands and there was also the rocklike quality he had early perceived. To Jack, David was a strange creature, someone who could never be taught to splice a rope's end, but who could visit places of the mind about which Jack could only speculate and of which he was in awe. At first he had been reserved about David—he was, after all, a Jew—but later as the length of their time together grew without mishap, their trust in each other also grew.

But what bound them more tightly than anything else was their passion for diamonds. They talked of little else in their spare time. They went over and over what they would do if they struck

it lucky. Jack's dreams were of riches, food, drink and women. But David spoke of the stones themselves, of weight and purity, of blue-whites and greens, of stones that were rose-cut or cushion-cut or table-cut. They would talk mainly at night in some bare room of a lonely farmhouse. Jack would lie back on his bed, his arms folded behind his head, and often David would think him asleep, and then Jack would say, "Tell me about the big one. The Indian one." And David would lean back against the mud wall in the light of a guttering candle and tell him about the "Great Mogul" or the "Mirror of Portugal" or the "Sancy" and the room would dissolve and again he would be seated in the big leather armchair with the steam rising from the hot chocolate, listening to his grandfather. At these times he would be overtaken by an ineffable feeling of sadness, of something lost forever.

It went on like this sometimes for an hour or more. It seemed that Jack could never get enough of the stories surrounding these great stones. Sometimes David would forget a fact or turn a story around in an unfamiliar way and Jack would always make him go back and tell it right. He was like a child to whom the shaping of the facts was vital.

Once he told Jack about his grandfather's room in Kiev where the old man would sometimes show him cut diamonds and make him look into them and describe what he saw. "Fire and ice," David would say always, to his grandfather's delight. The phrase seemed to delight Jack, too, for he said it over and over like an incantation, tasting it. "Fire and ice. I like that."

They reached Kimberley on a blustery autumn day with the first hint of a High Veld winter in the breeze, and all they could see was dust. They saw the cloud from fifteen miles away, a great brown smudge in the blue sky. As they drew nearer the dust thickened until it began to settle on them like dirty pollen. They left the road, for it was filled with wagons and traps and Scotch carts, all carrying wood and water, meat and vegetables towards the cloud. They cut straight across the flat desert. Neither spoke; neither knew what to say. Until then the desert had at least been clean under a blue sky; now everything, their clothes, the wagons, even the bushes, was covered by a patina of dust.

Abruptly they came upon the diggings themselves. At first they could hardly believe their eyes. Before them lay a gigantic hole,

cut deep into the earth, in which thousands of people were toiling like ants in a nest. The hole appeared to be about half a mile in diameter. Its bottom was uneven where some had dug deeper than others. It was like a great lunar crater from which stalagmites rose up, some as tall as buildings, with squared-off tops on which men—black, white, yellow, brown, all with cloths tied over their mouths and noses to stop the dust—were working.

"Sweet Jesus!" Jack said.

Both men registered the same shock. Nothing David had read had prepared him for the reality. And although Jack had spent hours pumping Delport for information about the diggings his imagination had not been vivid enough to create a true picture. It was the size of the thing that shocked them. The hole in the ground was so vast and the people toiling in it so tiny that it lacked human scale.

They walked on, across the parched and dusty desert to the town of Kimberley itself. The outskirts were unattractive: wooden houses mingled with tents, corrugated iron buildings with mud huts. The place appeared to have grown overnight. Once they reached the town proper things became more familiar, but even here famous European banks and shipping lines occupied dusty iron sheds. Both were reminded of London, not physically, but there was the same bustle, the same air of mercantile and commercial dealing, of good luck and bad, of money to be made and lost.

They walked along the wide, dusty streets and saw every shade of skin color, from the pink-white of the Nordic races through the darker cast of the Mediterranean, to the yellow of the Chinese and Japanese and Hottentots to the blue-black of the tribal African. They heard English and Dutch, German and Swedish, Yiddish and French and Italian, and frequently the nasal twang of America, Australia and New Zealand. Slowly the sheer exuberance of the place infected their spirits.

As they made their way to the center of the town, a man raced past them holding something in his hand and shouting, "I've found one! I've found one!" It took them some moments to realize it must be a diamond, and they felt a surge of excitement at the knowledge that what they had heard was true: you *could* come here and get rich if you were lucky. Then the man was gone and in his place, coming towards them down another dusty street, was a house. It had wooden walls and a tin roof, its

windows were in place, even its curtains were drawn. It was being carried to a new site by fifty black men whose sweating bodies supported it on posts the size of railway sleepers.

Drunks were being thrown out of bars that were called cosies. Lemonade sellers were shouting their wares from corner stalls. Pianos were tinkling in the brothels. There was the sound of a concertina. Everything was lively.

They came to a large square which served as a wagon park and marketplace, and on the far side, like some pot of gold at the end of a rainbow, was a wooden-framed building with a large painted sign above the door which said LEVINSON'S EMPORIUM.

"There it is!" David said, as though he had never quite believed in it.

It took a moment for his eyes to become used to the dim light inside the shop. A wide scrubbed pine counter ran along three sides of it, with shelves and drawers behind it. On the floor in the foreground were open bags of potatoes, loose maize, wheat, split peas, brown beans and coffee beans. Next to them lay coils of rope and wire, boxes of candles and soap, and hanging from the rafters were picks and shovels and sides of bacon and bunches of lanterns all tied together, and mangles and hand mills and a hundred other things which he could not make out. On the counter were bolts of cloth and ropes of chewing tobacco, huge cheddar cheeses and on the far side of the shop racks of woolen shirts, corduroy breeches, boxes of boots and stacks of hats. There were bolts of lace, dresses and hats imported from Europe, men's shoes from London and tweeds woven in Lancashire. Over everything was a smell that he discovered later was a mixture of strong yellow soap, ground coffee, bacon and paraffin. For the rest of his life these smells would remind him of that first day in Kimberley.

The shop was empty of customers at that moment. A short, very fat woman sat on a high stool behind a cash register and farther along the counter a second woman was bending over a ledger. She looked up as they advanced through the mass of goods on the floor and David saw that it was Hilda. He stopped a few feet from the counter.

"Yes?" she said. "Can I help you?"

He did not reply. She stared more closely at his dusty figure and a look of dawning recognition crept into her eyes. So softly that he almost did not catch it, she said, "It's you!"

"Yes, it's me."

Instead of putting out her hand to greet him she turned and fled down the length of the counter to a door at the back. "Father! Father!" she shouted. "Father! It's David! It's Mr. Kade!"

They were back in a matter of seconds, Mr. Levinson bustling in ahead of Hilda. "Lost and found!" he cried, taking David's hands in both of his. "The prodigal returns!" He turned to the woman at the cash register. "Rachel! It's him!"

"It's who?"

"The bag!"

"Mr. Kade, Mama!"

Mrs. Levinson smiled and nodded, her whole face wobbling with the movement. "Welcome," she said. "I have heard a lot about you."

"We thought he was lost," Levinson said, his bald head shining whitely in the gloom. "But here he is. The boy from nowhere!"

Everyone was talking at once. Mr. Levinson was shouting. Mrs. Levinson and Hilda were laughing. David, a smile on his face, was still shaking hands. Then Jack was introduced and because it was almost the end of the trading day the shop was closed and they went into the living area at the back, which had a wooden floor. They were given glasses of whisky and David was called upon to tell what had happened. "You said good night," Mr. Levinson said. "What happened then?"

It was not possible to advance the true reason for going out alone into the desert and so he made up a story about being unable to sleep and needing a walk. When he described how he had become confused and had wandered across the desert in the blazing heat until he had collapsed by the side of the track Mr. Levinson said, "People can die in this heat. Their tongues go black. I've seen . . ."

"Morris, please!" Mrs. Levinson said.

Then it was their turn and Hilda and her father broke across each other's sentences and told him how they had searched and how the coach had been held up, how they had sent messages to Victoria—which he had never received—and how they had thought of sending his bag—yes, the bag was there, the money untouched and the clothes intact—how they had thought of sending it by one of the southbound coaches but then had reconsidered and told themselves that since he was making his

way north it would be best to keep it.

Although it was not home, although he had never been there before, it was the kind of homecoming that David had always imagined when he had read of such things. The Levinsons were no kin of his, he hardly knew them, yet he felt almost like a son.

The room was furnished much as they might have furnished a house in Streatham, with heavy stuffed furniture and anti-macassars and mahogany chairs and tables and a patterned carpet in the Persian style, but bits of Africa kept intruding, like the corrugated iron that formed the walls and roof, and the lizards that scuttled about in the lamplight. David had noticed that while the front of the building had a wooden facade, the sides and back were made of mud bricks lined with corrugated iron. Wood was scarce and came as planks, first by boat from Sweden and then by ox wagon from the coast. Mr. Levinson was proud of his wooden floor; there were only three like it in the town.

But there was a sour note that became more apparent as the evening wore on: the presence of Jack. The more David talked and was the center of attention, the quieter and more sullen Jack became. Mrs. Levinson, who had spent the meal urging them to eat because of the long journey they had just completed, asked him about his own past and background and he mumbled about London and the sea and left it at that. David realized that though he had spent the last weeks closer to Jack than he had ever been to anyone else in his life, he knew little more about him than a few facts he had just revealed.

Levinson opened a bottle of port and held up a glass. "I said I'd found a young man. Didn't I say that, Hilda?"

"Yes, Father."

He turned to David. "Have you decided?"

"It's still the same, Mr. Levinson."

"Well, you boys must have your sport. You go off and do your digging. Maybe you'll find a diamond and maybe you won't. But when you become serious, then come to me. And Mr. Farson, well . . . Milwidsky and Rosenberg are always looking for good people."

Hilda lit them to a room at the back. "I must give you a spare candle," she said. David followed her to the larder. As she held out a candle in a holder she said, "I'm so glad you're here, Mr. Kade."

"You called me David a while ago."

She was smiling. The candlelight threw her cheekbones into relief and she was very pretty at that moment.

Two days later Jack and David formed their partnership. For both men it was a natural extension of what they had already been doing. It did not come easily. The problem was, they would need money to buy a claim and equipment and David had eighty pounds, which Jack could not match. But David was determined. In spite of Jack's silences and his truculence and anger, a bond had grown up between them, forged by hardship. David needed Jack to give him the confidence to do what he wanted to do, so when Jack spoke of getting work and saving up to put money into the partnership, he said impatiently, "That's just a waste of time. With my money we can start now, and the sooner we start, the sooner we'll make a find."

Jack sat on the edge of his bed and stared at his large white feet and shook his head. "I know you don't like to be beholden to anyone," David said, "but it isn't a question of that. We'll get Mr. Levinson to find a lawyer and we'll draw up proper papers. You can borrow the money from me and pay me back from your share of the profits. This will be our working capital, this will be the start." Finally, Jack agreed.

The first thing was to find a claim and register it. In the early days pegging a claim had been a matter of joining an organized footrace with a couple of hundred other diggers in a virgin area on the first-come-first-served principle. The thirty-foot-square claim was marked out with pegs and the digger went off to register it and hoped that claim jumpers were not already taking the topsoil out by the time he returned. Now things were different. Not far from the center of Kimberley was a large square tent which served as the registration office. Here were displayed lists of abandoned claims which were available for reregistration. There were also lists of claims which were for sale. Diggers interested in buying would record the numbers of a few claims and then go off and inspect them. This is what David and Jack proceeded to do.

It was a confusing time, for they did not know exactly what they were looking for. The claims were in and around the big hole and some were deep and some not so deep and some were on the rim and some were in yellow ground and some were covered to depths of nearly twenty feet by the topsoil—red

gravel—dumped there by neighboring diggers, which would have to be removed before the claim could be restarted. They spoke to diggers and they heard stories of good luck and bad luck in about equal quantities. They were offered advice by everyone, a lot of it conflicting. They only had the money to buy one claim and they knew it had to be the right one. But what was a good claim? What was a bad one? How to begin?

They had been looking for several days when on a Saturday afternoon, walking back from the registration office, they came across a public auction.

They were to know these auctions well, for they were a feature of life on the diggings. Each Saturday afternoon J. J. Rothschild would draw his wagon into the Market Square and sell anything anyone was offering. In a place where men could become rich in a single instant and go bust almost as quickly, the variety of goods for sale was wide. In the following years David was to see such diverse offerings as a pure white grand piano, a coat made entirely of ostrich feathers, a set of gold false teeth, a single glaring glass eye, a carriage which was inlaid with mother-of-pearl and furnished with watered-silk upholstery and drawn by four trained zebras, a large male monkey on a perch that masturbated continuously to the delight of the crowd, and a surgical sandal filled with a porcelain foot on which the nails had been painted in silver. But mainly the auctions comprised the effects of diggers who had died from typhoid, cholera, dysentery or one of half a dozen fevers, or who had lost everything. Shovels were bought for a few pence and so were picks and lanterns and boots and hats; everything told the story of failure.

On this particular Saturday afternoon they were watching the auctioneer sell off part of a bedroom suite which must have been brought up from the Cape at great expense, when David felt a tap on the shoulder. He looked round and saw the tall, thin figure and grizzled face of Joseph Malone. By his side was Daniel Halkett.

They greeted each other like long-lost friends. The two were dressed in clean khaki shirts and britches and both were sunburnt and thinner than when David had last seen them. He introduced them to Jack and then said to Malone, "You're the very man we've been looking for."

"How's that?"

David told him about their arrival, about the recovery of his money and how they were looking for a claim. "Let me buy you a drink," he said, indicating a saloon on the opposite side of the road. But Halkett broke in, "What about Madame's?"

So they went off to Madame Delatee's French Café and ordered ginger beer and lemonade and Joseph Malone drank tea.

That meeting set them on the road, for Malone knew of a digger ill with fever who wished to sell his claim, which was not far from one being worked by Halkett and himself. "How much can you spend?" Malone said.

"How much will we need to?" Jack put in.

"Between twenty and thirty quid. You could spend hundreds of pounds if you want to go near the center of the hole. But thirty'll buy you a decent claim and I've seen up to four carats come out of one in a day."

Halkett took an envelope from his pocket and the stub of a pencil—David was never to know a time, even years later, when Halkett could not produce a pencil stub from one pocket or another—and they worked out a scheme in which they could afford to spend twenty-four pounds on the claim, hire one black boy to dig, buy the minimum amount of gear, including a rocking sieve called a "baby," put down three months' rent on a bell tent, buy a couple of camp stretchers and blankets and have enough left over to buy food, fuel and water to last the same time. It meant simply that they were committed for three months; if they found nothing, they would have to think again.

The sick man lived on the outskirts of the diggers' main camp, between it and the hovels and shanties in which the blacks lived. It was a kind of slum area, the place you ended up if the luck was bad—a mixure of tar paper shacks and one-room dwellings of old packing cases, and tents that had seen better days, all festering in the burning afternoon sunshine.

The digger's name was Sandieson and he lay on a grass-filled palliasse on the floor of his tent in heat of more than 100 degrees Fahrenheit, yet he was shivering. He was in his thirties but looked sixty. His body was thin and wasted and the whites of his eyes were a dirty yellow.

His "boy," a large black man, was sponging his naked body. "This is Mackintosh," Sandieson said. The washing seemed to make him feel better. "Mackintosh, give us all a dram. I shouldna

be drinkin' it, my liver's gone to pot, but there's no hope anyhow, so it doesna matter." He drained his mug. "So you want to buy the claim? Can you afford thirty?"

"Yes," Jack said, without consulting David.

"It's no' a wonderful claim. I've had a few carats out of it, enough to live on, but it hasna made me rich. Still, who's to tell what'll happen? For thirty you can have all this." He indicated the tent and a large carpenter's chest which contained his food supplies. "And there's Mackintosh. Could you take him on?"

"We'd be starting immediately."

"Could you give me a day or two?"

"I didn't think you'd be leaving that soon," David said.

"Leaving!" He reached out and poured himself half a cup of whisky. "Leaving! Don't be soft, man. I'm finished, done. I'll no' be leaving here. I've only a day or so left. That's why I want to sell. I want a good grave and a good headstone. And I want my name on the headstone. I've paid for the grave but not the stone. Mackintosh has got the paper for that. It's all written down. Name. Place of birth. Date of birth. James McIver Sandieson, born Moy in the County of Inverness, twenty-seventh of February, 1843. Died, etc. . . . etc. . . . And nothing sentimental. No bits of verse. Just 'He Was a Digger,' at the bottom. It's all written down." He swallowed the whisky and lay back. The sweat burst out on him again. "At least they'll know," he said.

"Who?"

"The people who walk in the graveyard and look at the headstone. At least they'll know I was alive."

Sandieson died at evening two days later. Much of that time Jack spent at his bedside. They buried him the next day and David accompanied Mackintosh to the stonemason and arranged for the inscription on the headstone. The day after that they started their work on the diggings: the Kade-Farson partnership had begun.

6

"Pull . . . ! Pull . . . ! Pull . . . !" David Kade said the word over and over to himself. "Left hand . . . right hand . . . " Slowly the big iron bucket, filled with gravel, rose on the pulleys to the rim of the huge hole in the ground which the Dry Diggings had become. Beside David, Jack leant on his pick and stared down at the ground, too worn out to raise his eyes. "Pull . . . ! Pull . . . !" The muscles in David's back and shoulders felt as though they were going to tear. At last the bucket reached the top. He secured the ropes and then climbed up the long, rickety ladders to the rim. He heaved the bucket to his sieving machine, a metal frame which hung on leather thongs from four posts driven into the ground. It comprised two sieves of different mesh, one above the other. David placed the gravel in the top sieve and rocked the contraption sharply. The smaller gravel fell through to the second sieve, the larger pieces remained. These were called

coarse tailings and he searched through them, finding no evidence of diamonds. Next he searched the fine tailings. He placed them on a board supported by two rusty oil drums—his "sorting table." They were a mixture of small stones and fine yellow earth and, catching up a piece of metal shaped like a knife, he cut the pile into three and with a practiced motion spread out each pile in turn. He found several pieces of quartz, but no diamonds. He swept the tailings from the table and flung them onto a pile of detritus. Then he took the bucket to the rim, climbed down his ladders and lowered it. By this time Jack had dug another load with his pick and the two of them shoveled it into the bucket. They did not look at each other, did not speak.

"Pull . . . ! Pull . . . !" David heaved once more on the ropes and sent the bucket to the surface. Again there was nothing of value in the gravel, but he was not surprised; there scarcely ever was.

It was ten o'clock on a bitterly cold winter Sunday morning and they had been working since dawn. Like everywhere else in the world, Sunday on the diggings was a day of rest, a day when you cleaned your tent, did your washing, smoked a pipe with friends. But not if you were almost broke; then you worked seven days a week.

Two bitter years had passed since David and Jack had arrived in Kimberley. There had been times when they had found a small diamond, the sale of which put a few pounds in their pockets, but most of the time they struggled to stay alive. Mackintosh had been an early casualty of their ill luck; they had not been able to afford even his paltry wages.

David sorted the new load of gravel, found nothing and shouted down to Jack, "I'm having a smoke." Jack did not reply but dropped his pick, sat down and lit a pipe. David found the butt of a cigar which had once been an expensive Havana given him by Mr. Levinson, lit it and sat with his back to one of the oil drums. The smoke, on an empty stomach, made him momentarily dizzy.

He looked out over the diggings. Before him was the opencast mine, a huge gouge in the desert. The bitter east wind blew columns of dust across it and made the spider's web of cables that covered its surface shake and quiver in the yellow sunshine.

Because some men worked faster than others, the hole was uneven. Parts of it were deeper than others and there were

frequent rock falls from above into the deeper claims, with resulting injury to the diggers. Most dangerous of all were the "roads" that crossed the mine. These stood up from the bottom as though suspended in the air. They were only wide enough for one wagon at a time and a one-way system had been organized by the Diggers' Committee—the ruling power—so that no two wagons ever met. In spite of this David had several times seen oxen panic and drag a wagon over the road edge to plunge down the cliff sides and crash in a broken heap on the mine floor. Twice, such accidents had killed diggers below. It was a crazy place to work, he thought.

Beyond the mine the desert stretched away into the distance. He could see plumes of dust as a line of wagons made its way into Kimberley. At a guess these would contain water, wood—no trees remained around Kimberley—and pumpkins. But none of it would be for sale, for it was Sunday and the farmers—devout Calvinists—did not do business on Sundays. Behind each wagon walked one or two black women. Occasionally he would see one dart forward and bend down. He knew they were picking up the wet bullock dung and placing it in empty lamp-oil tins to take back with them to their huts where they would form it into small cakes, allow it to dry, then sell it as fuel. Once he had seen a white man, a digger, collecting dung in this fashion, and the memory had stayed with him: it was the ultimate failure, he thought.

The cold wind swirled around him. He was dressed, like most diggers, in heavy corduroy trousers, strong boots, short canvas ankle puttees, a thick woolen shirt, a brown jersey frayed at the elbows and a hat—his panama, now a sorry-looking object stained with sweat and dust. The cold wind made his nose run and he wiped it on his sleeve. His eyes were sore but the dust made everyone's eyes sore. His hands were the worst: the cold had cracked the skin across his knuckles and each time he pulled on the rope to raise the bucket the cracks would break open and blood would ooze to the surface. Hilda had given him one of the preparations they sold in the shop—a mixture of candle wax and paraffin—and nagged at him to use it. But the cracks never seemed to heal.

He heard Jack's pick crash into the earth and rose reluctantly. He wanted to stay where he was a little longer, perhaps close his sore eyes for a few minutes, but he knew it would never do. These days Jack's temper was uncertain and he did not want a

row. He climbed down the ladders and began loading the bucket.

At noon they stopped for half an hour and ate a meal of bread, cold beans and sugarless coffee, as they did almost every day. Their lives conformed to the general one at the diggings. In summer they would be up well before light. In the heady days when Mackintosh had still worked for them he would arrive about four, light a fire of dung and make them a breakfast of maize meal porridge. Then he would fill the billy with black, sugarless coffee which they would drink cold during the heat of the day. They would work until noon, when the heat became too fierce, then return to their tent for a meal of cold stew or cold beans and lie down for an hour before returning to the claim. But the summer heat had gone and so had Mackintosh and now they took their food with them and worked through the day until the light made it impossible to see. In the evening when they returned, dog tired, they were supposed to have their one hot meal of the day, but often they were too weary to cook it, and when they did, they sometimes fell asleep before it was ready.

The hard work and short rations had caused each man to lose weight and they wolfed down their food like animals. David watched Jack under his eyebrows. The big man stared, unseeing, into the distance as he stuffed pieces of dry bread into his mouth. At first, as on most claims, it had been a black man—Mackintosh—who had done the severe work, but after they had let him go they had taken it in turns to use the heavy pick. It soon became clear that David could not maintain Jack's work rate and so after several weeks the work had split naturally: Jack broke the gravel with the pick; David raised the bucket and sorted it; both filled the bucket.

It was unusual for white men to dig, although not unknown. It seemed that even the poorest miners could raise a few shillings a week to employ black labor and there was a convention that this was the way things should be. But even when they had employed Mackintosh, Jack had complained at his work rate, and David had to admit that since Jack had taken over the amount of gravel coming up for sorting had almost doubled. He recalled Mr. Levinson's phrase in the coach: working like a kaffir. That is what Jack was doing and at first diggers on their way to their own claims would talk in loud voices about the "white kaffir" until one day Jack had climbed the ladders and gone after one of them. That stopped the teasing but it did not stop the long-term effect

on Jack: it seemed to turn him against black people and when Mackintosh, down on his luck, had come to beg a drink of brandy, Jack would not even get off his bed to see him.

From the way Jack ate, David could see he was in a sour mood. He dug the spoon into the cold beans and thrust it into his mouth; he tore the bread as though it had given offense. Brutally hard work without much reward had given him a volcanic temper. Usually David waited for a better moment before discussing anything important, but today his own mood was gray and hopeless. This wasn't why he had come to Kimberley; this wasn't what he had dreamed. Before he could stop himself he said, "Jack, why don't we sell New Chance?" New Chance was the name they had given the claim.

Jack did not reply but moved the beans around his white enamel plate.

"There's still a good deal of yellow left," David said. "We could put the money into a different claim. Try our luck elsewhere." It was believed that diamonds were found only in the yellow gravel. Underneath that was blue gravel—the blue ground, as it was called—and once you hit that, any hope of finding diamonds was finished.

"I'm not giving up," Jack said.

"It's not a question of giving up. It's using our brains. Getting out in time."

"No."

"We're wearing ourselves out. Crippling ourselves. And all for what?"

With an angry gesture, Jack threw away the dregs of his coffee. "We'll never find anything if we sit on our arses."

They worked on into the cold afternoon. The sun disappeared into thick gray clouds. All color was leached from the landscape and it became monochromatic.

At five o'clock, when it was almost too cold to sort the tailings and too dark to see, David found a diamond.

He almost missed it. He had been about to sweep away the last of the fine tailings—as far as he was concerned, it was to be the day's last load—when he saw it in the middle of the table. So often had he found other "diamonds" in this fashion—there were many semiprecious stones that at first glance resembled the real thing—that he assumed this to be the present case. He picked the stone up with tweezers and fumbled for his loupe, but even

before he fixed it in his eye his hand began to shake. It was always the same; no matter how small the diamond, the moment of discovery caused him to tremble: the Kimberley shakes, they called it.

"Come on!" Jack called from below.

David hardly heard him. Under the loupe's magnification and in the last pale light of the setting sun, he examined the stone. This was the worst moment, for now would be revealed whether it was flawed, or afflicted by the dark area inside commonly known as a black spot. Either way its value would be greatly reduced. But looking into the crystalline structure he could see no faults.

"Get a move on!" Jack shouted.

"Jack!"

"What is it?"

"Jack!"

The ladders rattled against the rock wall as Jack climbed. His red hair and bony face appeared over the rim. "Have you . . . ?"

"Look for yourself!" He gave Jack the loupe.

After a moment Jack said: "It ain't flawed!"

David took back the stone and the loupe and examined it again. Jack watched, hardly breathing. Both men had been savagely disappointed in the past. The first half-dozen diamonds they had found had been flawed, so they were wary of jumping to conclusions.

This one was half the size of a coffee bean and resembled a piece of bottle glass smoothed down and dirtied by the gravel in which it had lain.

"Are you sure?" Jack said.

"Absolutely."

The two men looked at each other and slowly their tired faces broke into smiles. The smiles grew wider and wider and abruptly their lungs exploded in great guffaws of laughter. They caught each other by the elbows and whirled about in a jig, sending clouds of dust blowing away on the wind. Tiredness vanished, sore eyes and hands were forgotten. They pirouetted along the rim of the mine. After some minutes, when both were out of breath, they paused and Jack said, "What'll it fetch?" That was always one of his first questions.

"Hundred and ten, hundred and twenty if we're lucky."

The money would mean months of relative comfort, of decent

food, of wood fires instead of dung; it would mean a new shirt and a new set of underwear, an evening or two at the Lanyon Theater and the knowledge that they could go to the Digger's Retreat or the Cat and Gridiron and have a drink on a Saturday night to wash the dust from their throats. It would mean security.

They reached their tent in euphoric mood. "I'm going to have a bath," David said. "A proper one." He went out to buy wood and found a black woman to deliver two tins of water. Jack flung himself down on his camp bed, making it groan alarmingly, and laced his hands behind his head, a half smile on his face. When David returned he made a fire, heated the water and placed an old zinc bath between the two camp beds. He sat in it, luxuriating in the steamy warmth. Most of the time they washed themselves in cold water. The lamp was lit, the tent was warm. He felt his spirits soar. He had come to hate the dark chill of the tent; now it seemed positively cozy.

All the diggers looked after their tents with care and used every square inch of space. In their years on the diggings David and Jack would enter a hundred tents. Each was much like their own: two camp beds, a chest in which food was stored and whose top was used as a table, two kerosene lamps, a few white enamel plates and, suspended from the tent poles, walking sticks, rifles, shotguns, rolls of chewing tobacco and spare clothing. Those who could afford them bought animal skins to cover the hard-baked earthen floors. In spring and summer sudden storms would cause flooding. Blankets and mattresses would become damp, then moldy, and rot in a few weeks. Suitcases served as pillows and pickle kegs as chairs and the most useful single item was a billycan of gray enamel with a tight-fitting metal cup for a lid and a strong wire handle.

"A hundred and ten!" Jack said, breaking the silence.

"I'll take it to Peter. He'll give us the best price." Peter Arendt was a diamond dealer with whom they had done business in the past.

"I'll take it."

"I'm having supper with the Levinsons. Peter's office is on the way."

"I'll take it." There was something in the tone of Jack's voice which caused David to look sharply at him. He had not moved and was still staring at the roof of the tent.

"Why?" David said.

"I want to."

"But I know Peter. I always deal with him. I get us the best price, don't I?"

"I ain't saying anything about that."

"Well, what then?"

"I'm just saying as how I'm going to do it this time."

"But . . ."

"Don't you trust me? Is that it? Afraid I'll run off with it?"

"Of course not!"

"Well, then."

David shrugged. "If you put it like that. It's in my pocket." He always felt a wrench parting with a stone, even though he knew it was necessary.

Jack found the diamond. He stood up.

"I thought we'd have a drink to celebrate," David said.

"And then you go off to your friends."

"I suppose so. You could come too, you know."

"No, thanks." He pushed his way through the tent flap.

David lay back in the warm water, but the enjoyment had gone. Sometimes Jack's sudden changes of mood made his head spin. They had lived together as closely as any two men could for more than two years, yet he would never have said he knew Jack. There was something about him that was impenetrable and warned off expressions of intimacy. His life seemed to be split into three: work, rest and leisure. When he worked he did so with all his energy and strength. When he rested it was never with a book—in all their time together David had never seen him reading, nor indeed express any interest in books—but in the now familiar position, stretched out on his camp bed, hands behind his head, staring at nothing. His leisure, which depended on whether or not he had any money, he spent in one of the cosies or out at Portuguese Place.

It was obvious that the time spent with Frans and Marie Delport on the journey north had been important to him, for the one place he always seemed happy was Portuguese Place. David had gone there with him once to celebrate the installation of the pump. Marie and Susan had come in for supplies and had taken them out in the trap.

"It used to take us two days in the wagon," Marie had said. "Now it's only a few hours."

David's knowledge of the Delports had been based on one

evening around the fire with Frans and Marie at the village of Victoria. They had seemed to him to be similar to the poverty-stricken farmers he had met all the way up to the diggings. Now he began to revise this opinion. Their trap was new, their tack was of the best and the two horses were matched grays. The farm, when they came to it, was different from anything he had expected. It was approached through a large, imposing gate in the middle of nowhere. The gateposts were white, with PORTUGUESE PLACE picked out in black gothic lettering and, underneath, F. DELPORT. Barbed-wire fences ran out in either direction as far as the eye could see. David had not seen such fences before and realized that they must have cost a fortune. Once inside the gate he saw sheep, not in flocks, but in ones and twos wherever he looked.

It took half an hour to drive from the gate to the farmhouse and during that time he continued to see sheep until he realized their numbers must be in the thousands. There was a line of trees which marked the Green River and he was able to make out scores of red and black cattle standing and lying in the shade.

The house, though built of mud bricks, was large and rambling, the reason being, as Frans told him when he showed him over it, that bits had been added over the years.

"This was the first part," he said, indicating a wing which comprised the original two rooms and the stoep, shaded now by a substantial grapevine. "Then we built this section here, and a year ago that wing." It was a strange house, all on one floor, created without plans or drawings, so that in some parts they had to walk through one room to reach another. In others, there were little, dim passageways which wound to the left or right or simply stopped abruptly against a blank wall. It was only when David had viewed the house from below that he could follow the design. It was roughly L shaped. The foot of the L was the original part, with the stoep, onto which had been built a large sitting room which had a wooden floor. The upright of the L consisted of dining room, bedrooms, a sewing room for Susan and an "office" for Frans. The most recent addition was a bathroom which was to be fed by the pump with water from the river. The kitchen remained outside the house. There were a dozen or more huts at the back to house the Hottentot workers and there were several large stock pens made of river stones. A small field had been

plowed below the house and this was where Susan was to have her garden.

"Flowers!" Frans said at supper that night to David and Jack. "What will women think of next?"

The sitting room was very different from the early days. Auctions in Kimberley had proved a fruitful source of furniture, some of it in expensive yellow-wood, others in mahogany. Brass and porcelain lamps glowed softly, there were zebra skins on the floor and kudu skins casually thrown over the backs of chairs. Everything gave a feeling of substance and quiet wealth.

The food, too, was excellent: homegrown lamb roasted in its own juices, potatoes, maize fritters and rice. As Frans was carving he turned to Susan and said, smiling, "I suppose with all the flowers you'll grow you will have the house smelling like a—well, you know what I mean."

She took the teasing good-naturedly. "I'd rather it smelled like that than the way it sometimes does when you men light your cigars. Anyway, we'll have our own green vegetables. There'll be spinach and cabbage and maybe even lettuce if I can get the seeds."

"That's good," Frans said, looking down at the meal on the table, which consisted of nothing but meat and starches.

He served them and then said grace. David watched the others under his eyelids and saw Susan, in turn, watching Marie.

Susan must have been in her late forties or early fifties at that time and had the leathery look of someone who spends too much time in blazing sunlight. She seemed to speak very little yet it did not take long for David to realize that it was around her that the family existed; she was its heart. But now, as she looked at Marie, he saw that her plain, guileless face was worried. The moment he had arrived he sensed a tension. Was Marie the problem? he wondered. She must have been nearly twenty years old. She had an attractive, olive-skinned face framed by thick black hair but her mouth was turned down and there was a sullen air about her that he had not noticed before. It was a look that vanished when she was with Jack. She treated him with an easy familiarity, but the brother-sister bond had turned into something else. He was certain Jack had not noticed. He still smiled slowly when she teased him and threatened to put her over his knee and spank her.

"Don't you dare!" she would cry and spring away as he reached

for her, but David thought that in some circumstances she might enjoy being caught.

The following day they celebrated the inauguration of the pump. The Lessings and the Jordaans arrived about noon with their families and fires were lit down by the river to grill chops and sausages—David had never tasted sausages like these, sharp and spicy, dripping with juices. They drank white wine that had come up from the Cape by ox wagon.

Helmut Lessing inaugurated the pump. It was steam driven and a pile of wood had been cut and placed ready. A small holding tank had been built on the slope above the house and piping laid so that the pump would send water up into the tank and then they could bring it down by gravity to the garden or the bathroom.

Lessing lit the fire in the boiler and opened the draft.

"Speech!" someone shouted.

"Come on, Helmut," Frans said.

"I can't make no speeches."

He had drunk several glasses of white wine and now he stood, square and powerful, by the pump.

Jack, Marie and David were standing together and Marie turned to Jack and, in imitation of the thick German accent, said, "I can't make no speeches," and giggled.

Perhaps it was meant only for Jack, but it was loud enough for everyone to hear and David saw an angry look cross Susan's face.

Helmut Lessing pretended not to hear. He raised his glass and said, "Some men give der vives diamonds and pretty t'ings. Frans here gives his vife a pomp. But I now see why. It is the bathroom. He vill be the cleanest man in all Africa."

There was loud laughter at this which served to relieve the embarrassment.

"Come," Frans said, limping up the dusty slope. "Let us see if it works."

That was the only sour note, but it had spoiled the day and even though the Lessings and the Jordaans were asked to stay for supper, both men excused themselves and their families. David helped to round up the horses and harness them in the traps and he realized that these two farmers must also be doing well, for their gear and their horses were almost as good as the Delports'.

That evening Marie did not join them for supper, but stayed in

her room. Susan was grim-faced and Frans irritable and short-tempered with the maids. It had been a long day and everyone went to bed early except Susan, who sat on the stoep with a large black Bible on her lap, rocking gently backwards and forwards on a bentwood rocker. David was smoking a cigar and the two of them had been alone for a few moments.

Suddenly Susan said, "Do you read Portuguese, Mr. Kade?"

It was such a strange question that he was momentarily nonplussed. "I'm afraid not. Why?"

"This Bible is printed in Portuguese. Look." She opened it and he could see spidery writing on the top and bottom of each page. "Someone used it as a diary or a journal, I think."

"But you don't know who?"

She told him the story of the Bible and the crucifix and how she had met her husband. At first David thought she must be making it up, but when he saw her eyes in the lamplight he knew she was remembering.

He lay in bed that night thinking of her strange story; trying to imagine what it must have been like for her, all alone after the death of her husband, walking along the Great River. His admiration for her grew. He himself knew what it was like to be lost in the semidesert and he was not sure whether he would have survived her ordeal.

He had blown out the candle and turned over to go to sleep when he heard a sound of tapping on the window shutters. He was about to open one when he heard voices coming from the direction of Jack's room and realized this was where the tapping had come from.

"Jack!" It was a low hiss. "Jack!" He recognized Marie's voice.

Then Jack's voice, thick with sleep: "What is it?"

"Open the shutters. Let me in."

"What?" All trace of sleep had vanished.

"I want to talk to you."

"Don't be stupid."

"They're all asleep. Let me in."

"Go back to bed."

"Listen, Jack, I want you to take me with you."

"Take you where?"

"When you go back to Kimberley. I'll cook for you. I'll look after you. I can't stay here any longer."

"You're talking silly."

"I'm not! I hate this place!"

"Sssh!"

Just then a dog started barking.

"You'll wake everyone up. For God's sake, go to bed."

David heard a shutter close.

"Jack!" Marie hissed. "Jack!" Then he heard her feet on the gravel as she ran around the side of the house.

Next morning everything seemed normal. Marie was demure and helpful to her mother and treated Jack in the same semibantering way she always had. David wondered whether he had dreamt it all.

In late morning, much to his surprise, Mr. Levinson arrived. He spent a couple of hours with Frans and, after the midday meal, gave David a lift back to Kimberley in his trap. Jack was to stay an extra few days. As they drove along the winding farm road, David said, "I never knew that you and the Delports were friends."

"Not friends exactly," Mr. Levinson said. "Business acquaintances, more like. I got my start here through the Delports." He described how he had obtained the two sheep, slaughtered them and sold the meat. "It was fate. I've seen people come up to the diggings with the greatest schemes on earth and nothing come of them. But I hadn't been at the Dry Diggings more than a few days when I saw their wagon coming across the veld. I wonder who that is, I said to myself—they were coming from a different direction to all the others, you see—so I said, 'Come on, Levinson, go and find out.' It was nothing else but fate."

"They've done pretty well out of it."

"We both have. This whole valley is a gold mine, if you'll excuse the phrase in diamond country. There's Frans Delport back there, and over there Lessing and farther on Jordaan. All rich men now. Lessing and Jordaan used to try and grow corn and wheat but when they saw the money Delport was making out of sheep and cattle they let the fields lie fallow and went in for stock. A good thing, too. Kimberley can't get enough meat. It's only natural; if a man's been digging all day he doesn't want to come back to his tent for a supper of green beans or cabbage soup. He wants meat in his belly. I've seen men sell their spare boots and shirts for a good beef stew."

They talked about the Delports on and off all the way back to Kimberley, where they arrived towards dusk.

"But you don't still deal in meat," David said, not being able to recall ever hearing a butcher's shop mentioned at the Levinsons'.

"I don't kill sheep no more and I don't deal in meat. I'm what you might call a middleman. I buy livestock in the Green River valley and I sell to the butchers. I'll show you." He took him around the outskirts of the town and showed him the stock pens filled with scrub cattle and fat-tailed sheep. "There's a sale tomorrow and half of that stock is mine."

David sat silently pondering this new aspect of Mr. Levinson's "mercantile life." If he, Levinson, had made the Delports and their neighbors rich, then Green Valley had certainly changed Mr. Levinson's fortunes. Then he remembered Susan's story of the Bible and her meeting with Frans.

"Yes, it's a romantic story," Levinson said, turning the horses back to town. "Old Frans told me once. It was the sort of thing that used to happen in the old days. He's worked hard. They both have. Just a pity he hasn't a son to carry on."

"Marie will marry," David said.

Mr. Levinson turned to look at him and then flicked the hindquarters of one of the horses with his switch. "That's a different question," he said.

"How do you mean?"

Levinson hesitated, then said, "Well, there's some who say she's two coffee, one milk."

"What does that mean?" David had never heard the phrase before.

"A little touch of the tar brush."

"I don't believe it!"

"I'm just saying what the rumor is. I don't believe it either."

7

David finished bathing, put on his one remaining shirt, blew out the lamp, tied the tent flap and walked into town. It was a bitterly cold night. The wind had dropped, the clouds had cleared away and the night sky blazed with stars. Frost lay white and glittering in the moonlight and the roadway rang like iron to his footsteps.

He passed Peter Arendt's office, saw a light and guessed that Jack was there, bargaining over the diamond. For a second he paused, wondering whether to go in, but he did not want to embarrass Jack after what had been said in the tent. Instead he crossed to the Oporto Café and bought two Brazilian cheroots from Pereira, the owner, a sallow-faced Madeiran who stayed open eighteen hours a day selling vegetables, groceries, tobacco and confectionery.

The streets were beginning to liven up for the evening. After a

day of rest the diggers had energy for a night out and Sunday night, after the church services were over, was the busiest night of the week in the brothels.

He was a few minutes late at the Levinsons' and other guests had already arrived.

"Here he is at last: the late Mr. Kade," Mr. Levinson said, bustling him into the drawing room.

He shook hands with Mrs. Levinson, who was struggling out of a spoon-backed chair, then greeted the two guests. One was Peter Arendt, the diamond dealer. The other, talking to Hilda, was a man he had never seen before and who was introduced as Max von Holzman. He was tall and good-looking, with fair hair and blue eyes. He wore a well-cut English tweed suit in the latest fashion. When they were introduced he brought his heels together and bowed stiffly from the waist. He was an impressive figure.

"Herr von Holzman is from Essen," Hilda said. "He works with heavy machinery."

"Not works, dear Miss Levinson. It is *made* in our factory." He spoke very precisely and David noticed that his good looks were somewhat diminished by thin lips and eyes set too close together.

Peter Arendt was the son of one of the partners of Arendt and Meyer, the biggest diamond dealers in Berlin, and David had met him at the Levinsons' the year before. The two men had taken to each other. Peter was a few years older than David, a large, plump, pink and white young man whose interest in books coincided with David's own.

"Well?" David said when the conversation around von Holzman gave them an opportunity to talk privately. "Don't keep me in suspense."

"About what?"

"The diamond. Hasn't Jack been to see you?"

"No."

David frowned. "I thought he was going straight to your office."

Mrs. Levinson waddled into the room. "Come along, the food is ready."

"Allow me," von Holzman said, offering his arm to Hilda. As she took it, she glanced at David. There was a high color in her cheeks. He felt a sudden stab of jealousy. Their relationship over the past two years had remained one of close friendship. He

knew that Hilda wanted something more but since the very thought of marriage while he was continuing to look for diamonds was out of the question—he simply could not support a wife—it would mean finding some other way of earning a living, and that meant Levinson's Emporium. He had deliberately kept their relationship on the level of friendship.

There had been moments when something more might have developed. The first had been on a picnic to the Vaal River, twenty-five miles from Kimberley. Jack had been with them, but after lunch he had walked along the bank to watch the diggers fishing, and David and Hilda had been left alone. David, sleepy from drinking wine in the sun, lay back on the rug, placed his panama on his face and closed his eyes. Hilda began to tickle him with a piece of grass. At first, to tease her, he pretended not to feel anything, but then she tickled his ear and he exploded into laughter. He caught her by the shoulders and said, "Now I'm going to spank you." She was laughing, too, and her face, flushed by wine and sunshine, was very pretty. In the mock wrestling match that followed, he kissed her. She pushed herself up on her elbows, looked down at him and said, "I thought you would never do that." But Jack returned at that moment and there was no opportunity to take things further.

The second time was a few months later. They had been left alone in the house by the older Levinsons (David wondered later if this had been deliberate). It was a hot midsummer afternoon with the shutters closed to keep the house cool. Hilda had brought him a glass of lemonade and spilled a few drops on his trousers. She went to the kitchen for a damp cloth.

"I'll do it," he said.

"No, let me."

She began to rub at the spots. He smelled her then: a combination of soap and the dried lavender she hung in her clothes cupboard, over her own musky female scent, that brought up in him an overwhelming urge to feel and hold her. He pulled her down onto the settee and started to kiss her. These were different kisses, and he could hear the breath rasp in her nostrils.

"Do you want to touch me?" she whispered, and took his hand and placed it on her naked breast. He felt it contract under his fingers, felt the nipple rise and harden like an erection. But then the bell in the shop rang and she had to leave to serve a customer. By the time she returned the moment had passed.

He was caught in a dilemma. He knew that she expected his advances to continue. She may even have said something on the subject to her parents for they seemed to look at him with renewed interest. But she was indivisible from the shop; if he wanted her he would have to become part of the Levinson family, and he was not prepared for that yet. So he had given her only his friendship and she felt hurt and angered.

Now he watched in silence as she took her place next to Von Holzman, smiling and talking. Peter Arendt, aware of the situation, watched with cynical amusement.

The Levinsons usually kept a good table and tonight was no exception. They were fond of heavy, rich food and David found himself tucking into *schmaltz* herring with boiled potatoes and sour cream, pickled cucumbers and *gefilte* fish, and ending with cheesecake. The flavors brought back memories of his childhood.

As if divining his thoughts Mrs. Levinson, who ate very little but seemed to grow more and more gross, said, "Did your grandmother ever give you *schmaltz* herring in Russia?"

He nodded. "They were always cut up into small pieces."

"With chopped onions?"

"Sometimes."

"So, you are from Russia?" von Holzman said.

"Long ago."

"I have been there."

David had been watching him. The food was evidently not to his liking for he had only picked at it. Hilda, too, was aware of this.

"Eat," Mrs. Levinson said to him. "You cannot work with heavy machinery if you don't eat."

"Herr von Holzman doesn't *work* with it, Mother, he makes it."

"Work, make, what's the difference?" her father said, filling his mouth with a cucumber. He crunched it and juice squirted down his chin.

David saw Von Holzman's thin lips close in distaste. Hilda looked down, embarrassed. For a moment David had a flash of insight. He found himself looking at the room as von Holzman, newly arrived from Europe, would see it: the attempt to "civilize" it by stuffing it with pieces that might have looked good in Lewisham could not hide the corrugated iron walls and the scurrying lizards. He saw the two older Levinsons afresh: the father bald, plump, aggressively humorous; the mother gross,

quivering, a sheen of sweat constantly on her brow.

After dinner Mr. Levinson settled in a comfortable chair and unbuttoned his waistcoat. "Pickled cucumbers always give me gas," he said.

"Father, please!"

"Well, it's true."

"Cigar?" Von Holzman took out a fine leather case and offered Havanas.

"Thank you, my boy."

Von Holzman took one himself. "Do the ladies mind?"

"Oh, no," Hilda said. "Father smokes in here."

"Come, Peter," Mr. Levinson said. "Give us a tune."

Arendt needed no urging. The Levinsons' piano was a good instrument and he often entertained them.

He started with a Bach partita, and David went over to the piano. He loved watching the smooth, plump, white fingers moving like spiders over the keys. When Peter had brought the final fugue to a close and rested his hands on the keys he said, "There's not a diamond in the world worth ten bars of that." On several occasions David had heard him say that his first love was music and that diamonds bored him. At first he had thought it was affectation but when he knew him a little better he had realized it was true. He had studied at the conservatorium in Dresden and had wanted to make a career out of music, but his father had objected and had sent him to Oxford before taking him into the family business.

"I think that was a bit heavy for them," he said, and David saw that Mr. Levinson was dozing by the fire and Mrs. Levinson had settled down with a pack of cards to play patience.

"How do you like our Prussian friend?" Arendt asked.

"Did you bring him?"

"He arrived a couple of days ago with a letter of introduction. I thought it would be amusing."

David did not comment. "Play something else."

The fingers began to stray over the keys and he began to sing. He had a pleasant, light baritone and sang softly as though to himself rather than the room.

"What was that?" David asked, curiously moved by the song even though he had not understood the words.

"From *Winterreise*. Schubert. Something else you can't buy with diamonds." Then he said, "Is there an opera company in town?"

"I don't think so. Why?"

"On my way here I heard a woman singing from outside the Lanyon Theater. I haven't heard a voice like that since I left Germany."

Von Holzman and Hilda were on the settee, talking animatedly, and again David felt a stab of jealousy, which became part of a pervading unease that had been lying at the back of his mind since he had learnt that Jack had not taken the diamond to Peter's office. The music had brought temporary alleviation but now the unease returned: if he had not taken it to Arendt, where had he gone?

"David, come and sit down," Mr. Levinson said. "Here, next to me." His voice dropped. "I hear things are still going badly."

"Until today."

"A find?"

"Enough for a while."

"My boy, you're looking thin. Mrs. Levinson was saying only last week how thin you are. You're wearing yourself out. Now, I've got something to say to you." His voice dropped lower. "The shop is doing well. The best year so far. But it's getting too much for me. Mrs. Levinson and I—well, we'd like a house at Cape Town. Somewhere by the sea. And a trip home before we get too old. But someone must be here running things. That's why I wanted to talk to you. When you first came, I said, 'Have your fun, dig in the dirt and when you're finished, come and work for me.'"

"I remember."

"I'll say it again."

"Mr. Levinson . . ."

"Let me finish. I'll make you an offer. It won't be working for *me* but for yourself."

"I don't understand."

"A partnership. Seventy-thirty to start with, but then in a few years, when you know the business, fifty-fifty."

It was a magnificent offer. David looked around the room. Overstuffed it might be, but to him it was luxury, comfort. There would be no more cold beans, no more grinding hard work, no more flooding of the tent. And if he wanted Hilda, he could have her. It was a settled, secure future.

But was it what he wanted?

"Don't decide now, this minute," Mr. Levinson said. "Think about it."

Peter ended a Strauss polka with a flourish and said it was time to go. David rose with him but von Holzman gave no sign of leaving.

Outside in the frosty air Arendt said, "What about a nightcap?"

They went into the Digger's Retreat and took their glasses to a table at the side. A meeting was in progress at the other end of the bar. Twenty or thirty diggers were seated on bar chairs listening to a man standing on a low table. Meetings of diggers were dull and frequent. They met to air their grievances to the town council about a host of things, from the price of water and fuel to the state of the roads, from the poor hospital facilities to the need for proper sanitation. David and Jack were too exhausted by the end of the day to attend meetings organized by the Diggers' Committee and he had little interest in the present one until Arendt said, "That's C. J. Rhodes doing the talking."

David had heard of Rhodes, as had most diggers, but had never seen him. He was a man of medium height with a small moustache and a plump figure. His white, soft skin reminded David of Peter. His voice was light and curiously high. David had heard how he had become a power in Kimberley by buying up claims in the right places. He was said to be a sickly man; some even said he had suffered from consumption but the desert air had cured him. He was talking about the economics of diamond mining and his theme—David was to hear it repeated on many occasions—was that the only way the diamond industry would prosper was if the sale of stones was controlled by some central body. "If we can control the number of diamonds coming onto the world market, we can keep up the prices," he said. "If we allow a free-for-all the prices will drop."

A voice from the floor shouted, "But who's to judge? You?"

As David looked around, Peter pointed to a man in the front row on the right. He was dressed in a loud yellow and black checked suit and held a brown bowler in his hand. "That's Barney Barnato," Arendt said. "They say he's almost as rich as Rhodes."

"What you're saying," Barnato went on in a loud Cockney voice, "is that *you* aims to play God. You'll do the telling. You'll decide when the men will dig. Ain't that right, Rhodes?"

Rhodes looked down at him calmly. "Someone has to control the outflow of stones, Mr. Barnato, otherwise we shall all go bust: owners, dealers and diggers."

"He's right," Arendt said to David. "And Barnato knows he's right. But they hate each other, so it doesn't matter what one says, the other will take the opposite line."

"Why?"

Arendt shrugged. "Barnato thinks Rhodes is a snob, Rhodes thinks Barnato's a lower-class crook."

The swing doors opened and Daniel Halkett came in, saw David and Peter and crossed to them. "Have you seen Joe?" he asked. "He went to buy fuel and I haven't seen him since."

"How long ago was that?"

"Must be four hours." Halkett's eyes continually wandered to the door as though he were expecting Malone to walk in. His face had the worried expression of a parent whose child is missing.

"We'll come with you," David said.

They looked in at several cosies until in a street on the far side of the square they heard shouting.

"It's a road show," Halkett said.

The shouting grew louder and they went towards it. The first things David saw were three green and yellow enclosed wagons with MEECHAM'S MARVELOUS MAGIC SHOW stenciled on the sides. The last time he had seen them was on the Grand Parade in Cape Town. Just then the crowd gave a louder roar and Halkett said, "It's a boxing match. Joe'll be here all right. He loves a good set-to."

There were about three hundred in the crowd, most of them diggers, but there were some women as well. The platform was as David remembered it, with a roped-off section at one end where the boxing took place, and the same battered upright piano at the other. He began working his way around the crowd when he heard a choking noise coming from a shop doorway. He peered into the darkness.

"Hello," he said. "Are you all right?"

There was no reply. He lit a match and held it out; the glow illuminated the figure of Joe Malone. He was lying against the shop front, sprawled out on his back. There was a smell of vomit.

Halkett pushed past him. "On your feet, Joe," he said.

"I'll help you," David said.

"I can manage."

Arendt caught David's arm. "Jack!" he said.

"What about him?"

"Look over there."

It was easy to make out the huge torso of the tattooed man in the boxing ring, then David saw that the other one, his opponent, was Jack. He and Arendt pushed their way through to the ringside. Jack was taking a terrible beating.

"What's been happening?" he said to Peter.

"He is drunk. He forced his way onto the platform and started insulting the big man."

As he spoke Jack reeled backwards from a blow to the head. Blood and spittle flew. Jack was swaying from side to side, hands hanging limply, eyes glazed. The tattooed man was hitting him at will.

"Jack!" David shouted. "That's enough!"

But Jack did not hear.

The little gravel-voiced barker was acting as referee and David leant forwards and caught at his trouser cuff. "Stop the fight!" he shouted. "That's enough!" The barker ignored him. Jack was stripped to the waist and blood from his nose was smeared over his chest. The crowd was screaming. Across the ring David saw a girl whose face he recognized. She was the one who had sung so beautifully that night in Cape Town, the Surrey Nightingale, and she seemed hypnotized by what was happening. She held a gong in her hand. He elbowed his way to her, grabbed the gong and beat it as hard as he could.

"What the bloody hell do you think you're doing?" the barker shouted.

"He'll kill him!" David said.

Jack was hanging from the ropes. The Batavian Giant was hitting him on the face and head. Left. Right. Each time blood and foam flew through the air.

"'All right, Lothar," the barker said. "That's enough."

David and Arendt climbed into the ring. Jack was hanging on the ropes. Completely unconscious, he slid down first to a sitting position and then toppled over. There were rope burns on his naked back. A red robe draped about his shoulders, Lothar came over to look down at him.

"You might have killed him," David said.

The tattooed man touched Jack's ribs with his foot. "He shout. He talk big. I remember him from before."

"Bring him to my caravan," the girl said.

It was one of the closed wagons. Inside there was a bed, a table and chair, a small cooking range and a hanging cupboard. Everything had been lovingly made. The wood was mahogany, the lamps were expensive and there was a carpet on the floor; it was cozy and warm and feminine. They laid Jack on the bed. His face was covered in red blotches. The girl fetched a basin of water and a cloth and began to clean him up.

"He insulted Lothar," she said.

"He was drunk," Arendt said.

"It isn't wise to insult Lothar."

David watched her, spellbound. She had dark hair that fell about a gypsy face. Her body was slender but her breasts were surprisingly full. She had light blue eyes, and against her black hair they produced a startling effect.

"You are the one who was singing!" Peter said.

She began to put Jack's shirt on. He was still unconscious but his breathing had become less ragged and after she had sponged his face and neck he began to recover.

The wagon's rear door opened and the barker squeezed in. He opened one of Jack's eyelids and said, "He'll be all right." He backed out of the wagon, then said to the girl, "Lothar said to tell you he wants you."

She wet the cloth again and wiped Jack's temples.

"He said now, Lily."

She swung round at him, her eyes blazing, the skin tight around her mouth, and said, "You tell Lothar—" She checked herself and said, "I'll be there in a few minutes."

It took Jack another five minutes to recover his senses and when he did so he was sick into a basin which she held. She wiped his mouth and helped him to a sitting position.

"I'll do that," David said, trying to take the cloth from her.

"Don't worry. It's not the first time." She spoke with a London accent.

"You all right, Jack?" he said.

Jack touched the raw scrapes on his cheek and his swollen lips and he nodded.

"Come on, then." David and Peter helped him to his feet and out onto the road.

"He called Lothar a nigger," Lily said. "He shouldn't have."

"No," David said. "He shouldn't. Peter, you take one arm."

The rear door of the second wagon opened and Lothar appeared. He was still wearing his red robe. Jack saw him. He freed his arms and stood without help. He stared up at Lothar. Neither man said anything. Then Jack turned and walked unaided along the frosty road to the tent.

The following morning when David woke, Jack was still asleep. His face was a mess. There was dried blood in one ear and the left cheek was badly bruised and swollen. David decided not to wake him, but went off to the claim by himself. When he returned at midday Jack was still asleep.

It was a bright, clear winter's day with a warm noon sun and David did the work of two, breaking up the gravel with a pick, shoveling it into the bucket, hoisting it to the rim, emptying the contents into the "baby," separating it, sorting it and finally throwing away the tailings; then he went down to the dangerous line of ladders to the claim to begin the cycle again.

He worked until the sun sank behind a range of low hills. Instantly the air grew cold and the shadows became blue-black. He collected his tools and went back to the tent. All day he had worried about the diamond and had felt an uneasy frustration at not being able to question Jack. Now he would wake him no matter how he felt. But when he reached the tent Jack was not there.

He set off for Dan Halkett's tent.

"Joe hadn't touched a drop since Cape Town," Dan said. "It was bound to happen sooner or later."

"But *what* happened?"

"They had a few drinks and went to a whorehouse."

"Where did they get the money?"

Halkett opened his mouth, then closed it. Finally he said, "Jack stood treat."

David went into town. His initial anger had given way to fear. He looked into half a dozen canteens before he got onto Jack's trail. He had been into the Elephant and Castle, a one-room shack, had had a few drinks, sitting by himself, had bought a bottle of whisky and left. Where would he go? Jack had no friends. He would not go to Malone's tent, not after last night, not with Dan Halkett there. But there was one place he would have to return to eventually: his own tent. David reached it and sat on his bed. He tried to read but he was filled with anger and

apprehension which grew worse as the time passed. Shortly before midnight he heard the crunch of boots on gravel. They faltered, stopped, came on. The flap of the tent was swung aside and Jack entered. They looked at each other without greeting. Jack's face in the lamplight was a mixture of red and purple blotches. He dropped his eyes and sat on the bed, picked up a tin mug and poured himself a whisky from the bottle, which was now half-empty.

"Help yourself," he said after a moment. He pulled out his pipe, filled it and inhaled the smoke from the rank, locally grown tobacco.

"How are you feeling?" David said.

"I'm all right."

"What happened last night?"

Jack looked down at his big hands and did not reply.

"Have you still got the stone?"

"No."

"You sold it?"

"That's right."

"Who to, then?"

"Don't know his name."

"Come on, Jack!"

"It's true."

"You mean to say you took a good stone and sold it to someone you didn't know? You don't expect me to believe that."

"I don't care tuppence what you believe."

"Be reasonable. I'm only trying to find out. I own half the diamond, you know."

Jack did not reply and David went on, "How much did you get for it?"

"Not as much as we thought."

"How much?"

"It had a flaw."

"We looked at it. It was perfect."

"We were wrong. Ask Malone."

"Joe was drunk."

"He was there."

"How much?"

"You said it was perfect. You were bloody wrong. There was a black spot."

142

"I don't believe it. We'd have seen it. You looked yourself. How much?"

Jack poured himself another whisky and threw it into the back of his throat.

"How much?"

"Forty."

"Forty pounds!"

"I told you. It was flawed."

David half rose, then subsided. "You said yourself it was worth a hundred."

"That was before I knew it was flawed."

"I don't believe in the flaw. I don't believe it had a carbon spot." He was leaning forward, his face close to Jack's. "I think you were drunk and you wanted the money for women. I think you sold the stone to the first person who offered you money." He put his head in his hands. "We work and work and finally find something good and you . . . Why, Jack? Why?"

Jack looked down at his hands as though to find an answer on the raw knuckles.

"You don't know why! That's the trouble with you, you can't think straight. You simply do things because you want to. All right, you got forty pounds for it. I suppose you spent some of it. At least there'll be something left to live on." He said it wearily as though coming to terms with what had happened.

Jack looked up and said, "There ain't much left." He put his hand into his pocket and emptied a pile of silver and copper coins onto the top of the wooden chest. David waited, but there was no more. He poked at the pile with his finger. "Is that all?" he whispered. "Out of forty quid?"

Automatically, he separated the silver from the coppers. "Twenty-two and ninepence. One pound, two shillings and nine pennies. Jack, what the hell happened?"

Some of the truculence had gone from Jack's tone and he looked abashed. "Honest to God, I ain't got a memory for what happened. It's the truth." There was a humility in his voice that David had never heard before, and it was at that moment that he should have left things as they were; cut his losses and tried to forget it. But the days of work, the split knuckles, the aching shoulder muscles, the cold, the dust that irritated his eyes, the strain of living from hand to mouth, the tension produced by

Jack's often uncomfortable presence—all these things had a cumulative effect.

"Didn't you know what you were doing?" he said. "Didn't you realize what might happen?"

"I didn't think."

"But you realize now, don't you?"

"Yes."

"I mean, it was foolish; no, more than foolish, stark raving insane to go into a brothel with a diamond in your pocket. I suppose that's where you sold it?"

"Yes."

"But why, Jack? That's what beats me. Why?"

The big man shrugged. He opened his mouth and began to speak, but stopped and there was a moment of silence. David could almost see him trying to marshal his thoughts, could almost hear the creaking machinery of his mind grind into action. At last he said, "I dunno. Maybe it was just seeing you go off to the Levinsons'."

"But you could have come, too. You know you're always welcome there."

"They're your friends, not mine."

"That's not my fault."

"I'm not saying it's your fault. It's just the way . . . the way things are."

"They were good to you when we first came. You know they were."

"I'm not saying nothing against them. It's just . . ." He groped for thoughts that would not come.

"And why didn't you go to Peter Arendt? You said you would. You said didn't I trust you and I said I did. But you didn't go to him. That's another thing I don't understand. We've gone to him for a year now when we've had something to sell and we've got the fairest prices."

"You've gone to him."

"But for both of us. It's been for the two of us."

"But it's been *you. You* sort the diamonds, *you* keep them, *you* sell them."

"But that's how we divided the work. You remember that. You agreed."

"Divide the work! That's a good one. I do the digging. That's all."

"I did, too. We agreed it was slower when I dug. I'll go back to it if you like. I'll dig and you haul and sort. And then we'll see how much spoil we shift."

"No . . . it's not that. It's just that it's you all the time, *you* . . ."

"That's just your damned excuse," David said, his anger mounting again. "You've done something wrong and now you're like a little child looking round for someone else to blame. You haven't even said you're sorry."

"*Sorry!*" The word came out as a roar. "Sorry! Why you bloody little . . . !"

"Say it!"

The colors on Jack's face turned darker.

"I know what you were going to say!" David said. He began to scrabble for something under the bed. "Just remember it wasn't *me* who got drunk. It wasn't *me* who sold the diamond." He pulled out a small japanned box, opened it and took out a document. "It wasn't *me* that blew the money in a whorehouse." He thrust out the document. "That's our partnership agreement. It says we split the money. That we share it. Read it!" Jack was forced to take the paper. "Read it! Show me where it says one partner has the say-so about anything!"

As though in a trance Jack stared at the document. "Well?" David shouted.

He did not reply. His eyes were on the paper but he was frowning helplessly. In a flash, David realized something he had not known before. Without thinking, he blurted, "Why, you can't even bloody read!" and threw himself back on the bed and laughed bitterly.

There was a sudden movement and the tent shook. Jack was standing over him. He released the document and it floated down to the floor. For a moment they stared at each other, then Jack caught up the bottle of whisky and went out of the tent. David listened to his boots on the gravel until they gradually faded out.

He lay on his bed for a long time. He had never seen such an expression on anyone's face. It had frightened him with its hatred. When his own anger vanished, he knew that he had done something unforgivable. He had recognized too late symptoms he should have seen earlier; he should have known Jack would become jealous of his friendship with the Levinsons and with Peter Arendt; he should have known that this evening Jack had gone to the Elephant and Castle to fortify himself for a meeting

with David; he should have recognized Jack's tone when they began their discussion. Jack had been trying, the best way he knew, to apologize for what he had done without saying the words "I'm sorry." People like Jack *never* said that, and David should have known it. And then had come the discovery that Jack could not read, and his humiliation.

When he thought of what he had said he realized that nothing would ever be the same between them, even if on the surface they managed to repair their friendship, and something inside him cringed.

Like a small boy who wants to be forgiven he went in search of Jack. Again he wondered where to begin: bars and brothels? But now Jack had no money; what was left of it lay on the wooden chest. Instinctively, David knew where he would have taken the remains of the whisky: to the claim. He hurried along the road towards the diggings. The gigantic hole gaped blackly; the spider's web of cables looked like ghostly threads in the starlight. He crossed the hole on one of the roads, trying to keep to the middle, sensing the drop on either side. He came out on the far rim. The area was dotted with sieves, sorting tables and mounds of spoil. He saw a bulky figure leaning against one of the sieves. "Jack," he said. "I've come . . ."

"Get away."

"I want . . ."

"Get away or I'll kill you." Jack stumbled away onto the road across the mine.

"Jack, for God's sake be . . . !"

It was too late. Jack's body dipped to one side, there was a scraping noise and then he disappeared.

8

Jack came awake slowly and for a few moments was completely confused. He had expected to see the dirty white tent canvas above him, but instead he was looking up at a corrugated-iron roof. The room was lit by tendrils of sunlight that crept through shutters and gave enough light to make out other objects: the chair with its seat made of rawhide thongs, the washstand and basin, the hanging cupboard, the mud walls. Then he knew he was in his room at Portuguese Place. It was one of the rooms in the original part of the house and he had slept in it so many times that he thought of it as his. He had been there nearly three weeks now and was feeling almost well again.

As the days passed he had begun to put together what he knew and what he had been told. He could remember hazily the fight with Lothar, but he could not recall what had happened at the mine. He had no recollection of David's arrival there, but he did

remember clearly and with a deep sense of bitterness the row they'd had before his fall. He did not remember the fall. They said he had been unconscious for several days and certainly he had no memory of the journey out to Portuguese Place, nor of the first few days at the farm.

The wool mattress was lumpy and he shifted to another part of it. There was some pain as muscles protested, but nothing like it had been when he had first left his bed to stretch his legs a few days before.

His body was big, strong, well muscled, supple. It was at its best, hard from the work of mining, but it had not coarsened yet, as it would with time. His white skin was almost silky with the sheen of good health and vigor, except where it was covered in fading bruises. It was a strong body, stronger than most men's, but no frame could stand the kind of beating it had taken from Lothar without effect. Jack had suffered a concussion from his fall, but it was the beating which had done the real damage.

But now he was feeling distinctly better and he decided to get up. The day was crystal clear. Above him was a deep blue sky, the sun was just lipping the eastern horizon and the last of the frost was turning to dew in its warmth. It was a golden-blue day and he felt his spirits rise to meet it.

He had always felt good at Portuguese Place. There was something about it and about the Delports that made him a different person. They had become like a family to him and there was a bigness about the land and sky which made him feel equally big. Once David had come with him to spend a few days on the farm and he had hated that. Susan had been comfortable enough in his presence but Jack had seen that both Frans and Marie were uneasy. They had tried to entertain him. He had tried to show interest in the pump, the water tank, the stock and the work Frans Delport was doing, but Jack knew that his interest was more polite than genuine. He was a person who worked with his mind. Frans Delport—and Jack—used their muscles. There was a difference.

On this glorious late-winter's morning, he found himself walking down towards the river. It lay some two hundred yards below the house, marked by a thick screen of mimosa and willows, winding its way through low brown hills like a green snake. It was the one most important factor in the life of the surrounding land, for it never quite dried up. In summer, if the

rains were good, it would become a brown torrent fifty yards wide, but for most of the year it was a necklace of pools linked by narrow channels through which the current ran. The pools were lined by weeping willows and had a bottom of sand. Father John, Dom Manuel and Barreto, who had come this way so long ago, would have seen little change.

He reached the bush which grew to a depth of twenty or thirty yards on either bank and took a well-worn track to the water. There were game trails made by antelope and warthogs coming to drink, but this was a wider path which he had helped Frans to cut on a previous visit. The pipeline came this way. He walked to the water itself, where the pump gleamed under its coating of grease. He saw the big die-stamped makers' label and his fingers went out to trace the letters. The Invincible, G. A. Gwynne, Hammersmith, London. He knew what it said, for Frans had repeated the words so often like a magical incantation, but he could not read it. He frowned as he remembered what had happened in the tent: David's face close to his, shouting at him to read the partnership contract. His shame had been so deep, his anger so violent, that even now as he traced the lettering on the pump, his hand shook, his face darkened with anger and it took an effort of will to switch his thoughts away.

He put his hand in the water. It was cold but not as cold as he was used to for already the sun was warming it in the shallow runnels. He was still wearing the clothes in which he had been brought to the farm and while he had washed once or twice in bed, that was not the real thing. He stripped off his clothing and walked into the Breakfast Pool. The chill took his breath away. He could not swim but he splashed water over his head and shoulders and watched the droplets glitter in the morning sunshine. He came out onto the sandbank and allowed the sun to dry his body. He inspected himself carefully. Bruises remained on his chest and stomach and high up on his shoulders. They had turned sulfurous yellow and some had dark gray centers. Soon, he knew, they would disappear and he would be as good as new.

He walked across to fetch his clothes and Marie stepped out from behind a screen of willows.

"Who gave you permission to get up?" she said, smiling at him.

He stopped, covered his scrotum with his hands and said, "What are you doing here?"

"Why are you shy?"

He turned his back to her. His clothes were at her feet and out of reach.

"Pass me my clothes," he said.

"Why?"

"Why are you doing this?"

"Do you think I haven't seen your body?"

"You haven't."

"Who washed you?"

"Your mother."

"I did."

"I don't believe you."

"Only your face and hands, Mother said."

"Well, then . . ."

"But you've got a mole in a special place."

She had come up silently behind him, then reached around and touched him just below his navel. "About there."

"Christ!" He leaped a foot in the air and doubled up as though his hands and arms could hide his whole body. "Go away!"

"No."

"Please."

"No!"

Jack, who knew the inside of brothels in most of the major ports of the world and quite a few in Kimberley, did not know how to handle the situation. He ran forwards and entered the safety of the water.

She laughed at him.

"Get away!" he said. "Ain't you got no shame?"

"You look beautiful, Jack."

"I want my clothes."

"Don't you want to swim?"

"No."

"*I* want to swim."

"You can't."

"It's my river."

She was wearing only a coarse wool nightdress and in a moment she had pulled it over her head and was standing naked in the sunshine of the riverbed. She looked beautiful in the early light, her skin the color of wild honey and her hair black against the morning sky. But Jack only saw her as an embarrassment, a threat to his relationship with her family.

"For God's sake," he said. "What if your father . . . ?"

As though at a signal they heard Frans Delport's voice: "Marie!"

"Jesus!" Jack whispered. "Get out! Get away!"

"No," she said, dipping down into the water so that her pale breasts floated just below the surface. There was a wildness about her that he had never seen before.

"Marie!" Delport's voice came from the thick bush on the far bank.

Jack felt his heart seize up.

They could hear him moving through the bush about forty yards away. "Marie!" he shouted again. "Are you there?"

She turned to Jack. "Promise you'll take me away. Promise, or I'll call."

"How can I . . . ?"

"Promise!"

"Listen . . ."

She opened her mouth and he grabbed her. He put one hand over her mouth and pulled her behind the long fronds of a weeping willow. She tried to struggle but he used his strength and held her while her father walked along the bank above them. He stood there in the freezing water until Frans had walked away downstream. Then he let her go. He took his hand from her mouth first and she bit him. She sank her sharp teeth into his arm and he pulled away in pain. When he recovered his balance she had scrambled up the bank, had caught up her nightgown and was gone. He walked out of the water and put his clothes on in spite of his dampness. He was chilled and at the same time apprehensive. This was a new feeling and he could not put it into words. He found he did not want the Delports to think badly of him. He respected them, and respect was as close as he had ever come to love.

"It's called the *vet derm*," Frans Delport said. They were at breakfast on the veranda. Jack had eaten a plate of maize-meal porridge and was now being helped to a portion of lamb's fry. There was a kidney, a piece of liver and this thing which Delport called a *vet derm*. "It's like a sausage," he said, cutting it up and giving Jack a small piece. "Only it's filled with fat. You fry it until it's crisp."

"You'll enjoy it," Marie said. She was dressed and looked as demure as a nun. Jack was bewildered at the memory of what had so recently happened.

"Some are long and thin," Marie said.

"That's true," her father said.

"And some are short and thick. And some are long and thick. They come in all sizes." She looked up innocently from her plate. "I like the big thick ones best."

Jack tasted the delicacy. It was neither one thing nor the other. He was chewing it when he realized what Marie was talking about. She was laughing at him.

Susan poured him a cup of coffee from the tin pot. It was harsh with chicory. "So you went to the river," she said. "You must be feeling better."

"I'm well enough," Jack said.

"You could do with a week or two more of good food and rest."

"He's as thin as a winter lamb," Frans said.

"He's not thin all over," Marie said.

Frans looked up from his plate. "How do you know?"

"I saw him down by the river."

"You watched him bathing?" Susan said.

"I didn't watch. I was having a walk and he got into the Breakfast Pool."

"I thought I heard someone down there," Frans said. "I called out to you. Didn't you hear?"

"No," Marie said. "Did you, Jack?"

He shook his head and Susan saw him color. The problem with Jack, she thought, was that his skin was so fair that the slightest blush could be seen.

There was something going on that she did not understand. The bantering had a sharper edge to it than normal. For some time now she had been aware that Marie had developed a passion for Jack. He was not the sort of person that she, Susan, would have chosen for her daughter. She looked at him across the breakfast table and saw the gingerish hair, the craggy, freckled face, the big, angular frame. She supposed that he was attractive to some women. She sensed that deep down there was a violence in him that might be exciting. And then there was his rocklike strength: that had an obvious appeal.

She had always hoped for someone special for Marie. She supposed all mothers did that. Someone with a bit more brain, a little more polish. She knew Frans liked Jack, but she did not know whether he saw him in the role of son-in-law. He liked to have him around as he had once liked to have the Lessing boy,

Hans. They were substitutes for the sons he had never had.

Both of them had hoped that Hans Lessing might marry Marie, but from the moment she had returned from school in Cape Town, Susan had realized that this was never going to happen. Her friendship with the Lessing children was never reestablished. Marie had learned too much and too little. She had a veneer of culture and sophistication which went skin deep, but the Lessing children had nothing. They had grown up on the farm and been taught by itinerant teachers. They could never match Marie's experience; she felt superior to them. Susan remembered one incident soon after she had returned. They had given a homecoming party for her. The Jordaans and the Lessings had come, the girls in their newest dresses. Family gatherings usually split into two, the adults sitting together in one group on the stoep and the children in another. This time Marie chose to sit with the adults. "You're being rude to your guests," Susan had whispered to her. "Why don't you go and talk to them?"

But Marie had ignored them all day and had stayed with the adults. After they had departed Susan had followed her into her bedroom and said, "You were cruel to them. They came specially to see you and you hardly spoke two words to them."

"They're children!"

"They're your own age."

Marie's face paled with rage. "They don't even wear shoes!" she said.

Susan realized how much she herself had become used to the roughness of farm life, for she had not even noticed that underneath their best dresses the Lessing and the Jordaan girls were barefooted.

Marie's anger had an edge of hysteria and Susan had closed her bedroom door, thinking it wiser to leave her alone. Her temper was unpredictable and sometimes she showed a wildness that Susan feared. Once, soon after she had returned from school, they had gone into Kimberley for supplies and she had vanished for five hours. Susan had eventually found her in the Elephant and Castle, a low-class bar, with an elderly man.

"His name is Joe Malone," Marie had said in the trap on the way home. "There's nothing wrong with him, he's a friend of Jack's."

"I don't want you in places like that."

"Why not? Is it because we're rich now? Because we're the Delports of Portuguese Place?"

"It wouldn't matter if we had nothing at all. Ladies don't go into bars."

Marie laughed shrilly. "But I'm not a lady! Don't you understand that? I'm just a . . ." She stopped.

Susan was about to say, "Just a what?" But she, too, stopped herself and they both took refuge in silence.

"What happened to your arm?" Marie said across the breakfast table to Jack.

His shirt sleeve had ridden up and displayed the place where she had bitten him. He tried to pull it down but she was too quick for him.

"Look at that," she said, holding his arm and peeling back the shirt. "That looks like a *leguaan* bite." Monitor lizards, though harmless, were sometimes seen down at the river.

"I scraped it on a rock," Jack said, and once again he flushed.

Susan looked at the mark more closely. It did look like a bite, but one made with human teeth. She had bathed Jack when he was unconscious and it had not been there then. The bite was on the inner forearm. Marie was holding his wrist and suddenly Susan noticed the difference in skin tone: the pure white of Jack's arm with Marie's olive-colored hand superimposed. She felt her stomach clench and she looked down at her plate.

"It's nothing more than skin tone," she told herself. "We all have different shades. It's just because Jack is so fair."

But thoughts like these had been occupying her mind for a long while, ever since Marie had returned from school. When you live with someone and see them every day you don't see change, she thought. But after three years Marie had been a different person. The olive tone of her skin was the first thing Susan had noticed.

Many times since then she had said to herself, what if she did have colored blood? What if the half-caste girl at Galilee had recognized Marie as one of her own?

Susan had seen octoroons and quadroons in Georgia. Selina the cook had herself been what the male slaves had called a "high yeller."

"Why is Selina yellow?" she had once asked her father.

"Because God made her so."

"But why?"

Her father had paused, as though to explain, and then he had said, "One day you'll find out."

And one day she had. Selina's father had been a white overseer on a neighboring farm, her mother a coal-black slave from Whydah. For a time she had been bothered by the fact that her friend Jim was deep black while his mother was yellow, and later she had found out about that, too: black blood could come out at any time. Even though it skipped a generation or more, it was there like some time fuse.

But the half-castes, the high yellows, of Georgia, were the result mainly of white men on Negro women. What could be the result of a half-caste Koranna Hottentot on a white woman? She could not even guess.

She studied Marie. She did not look half-caste; her features were regular and her skin was only slightly darker than Frans's. Her fears were rubbish, Susan told herself. Absolute rubbish! Marie must never know what she had been thinking. She must never know what had happened to her mother.

Marie and Jack were teasing each other and Frans was smiling and drinking his coffee and filling his pipe. It *was* nonsense to worry, she thought. If there was any ground for suspicion, Frans would be aware of it. Then she remembered how often she had caught him, a worried expression on his face, studying his daughter. She had told herself his concern was at the girl's behavior.

"Diamonds?" Frans was saying. "Here? On the farm? I've never found one."

"Would you let me look?" Jack said.

"Father doesn't like money," Marie said, laughing. "He doesn't trust it. But think of the stock you could buy. And a house in town."

Marie was rarely allowed into Kimberley so she had recently begun a campaign to persuade her father to buy a town house.

"The surveyor who came out to mark the boundaries was an expert," Frans said. "He told me there wasn't a sign of anything."

"I'd like to try," Jack said.

"Mother says he should stay another two weeks," Marie said.

Frans shrugged. "I don't understand you people. Here's a country that has everything: sunshine, space, and where there is water you can raise stock and grow crops. Yet you choose to spend your lives covered in dust digging in the dirt. Even Mopedi

thinks you're mad. When the diggers first came I showed him a cut diamond. He looked at it closely and then he licked it and smelled it and said, 'It's like a flower of stone. It has color but you cannot smell it. It is dead.' He's right, but I suppose if you want to dig in the dirt I'm not going to say no."

So for the next two weeks Jack prospected for diamonds within a mile or two of the house, sometimes walking, sometimes on horseback, always carrying a pick and shovel. At first Marie went with him but after a couple of days she stayed at home, a sullen look on her face, and Susan assumed they had had an argument. She began to consider Jack more closely. If Marie wanted him so badly, why not? He seemed a straightforward man and if he failed to find diamonds—as most people failed—he would probably go back to England and take Marie with him. In which case she would be removed from possible unhappiness. If he struck it rich, he might still go back. She could do worse.

9

Everything was the same when Jack returned to the diggings. The weather had turned gray and an icy wind was blowing the dust. It was as though he had never been away. At another time this might have been depressing, but now it was a relief to be away from Marie. He knew she was trying to use him as a way out of a life that bored her, and he did not like it. He reached the tent about dusk. David had come in from the day's work and was washing in a can of cold water. They shook hands warily. "Feeling better?" David said.

"I'm all right."

David searched through the pockets of his coat and took out a thin wad of notes. "I found a stone yesterday. Not much. Here's your share." He counted out fifteen one-pound notes.

"You keep it," Jack said.

"How will you live?" David put the money on Jack's bed. "I'm going out," he said.

As the winter wore on it grew colder and there were occasional snow flurries. Jack and David became like automata.

They rose at daybreak, dragging themselves out of bed, already tired before they had shifted a bucketload of gravel. Then came the walk to the mine: the endless picking, shoveling, sorting; back to the tent and the evening meal. For most of the time they said nothing to each other. They spoke when they had to, in laconic phrases that dealt with the day's work. Sometimes after supper David would go off to the Levinsons' or to Peter Arendt's house and Jack would be left to his own devices. He took to going to Malone's tent for company, but soon wearied of his stories. He sensed, too, that Dan Halkett was not happy about his presence.

They scraped a living. Just when it seemed they must run out of food, they would find a small diamond and replenish their larder. He guessed that, given encouragement, David would try to sell the claim, so gave him no opportunity to discuss the matter. The claim was the first thing he had possessed in his life and he was not going to give it up.

The nights were the worst. During the day he had other things to think about but at night, after David had left the tent, he would lie on his bed, arms behind his head, killing time. On the chest near the door was a wooden box on which had been stenciled the words "Dingler's Tobacco" and alongside it was a metal tea caddy with the words "Mazawattee Tea" painted on it. He would mouth each letter and after a time he was able to understand what the lettering of the tobacco stood for, but that on the tea caddy was indecipherable. Once he picked up one of David's books and, with his finger under each word, tried to make them out, but it was no use. He could recognize individual letters, but once they were placed in conjuction with others to form words, their patterns defeated him.

Often he would think about the tattooed man, Lothar. Sometimes he would relive the fight, or what he remembered of it, which was hardly anything at all. He saw again the smudges under Lothar's eyes which hinted at age, and the soft paunch which hinted at weakness, and knew that if they fought again the result might be different. But there was no opportunity to prove it one way or another for by the time he returned from the Delports', Meecham's Marvelous Magic Show had gone.

Winter gave way to spring and then, almost as soon as the wild

flowers spread over the desert floor, summer arrived and, with it, baking heat and violent storms. Diamond production, except, it seemed, in their claim, was up and prices, as C. J. Rhodes had forecast, were correspondingly down. For several days panic gripped Kimberley because of rumors that an American chemical company had found a way of creating diamonds artificially; then the rumor was denied. Malone got drunk again after he had found a stone of twelve carats; Mr. Levinson had a bad attack of jaundice which left him weak; Herr von Holzman rented one of the best houses in Kimberley and he and Hilda were seen together several times at the Lanyon Theater. David was approached by the Diggers' Committee to become a member, but turned them down.

All this passed Jack by. Work had become like a drug taken for its own sake. The struggle to keep going dominated everything. Even the possibility that one day he might find a diamond which would change his life forever no longer entered his thinking.

One sultry summer's evening when the black thunderheads had built up on the northern horizon and there were growls of thunder, he was sitting outside the tent mending the leather upper of one of his boots when a voice said, "Good evening!"

He looked up and saw a woman standing a few paces away. Her back was to the light and for a moment he could not make out her features. "Do you remember me?" she said. "Lily Bartlett. They brought you to my wagon when you fought Lothar."

He got slowly to his feet. "He ain't in," he said.

"Who?" She was taller than he remembered. Her light blue eyes were a startling contrast with her dark hair.

"My partner," Jack said. "Mr. Kade."

She laughed. "It's you I've come to see. I've been wondering if you had recovered after the fight."

Jack had become so enclosed by his own walls that such a possibility had not occurred to him.

There was a moment of silence. "What are you doing?" she said.

"Mending a boot."

"Are you a good boot mender?"

He smiled. It was the first time for many weeks. "I'm better at making coffee. There ain't no sugar though. I'll get a chair." He brought up the fire and heated the coffee.

"I heard you sing," he said.

"Here?"

"In Cape Town. I was just off a ship and you was singing in that big square."

"We're going back there in a week. We've been to all the camps around here and every village in the country—or it seems like it."

"It's called a magic show," he said. "But I ain't seen no magic."

"Mr. Meecham died three years ago come July. We were in India. He did the magic tricks."

"Did you go to Bombay? I know Bombay."

"That's where he died. A fever caught him."

They talked for an hour. She told him how the show had nearly come to an end with Mr. Meecham's death but that Lothar and the barker, whose name was Wilkins, and Lily herself decided to go into partnership. From India they had gone to Ceylon and thence by ship to the Cape of Good Hope. They had been touring Africa for nearly three years and were on their way back to the Cape. From there they would make a passage to England.

"I haven't been home for nearly six years," she said. "I wonder if the old place has changed much?"

"Which part?"

"Whitechapel."

He was astonished. "But you talk so . . ."

"High class? Don't you believe it. I can still take you to the best oyster stand in the Whitechapel Road. Charlie Booth's."

"I know it!"

"And Auntie's for jellied eels."

"And Mr. Pasco's for kidney pies and black puddings!"

They laughed. "I could do with a plate of jellied eels right now," she said. Then she rose. "It's getting on. Thanks for the coffee."

"Have another cup?"

"I must go."

Jack found himself struggling to say something. "I've not had . . ." he blurted. "I mean I don't eat till late. I don't mind waiting. That is . . . when you've finished your singing . . . supper." The word finally emerged. "Would you have supper with me?"

There was amusement in her eyes. "All right," she said. "Nine o'clock. That's when I finish."

He watched her go down the dusty road between the tents and

the wooden shanties, a tall, well-built woman who carried herself with an independent air. Many of the other diggers were sitting in front of their tents drinking coffee and smoking their pipes and he watched their heads swing as she walked past. How different she was from Marie, he thought. He could not imagine her giggling and flinging off her clothes and carrying on. But by God, he thought, if she cared for you . . . He felt a shiver go down his spine and a weakness in the legs. If she cared for you! There was something about her eyes and her mouth, a feeling of maturity, of female knowledge, of . . . he didn't know what, only that he wanted to be walking between those tents with her while the others looked on.

He ran back into his tent and washed as well as he could in half a tin of cold water. Then he took out a clean set of underwear and a clean shirt, his best britches and a bandanna for his neck. He counted his money: there was nearly six quid, more than enough.

A small crowd had already collected for the show and Jack stood at the back. Lily was singing, but the crowd had come mainly to see Lothar. He did not know the song but again he was transported by her voice. This time there was no quality of sadness. He felt tremendous. He had money in his pocket and he was waiting to take out the most beautiful woman he had ever seen. He wanted to turn round to others in the crowd and say, "That's Lily Bartlett and I'm the one who's giving her supper." Not even the thought of Lothar lurking somewhere in the painted wagons could damp his excitement.

The recital came to an end and she took her applause.

"And now, ladies and gentlemen," the barker shouted. "After Beauty comes the . . ." He paused and cupped his hand to his ear.

"Beast!" they shouted, and Lothar stepped onto the platform.

Jack felt a tug on his sleeve and turned to see Lily. "Here I am," she said.

They went to the Diggers' Delight, a chophouse that catered to miners and their women. It was a place of some elegance, with a sign which forbade spitting on the floor, and it had a piano player. It also had separate tables, which was why Jack had chosen it. He had never been there before.

The place was almost full but there was a table vacant on the far side of the room. Lily was strikingly dressed in a red dress

with a black silk shawl. With her black hair and her red lips she was a complete picture in red and black. As they walked between the tables heads turned to follow them.

"Lily!" She paused at a table of four men. One rose and kissed her hand. He held on to it as he introduced her to his friends. "The most beautiful woman in the country," he said. "With the most beautiful voice." She laughed and patted his arm. Her eyes were shining and she had color in her cheeks. They looked past her at Jack.

"This is Mr. . . ." She stopped.

"Farson," he mumbled.

"Mr. Farson."

The men smiled and eyed Jack speculatively.

When they were seated, she apologized. "No one introduced us," she said. "I only knew your name as Jack and that you shared a tent with someone called Kade. That's all I knew."

"It doesn't matter."

"But it does. It was embarrassing for you and I'm sorry."

She touched his arm in a gesture similar to the one she had recently used.

A waiter in black with a white apron brought them a menu written on a wooden plank.

"You choose," she said.

"I ain't much of a hand at café food," he said hurriedly, for the hand-printed words made no sense to him. "You best look for yourself."

"There's a hot pot or there's . . . no, I think I fancy venison stew. Won't get much of that in London."

"Make it two," he said.

"Something to drink?" the waiter said.

"Beer."

"For the lady as well?" His eyebrows rose.

"No . . . well . . . I mean . . ."

"Yes, please," Lily said quickly. "Beer."

Jack looked down at his place and found several knives and forks and spoons, and had no idea why they were all there. He usually ate beans with a spoon and meat off the point of a sharp sheath knife which he carried at his belt. He decided to watch what Lily did.

The ease with which they had talked together only a few hours before had vanished. Instead, there was a vacuum which he did

not seem able to fill. Lily, sensing this, asked him about mining and diamonds. When there was a hiatus in her questioning, as there was several times, he sat rubbing his hands under the cloth. The four men rose from their table, laughing. They waved to Lily as they left. Were they laughing at him? Jack wondered angrily.

The food came as a relief. He ordered more beer. The room was hot and he was sweating freely. Lily, as though sensing that the only common interest they had was London, steered the conversation back to places they both knew, but even then Jack was uncommunicative. So she began to tell him her own story: how she had been born in the East End, had gone to work in a candle factory when she was little more than a child and had begun to sing there in concerts organized by the workers. Later she had won a singing competition run by a magazine which had offered a prize of fifty guineas. She had used the money to pay for speech and singing lessons but it had run out within a year and she had joined a music hall group called the Troubadors. From there she had moved to Meecham's and had started on her travels.

Jack listened with half his attention, the other half concentrating on how to balance bits of meat on a fork, something Lily seemed to do with ease. Several times his hand went out to grasp his spoon but each time he stopped himself. It was a relief when he came to the end of his meal.

Then she did something which astounded him. From her reticule she took out a small tortoiseshell cigarette case and lit up. He had never seen a woman—he excepted whores—smoke.

"Have one yourself?"

"All right."

A voice above them said, "Well, Jack."

He looked up and saw Peter Arendt. As he mumbled the introductions Arendt took Lily's hand and held it slightly longer than was necessary. "Your voice is truly magnificent," he said.

She smiled with pleasure. "Thank you. That is kind."

"No kindness, I assure you."

"Won't you join us?" she said.

There was a shuffling of chairs and Peter said, "Allow me to get you something." He looked at her glass. "Beer? I think something better than that." He ordered a bottle of champagne.

Jack felt left out. The champagne came and the waiter brought

three glasses. Although it was the best French champagne it tasted peculiar after beer. Peter was talking about opera and singers. Jack knew nothing about this and although Lily knew none of the names either, she seemed impressed with Arendt. Jack stubbed out his cigarette and lit his pipe. The smoke swirled about their heads and Arendt waved it away as he talked. Sometimes Lily would say, "What do you think, Jack?" to bring him into the conversation, but he did not reply. Arendt ordered a second bottle of champagne and a plate of kidneys for himself. He talked continuously about the singers he had heard and the operas he had seen in Europe and how he thought Lily could be a great star.

"In my opinion," he said, "your voice could go to a higher register. Become a coloratura instead of a mezzo. That's where the great roles are. Bellini. Donizetti. You should be singing bel canto."

Jack helped himself to several more glasses of champagne. He had a tremendous thirst. Arendt was continuing his thesis about the need for Lily to expand her repertoire when he suddenly broke in, "What does Lily say? You *tell* her this and that. But what does *she* say?"

She turned to him. "I'm not clever at this sort of thing, Jack. He knows ten times more than me."

"It's you that's got the voice."

"But he's got the knowledge."

"About what?" His voice had grown louder.

"About everything."

They were aware of someone standing by the table. It was Wilkins. "Lothar wants you," he said to Lily.

She flushed.

Jack had had enough. "You tell that bastard she ain't coming," he said.

Wilkins ignored him. "You comin', Lily?"

"Ain't you got ears?" Lily tried to restrain him. "Go and tell that bloody half-caste . . ."

Wilkins backed away. Lily pulled Jack down. "You shouldn't have said that."

"You're drunk!" Peter said. People were looking at them. Then heads turned in a different direction. Lothar was standing in the doorway. He was dressed in Turkish trousers caught at the ankles and a white Russian blouse. He made a striking figure.

"Lily!" he called across the room. "Lily!"

"By Christ!" Jack said.

But Lily was too quick for him. "Don't let him make a scene!" she said to Peter, and she hurried across the restaurant.

Jack became entangled with his chair. It went over with a crash. Waiters were converging. Lothar stood at the doorway long enough for Lily to reach him, long enough for Jack to see him take her arm.

All the next day in the broiling sun he worked without pause. He attacked the ground as though he had a grudge against it. Memories of the evening before were going round and round in his mind and he was trying to fathom what had happened and why. His whole body was charged with frustration and anger and a yearning for Lily as he had never yearned for anyone before. He felt sick whenever he wondered what she must think of him. He knew he had to find some way of making things up to her. But how?

That evening, depressed and coldly angry, he wandered into town and found Malone in the Elephant and Castle. "Drink up," Malone said. "I'm way ahead."

Jack realized he must be in the early stages of a binge. "Does Dan know where you are?"

"Dan doesn't know everything, old friend. Have a drink." He had a bottle of cheap Cape brandy on the table.

"I ain't drinking that stuff." Jack fetched himself a whisky.

They sat together for an hour. Jack's mind was elsewhere. Malone became steadily the worse for drink. ". . . the eastern Transvaal," he was saying when Jack gave him a moment's attention. "They've been panning it in the rivers. Tons of it."

"What?"

"Gold, my friend."

"Gold?"

"This place is finished. Once we get through the yellow ground and into the blue, it's over. And there are some that's got into the blue ground already. The Transvaal—that's where I'll be heading as soon as I've got a poke." He drank from his glass of brandy. "I never did like diamonds. Cold, miserable things. Gold's the stuff. I've been after gold in California and Mexico. It's warm. Got a heart to it. Friendly stuff." He was mumbling to himself now.

Jack looked at him and the chill of depression grew. Was he

also going to be a drunk when he was Malone's age? Was he also going to bore everyone with histories of past strikes and future hopes?

". . . nuggets in the pools. Why, I heard of one the other day that weighed nearly three pounds. . . ."

Money, Jack thought. He had to have money. He recalled the four men in the restaurant the previous evening. They had all looked prosperous. And then Arendt, airily saying, "Put it on my account," when the waiter had presented the bill—and thank Christ, too, for it was more than he had. The key was money. It was the key to Lily, the key to happiness itself. But how to make it?

". . . a few bob in my pocket and you won't see me for dust . . ." Malone said.

Was that Lothar's secret? Money? Why else was a woman like Lily . . . ? He tried not to think about it. He wanted to take Lothar in his hands and . . . a thought came, fully formed, into his head. He stood up.

"Have another drink," Malone said.

"I'm off."

"Come on, ol' friend. . . ."

Jack hurried across the square to where the Meecham wagons were parked. Wilkins's was the last in the line. He knocked at the door.

"What the bloody 'ell do you want?" Wilkins said.

"I got something to put to you."

"If it's about Lily you can forget it, yo bastard."

"It's about money. Money for you."

Wilkins scowled but moved back and Jack followed, bending his head and sliding onto a chair. The wagon was of the same design as Lily's but without the atmosphere of luxury and care. Wilkins sat on his bunk. There was a table, an enamel basin, a cheap enamel jug for his ablutions and a cupboard which contained food. On the table was a half-finished bottle of brandy.

"You havin' one?" Wilkins said, with ill-concealed dislike. He was a small, bandy, runty man with hair parted down the middle and bad teeth. Years of shouting had given him a gravel voice.

Jack shook his head. "I got something to say to you."

"About money, wasn't it?"

"That's it."

"You got my attention."

"You got a boxer in Lothar, only he don't fight proper."

"What do you mean by that? He half killed you."

"I'm coming to that. It's this three-round stuff. How do you make your money?"

"Collection."

"That's it, passing round the hat. That ain't a very certain way."

Wilkins drank a mouthful of brandy and said, "You got a better way?"

"Why not box him proper? He's a champ, ain't he? Put 'im against someone good. Then stage it right with a proper ring and chairs and everything and charge entrance."

Wilkins shook his head. "You got to 'ave a decent challenger for that. There ain't no one here who could challenge the Batavian Giant. Not enough to bring in the paying customers."

"I could find you one."

"Who?"

"Me."

"You! Don't make me laugh, sonny. You been done already by Lothar. He made mincemeat of you."

"I was drunk. Listen. I knows how to fight. Did my share of it before the mast. Now there's a lot of people in this town knows that Lothar and me don't get on—and that's puttin' it mildly."

Wilkins eyed him with more interest. "We could stir things up a bit. Make out it's a hate fight."

"That won't be far wrong," Jack said.

"What do you get out of it?"

"A share in the money."

"How big a share?"

"That's what we got to talk about."

They talked for nearly two hours and it was late when Jack got to bed.

Wilkins worked quickly and by the following afternoon Jack found he was something of a celebrity. Diggers spoke to him as he worked in the claim and men he had never met came up and wished him luck. Some even gave him advice.

It was an easy fight to promote. With his dark skin, his exotic tattoos, his ugly manner, his very foreignness, Lothar was roundly disliked. He knew it; it was part of his trade. He was, as Wilkins told Jack, "the one they loves to 'ate." He suited the place and the time, for Kimberley was a town of men who saw fraternity in what they were doing. They were all struggling to make a living, all in the same boat. This gave them unity. The

town came down heavily on the side of Jack.

The *Diamond and Vaal Advertiser* published a story about the fight, it was talked about in every bar and cosie. But while Jack was known as "the diggers' choice," which meant that popular sentiment was behind him, it did not mean people thought he would win. They did not. They had seen Lothar in action; some had even seen his previous fight with Jack.

The fight was set for five o'clock in the evening in four days' time. This would give everyone the chance to get back from the diggings. Wilkins had decided not to bother hiring chairs but to put the ring up at the base of a small hill, called a *kopje*, the side of which would act as a natural ramp.

At first there were to be no rules but then the Diggers' Committee decided that Jack might be killed, so they would fight with mufflers and according to Queensberry. There would be no gouging, kicking, or biting. At first Wilkins had wanted a fight to the finish, but now a limit of thirty rounds was agreed.

Not everyone was happy. Lily went to see Jack at the claim two days before the fight. He had kept away from her, promising himself that after the fight things would be different between them. He would have real money then, even if he had lost.

"Jack," David called down to him. "You've got a visitor."

The heat was bad and Jack was covered in a layer of sweat and dust. He came up the swaying ladders to the rim of the mine and saw her. Men in other claims had stopped to look, not only because any woman was rare on the rim, but because it was said that she was the cause of the fight. It gave her an aura of mystery and romance.

She was hatless and her black hair hung down to her shoulders and shone in the strong sunlight. Again her colors were red and black.

Jack felt embarrassed at his own dirt and nakedness and put on his shirt.

"I've come to ask you not to fight," she said.

"Why not?"

She hesitated, then she said, "Because I like you, Jack, and when Lothar wants to, he . . ."

"I can look after myself."

"I know you can. But he's a champion. He's been trained for it. Remember what he did to you last time."

"I was drunk."

"Are you set on it, then?"

"Yes."

"Is it . . . is it because of me?"

He looked down at his work-stained hands.

"Because if it is . . ."

"The arrangements have been made," he said.

Susan Delport was also against the fight. She and Marie had come into town to shop and they took him to Madame Delatee's French Café for Cornish pasties and tea. As he was shaking the bottle of vinegar sauce over his plate Susan said, "You were lucky last time. He might have killed you."

Marie took a different line. "Father's going to take me. The whole town will be there."

"I wish you wouldn't," Susan said. "I saw your bruises."

"It'll be all right," Jack said. But inside he was not so sure.

10

The fight was scheduled for Saturday. Word had reached the outlying districts and farm wagons began to arrive in Kimberley from early morning. Many people had scheduled their monthly shopping to coincide with the fight and all the roads carried plumes of dust as wagons, traps and Scotch carts converged on the town. Few of its residents could remember seeing it so full: the square was packed by breakfast time, the bars opened at eight, the whores were woken and set to work and it was queuing at Madame Delatee's for a cup of coffee. By midday many wagons were heading for the boxing ring which stood at the base of the *kopje*.

Wilkins had done well. Seeing for once the chance of a lifetime, he had spent money to make money. He had hired a dozen large diggers to act as ushers and they spread the wagons in a semicircle on the side of the ring opposite the slope of the small hill. So on one side was the hill, giving a good view, and on the other the wagons, from which spectators could also see. Soon the expanse of veld around the ring was filled by wagons and

bullocks, and stalls which sold lemonade and pies, sandwiches and beer. There were sideshows: darts and shove ha'penny, crown and anchor, dice; even a fortune-teller. Some people were reminded of Epsom Downs on Derby Day.

The only thing wrong was the weather. The day had dawned clear, but black thunderclouds had quickly covered the sky and by early afternoon the atmosphere was heavy and sticky. Wilkins was seen to look up at the sky every few minutes and once he shook his fist at it. People said he was threatening God.

Jack woke early. David was already dressing. Jack said, "I'll not be coming today."

"I didn't think you would."

David took his food and cold coffee and left. It was almost the first time the two men had spoken to each other for days.

Jack lay back in his bed, a luxury he would have given good money for on many a morning, but now he was uneasy. He was not used to being in the tent at this hour, especially by himself. He began to think of David. What had gone wrong? When they had started off they had been pals. He'd never had a friend before. And then everything had disintegrated to a point where now they hardly spoke to each other.

There was one thing he had been putting off: who to ask to be in his corner and act as his second. He had thought of Dan Halkett and had intended to see him that morning; now he decided to ask David. He dressed and went to the claim.

David was filling the bucket with spoil and he waited until it reached the rim.

"What are you doing here?" David was covered in dust and seemed already worn out from the work. "You should be resting."

"I wanted to . . ."

"What?"

". . . to ask . . ."

Jack stopped. It was no use. They stared at each other for a few seconds, then he turned and walked down towards Halkett's claim.

By a quarter to five that afternoon the veld around the boxing ring was packed and so was the slope of the hill. Money had come in like a silver stream and many farmers had taken down the hoods on their wagons and were charging standing room, much

to Wilkins's chagrin. Jack, Dan Halkett and Joseph Malone arrived with Frans and Marie Delport. A space at the ringside had been reserved for their wagon. Marie saw herself at the center of things and was flushed with excitement. Even Frans had been caught by the crowd's restlessness. As usual Dan left the talking to Malone.

"Watch his eyes," Malone was saying. "Don't worry about his hands. I handled a boy in Cripple Creek, Colorado, once. Fight like this except they'd fallen out over money. Big, slow-moving boy; came from Missouri as I recall . . ."

Jack was not listening. As the Delports' wagon came to a halt a few diggers recognized Jack and started to cheer. It was taken up by others, and grew in volume.

"Stand up, Jack," Malone said. "Let 'em see you."

Jack stood and Marie stepped up onto the box with him.

"Wave!" she said, and raised her own hand.

"Get down!" Frans said.

The cheering turned to booing. A small trap had reached the ringside. Lothar, in his dirty red silk dressing gown, was stepping down. With him were Wilkins and Lily. The booing reached a crescendo as he climbed through the ropes and stood in the ring. He stared at the crowd, contempt on his face. Jack was watching Lily. She took one of the few chairs at the ringside and then he saw that just behind her were Peter Arendt, David, Hilda Levinson and the German, von Holzman. Arendt moved to sit next to her.

"Come on," Halkett said. "It's time."

Jack did not hear the voices wishing him luck nor feel the pats on his bare back as he moved to the ringside and climbed through the ropes. He looked down at Lily. Arendt was talking animatedly but she was not listening. She was looking up at Jack and her face was white and still. He tried to smile, but his lips were frozen. Wilkins threw him a pair of mufflers, light gloves with a minimum of padding. They did not have laces and were kept on by the act of clenching the fists. Dan and Joe were in his corner. Someone had placed a chair there and he sat down. Joe began to massage his arms and legs. "Watch his eyes," he said. "Don't forget now." Dan said nothing.

Jack looked across at Lothar. He seemed massive. He had disdained the chair in his corner and was leaning against the ropes. His dressing gown lay on his shoulders and his arms were

folded. He looked for all the world like a man deep in thought. He can't be that calm, Jack thought. His own stomach was crawling with nerves. As he looked closer he could see the pouches under Lothar's eyes, the bulge of his belly under his folded arms.

The referee, a big Belgian who had once been champion of Antwerp, entered the ring. The crowd fell silent.

"Queensberry rules," he told each man in turn. Then he said, "Come on." Wilkins hit a gong, and the fight started.

Those who saw it that afternoon, under the lowering sky with thunder rumbling on the distant hills and the occasional flash of lightning, would remember it because of its aftermath, and that would color their stories. But while it was taking place few saw any pattern to it. There *was* a pattern, though.

In a fight scheduled to last for more than two hours neither man wanted to start badly. A few blows were thrown and one or two landed, and each was surprised at the other's strength. Soon, in the heavy, hot atmosphere, both were dripping with sweat and Jack felt it stinging his eyes. For the first half-dozen rounds they traded blows and broke away, then came forwards again. In one of the exchanges Jack was caught on the side of the nose and he felt tears come to his eyes and tasted blood. He had told himself to be calm, that anger would lose him the fight, but he felt it flare up suddenly, for the blow had hurt.

Lothar seemed too relaxed and too uncaring. Jack launched himself in a vicious attack. Lothar fell back, taking some blows on the gloves and allowing others to whistle past his head. Jack pressed on. He heard Malone's voice yelling behind him.

He did not see the blow. One moment he was flailing forwards, trying to get his right hand to Lothar's head, the next he felt a tremendous blow over his heart. He fell and tasted damp sawdust.

"Get up!" the crowd roared. He could not breathe. He heard a voice begin to count. He came forwards onto his knees and pulled himself up to the ropes. At that moment the gong went and with legs like jelly he managed to get back to his corner and flop on his chair. He was giddy and felt slightly sick. Then there was a sudden chill as a sponge of water was pressed against his face.

"What round is it?" he said.

"Seventh," Malone said. "You nearly had him, Jack. I thought

he was going then. That's the only way. You've got to get in one good one, then it'll all be over." Halkett said nothing.

By the end of the twelfth round Jack was marked on his face, chest and arms. He was swallowing blood from the blow to his nose and his left eye was beginning to close.

"You've got him," Malone said excitedly. "Another round like that one and you'll finish him off."

But Dan Halkett, who had been using the sponge to try and reduce the swelling of the eye, turned and said softly, "Be quiet now, Joe." He turned back to Jack. "He's a boxer, you're a fighter. The only way you can beat a man like that is to wear him down. You've got to dance, Jack. Keep away from him. Dance."

The ring was a big one and it was easy enough to keep his distance. Lothar had been used to standing his ground or moving slowly backwards as Jack came at him. Now he was forced to attack. Each time he came forwards Jack slid away either to the right or to the left. "Dance," Dan had said. It was the one word that stayed in his mind. The crowd did not like it. They had been shouting for Lothar's blood, anyone's blood. They felt they were being cheated. They began to jeer.

The light had gone out of the day and, with the heavy dark clouds, visibility was poor. After an hour Wilkins lit the torches. Jack realized that for three or four rounds he had been boxing a shadow. Now he saw Lothar more clearly. He saw the reds and blues of the tattoos, the rivulets of sweat. But he also saw something that gave him hope: Lothar's face looked ten years older. Dan was right. The only way to beat him was to tire him out. "Dance," Jack said to himself.

He also began to use his left hand. He flicked it out and caught Lothar in the mouth and this time there was no reply for Jack danced out of the way, his bare feet holding the boards as they would have held the deck of a ship. Flick! Flick! Lothar came on with his slow shuffle. There were other indications of his exhaustion. His hands, which at the start had covered his face and body and seemed to form an impenetrable wall, had dropped, leaving him open to Jack's long left arm.

The look in his eyes had changed. Earlier they had been filled with contempt both for Jack and the crowd. Now they seemed almost like a dead man's eyes.

The eighteenth round passed. The nineteenth. The twentieth. The pattern remained the same, Jack flicking his left into

Lothar's face and the Batavian Giant himself coming forwards like a clumsy bear as the strength drained out of him.

Jack was able to hit him with his left at will. Each time a blow landed the crowd bellowed. Sometimes in the clinches the two men's faces rubbed against each other, mingling the blood that dripped from both.

The crowd was yelling to Jack to finish him and he thought: "I'll give them their money's worth!"

He suddenly reversed his tactics. He moved forwards, jabbing, waiting for a chance to use his powerful right. Lothar began to retreat. Jack moved in quickly for the kill.

Then things went wrong. Lothar held his ground and as Jack threw his right, he saw too late Lothar's left hand go up. Jack's blow was taken harmlessly on Lothar's muffler, then Lothar hit him on the side of the head. It was a terrible blow and he felt as though his eyes were coming out. Lothar hit him again. He crashed backwards against the ropes, then was catapulted forwards. He grabbed Lothar for support. For a moment the two men were entangled and unable to get at each other. Jack's head was against Lothar's chest and below him was the soft bulge of the belly. He had Lothar's right arm trapped against his side. He knew he had only one chance, and he drove his fist as hard as he could into the soft, brown, tattooed mass.

There were some among the spectators who would always maintain that he had struck Lothar below the belt and that it was a foul blow. Others were as certain that it had been fair. No one would ever be sure: not Lothar, not Jack, not even the referee, whose view had been blocked at that moment. Malone thought it a fair blow and said so whenever the fight was mentioned—and it was talked of a great deal then and in the years to come. Dan Halkett was never heard to give an opinion. Peter Arendt, Lily and David had been on the far side of the ring, with Lothar's broad back blocking their view.

On one thing there was no disagreement: it was the blow that finished Lothar and stopped the fight. It is true that Jack hit him several more blows as he stood swaying on his feet, but everyone agreed that they had no sting in them by that time.

There was also general agreement that Lothar could not have been expecting the blow. "Jack's whole fist went in," Malone said later to anyone who would listen. "In and in. I thought it was going clean through him."

Jack himself remembered little about the fight, but he did remember how it ended. He remembered his own desperate plight, he remembered hitting Lothar as hard as he could, he remembered feeling his fist travel deep into the soft interior of the belly. Lothar had staggered backwards holding his stomach, his mouth working, trying to pull air into his exploded lungs. Then Jack had hit him three times in the face. Slowly the Batavian Giant had toppled sideways and collapsed like an uprooted tree. The crash of his fall was heard above the thunder of the oncoming storm; many spectators thought it *was* thunder. There was something about the manner of his fall that told people he was finished, and Lily jumped to her feet as the referee counted him out. Jack raised his tired arms above his head and the crowd cheered him. Marie was jumping up and down on the wagon, Frans was waving his hand. He saw von Holzman take Hilda by the arm and say something to her. He saw Peter Arendt clapping slowly. He saw David look at him, then look away.

The ring was full of people. He felt himself hoisted onto shoulders and carried about in triumph. Wilkins was bending over Lothar, who had not moved. Lily had come through the ropes. Few were paying attention to the Batavian Giant; most were cheering Jack. Then he heard a voice saying, "Let me through, I am a doctor." A man with a Gladstone bag climbed onto the sawdust. The big ushers restored order and Jack saw several policemen form up at the base of the hill to stop the crowd from surging forwards.

He managed to release himself from the diggers who were carrying him, and scrambled up onto the wagon. "Jack! Jack!" Marie said, breathless with excitement. She flung her arms around his neck and kissed the blood and dirt. Frans was patting him on the back. "Man, you fought like a champion! I thought you were going to go down. But then . . . Man, it was something!"

Malone arrived with his congratulations. Jack looked past him and saw Dan Halkett. "I danced," he said.

"Yes. You danced."

The wagon was surrounded by people who had come to shake his hand and it was not until Malone said, "They're taking him away," that he saw Lothar being carried to the trap by four men, with the doctor and Lily walking alongside him. He was still unconscious.

There was a bucket of water and Jack washed himself as well as

he could. He was putting on his shirt when the storm which had been threatening for hours finally broke. Rain lashed down for ten minutes, sending the spectators hurrying back to town and then, as quickly as it had come, it passed south, leaving the air fresher.

"What are you going to do now?" Frans Delport asked Jack.

It was something to which he had given no thought. "I don't know."

"We'll all go into town," Marie said. "We'll celebrate."

"That's it. We'll make a night of it," Jack said, wondering how he was going to find Lily.

"You can't just leave," Frans said. "Don't you care what happens to him?"

Chastened, Jack said, "I'll go and find out."

The hospital was a one-roomed building made of the usual corrugated iron. It was the size of a small chapel, with a waiting room at the front. Lights were on when he arrived.

He pushed open the front door and saw Lily. She was sitting on a hard wooden bench, the only piece of furniture except for a raised desk where a nurse would have been sitting during the day. As he entered, she turned towards him. For a moment he felt afraid of what she might say. He thought he saw anger in her face. He stood in the doorway, rubbing his huge hands together like a child.

Her expression changed. "It's good of you to come, Jack."

"How is he?"

"The doctor is with him."

"I don't think . . ." he began. "I mean, it wasn't as though . . ."

"It wasn't your fault. It might have happened the other way."

The doctor came out. He was a tall, rawboned Swede called Axelson who owned a claim near New Chance. "Not good," he said to Lily's inquiry. "He has injury here." He pointed to his midriff. "Something is damaged. The spleen, I think. We must wait to see what happens."

"Is it very bad?"

"Ja, I think so. Very bad."

"Can I see him?"

The doctor shrugged. "It cannot do harm. I go now for my meal. Later I come back."

Jack followed her into the ward. Lothar was the only patient. A nurse was sitting at the desk lit by a small lamp at the far end of the ward.

"Please be quiet," she said.

They looked down at Lothar. He appeared very different from the big man Jack had fought. His face was relaxed and the lines of age were plainly visible. His skin was a dark yellow in color. It was very hot in the ward and he was sweating. Lily took a cloth and wiped his forehead.

"Are you going to wait?" the nurse asked.

"Yes," Lily said.

"I'll call you if there's any change."

They returned to the front room.

"Your friends must be waiting for you," she said.

He shook his head. "I'd rather stay, if that's all right."

She smiled slightly. "You're a strange man. Come and sit down." She moved along the bench, giving him a space.

"This is what he feared," she said. "Getting hurt."

"If you do what he did for a living you take your chances."

"He was going to stop. This was his last tour. He wanted to buy a lodging house down the river near Gravesend. Wanted me to come and run it for him."

"Would you?"

She shrugged. "Hadn't made up my mind. Sometimes I think, 'Well, it's better than the life I've got.' But sometimes . . ."

"What is he to you?" Jack said.

"That's no business of yours." Two spots of color had appeared on her cheeks.

It was the question foremost in Jack's mind and he had blurted it out without thinking. He was startled at her reaction.

"People are always asking about Lothar," she said. "They don't understand him so they hate him. They wonder about him and they wonder about me. As if it's any of their business."

"He wants to be hated," Jack said.

She looked up at him sharply, surprised at his perception. "The more you hate him, the more you come to see him. That's what Mr. Meecham always said. He wasn't always like this. When I first knew him he was a strong man. There were no tattoos then, no boxing. He'd bend iron bars and lift things with his teeth. When I first joined Mr. Meecham I was only sixteen and we had an act where Lothar would swing from a bar and I would swing from an ankle rope he held in his teeth. But we had to give that up after a time because of his eyes. Sometimes there'd be bleeding when little veins burst and sometimes he'd see double.

Then he had to give up his strong man act because he injured his stomach picking up the weights."

Jack had a momentary vision of the soft, tender belly and his fist going into it.

"We were in Australia then and when he healed he couldn't lift anymore. So Mr. Meecham said he should get tattooed and start the boxing booth. He never used to be tattooed. He never used to box."

"I thought he'd been at it for years, him being the Batavian Giant."

"That was Mr. Meecham's name for him. He's no champion of Batavia or anywhere. He was born in Singapore. His father was a German seaman, his mother was a Chinese girl. He lived there until he was grown up. I taught him what little English he knows. He was good to me at first, but then . . ." She raised her hand and let it drop.

They heard the crunch of footsteps on the gravel outside and Wilkins came in. His small monkey face was red and Jack realized he'd had several drinks.

"Well, you done it, lad," he said. "And there's a good lot comin' your way. How's Lothar?"

"Very bad," Lily said.

"Stomach?"

"The doctor says there's something smashed inside him."

Wilkins shook his head slowly. "It had to be. I knew it from the first. Once he'd done himself lifting those weights I said to Mr. Meecham, 'That's 'im finished,' but there weren't nothing else he could do. And he had to do *somethin'* if he was to stay with us." He lit a large cigar. "Well, I got business. There's payments to be made. I'll look in later."

Jack followed him into the street. "How much?" he said.

Wilkins cleared his throat. "Well, now, Jack, I ain't absolutely sure. . . ."

"Guess."

"It's got to be four hundred quid."

"For me alone?"

"That's it, lad."

"Christ!"

"Come and see me in the morning."

Jack went back into the hospital in a daze. Four hundred quid! It was better than finding a diamond.

The doctor came about eleven, but there was no change. At midnight the nurse made them cups of tea and then she went into the ward and slept on another bed.

"You've never told me about yourself," Lily said. "I know you come from London, but that's about all."

"You'd not be interested in my past."

"If we're not to fall asleep we're going to have to keep ourselves interested. You tell me, and I'll be the judge."

But Jack's early life was closed to others as well as to himself. The horror of his mother's death—and life, for that matter—had made him shut out the past. He never thought of Mary or Mr. Berkis or Truman Rutter. They were all part of another life.

"Come on, now," Lily said. "Fair's fair."

The very thought of exposing his past made him nervous and he began to walk up and down. Sensing that he could not be pressed, she said, "Have you eaten?"

"I'm not hungry."

"Nor I."

He sat down at the desk and suddenly felt overwhelmingly tired. The physical energy drained out of him and he rested his head on his folded arms. In an instant he was asleep.

He awoke stiff and sore. Lily had stretched out on the bench and was sleeping on her side. Her mouth was slightly open and he could see her white teeth. He had an overwhelming desire to kiss her, to force his tongue inside her lips, but even as he thought of it he smelled his own rank body smell. He had only washed perfunctorily after the fight; he was filthy.

He left the hospital without waking her. It was later than he had thought and the day had begun. He went to the tent, but David had already left for the mine. He took a change of clothing to the Anglo-African Slipper Baths. People in the streets recognized him. Some shook his hand, some patted him on the back, some waved.

After bathing and shaving he returned to the hospital. He was crossing the square when he remembered that the Meecham wagons were parked nearby. He decided to collect his money. He knocked on the door of Wilkins's wagon and, getting no reply, pushed open the door. Wilkins was not on his bunk. He went to the other wagons, but they were empty, too. Wilkins had said he would be returning to the hospital and Jack hurried in that direction. Lily was no longer in the waiting room. He heard a

noise from the ward, a cry and sounds of a struggle. He flung open the door. Lothar was out of bed. His body was naked and he was drenched with sweat. Lily and the nurse were trying to hold his arms. His eyes were wild and there was blood on his lips.

"For God's sake, help us!" Lily said.

Jack ran to her. There wasn't much strength left in Lothar's body, but it was still too much for the women.

"Easy now," he said, pinning the man's arms from behind.

Lothar tried to turn but Jack held tightly.

"Come on!"

He began to pull Lothar back towards the bed. For a moment he seemed to understand.

"Be careful!" Lily said.

"I've got him."

Then Lothar stopped. His eyes cleared and he looked directly at Lily. For a second everyone stood still. Then he gave a great cry: "Lily!" All his life Jack was to remember it. Then the Batavian Giant flung him off and stepped towards Lily. At that moment a wave of blood came up his throat and gushed from his mouth and he fell back across the bed.

The nurse ran to him. She put a basin under his head and then stood uncertainly.

"Get the doctor," Lily said. The nurse ran out and she and Jack lifted Lothar's legs onto the bed.

"He's dead," she said.

Jack put his head on Lothar's chest. He could not hear a heartbeat nor feel breathing. "Christ!" he said. "I've killed him!"

She took him into the waiting room.

"You *asked* me not to fight!" he said.

She started to speak and then shrugged her shoulders.

"You knew this would happen," he said. Again he saw his fist sinking into Lothar's broken belly.

"He wanted the money just as badly as you," she said. "You can't live someone's life for him."

"But you tried to stop me."

Her face had hardened. "It wasn't my business. I shouldn't have."

He was thinking of the other man he had killed. He saw again the body of his mother, the flames licking up Mary's back, the pulpy head that had once belonged to Truman Rutter. . . .

"I must tell Wilkins," she said. "He can get the grave dug."

"I looked for him. I thought he was here."

"If he's not at the wagon he'll be in the Red Mill. He doesn't drink anywhere else."

"I'll go," he said, glad to leave the hospital.

But Wilkins was neither at the wagon nor the Red Mill. The barman denied seeing him that morning and so did the waitress who usually served his breakfast. Jack went back to the wagon. This time he looked more carefully. A drawer which had held clothing was half-open. A few things remained but were rumpled as though hands had rummaged quickly though them. Jack began to feel sick. There was a washstand with a basin on which Wilkins's shaving soap, razor and brush had stood. They were gone. He ran back to the Red Mill.

"When did you last see Wilkins?" he called to the barman.

"Last night. After the fight. He was standing a few rounds."

A man at the bar said, "I saw him later than that."

"When?"

"Midnight. A little before, maybe."

"Where?"

"Crossing the square. He was carrying a bag."

Jack ran across the square. At the transport office of Arnholz and Company, he pushed his way to the head of a crowd of diggers waiting for mail and shouted at the clerk, "Did you have a coach out last night?"

The clerk, who was sorting letters, took his time; he did not like being shouted at. But when he did look up and saw the size of the man and the expression on his face, he said hastily, "There was a southbound mail left at midnight."

"Was it full?"

He looked at the manifest in front of him. "There was one place left." Then he looked more closely. "No, there wasn't. It was taken. The coach left full."

Jack walked out into the hot sunlight. It was early afternoon. The coach would be nearly fifty miles away. There was no way in the world that he was ever going to catch up with Wilkins, even if he had the money to hire his own coach. He walked slowly and aimlessly out into the desert.

"There is always the possibility of doing something," Peter Arendt said. "Nothing is hopeless, Lily."

Arendt, Lily and Jack were in Arendt's house, in what he called

the music room. It was elegantly appointed, with a wooden floor and wooden walls, the first Jack had seen. The prevailing color was blue: there were two blue velvet button-backed chairs and a settee. There was also a Blüthner grand piano and two music stands for string or woodwind players. When he could find them, Peter liked to play piano trios. It was a few days after Lothar's funeral and Arendt, to Jack's annoyance, had put himself in charge of organizing Lily's future.

"Let us see," he continued. "On the one side Wilkins has gone with the money, but you are not penniless. There are assets."

"Assets?" Jack said.

"Property. The wagons, for example. There are three wagons and the platform from which you sing, Lily. Not much, but something."

"And the mules," she said.

"And the mules."

"I've got to have somewhere to stay. I must keep one wagon."

"So there are two wagons and mules. As you say, not much."

Suddenly she laughed and in a second the depression which had gripped her since Lothar had died and Wilkins had decamped seemed to vanish. "I'll be all right," she said. "I've been in worse fixes than this. I've got a roof over my head and a few pounds. Some of the poor devils here haven't half as much."

"And you have two things much more valuable," Arendt said.

"What're those?"

"First your voice. Second your beauty."

"That's very gallant."

"It is nothing but the truth."

Jack hated him, hated him for saying the things that he, Jack, would never have dared to say.

"If you will forgive me, I have a suggestion," Arendt said. "Stay in Kimberley a while. You have nowhere better to go. I know Mannie Lipschitz, the owner of the Grand Music Hall. Why should you not work there?"

"You mean permanently?" she said.

"Why not?"

"I've never stayed in one place for long."

"It is worth trying. I've talked to him about you."

"What do you say, Jack?"

There was nothing he wanted more than for her to stay in town, but this was not the way he had visualized it happening.

"You'd best make up your own mind," he said.

"Will you come to the music hall with me?"

He hesitated.

"Please."

The Grand Music Hall modeled itself on the Argyll Rooms in Leicester Square, London. Mannie Lipschitz interviewed Lily in his office. He was a thin man of middle height, stooped and balding, with a permanently weary expression on his face. He was wearing a dark blue smoking jacket with food stains down the front.

His eyes brightened momentarily when he shook Jack's hand. "What a fight!" he said. "What fisticuffs! I never saw better, not even in London." He had a habit of sucking noisily through his prominent front teeth.

Reluctantly, he turned to Lily. "So you can sing. Arendt says you're the best. But singers I can get by the dozen."

"Not like her," Jack said.

"Any sort. Juggling singers. Fire-eating singers. Acrobatic singers. Singers who dance; dancers who sing. What can you do, dear?"

Jack shifted angrily and would have spoken, but Lily stopped him. "I'm a standing singer," she said sharply.

Lipschitz shrugged. "So you better sing."

He led the way into the interior of the theater. It smelt of stale tobacco smoke. Along one side was a wine bar. "I ain't got a pianist tonight. Can you sing without one?"

Lily sang three songs. Two were popular romantic ballads, the third an aria from an operetta. Jack had stayed in the rear of the darkened room. The stage was lit by a single lamp and he could hardly see her. But her voice, thin at first without an accompaniment, swelled to fill the theater. When she had finished, he rose from his seat, clapping loudly.

"Very nice, very nice," Lipschitz said. He sucked through his teeth. "You got a nice voice there. But . . ." He raised his hands and shoulders. "Like I told you. Singing ain't enough. Not in this town." He turned to Jack. "But you, my boy. I can use you."

"You want *him* to sing?" Lily said.

"Have your joke. Fighting. That's what I'm talking about. You're a famous man, Mr. Farson. What I'm offering is what that big tattooed man was doing. Three rounds against all comers. Fifty quid if they knocks you out."

Jack was taken by surprise. He looked first at Mannie Lipschitz, then at Lily. Seeing her flushed and angry face he suddenly knew what to do.

"I'll fight," he said, "but only on one condition."

"We ain't even got a contract yet and he's making conditions!"

"I'll only fight if Lily sings."

Lipschitz paused, sucked his teeth, then gave a weary sigh. "Everyone always said Mannie Lipschitz was an easy touch."

So Jack began a new way of life. He continued to work on the claim by day but then, instead of returning to the tent, would go directly to the Grand. He would wash there in real hot water and put on the calf-length trousers and soft leather boots which Lipschitz had bought for him. The show included the usual music-hall players, the baritone, the juggler and magician, the dance duet, the declaimer of verse, the stand-up comic. Most were employed for a few nights at a time or at best a week. Or else there were touring companies that might present a revue— the strong theatrical meat like Shakespeare woud be found at the Lanyon or the Theater Royal, not at the Grand. Lipschitz catered for the digger out for an evening's entertainment with a few quid in his pocket and a liking for broad humor and language. Jack and Lily were the only permanent members of the company.

Getting there early meant that he could eat a decent meal at the wine bar for half the cost to the public but, above all, he could see Lily. In spite of putting a little aside each week to pay David some of the loss he had incurred when the diamond had been sold in the brothel, Jack would often have enough left over to buy her a glass of wine or a plate of food.

In later memories it was Lily who colored this time for him. In reality he did not see very much of her. His own toil kept him occupied during the day and in the evening she would arrive only a few minutes before her first song and leave immediately after her last. Jack had no idea how she filled her time. Once he had asked her and she had said, "I read a lot." When he pursued it she said, "Jack, I'm more grateful to you than I can ever say. But don't question me. I've lived my own life since I was sixteen. I don't owe explanations."

He had to put up with that. His problem was that though he wanted her, he had no idea how to get her. His usual rough-and-tumble methods, learned in a hundred brothels, were not, he knew, going to work with Lily. So he bided his time.

Lily, on her side, treated him with a friendliness he had never experienced from a woman. She treated him like an adult and made him feel a man; Marie treated him like a youth.

This period was also marked by his physical exhaustion. By day he still did the brutal work at the claim and by night he boxed at least one match of three rounds. Sometimes on a Saturday night he might have two matches. Occasionally young men would challenge him to a private fight with money on the side. Lipschitz was delighted with him and built the evening around his appearance. Sometimes he would keep him late if he thought he could get a better house and Jack would stumble off to the tent at midnight or one in the morning, knowing he had only four or five hours' sleep before returning to the claim and the endless digging.

The claim yielded just enough to make it worthwhile continuing. Jack did not mind the work; he liked being outside in the sun, liked the feeling of strength in his body. But there were dark clouds. He and David had not spoken to each other for weeks. He knew he had hurt him by asking Dan Halkett to be his second in the fight, but he also felt that things were not entirely his fault. He had done wrong to spend the diamond money—and it was a measure of his changing sensibilities that the thought touched him at all—but he was paying it back.

Sometimes he felt David was on the point of saying something, anything—a remark on the weather would have been enough to start the healing process—and sometimes he, too, felt an overwhelming urge to speak. But the moment would pass and they would look at each other and turn away.

Lily had heard about the situation and one night she said to Jack, "Couldn't you bring yourself to make it up?"

He had replied angrily, "Why don't you ask *him*?" She had not mentioned the subject again.

Then there was Peter Arendt. Lily was seeing him. Jack told himself that it was because Arendt knew about music and this gave them common ground, but there was more to it than that and he had transferred the jealousy he had felt for Lothar to Arendt.

He did not like the plump young German, but had to acknowledge that his feelings had nothing to do with Lily, for he had disliked him before she had arrived in Kimberley. Arendt had been decent to him, yet there was something about the soft

white skin that repelled him. Months ago he had mentioned this to David, who had replied, "He's different, that's all."

He began to brood about Lily and Arendt. The long hours on the claim with nothing else to think about were fertile ground for such thoughts and his frustration became so great he was like a volcano, with anger bubbling just below the surface. The only time he could release the pressure was when he boxed. When he had first started, his idea had been to stay on his feet, keep his opponent's fists away from his face and last out three rounds without being marked or hurt. Now things changed. He began to fight, to hurt people, to knock them out. The diggers in the audience did not like it. Just as they had paid to see Jack fight Lothar and cheered him on, so they liked to cheer their fellow diggers when they got into the ring with Jack himself. They hardly expected them to win but the bond of fraternity allowed them to hope. As Jack began to savage one challenger after another, they began to hate him for it.

Lily spoke to him about it. "It almost looks as though you *want* to hurt them," she said one day after a young digger had been carried out with a smashed nose.

"It's them or me."

"They're only boys."

A week later he went into the ring with a big Italian. The man had come into the Grand with three or four other Italians whose claim had produced a good-quality stone. They made a noise and drank a lot. When Lily sang they had set up a chant—*"Bella . . . bella . . . bella . . ."*—and carried her from the stage at the end of her number and bought her a drink at the bar. It was nothing more than high spirits and Lily enjoyed it as much as the Italians. But Jack watched them dourly. Then one of the men put his name down for the fifty-pound challenge and Jack beat him about the head so severely that he broke his jaw and closed one of his eyes.

The diggers booed him and the Grand emptied rapidly, few people remaining to hear Lily sing her final song.

Lipschitz told him, "You're overdoing it, son."

Jack produced Wilkins's aphorism about being the one the audience loved to hate. Lipschitz shook his head. "Some people can do it and some can't. That tattooed man was a foreigner, a stranger. He looked as though he could be downed and people came because one day they knew he would be. One day you'll be

put down, too, son, but no one thinks it at the moment. You're one of them, but you're doing it to them and they don't like it."

Takings fell, the number of challengers diminished and some evenings Jack found that he was not boxing at all.

A week later his worst suspicions about Lily were confirmed. He had broken the handle of his pick and had come into the town to buy a new one. It was midafternoon and very hot. He was about to turn into the shop when he saw her. She was hurrying along Stockdale Street, her red dress making a splash of color in the bright sunshine. He opened his mouth to call her, but something stopped him. Instead he waited until she had gone a good distance and then followed. She turned into an alley and knocked on the door of a wooden-framed house. It was opened immediately and she disappeared inside. It was Arendt's house.

He stood in the alley, feeling anger build up inside him. Christ, he thought, she had gone to his house like a whore in the afternoon! Anyone might have seen her and she hadn't cared! He waited outside for about ten minutes until, of their own volition, his legs carried him to the door. He knocked. He heard voices, but no one came. He opened the door and stepped inside. The voices were loud and were coming from the music room at the end of the short corridor. He realized he was trespassing but he could not stop now. He went along the passage, paused and listened.

"Why not?" It was Arendt's voice.

"Because I can't," Lily said.

"Cannot or will not?"

"It's the same thing. Don't you understand that?"

"I will drive you. I will *make* you!"

"You wouldn't dare."

"You have a beautiful chest."

"I won't!"

Jack threw back the door and crashed into the room, half expecting to see Lily's clothes being ripped off. There were the piano and the settee as he remembered them. Music was strewn over the chairs and piles of it lay on top of the piano. Arendt was standing near the instrument and Lily was in the middle of the room. With a roar Jack grabbed the German and threw him against the wall so that the house shook. Lily screamed.

"He won't touch you again!" Jack shouted. He took her by the arm and pulled her from the house. She struggled every step of

the way and when they reached the boardwalk she managed to turn and, using her free hand, slapped him across the mouth.

He shook himself like a dog.

"What are you doing?" she shrieked. Passersby stopped in their tracks and stared.

"You ain't never going to see him again," he said.

"You don't own me!"

"If he touches you again I'll kill him!"

"If he . . . ?" She suddenly threw back her head and laughed. "God, Jack, you *are* a baby!"

"What . . . ?"

"Come." She caught him by the sleeve and tugged him back into the house. Arendt looked out somewhat fearfully from the door of the music room.

"Jack thinks . . ." Lily began. "Well, never mind." She turned to Jack and pointed to the settee. "Sit!"

"But . . ."

"Not a word. Not a single word. Just listen. Now, Peter, you tell him."

Arendt eyed him speculatively. "My God!" he said. "Save me from jealous lovers."

"Don't exaggerate," Lily said, smiling. "Now, tell him."

"Do you know anything about singing?" Arendt said.

"No," Jack said grimly. He sat hunched on the settee, making it look flimsy, his big hands clenched on his lap.

"Lily has a good voice. You know that?" Jack nodded. "But it is better than good, or at least it could be. She has the possibility to be a great star in opera if she wishes. But her voice lacks training. We are trying to give it flexibility." Jack watched Lily as Arendt spoke. She was listening intently.

"She has what we call a mezzo range. A middle range. I think her voice can go up higher than that, to coloratura. There are many who can sing mezzo, but few can be coloraturas. She thinks differently."

"I know what I can do."

"Nonsense, my dear! You are made for the Italian *ottocento* operas. Bellini. Donizetti. You will be famous one day. I will make you famous."

"I can't do it."

"Of course you can. You have a throat of steel and stomach muscles like a horse." They had forgotten Jack. "Now. Please. We

will try "Qui la voce sua soave" from *I Puritani. . . ."*

Jack was cowed when they left the house but Lily, who had been flattered by the wildness of his jealousy, took his arm as they walked to the Grand.

Lipschitz saw them come in and called Jack. In his office he pushed a small bundle of notes across the table.

"What's this for?" Jack asked.

"Notice."

"Of what?"

"You don't work here no more, son. I like you. Don't make any mistake. But . . ." He raised his hands, palms up. "I got to cater for the public. You understand?"

It did not come as much of a surprise and Jack took the money. "I'm sick of it anyway. What about Lily?"

"She's a good girl and she's got a nice voice. This ain't the place for operas, but if she wants she can stay."

He found Lily backstage and told her.

"It's a shame," she said. "But perhaps it's for the best. You'd have been hurt one day like Lothar."

They went out for a late supper and he took her back to her wagon, which was parked on the square. "I've got a drop of French brandy," she said. "Do you fancy a glass?"

She lit the lamp and closed the curtains and the wagon was suddenly feminine, intimate.

"It's strange how things fall out. Without you I'd never have got the job. Now it's me that stays and you that goes. I'll never forget what you did for me, Jack." She sipped the brandy. Then she said, "You know, digging isn't everything. There are other things. Someone like you should be able to get on, especially now that people know you. There was something in the paper today about a job in the transport business." She found the *Diamond and Vaal Advertiser.* "Here you are." She turned a page and folded it. "Read that." She tapped a boxed advertisement and passed the newspaper to him.

He held it at arm's length and scowled at the page. Then he cleared his throat. "Which one?" She came closer and pointed to the place. "Just what you'd be good at."

He strained to concentrate. He could make out individual letters just as he had been able to make out those on the box in the tent, but they would not form any recognizable pattern. He brought the paper close. He suddenly seemed to have become

nearsighted. He felt that, like David, Lily must realize what was wrong, and all at once he said in a low voice, "It ain't no use."

"What isn't? The job?"

"I can't read it. I never have been able."

"Oh, Jack!" She put her hand on his arm. The blood was in his face. "Never mind! Not everyone gets the chance to learn. It's nothing to be ashamed of. If you'd like, I'll teach you."

"Would you?"

"Of course I will." On impulse she put her arm around his neck and kissed him on the cheek. It was like touching off a charge of powder.

He grabbed her.

"Jack!"

He turned so that he was facing her and kissed her on the lips.

"You're hurting me!"

But he could not wait. Something the size of one of his own fists seemed to grab his stomach and squeeze it. His legs felt as though they had become water.

"Christ, Lily!" he said.

"Wait now!"

But he would not. She was a strong woman but he held her fast. He heard fabric tear, then felt the heat of her skin under his hands.

"Jack, for God's sake!"

He was past hearing. He was feeling her flesh, seeing its pink and white tones. Nothing, except a blow on the head, would have stopped him. He had never in his life felt power like this.

He found himself on top of her and then realized she was no longer struggling but had locked her arms behind his head. He clawed at her dress and heard the fabric tear again, and then felt himself sinking into her. She gave a cry of pleasure.

The bed was a narrow bunk, far too small for such goings-on, and his feet were flailing the air. Pots and pans came crashing down. There was a thud as one of his boots struck the wooden wall. He was hardly aware of the wagon rocking and shaking.

They came to like drowned people slowly breaking the water's surface. By some miracle the lamp still hung from its hook in the roof and out of the corner of his eye he saw the wreckage. At first glance it appeared that a tornado had struck the wagon: books, papers, pots, pans, cups, saucers, all lay in a heap on the floor. He was still on top of her, quiet now, and relaxed, his body a dead

weight. She was naked from the waist up and from the waist down, and her dress was bunched around her hips. Jack's onslaught had been so violent that his own shirt had lost all its buttons and was torn away. Between them was a warm, slippery sheen of sweat. He had bruised her and there was blood on her lips; at the same time, every muscle in her body was slack and unresisting.

"Jack!" she whispered, and stroked the back of his head. "My God, Jack!"

Then suddenly a voice from outside called, "Are you all right in there?"

Jack stiffened. His lips were by her ear. "Who's that?" he said softly.

"I don't know."

"You in there," the voice said. "Are you all right?"

She laughed quietly. "Yes," she called. "Yes, thank you."

Jack tried to picture what the past minutes must have sounded like to people in the other wagons parked in the square: the crashing of his big feet, the clatter of the pots and pans, the shaking of the wagon. She bit his ear and said, "Next time, take those boots off."

And there *was* a next time and a time after that, many times, for they were like two people starved of food who were eating as though they might never find a bellyful again.

Jack became a changed man. As usual, he worked on the claim during the day and, as usual, hardly spoke at all. But David noticed something that he could not, at first, understand: while Jack was still uncommunicative, his surliness had disappeared. He seemed to have found something deep down inside himself which he was exploring, something new and unfamiliar. David's impression was true. Nothing like this had ever happened to Jack before.

As though fate had decided to smile on him in other directions, they found, in one week, three small diamonds, the most they had ever found, and once again he had a wad of notes in his pocket.

Each evening after work he would wash and change his clothing, wait for Lily to finish work, go out to supper and then to her caravan. The thought of the rattling and the shaking which must provoke the curiosity of nearby wagon owners or passersby was inhibiting, so they fell into the habit of hitching up the mules

and letting the animals wander through the streets of the town. These were in poor repair and the wagon naturally lurched and banged and shook and they would cross the market square and make their way down Stockdale Street and the motion and the noise would enable them to let themselves go. Soon there was hardly a square yard of the town's roads which they had not put to good use.

As the summer wore on, Jack found it irksome to return to the tent at night—the wagon was too small for two to sleep comfortably—and one night, as they were walking back after supper, he said, "I've got something to ask you."

She sensed what was coming, stopped, touched his arm in the gesture with which he was now familiar and said, "Don't say it, Jack."

"Why not?"

"Don't change things. You're happy, aren't you?"

"Yes."

"Leave it be, then."

That night as he lay in his tent listening to David's breathing he felt, for the first time in weeks, a sense of depression and insecurity. Had he taken too much for granted? In all the hours and days they had been together, she had said many things, but never "I love you." Why was that? he wondered. It couldn't be because they didn't. They could not be as close as they were and not love each other. Then he thought, is this what she had had with Lothar?

But he did manage to persaude her to agree about one thing, to sell the wagon and the mules, and live in a house. They found a simple two-roomed shack with a roof that let the water in when it rained. But by comparison with the wagon it was vast. He tried to give her some money to buy furniture but she bought what she needed out of her own pocket at the Saturday auction and her first purchase was a big brass bedstead. She furnished the place on next to nothing and soon he was spending every spare minute there. He painted it and fixed the leaks. He managed to buy some planks cheaply and he put in a floor. Soon the house was comfortable and cozy. Sometimes she would let him stay for a whole night and sometimes not, depending on her mood, and he had to be content with that.

11

Susan was alone in the big living room at Portuguese Place. It was eight o'clock in the evening and already dark. She had had a simple meal and the servants had gone out to their huts. She took up her sewing and sat by an oil lamp, but after ten minutes she put it down again. She picked up the previous week's newspaper and read one or two items about cattle sales, but lost interest in that, too. She felt unsettled, without knowing why. It was something that was happening to her more and more frequently: a kind of boredom which she hardly even admitted to herself, for with her background, boredom was equated with sin.

When Frans was with her it was all right, but more and more frequently he was making the journey to Kimberley to buy and sell stock, and Marie went with him. He had tried at first to dissuade her but the arguments had been so fierce that he had finally given in. This meant that Susan was increasingly left on her own. In the early days there would have been a thousand things to do. But not now. If she wanted curtains made for the

sitting room, there were half a dozen women in Kimberley who could make them better than she could. If she wanted soap she bought it at Levinson's; if she needed a new dress she found it at Timpson's Modes; shoes she bought at Thomas's. The servants did everything she used to do in the house. "Why should you do it?" Frans had said many times. "You've had your turn. Now we have money to pay others." In a way he was right; it would have been pointless to try and turn the clock back and work as she had done when they had first married.

She spent as much time as she could in the garden she was creating down near the river. For weeks she had planned paths and had walls built. The original scheme to grow maize had been supplanted by her need to create something more personal. In any case, as Frans had pointed out, this was cattle and sheep country. But she could not be supervising the garden every minute of the day.

The gap in her life had a profound effect on her: it gave her time to think, and thought meant worry. She worried always about what was to become of Marie, and thoughts of Marie took her mind back to the past. She had hoped to bury it, to erase the memory of Kaptein, but it had lain in her subconscious, festering away without her knowing it, until now it reemerged as a kind of sore in her psyche. She remembered again things that had long since seemed forgotten: the little Bushmen women who had looked after her. Whatever had happened to them? She knew that nowadays white men hunted down Bushmen as vermin. People said there were few of them left. She recalled Mr. Parker in his dusty black with his two services every day, one for white people and one for nonwhites. She even remembered the hard ship's biscuits that she had dunked in the tea which tasted of earthy river water.

When these memories crowded in as they did now, she would go in search of the big Portuguese Bible.

She had a Bible of her own in English from which she read every day, but she drew a strength from holding the old Portuguese one which seemed to come from nowhere else. Now she crossed the room, fetched it from its shelf and took it back to her chair. Slowly, as she so often did, she turned the thin, stained pages. Genesis, Exodus, Leviticus, Numbers. She tried to pronounce the Portuguese words, but they defeated her. She looked again at the spidery writing that covered so many pages in the

margins above and below the black biblical type. And, as she had so many times before, she wondered who had written it, and why, and what it said. She could make out occasional figures and had decided these must be days of the month. But that was all. In some places the writing was almost illegible. How had it come to their mudhole? How had the crucifix got in the river? Had this Bible once belonged to Portuguese settlers? But she had never heard of any Portuguese settlers. A Portuguese woman, perhaps, who had married an Englishman or a Frenchman. Was this her Bible? And what had happened to her? Had the Korannas found her, too? Immediately the picture of Kaptein arose again in her mind: the skin the color of old ivory, the long black hair, the dark brown eyes, the handsome face. Were these some of the features she saw in her daughter? She gripped the Bible again, smoothing the rough leather cover. If only she could tell someone, she thought. If only she could tell everything as it had happened. Perhaps that might exorcise these ghosts from the past which rose up now so frequently to haunt her. But she could not tell Frans and she could not tell Marie, and there was no one else.

She heard the dogs begin to bark behind the house and soon there came the noise of the trap arriving and Frans's voice shouting for the servants to unharness the horses and carry the parcels into the house. She rose and went to the door. Marie came up the steps and pushed past her without a greeting, a thunderous expression on her face. She went on down the passage to her room and slammed the door.

In a few minutes Frans limped in and she made herself busy fetching him coffee, cold meat and bread. She could have rung a handbell for one of the servants, but it gave her pleasure to be doing something. When he had finished he sat in his chair and filled a pipe and drew on it slowly and all at once her world became a less thorny place.

"What did you do?" she said.

"I sold all those *hamels*," he said, referring to a couple of hundred sheep he had kept back from the previous week's sales because of low prices. "Old Levinson thought he'd get them cheaply, but I said to hell. If I have to drive them back to the farm, I'll do it. He wanted to give me a check—you remember he tried that about a year ago—but I said, no checks. He says he's afraid I'm going to lose the cash if I don't put it in a bank. He says checks are easier. I said, you just give me the cash. Don't you worry about me."

"Don't you think you should open a bank account?"

"What for? I'd just have to take the money out again. We've got enough for day-to-day expenses. The rest goes back into stock. That's my bank." He jerked his thumb at the invisible animals beyond the walls of the house.

"Did you buy anything?"

"Ja. Cattle. There were some brought down from the north. I'm not sure where, but they looked good. Tough. I thought we might fatten them up. Maybe even breed them with our own. Helmut bought some, too. Is there any more coffee?"

She poured him another cup.

"Marie seemed upset," she said.

Was it only her imagination or had the quality of her voice changed when she used Marie's name? They did not discuss her much. Both seemed to shy away from the subject.

"I don't know. She disappeared, of course. Went to see her friends. When she came back to meet me in the square she wasn't herself. I didn't like to ask why. She didn't speak all the way home."

"What's the news?" Susan said, changing the subject with some relief. Frans always picked up a little gossip.

He shrugged. "The prices of diamonds are down, because of overproduction. They say that chap C. J. Rhodes is trying to control production by buying up claims."

"Did you see Jack?"

"No. But old Levinson tells me he's not at the tent much anymore. He's taken up with some actress or singer. My God, but I'm tired."

Sometimes his face looked ash-gray with fatigue after a trip into Kimberley. He had lost a lot of weight in his late forties and now he was a rather gaunt, thin, sun-wrinkled man who looked older than he really was. Sometimes she thought that of herself, too. Once, she remembered, she had looked at herself in a cracked glass in Mr. Parker's wagon and faced the reality of her plainness. Now she avoided looking in mirrors and was thankful that there was still something left between Frans and herself.

As she undressed and got into bed beside him she remembered what he had said about Jack and knew exactly why Marie had been upset.

During the next few weeks he went into Kimberley on average twice a week and each time Marie made an excuse not to go. She

kept to herself. When she was not brooding in her room Susan would see her walking down by the river. This gave her something new to be concerned about.

She had worried at the thought of her daughter, headstrong and willful, being let loose in Kimberley, with its undercurrent of low life; but it was equally dangerous, it seemed to her, for the girl to be isolated at Portuguese Place. She had always hoped that one day Marie would marry and that she would live on the farm. Susan and Frans could build a smaller house some distance away, a kind of dower house, and she could watch her grandchildren growing up. But how would Marie marry if she never met anyone?

Slowly, she began to reconsider something which Marie had talked about, but which both she and Frans had dismissed as nonsense. That was her idea of buying a house in Kimberley where they could spend part of the year. The more she thought about it, the more it seemed to give promise of an answer to her problem. Marie in Kimberley by herself was one thing, but Marie chaperoned, as part of a family, Marie with a house and a background in the town—that was quite another. But she knew that Frans would not agree. It was something she would have to come at obliquely; better still, it was an idea which should appear to come from Frans himself. She waited for an opportunity.

It came sooner than she expected and in a way she would never have wanted. Late one afternoon he brought in a lamb that had been bitten by a jackal. He had found it about a mile from the homestead and, as he usually did, had slung it over his shoulders. She had seen him do this a thousand times without coming to any harm. But that evening after supper he stumbled while crossing the living room and steadied himself like an old man by grasping the back of a chair. His legs seemed weak and wobbly.

"What is it?" she said, coming to help him.

"Nothing. I feel a little giddy. I think I'll go to bed. I'll be all right in the morning."

But he was not all right. He found that the moment he put his feet on the floor he could not hold his balance.

"I'm going to get you into town to a doctor," Susan said.

"There is nothing the matter with me. I'm a bit tired, that's all."

But she called the servants, told them to get the trap ready and she and Marie took him into Kimberley. He sat, slumped and old, between them.

Their doctor—whom they had hardly ever consulted—was an Englishman called Hibbert. His rooms were above a bank in the square and after he had examined Frans he came out to the waiting room. He was a small, thin-faced, precise man who wore pince-nez and had a nervous mannerism of polishing them with a silk handkerchief. Now, as he breathed on the lenses, he said, "There's nothing seriously wrong with him except *anno Domini*. He's been overdoing it." He tapped himself over the heart. "This is where it tells. He's not as young as he was and his heart is not as good as it was. What he needs is rest and he's to stop carrying heavy loads. The main thing is to take it easy. He must let someone else do the picking up and the carrying. That's what servants are for, isn't it?"

They went to Madame Delatee's for a cup of tea and by the time they had done their shopping it was nearly five o'clock and Susan said, "It's too late to go home now."

"Of course we must go home," Frans said. "Where will we sleep?"

"At the Central Hotel."

"At the hotel?" He said it as though the idea were totally outlandish.

"Yes," she said firmly. "That's exactly what we're going to do."

He had never slept in a hotel before and was dead against it, but she would not listen. She marched both him and Marie across to the hotel and booked the top-floor suite. They had a miserable night. The beds were uncomfortable—much too soft for Frans—and the food, he said, was inedible. His normal daily diet was roast leg of mutton at midday and the same joint cold at night. The Central Hotel gave him what he called made-up dishes which he hated. Susan and Marie found the change pleasant enough.

That night proved to be a blessing as far as her campaign was concerned. Once they returned home she inaugurated a strict regime for Frans. She made him delegate more authority to Mopedi, who was in any event an outstanding farm foreman. She made him lie down—much to his disgust—after the midday meal and she began to nag him about his journeys into Kimberley.

"How are we to live if I can't go in and sell the stock and buy more?"

"Let Mopedi handle the sales."

He shook his head. "He's a good boy on the farm but he could

never bargain with old Levinson."

She left the subject for a day or two, then she said, "What if Mopedi was to look after the stock and you were to do the business in Kimberley?"

"That's what we do already."

"Remember what the doctor said. It's all this traveling backwards and forwards that is tiring you out."

"Aah, doctors!"

She decided to attack. "If you won't think of yourself, think of Marie and me," she said severely. "What would become of us if something happened to you?"

He paused. She rarely used this tone of voice and when she did, he listened. "What do you want, then?"

"I want you to travel less, and the only way that can be achieved is to stay overnight in Kimberley on the days of the sales."

"In that damn hotel? That would finish me sooner than anything."

She decided to let the matter rest. They did not discuss it for a few days, but from Frans's silences, she could tell he was brooding. At last, one evening after supper, he said to Marie, "How would you like a house in Kimberley?" Marie dropped her sewing and looked up. "Well, your mother thinks I shouldn't be traveling so much. I can't stand the hotel. So there isn't any other way."

"What a good idea," Susan said, her eyes on her own sewing.

"When shall we start looking?" Marie said.

"As soon as you like, but remember, every penny we have is tied up in cattle and sheep. It will take me a month or more to get the money."

When Susan had first known Kimberley—or the Dry Diggings, as it had been called then—people had lived in wagons or tents. Then had come the first wooden buildings, shops brought over in pieces from the abandoned diggings on the Vaal River. Slowly, as wealth accumulated, as merchants came, followed by professional men bringing their wives and children, people wanted more substantial homes and these—like the Levinsons'—were made of corrugated iron, mud and wood. Then a brickyard was started and those who could afford it had their houses built of bricks and mortar. Some were even built beyond the limits of the town, clusters of houses forming tiny suburbs.

The market for houses, as for anything else, depended solely on diamonds. When prices were high the real estate market was strong; when there was overproduction, or when heavy rain flooded parts of the diggings, or when it looked as though international events were going to cause a shortage of money to spend on diamonds, then prices for real estate sagged.

Marie and Susan began to make regular journeys to Kimberley, sometimes staying overnight at the hotel while they searched. At this time houses were scarce. They could have had any number of wooden shacks, but Susan knew that Frans would never tolerate life in a place he hated. He had built much of Portuguese Place with his own hands and to wean him away from it she would have to find a house where he was comfortable and in which he took pride as well.

As autumn turned into winter, nothing offered itself, so she did the next best thing: she took the suite in the Central Hotel on a permanent basis, put in good beds, changed the furniture, and, while Frans did not actively like it, he disliked it less than he had the first time.

Her plan seemed to have worked. One of her main worries had been what would happen to Marie. In the event, the girl now seemed content to stay close to her mother. She was caught up in the search for a house, which gave her an interest she had never had before. But Susan knew there was more to her changed behavior than that, and it had to do with Jack. She heard that his affair with the singer was continuing and, once or twice, when she had asked Marie to invite him and David to dinner, she had made an excuse. She was spending more time at the Levinsons' and through Hilda she met other people of her own age, the sons and daughters of men like Dr. Hibbert, Mr. Agnew, the advocate, and Mr. Louw, the magistrate, professional people, people of substance. She went to teas and dances and concerts and Susan congratulated herself. For the first time Marie seemed to be mixing with people of whom both she and Frans approved.

It was a calm period in her life. Frans seemed better, Marie was occupied and the farm was going well. She felt a sense of happiness, peace and, especially when she went down to her garden at Portuguese Place, achievement.

Winter was the time for planning. She was going to have a quince hedge and several peach, plum and apricot trees. Her flower beds, bare now, were ready for the spring planting. From

the garden she could look up at the house standing on its south-facing slope. The grapevine had grown across the front and its leaves were oxblood and gold. Her garden was the place to which she came more and more: it fulfilled a creative need in her.

She was working there one day when she saw a movement over the low wall of river stones which separated her flowers from the orchard. She found she was looking at a reedbuck, a medium-sized antelope that lived in the heavy bush farther down the river and was rarely seen up at the farm. It was a doe, brown in color, and she was close enough to see the huge eyes. Fortunately, there was nothing green in the garden for it to eat. They stared at each other for a few moments and then, instead of running away, the antelope took a few shaky steps towards her, fell onto its forelegs, struggled to rise, then rolled over on its side. She went to it. It moved its legs again, trying to stand up, but there was no strength left in them. She noticed that the breathing, quick at first, gradually grew slower. It was clearly in great distress and she wondered if it had been bitten by a snake. She looked as closely as she could without touching it, but could see no lesion. Its breath stank. Even as she was examining it, the breathing grew slower and finally stopped. The liquid eyes filmed over in death. She had never seen anything quite like it before and she strolled thoughtfully back towards the house to tell one of the servants to remove it.

She had still some way to go when she heard the sound of a horse at full gallop. She saw Mopedi bring his Basuto pony to a stop at the bottom of the veranda steps in a flurry of dust. "Baas!" he shouted.

Frans had been working at his stock books and he came out. They talked for a moment and then Mopedi pointed down towards the river past her garden where the cattle camps were. Frans limped around the back of the house, shouting for a horse.

"What is it?" Susan said, catching up with him.

"Mopedi says there is something wrong with the stock."

In a few minutes he and Mopedi were riding towards the river. She gave her own orders about the removal of the dead antelope and went to see how the midday meal was progressing. But Frans did not come back at midday and it was not until later in the afternoon that she saw the two horsemen walking their animals slowly back towards the house. The light was going out of the winter afternoon and there was a crackle of frost in the air.

Frans was covered in dust, his lips rimed. She brought him a glass of sack milk and he slumped in his chair in front of a huge fire of camel thorn. Again she thought how old and tired he looked.

"There's something wrong with the cattle," he said. "Mopedi found four bullocks dead—there are more downstream."

"How many?"

"Six. There were also some dead sheep."

"What's caused it?"

He shook his head. "I don't know."

"It's nothing they've eaten?"

"There's nothing growing now. I've told Mopedi to go into the hills early tomorrow and see what's happening up there."

The following morning they were at breakfast when Mopedi came back. He told them he had found dead animals in the hills. He reported several dead springbok, and Susan remembered the reedbuck who had died in her garden the previous day. She told Frans about it.

"What do you think it can be?" she said.

"God knows. Anyway, we must go and look. I want you to come with me. We'll take the wagon. Marie can come, too."

They filled the wagon with supplies and blankets. Frans, Mopedi, Susan and Marie were on horseback, as were half a dozen shepherds. They rode out into a gray, cold morning. A bitter wind was blowing the surface of the desert and soon they tied kerchiefs over their mouths. Their faces were as gray and drawn as the day.

They did not take long to come across the first dead beasts. Some cattle had died a day or two before and their bellies were distended by gas. Others were in the process of dying, struggling to rise, falling forwards and then collapsing on their sides. Many animals had died alone; others had come together in their distress and lay huddled together in death. Vultures were everywhere, some so bloated they could no longer rise as the Delports and their servants went past. It was like riding in a dead land and Susan thought it had the apocalyptic horror of the Old Testament, as though God, for some angry reason of his own, had decided to strike down every living thing.

All morning they passed dead and dying animals and when they stopped in the middle of the day no one could face the thought of eating.

"Someone's riding," Marie said suddenly, squinting into the wind and pointing to a plume of dust a mile away. They watched the rider close with them and she said, "It's Uncle Helmut." Susan was reminded of the time he had come to tell them about the first prospectors. Now his face was even grimmer. His beard was whitened by dust.

"I ride to warn you," he said. "But I am too late."

"So it's happened to you," Frans said.

"Ja. And the Jordaans."

"What is it? Does anyone know?"

"I know. I see it in Germany before I go. It is *rinderpest.*"

"Oh, my God!" Frans said.

Like all stock farmers he had heard the German word for "cattle plague" but he had never knowingly seen a case, although he had heard of one or two isolated outbreaks. Most people thought the disease was still confined to Asia and Europe.

"Is there any hope?"

"None," Helmut said. "Have you seen the buck? They die, too."

"We saw springbok on the way here," Susan said.

"Where did it come from?" Frans asked.

"From those cattle we bought," Helmut said.

Frans nodded. "It must be so. Is anything safe?"

"Only horses. Not so many sheep will die as cattle."

"What must we do?"

"Burn the corpses."

"That's not possible; it would take months."

"As many as you can."

"And then?"

"Only pray it never come back."

For nearly two weeks the Delports and their servants stayed with the wagon, moving slowly from one stock camp to the next. The death rate was fearful among the cattle—nearly ninety percent—and Frans had to send the servants into Kimberley to bring out supplies of lamp oil with which to drench the corpses before setting them alight. They did not bother with single beasts, but where there were a dozen together they would pull the bodies into a heap, saturate them, cover them with dry brush and set them alight. The desert air became charged with the smell of burning flesh and wool. Where they could, they buried the bodies in small ravines. Occasionally they would find groups of live sheep or cattle and these Frans ordered to be driven into

dry riverbeds and there shot and buried.

"Who would eat this meat, knowing what had happened here?" he said.

At the end of the fortnight they had all had enough. They knew that there were still scores of cattle rotting on the veld but there was nothing they could—nor indeed had the will to—do about them. They would be left to the sun and the rain, to the vultures and the hyenas and the ants. In a year or two there would be nothing left but whitened bones.

They returned to the homestead late one afternoon. They were all tired and depressed, but Susan bore the extra worry of having seen Frans turn from a middle-aged into an elderly man. He seemed to have shrunk even further into his skin: his dusty clothes hung on him as though they had been given as handouts from someone much larger. But the change was not only physical, something inside him seemed to have been damaged by what had happened and she knew it might take a long time to repair.

Their future was made plain to her within the first day or two of coming home. There was no meat in the house and nothing now to kill. She had to send Mopedi out with the shotgun and he brought back guinea fowl and a wild duck. Frans seemed to be overcome by a great lassitude. For two days he simply sat on the veranda staring out at the empty veld. There were a dozen things she wanted to discuss but she knew it was not the time. They needed supplies and she took Marie into town.

All Kimberley knew of the tragedy on the farm and as Susan walked through the streets she felt the glances of the other pedestrians. Some people, she thought, would not be too displeased at what had happened, for there were those who envied their rise in the world. But that was only human nature. Others sympathized, saying what a terrible thing it was; some even inquired if there was any way they could help. ("Not unless you know how to give a man back his spirit," Susan thought.)

One of these was Mr. Levinson. He had wanted to go out to the farm when he first heard of the *rinderpest*, but Mrs. Levinson had stopped him because of his increasingly poor health.

David had agreed with her, but for a different reason. "We'd only be in the way. We're not country people. Let them finish what they have to do; then we can help."

And so they had waited, and now Susan Delport was in town.

She always bought her supplies at Levinson's and this day was no different. "I heard what happened," Mr. Levinson said, coming round the counter to greet her. "And to Frans, too. It is a tragedy. Mrs. Levinson and I were saying only this morning, 'It is a real tragedy!'"

"Thank you."

Mr. Levinson looked carefully about him, but there was no one in the store. "I have something to say. Mrs. Levinson and Hilda and also David . . ." He paused, fumbling for the words. "We talked. We said to ourselves, 'What is happening is a terrible thing; what can we do?' That is what we asked ourselves, you know."

Susan waited.

"You are going to need capital. Money for this, money for that. It takes a lot to rebuild. And we . . ."

Susan felt afraid to open her mouth, afraid she would not be able to speak. Slowly, she shook her head.

"Look," said Mr. Levinson, "think of it this way. A loan. You build up your stock. We do business together again. The sooner the better. It's good for both of us."

When she found her voice, Susan said, "It's good of you, Mr. Levinson, but we can manage."

"Manage? I'm talking about business, not *managing*."

She smiled and shook her head again. "We'll be all right. Once Frans gets over it. He's built it up once, he can do it again."

"Well, when you need it, it's here. Remember that."

"I'll remember."

It was late when they got back to Portuguese Place. The first thing she noticed was that the lamps were not lit. She ran up the steps into the living room and found Frans sitting in his chair by a dead fire. She thought he was asleep until she saw that his eyes were open. "Frans, are you all right?" she said.

His mouth began to work on one side and saliva dripped down his chin. She realized he was trying to speak, but could not.

"What's wrong?" Marie said, bringing a lamp.

"I think he's had a seizure. Tell Mopedi to ride for Dr. Hibbert."

12

It was a Sunday morning and Jack was at his lessons in Lily's house. They had become a regular feature of his life. Every Sunday morning he would come to her about ten o'clock and she would seat him at a small table with a writing block and a pencil. While he worked she would tidy the house, dress, prepare a meal, make them both coffee. She would come regularly to see how he was getting on and later she would make him read to her. Now she came to the table and looked over his shoulder.

"What's that?" she said.

"An *h*." He no longer pronounced it "haitch." Under her influence he was losing his Cockney accent.

"It looks more like an *n* to me. Put a decent loop on it, Jack. Don't be afraid to write big. Everything else about you is big; I don't see why your handwriting shouldn't be."

At first he had had to copy out line after line of single letters until he knew them both in upper and lower case. Then she had given him simple sentences. Now she was making him copy out verses from Moore's *Irish Melodies*.

"Read me what you've written. Start at the top," she said.

He put his finger under the first word and began to read. "Believe me, if all those endearing young charms, Which I ga . . . Which I gace . . ."

"Gaze."

". . . Which I gaze on so fondly today, Were to change by tomorrow and fleet in my arms, Like fairy gifts fading away . . ."

"That's good, Jack. That's really good."

She pointed to the word "gaze." "Say that one again."

She was very close to him. She was still in her nightgown and peignoir and he reached up and cupped her breast in his hand.

"Stop that," she said briskly. "I can't concentrate if you do that."

"I like to feel you," he said.

"Tell me something new!" She drew away. "That's not the way to learn how to read, my lad."

"You know, I been thinking . . ." he said.

"I know what you think about. I never met such a man for thinking about it."

"I don't mean that. I mean I been thinking about something in the future."

"Oh, yes?" Her voice changed subtly.

"Yes. When we have a house. A proper house. I seen books in some houses. In bookcases." His fingers smoothed down the pages of Moore's *Irish Melodies*. There were engravings to illustrate each song. "I'd like some books with pictures in them. What sort of a house do you want, Lily?"

"You get on with your work," she said, with mock severity. "It doesn't do to talk to the teacher."

The Sunday mornings were unique in his experience. They were a mixture of learning and domesticity which he had never known. There was an unhurried but deep pleasure to be found in watching Lily go about the shack tidying up and washing and dusting, while he worked with his brain. It was the first time he had ever used that part of his anatomy for any academic purpose and at first it tired him more than swinging a pick, but after a time he became used to it and would look forward to the Sunday mornings more than any other time of the week.

Often now he would not see Lily for two or three days at a time. She was expanding as a singer under Peter Arendt's tutelage. Every morning he gave her singing lessons and in the

afternoons she would practice. In the evenings she would sing at the Grand.

She was being sought now by other managements. The Lanyon Theater, after pressure from Arendt, had engaged her for a recital at which she had sung Schubert and Brahms, very different fare from her usual repertoire. After that she began to be invited to give recitals at private parties and men's smokers. Jack had been to her recital at the Lanyon. She had been surrounded by Arendt and David and other people who made up "cultured" Kimberley. He had felt out of it and had left early, far preferring the bawdy but—as he saw it—honest atmosphere of the Grand.

Lily came back with coffee and stood at the door. He was bent over his work as though his life depended upon it.

"All right, love," she said. "Coffee time and then reading."

Today she gave him a printed pamphlet containing the reminiscences of a British settler, which David had lent her to read.

"Start there," she said.

"Health, long life and growing . . . pros . . . prosperity . . ."

"Good."

". . . made existence pleasant. But pros . . . perity brought growing peril. The little flocks and herds of the settlers were at first tended by the sons and daughters of their owners." He broke off and said, "Would you like a farm? I mean, when I've made my fortune. I've wondered myself. It's a good life, you know."

"Don't worry about that now. You get on with your reading."

He was about to start again when there was a knock at the front door. It was Susan Delport.

"I'm sorry to intrude on a Sunday morning," she said to Lily. "But they told me I might find Mr. Farson here."

It might have been a moment of tension and embarrassment, but Lily smiled and said, "You're Mrs. Delport, aren't you? I've heard Jack speak of you often. And you're not intruding at all. This is where you'll always find him of a Sunday morning."

Jack rose, embarrassment plain on his face. The contrast between the two women was enormous: Susan short, dumpy, with a strong, lined face; Lily tall, white-skinned and sensual. Yet somehow they seemed to complement each other.

Lily brought Susan a cup of coffee and said, "I'll leave you two together."

When she had gone Susan said, "You've heard?"

Jack nodded. "I would have come to help only . . ." Susan was silent, waiting for him to finish. "Only . . ." He flushed.

She helped him. "There wasn't much you could do. The stock died, we burned what we could. But it finished Uncle Frans."

"I *would* have come out to see him," Jack said abruptly, "only the days ain't been long enough. . . ."

"I know."

"I mean, there's been the digging and the work on the claim and then in the evenings . . ."

"You don't have to apologize, Jack. I understand."

"It's just that I don't want you to think . . ."

"You've got your own life, your own way to make."

By agreeing with him she seemed to make it worse.

"I been boxing at night. At the Grand."

"Yes, I heard about that. We could do with a little help now, though, Jack."

"That's what I'm trying to say, Aunt Susan. I ain't got no time at all."

"Uncle Frans needs help. And it won't be for long. A couple of weeks, just till we're on our feet again."

"And there's David. I can't let him work on his own."

"I saw David on the way here. He offered to come himself, but it's your muscles we need, Jack, not David's . . ." She caught herself just in time, but the word "brains" hung in the air like a ghostly sign.

Jack rose and let the anger come to him. It was what he needed, an excuse to do what he had intended all along: to refuse her. For the first time in his life things were going for him, he wasn't going to jeopardize that because ill luck had struck at someone else. He knew ill luck of old; it had been his constant companion. You had to get on with it as best you could.

"Wait, Jack," Susan said. "I guess I made that sound bad. It wasn't what I meant. What I meant was that the job's too big for David. Too big for most people. It needs a big man."

"It's like I said, Aunt Susan. I ain't got a minute of my own. Why, look at me now, even on a Sunday morning."

A shadow seemed to pass over her face, then she said, "We'd pay, Jack. We wouldn't expect you to work for nothing. There's no money, no cash, that is, but there's land; there's enough land at Portuguese Place to spare some."

"I'd like to, but . . ."

"I'm talking about a farm, Jack. Something of your own. You can't dig all your life." Abruptly, her own anger, created out of days and weeks of worry, began to flicker inside her. "I've said enough. I'll be in the square until noon. If you're coming, find me there."

She closed the door quickly behind her. Jack stood uncertainly in the center of the room. Lily came in. Her eyes were angry.

"She wanted me to go out to the farm," he said. "They've had that cattle plague. . . ."

"I know all about it! I heard. I didn't listen by choice." She banged on the thin walls. "And by God, Jack, I tried not to when I heard what was said!"

"Now wait a minute, Lily . . ."

"What are you, Jack? I thought we were the same." She shook her head. In a way, they were the same: from the same background. This was partly what had attracted her to him, the sympathy for someone struggling—as she had struggled—to get away from the London slums. It was true that in the London she knew, and from which they had both emerged, life was so hard that altruism was a luxury no one could afford. And yet . . . yet those very slums produced a kindness and a concern for the downtrodden, *because* they were downtrodden; a camaraderie, a sentimental affection, a rough and bluff concern for your fellowman. In a word, humanity. And it was this that was lacking in Jack. Perhaps, she thought, his life had been too brutal, perhaps he had not lived long enough in London for some of its benefits to accrue. Perhaps the life he had led had not prepared him for situations like the one he now faced.

"I wanted to stay with you," he blurted.

"I know, Jack, I know. And I'm flattered." She was speaking to him as though he were a small boy. "But you love the Delports. You've told me before how they helped you."

"I know, but . . ."

It was as though she were seeing him for the first time, the big rawboned miner, whose very roughness and animal quality had taken her fancy. She had seen in him a quality of simplicity, almost of innocence, which had attracted her. He needed someone's help and she had offered it.

But now all the instincts which had developed in her since, as a girl of sixteen, she had taken to the road began to send up

warning signals. More and more, Jack was talking about a future which encompassed her; more and more, he was trying to exert rights over her that did not exist. She was her own woman; no man was ever going to swamp her.

Subtly, she changed her tack. "You've had a bit of luck with diamonds lately, but you know it can't last. You know it's here one day and gone the next. I heard what Mrs. Delport said about giving you land. Think of your future if you won't think of anything else. You don't want to end up like that Scotsman you told me about, do you? Dying in your tent with only a black man for company?"

Jack absorbed what she was saying and then said slowly, "When I've made my pile I could build out there. I've always liked it. There's space and clean air, not this bloody dust all the time. We could build a great house, Lily, and come into town when we'd a mind to, and keep horses. You'd like horses. And . . ."

"Steady, Jack. That's looking far ahead." The thought of living on a farm in the desert appalled her. She was no Susan Delport. No, she was going to make something of herself; that had always been her dream. Her future seemed more and more to be tied to Peter Arendt. He had said that if she was properly trained there was nothing she could not do. She wanted very badly to believe him.

"But you'd come, wouldn't you? I mean, we'll get married, won't we?"

"First things first, Jack," she said. "First you've got to help the Delports. Then we'll talk about the future."

It took her another hour of gentle persuasion and when he left, at last, a little before noon, making his way to the square, she felt as though a load had been raised from her.

On the journey to Portuguese Place, Susan expanded on what she had already told him. There was no money or food left to pay servants, so she had let them go, except for Mopedi. Her plan was to cut all the timber along the river and sell it in Kimberley. Jack was to be in charge of the operation on the farm, the felling itself, and she and Marie would take the wood into town in the wagon and the Scotch cart, which would be drawn by mules, not susceptible to cattle plague. She had already negotiated to buy the mules from Jordaan, who had survived the epidemic better than either the Delports or the Lessings, because at least half his

operation had been breeding horses and mules.

"We'll only need you for a couple of weeks," she said. "If I can build up a little capital I'll hire some Hottentots to do the cutting. Then in the spring I'm going to plow the fields down by the river and put in maize and use the pump to irrigate it. With the money from the maize crop I'll buy horses and some cattle and sheep, but I'll also have pigs. I'm going to have a mixed farm. I'm not going to be caught again."

They were on Portuguese Place now and Jack could see the occasional carcass lying near the road. There was a feeling of death in the air.

In spite of his mood, which was one of resentment at somehow having been forced into doing what he was doing, he was conscious of the way she spoke. How *she* was going to do this and *she* was going to do that. She had told him that Frans was ill and he wondered just how bad he was.

As if divining his thoughts she began to talk about her husband. "He's changed. Be prepared for it." She drove on in silence for a while then said, more to herself than to him, "He's like some nomadic chief. His wealth and stature are measured by the size of his flocks. Now that the flocks are gone he has nothing. Always put some money in the bank, Jack. Don't have all your eggs in one basket."

The river was away to their left and Jack looked at the gray-green line of trees in the fading afternoon light. She followed his glance. "Yes, it's a pity, but they'll grow again. If we don't sell the wood, we'll lose the farm and if we lose the farm, Frans will die."

They came to the house sprawling on its hillside. The last time Jack had been there the cattle and the sheep kraals had been full; now they were empty, their concertina gates lying in the dust.

"Don't forget what I told you," Susan said.

It was as well she had reminded him for he was totally unprepared for what he saw. Frans was sitting in a chair near the fire. He was a shell of a man, shrunken and thin, his skin hanging on him in folds. His hair was white and so was his beard, and his eyes seemed to have gone back into his skull. He was wrapped in a blanket and Jack could see one thin, mottled hand.

"Here's Jack come to see you," Susan said.

"Hello, Uncle Frans." Jack put out his hand. The hand on the blanket twitched and Frans's mouth began to work. Slowly a dribble of saliva ran down his chin.

"He can hear perfectly well, but he can't speak yet," Susan said, taking a cloth and wiping his chin. "It won't be long, though; he's getting better every day and the doctor says it's only a matter of time."

Later that night after they had eaten and Frans had been fed at the table like a child, Jack helped to put him to bed in one of the spare rooms. Susan stayed with him and Jack was left alone with Marie. She had hardly said anything since his arrival; the boisterousness and the teasing had not surfaced at all. He had put this down to the shock of her father's illness and the natural result of the tragedy on the farm. She had thinned down and her cheeks had become slightly hollow.

"It's good of you to come," she said formally.

"I was glad to."

"Were you?"

"Of course."

"I thought it might be interrupting something." She turned to the door. "Good night."

She knew about Lily, he thought.

Early the following morning, in the bitter winter cold, he began the work of cutting down the river trees. It was a Herculean task even though he was helped by Mopedi part of the time. The tools they had were long-handled axes and bow saws and the trees were camel thorns and anas, wild figs and willows. Although the trunks were not more than a foot or so in diameter—except for the willows, which were bigger—the wood was fibrous, tough and springy and the axes were not sharp. As each tree came down it had to be cleaned of its small branches, then sawn into logs and loaded on the wagon and the Scotch cart. It was the same kind of brutal work he was used to on the diggings, but there he had Lily's company to look forward to. At Portuguese Place he worked alone or with Mopedi. Susan and Marie were away most of the time and Mopedi's wife looked after Frans. Sometimes Jack would sit with him in the evenings but mostly, dead tired, he would go to bed. He found that he missed Lily more than he could ever have imagined.

Susan had said that he would only be needed for a few weeks but she could not have foreseen what would happen. Spring came early and the days were unseasonably hot. The result was that there was a sudden drop in the demand for firewood and prices plummeted. Instead of saving money, they were spending

everything they made just to keep alive.

At first Jack seemed to make no impression on the trees but one day, after he had been on the farm for a fortnight, he was helping to put Frans in the sun on the stoep and wrap him in his blanket when the old man—that is how Jack now thought of him—started to say something. His speech was returning and so was some hand movement. One hand came up and his lips moved and Jack thought he said, "Trees."

Jack looked down to the river and for the first time saw the gaps he had created. As the days passed the gaps grew and joined until after six weeks the whole area in front of the house was devoid of trees and scarred by the wheels of the wagons. Frans no longer wished to be brought out onto the stoep and kept to his chair in the living room, with his back to the windows.

Susan realized they could not go on living from hand to mouth as they were. Things had to be done: lands had to be plowed to plant maize, stock had to be bought for fattening; in other words the farm, which had lain dormant since the *rinderpest,* had to be started again. But where to get the money? The sale of the wood was barely paying for their food and doctors' bills. She went into town to see the manager of the bank. She knew him slightly, for Marie had once had tea at his house. His name was Mitford and he was a solemn, plump, middle-aged man. He had a habit of sorting through papers on his desk while he was talking as though they contained vital information about the subject under discussion. Now as he spoke he began to rummage among letters and documents. "Let me see, Mrs. Delport. You wish the loan to restock the farm?" He lifted a batch of papers and looked at them.

"Yes." Susan was sitting primly on the edge of her chair.

"I was sorry to hear of your misfortune. The bank was sorry."

"Thank you."

"Your husband, Mrs. Delport, as the bank understands, was in a substantial way of business, was he not?"

"He was the biggest stock owner in the district. The farm can be put on its feet again. I know it can."

"What about the disease?"

"It's run its course. We keep a check on the antelope. We haven't found a dead one for months."

"As I recall, Mr. Delport did not use the facilities of the bank."

"He invested in the farm."

"I see. He thought that was safer, did he?"

"I don't know about being safer . . ." Susan heard her voice stumbling.

"No. Nor does the bank." Mr. Mitford read the address on a letter and pushed it away. "Please don't think the bank is unsympathetic, Mrs. Delport, but these are troubled times. Now had you been clients of the bank—had we an *association*—then the circumstances might be different. But as you can appreciate, it is not the bank's money. . . ."

She rose abruptly. "I shall not trouble you further, Mr. Mitford."

"So good of you to come in." He shuffled his papers. "And how is your dear daughter?"

But Susan left without answering.

She stood out on the pavement, angry and confused. Where to next? She saw the sign LEVINSON'S EMPORIUM. She supposed—but no. She would not go to Mr. Levinson, even though he had offered to help, nor to David for that matter. She remembered what her father had often told her: never do business with friends. Never borrow money from them, never lend money to them. What if they had changed their minds since their first offer? What if they even *looked* as though they might refuse her? That would be enough to ruin their relationship. She remembered the look on Jack's face when she had come to him for help. It had cut her to the heart. No, she would ask nothing of her friends. Who then? Well, there was always Mr. Bulchand.

She knew of Bulchand, as did most people in Kimberley, but had never had any dealings with him. She had heard stories of people who had gone to him to borrow money and, because his rates of interest were so high, had never been able to pay off the principal. One man was said to have shot himself because of this. She told herself that such stories always clung to moneylenders and she made her way to the outskirts of town, where he had his office.

There were two views of Mr. Bulchand. Those who owed him money looked upon him with an anxiety often amounting to fear; those who did not do business with him sometimes described him as "a funny little coolie."

Mr. Bulchand was neither funny nor a coolie. He was the illegitimate son of a Turkish father and an Armenian mother who had grown up in the stews of Smyrna. He had come to

Africa with a great sack of dried figs, left the boat at Port Elizabeth, sold his figs, bought a cartload of pumpkins, sold the pumpkins, bought thirty boxes of cheap shoes just unloaded from Northampton and carried the shoes on his back until he sold them at a profit of nearly four hundred percent. He reckoned to himself that if he could achieve this kind of profit knowing only a dozen or so words of English, this was the country for him.

He walked the hamlets of the eastern Cape trading as a *smous,* a peddler, and in a few years had made enough to set himself up in the commodity he knew best: money. When diamonds were found in the northwest he was attracted as a bee to nectar. He knew little about diamonds and had no wish to learn, but he knew exactly how much a pound note was worth to a man who needed it badly enough.

It was not possible simply to see Mr. Bulchand; arrangements had to be made. And when Susan arrived at the small office one of his sons, Niki, went to make the arrangements. She sat in the corrugated-iron room, bare of anything but a cheap wooden table and two chairs, and waited. Ten minutes later, Bulchand arrived. He was in his early sixties, small and dapper, dressed in a dove-gray suit and waistcoat, gray spats, a gray cravat. His hair was gray and brushed smoothly back over a high-domed head. His face was thin and he had little tufts of hair growing from his ears.

He bowed formally over Susan's hand and sat at the table. She noticed that his nails were beautifully kept. His only recognition that he lived in a diamond town was a solitaire ring on the third finger of his right hand; the diamond glittered against his brown skin.

He spoke to his son, who stood behind his chair.

"My father says, how can he help you?"

"I've come to ask about a loan."

"My father says, how much?"

She spoke to Mr. Bulchand, but the mouth that answered was Niki's. He was a smooth, dark-visaged young man with oiled hair, but as soberly dressed as his father.

"One thousand pounds," she said. She had calculated that eight or nine hundred would probably do but had decided that the higher figure would gave her some leeway.

"My father says, what this for?"

"Investing in stock."

"My father says, what is stock?"

"Sheep, cattle, pigs. Farm animals."

Bulchand smiled and Susan realized that he probably understood every word she said.

"My father says, what farm is this?"

"It is called Portuguese Place. My name is Delport. Perhaps he has heard the name."

"My father says he know the name. He says, do you know what interest he charging?"

"No."

"Twenty percent. We take at beginning. You borrow one thousand pounds. We give you eight hundred. You pay us back one thousand. You understand?"

Eight hundred, she thought. Could she do it on eight hundred? But there was no question of *could* she; she *had* to.

"All right," she said.

"My father says he must see title deeds of farm. He says, tell your husband to bring them when he come to sign papers."

"My husband is very ill."

"My father says, when he better?"

"He will never get better. I run the farm."

Mr. Bulchand smiled and stood up. Then he said something to his son.

"My father says he don't do no business with ladies. He never has and never will. My father says ladies do not have farms, this is work for men."

Mr. Bulchand bowed.

Susan opened her mouth and closed it with a snap. "Thank your father," she said flatly, and walked out into the street.

During the following days she fought to save the farm.

She tried several other banks as well as the Kimberley Trust and Loan Company, but the fact that *rinderpest* had struck the farm, and that a woman was now trying to salvage it, was too much of a risk. She was tempted several times to go to the Levinsons or even to David, who knew wealthy people, but each time she recalled the expression she had seen on Jack's face, and drew back from the idea of asking help. So she did what she could in other ways. She decided to sell some of their possessions. There was furniture with which she had refurbished the hotel

suite and there was a great deal at Portuguese Place which she could manage without.

She arranged for J. J. Rothschild, the auctioneer, to come out to the farm to collect the pieces. In preparation for that she had given Frans a little laudanum to make him sleep so that he would not hear his possessions being removed, and had sent Marie down to the river to fetch a load of wood so that she would be out of the way as well, not wanting to see the effect on her when she realized that things she had grown up with were being taken away.

Her plans went somewhat awry. Frans slept peacefully enough, but Marie was quicker than she had expected and Rothschild and his "boys" were only halfway through the job when she came up from the river with Jack. Susan watched them from the veranda. They stood below the house, watching for a few moments, and then Marie ran to the bottom of the steps, her face alive with pleasure and excitement.

"Are we moving?" she called. "Are we going to live in town?"

When Susan told her what was happening the change was dramatic. Her face became sullen, her eyes bitter, and she backed away to stand with Jack again. For a moment, Susan felt anger in herself, but she controlled it. There was no reason why Marie should love Portuguese Place as she did, but why did she hate it? Or did she? Perhaps it was only her natural reaction to her parents and to the rigors of her life. What if she married and the place were hers? Would her attitude to it be different then? She looked at them, standing below the house. What if Jack were master here? Jack . . . She had never discussed the land deal she had first mentioned to persuade him to come out to the farm. She had thought of it many times, but each time something had stopped her from talking about it: it would break up the farm, and this was akin to breaking up her own self. Everything she was came from the land she stood on. Frans had fought to keep it; she would fight even though she saw no future. And Jack? She would pay Jack somehow, but in money, not in land.

By the end of the day the house was bare of anything except the furniture that was necessary to continue civilized, if not comfortable, living. She watched Rothschild's wagons leave, expecting to feel a wrench at the sight of their possessions disappearing. But she felt nothing. Her mind was too full of

Frans's illness and Marie's future and what to do about Jack. Anyway, the most important things remained: the pieces of furniture Frans had made all those years before when they were starting their life on Portuguese Place.

But her reaction was not the same when she saw them in Kimberley. She had not meant to attend the auction, but Frans needed one or two things, so she had left Marie and Jack to look after him. When she came through the square the auction was already in progress. A crowd had collected around Rothschild's wagon. She made her way to the front and, with a shock, saw a mound of familiar articles: old Cape Dutch chests, tallboys made from yellow-wood, a wardrobe of stinkwood, a military chest with brassbound corners, inlaid tables, bookcases of mahogany, a four-poster bed. They were piled anyhow, dusty, almost abandoned. She did not see them as inanimate pieces of wood, but as things with a life of their own. She knew exactly where the tallboy had stood; the chest had been near the door; in which room the bed had been. Instead of a picture that lay on its side in the dust, her mind's eye now saw only a discolored patch on the drawing room wall. Something twisted inside her as though these things were being harmed and she was feeling their pain.

She told herself she was being silly. What did they amount to anyway? They were simply material possessions she could do without. She forced herself not to think about them and, instead, concentrated on the bidding. And soon her thoughts vanished, replaced by a feeling of astonishment. A chair which had stood for years in one of the spare rooms, for which she had paid half a crown at one of Rothschild's auctions, was being knocked down for five guineas. She thought she had misheard. A tallboy fetched a hundred; she had paid thirty. A bolt of curtain material, bought but never used, was sold for nearly twice what it could be bought for new. Could these be her possessions?

An old desk made of planks which Frans had used in his office and which she had once thought of as firewood was started at ten guineas. Immediately the bidding leaped up to fifteen, to twenty, and finished at twenty-two. She looked round to see who was bidding. For a moment she thought Joe Malone had nodded his head. But that could not be.

The next item was an old rocker which she had replaced years before and which squeaked badly. She watched it being sold for eight guineas. This time she was sure Malone had bid. It was

followed by a hanging lamp which she had bought in Cape Town. It went for three guineas—about twice its value—to a bidder on the far side of the crowd. She was sure it was Dan Halkett.

Everything went at inflated and sometimes ridiculously high prices. She could not understand it. She would have heard if Joe or Dan had suddenly struck it rich. And then, towards the end of the sale, she saw something occur which gave her a clue. A table had come up and the bidding had been less brisk than before. She was watching Malone. He had turned away and was looking towards the door of Levinson's Emporium. She thought she could make out a figure in the doorway. Just then he stepped forwards and she saw that it was Mr. Levinson himself. He raised his finger in a signal to Malone. Joe nodded and turned back to bid.

Susan walked away and found herself, without knowing how she had got there, in Madame Delatee's, with a pot of tea in front of her. A storm of conflicting emotions raged in her mind: shame, gratitude, humiliation. At first the thought of charity made her feel physically ill, but slowly she realized that there was no way she could make Mr. Levinson take his money back without causing a rift between them. In any case, how was she to tell which pieces he had bought and which had been bought by others? She brooded about her position for several days before deciding that there was nothing she could do to change things— not at the moment, anyway—except be grateful and use the money to save Portuguese Place.

So she bought a plow and six bullocks and soon her garden was torn down and long furrows cut the flat land down near the river as maize lands were created. The rains came early that season and prospects for the crop looked good.

Jack had been on the farm for nearly two months when one of the wagons broke a wheel near Kimberley and had to be mended. He took the opportunity to go and see Lily. It was a Sunday evening and he arrived at her shack about seven o'clock.

She was not there, so he went to the Grand, but there was no performance that night and it was in darkness. He wondered if she was giving a recital at a private house or a party. There was one man who would certainly know. He went to Arendt's house. He heard her voice even before he reached the door. It was one of what he thought of as her "serious songs," and he could hear

the tinkle of a piano accompaniment. He knocked, but there was no reply and he let himself in. Her voice was coming from the music room. As he went up the passage the song came to an end and he heard clapping. The door was slightly ajar and he could see into the room. It was full of people and was very hot. The night was close and occasionally there was a rumble of thunder. Lily was at the far end with Arendt. He could see David, his face red above his starched white collar, with Hilda Levinson on his arm. He did not know the names of the others, but had seen many of them before; they were the "culturals." Lily was wearing her red dress with the black silk shawl and looked more beautiful than he had ever seen her. Her face was alive with pleasure and excitement and he felt a sudden pang: she never looked like that in his company. The clapping continued for almost a minute. He saw that everyone held a glass of champagne. As the clapping came to an end Arendt put his hand up and said, "Now, ladies and gentlemen, we come to the real reason for being here." He took a long white envelope from his inside pocket. "You all know what this is, so I will not talk too much. I only say this, that it comes to dear Lily from every member of the Kimberley and District Music Society with all our best wishes for good fortune." Jack listened, puzzled. It was clearly some kind of presentation and he wondered if it was her birthday. Then Lily saw him and her eyes widened. She tried to smile, but it was tentative and a sudden shadow crossed her face.

Arendt finished what he was saying and then a woman began to speak. She was thin, elderly, and wore a dress with much gray lace on it. Jack had seen her before, and knew she was a leading light in the music society.

". . . and our greatest thanks," she said, "are for Herr Arendt, who has put up two-thirds of the money himself. Miss Bartlett could not have had a finer teacher. I think we all agree that he could have brought her to the highest standards himself. It is a mark of his modesty that he feels she should continue her training in London, and a mark of his generosity that he has made so handsome a contribution towards that end. When Miss Bartlett is a famous diva singing in Rome and Paris she will have Herr Arendt to thank for it. Ladies and gentlemen, I give you first of all our Lily who, we know, will reach the greatest heights but who, we hope, will not forget her friends of the Kimberley and District Music Society; but I also give you Peter Arendt, who

discovered her and to whom we are all so grateful."

Again there was a burst of clapping and someone shouted, "Come on, Lily, speech!"

Another called, "Never mind the speech, give us a song!"

In the silence, Lily said, "I can't make speeches, but all I can say is thank you—from the very bottom of my heart." She was looking everywhere except at Jack. The clapping continued as he began to push his way through the crowd. His face was like granite. She watched him come towards her, shouldering people aside. He was still several yards from her when there was a commotion to his left, and a thud. He heard a voice say, "Make way!"

"Give him air," someone said.

"It's the heat."

"Loosen his collar."

Jack turned and saw that David had fainted. Arendt bustled forwards. His white, perspiring face passed Jack without greeting. People hurriedly left the room, opening the door to the street to let air in. The night sky was slashed by lightning. David was lifted and carried outside and in a few seconds Jack and Lily were alone in the room. Neither moved.

Jack looked at the envelope in her hand. "Is it true?" he asked. "Are you really going to London?"

"Yes, Jack."

"Is there money in that envelope?"

"A check. Jack, it's all been so sudden. I wanted to tell you, but you weren't here. Don't you see? It's the one chance I've got." She put her hand on his arm. "My dear, I tried to warn you not to become too involved. I tried not to encourage you to plan for our future. But you always would. Don't you see, Jack, it would never have worked."

"Is that how you treated Lothar too, the poor bastard?"

She flinched. Then she said quietly, "My life is my own business, Jack, but I'll tell you this much. Lothar was a good man once, kind and simple and loving."

"Don't talk so soft!"

"For God's sake, try to understand."

"There's one thing I understand: only whores take money from men."

13

David lay against the pillows watching rain lash down on the window pane. He was in the Levinsons' spare bedroom, where he had been for nearly a fortnight since collapsing at Arendt's house. He had no recollection of the first week when he had been delirious with fever. It was well past noon and any time now Mrs. Levinson would arrive with a tray. He was not hungry and the thought of food bored him. The rain bored him, too; it had been raining on and off for days, one storm following another, clouds so black as to make daytime seem like dusk.

On the table next to the bed was a pile of books. A copy of Goldsmith's *She Stoops to Conquer* lay open on his chest. "Such an intelligence!" Mrs. Levinson had said when he had given her a list of books he would like to read. "Such taste!" But he had hardly looked at them. Dr. Hibbert had warned him that he would feel weary and depressed most of the time during his convalescence, for that always followed a bout of camp fever.

There was a soft knock on the door.

"Come in."

Mrs. Levinson entered, carrying a tray, and was followed by her husband. "We thought you might be asleep," she said. If anything, she was stouter than when David had first met her, and her flesh still shook as she walked. "Chicken soup! A real broth to put flesh on those bones again." He had lost nearly ten pounds. His hair, which usually sat on his skull like a smooth dark cap, had grown during his illness and made his face seem thinner. His skin was a sickly white. The smell of food made him feel queasy, but he knew he would have to eat it, for Mrs. Levinson became hurt if her cooking was rejected.

"How are you today, my boy?" Mr. Levinson said.

"Better."

"That's the spirit. We'll soon have you up and about."

"Such talk!" Mrs. Levinson said. "Look at the poor boy, he can hardly lift the spoon and you talk of up and about. He'll stay in this bed until Dr. Hibbert says he is ready. Eat! Eat it while it's hot."

They stood watching him. They did this at almost every meal, willing the food down his throat, tasting as he tasted, enjoying the flavor with him, *being* him.

"Good boy," she said as he finished the soup. "Now a little fruit?"

"No, thanks. I've really . . ."

"What about some cheesecake? I made it myself."

Just then Hilda came in to shoo them out. "You stand and stare at him while he eats! What is he, some sort of python? That's not the way to get him well."

David watched the two older Levinsons move out of the room under her stern eyes. It was a measure of how much she and they had changed that it seemed more and more that it was Hilda who ran the family now. Her father had never really recovered from his jaundice attack; he seemed much older than when David had arrived in Kimberley. Then he had been plump and energetic; now he was often tired.

She smiled and shook her head in a kind of mock exasperation. "Always fussing," she said. "I don't know what they'll do when they don't have anyone to fuss over." She began to plump up his pillows and straighten his sheets, which she did three or four times a day.

She was an attractive woman, he thought, as she bent over him. Attractive and capable. He caught the smell of lavender and remembered the hot afternoon when he had put his hand inside her bodice. For the past two months they had been seeing each other more frequently, and had taken up almost where they had left off when von Holzman had entered the picture. Von Holzman. One day he had been there and the next he was gone. When David had asked Hilda where he was, her lips had formed a thin line and she had said, "How should I know?" She never spoke of him, nor did her parents; it was as though he had never existed. But for quite a long time David had seen the anger in her eyes. Perhaps that was when she had grown up.

Their renewed friendship had meant a lot to him, for his own life was barren. They had gone out together to hear Lily sing at several private recitals and also to the Lanyon Theater. He had seen the glow on her parents' faces as they watched the friendship progress. Now here she was looking after him better than he had ever been looked after in his life. He watched as she went around the room, straightening and tidying: organized, deft and, at the same time, very pretty. "Are you ready?" she said.

She passed him a dressing gown and turned her back while he put it on. He swung his feet to the edge of the bed and she put her hand under his arm. "How do you feel?"

"Wobbly."

She walked him up and down the room for nearly ten minutes. They had been doing this for the past three days. He liked to feel her hands on him and smell her smell and be close to her. And she seemed to like being close to him.

"May I sit in the chair?"

"All right." She tucked a blanket around him. "Would you like a cigar?"

"Don't you mind the smell?"

"I love it when you smoke."

He drew on the cigar and she sat opposite him and they watched the rain on the windows.

"Have you thought what you're going to do?" she said.

He knew what she meant. No one pretended anymore. They knew, and he knew, that a period of his life was ending. The thought of going back to the claim by himself, of the endless work, of the lonely nights in the tent made him even more depressed.

And then she said, in a softer voice, "I know what you're feeling. You're thinking it would be giving up, but it wouldn't. You've struggled and fought. No one could have worked harder."

She was saying what he wanted to hear. He knew that the Levinsons needed him and he knew why. Mrs. Levinson was fearful of her husband's health. She wanted him to live in the Cape and she saw in David the means of achieving this. Mr. Levinson himself wanted to go and he saw in David the means of his own release. And Hilda? He assumed that she saw what she had always seen in him: a husband and a partner in the store. He knew he was in a kind of spider's web, but he also knew that it contained comfort, security and love, things he had almost forgotten existed. But at the center of the web was the store. Would he really want to serve behind a counter for the rest of his days?

He put out a hand and gripped one of Hilda's. There was answering pressure.

"You've been so good to me," he said.

She colored and seemed to wait for him to go on, but he withdrew his hand and said, "Would you read to me?"

"Cotton braiding?" David said.

"Cotton braiding." The customer was a large lady in black bombazine. "Off-white."

"Cotton braiding. Off-white." He repeated it as if it were some magic incantation. "One moment, please."

Hilda was serving another customer farther along the counter. "Cotton braiding," David whispered.

"In the haberdashery drawers. The top one."

He hurried back. The woman was looking impatient. "You must be new here," she said.

"Yes. I'm helping out." He opened the top haberdashery drawer and saw rolls of colored woven cotton which he assumed was braiding. He picked up one and showed it to her.

"That's beige," she said. "Don't you have off-white?"

"It seems that's all we have."

"Give me two yards, then."

He measured two yards against the brass rule set into the counter top, cut it off with dressmaking shears, placed it in a small box, wrapped it up in brown paper and tied it with string.

"That'll be ninepence," he said.

She paid and left. He turned to put the braiding away. As he did so a voice said, "Half a pound of iron filings, please." He turned and saw Peter Arendt.

"So they've got you at last," Arendt said, softly enough so that neither Hilda nor her mother, in her usual place on the high stool, could hear.

David smiled. "The old man wasn't feeling too well this morning. Anyway, I need something to do. That room's driving me mad."

"What you really need is a glass of beer." He turned to Hilda and Mrs. Levinson. "Does anyone mind if I steal David for a little while?"

They went to one of the cosies. The day was close and sticky, with thunder on the horizon, and David was thirsty.

"Where do you think Lily is?" he said when they were settled.

"It depends how long she had to wait for a ship. She could be halfway to England."

"Do you really think she's that good?"

"I would not be wasting my time if I did not. I wrote to Mantelli two months ago telling him about her. I said he would be lucky to get her."

"Who's Mantelli?"

"The best voice teacher in London. But I do not think she will need him for long. I, too, am going to Europe in a few months, did you know? I must go to Berlin to see my father and to Amsterdam to see Asscher's about cutting some stones, so I will also go and see how Lily is getting on." He paused. "What are you going to do?"

David shrugged. "Everyone's asking me that. The Levinsons are always watching me as though they're trying to read my mind."

"They need you."

"It's hard to decide what to do."

"It seems simple to me," Arendt said. "You have been digging in the ground for more than two years. You have found nothing worthwhile. You only keep going by miracles." He held up his hand. "All right, I know you always wished to do it, but there comes a time when you must regularize your position."

"You sound like Mr. Levinson—a good Jewish father."

"Listen, unless you have great luck, what you are doing is

hopeless. It is like swimming in the sea with your eyes closed, trying to catch a fish with your hands."

"Lots of people find good stones."

"Do you know anyone who has found a really good stone?"

"Not personally, but . . ."

"You see? Understand something. You are working for chance. Now I work for certainty. You say *some* people find good stones, I say whoever finds a good stone must come to a diamond buyer, and there are very few buyers compared to diggers. You should be a buyer."

"You need money for that. Anyway, I don't know enough about diamonds."

"I could teach you."

"I thought you hated them, that they bored you."

"They are a means to an end. I wish to make a fortune quickly so that I can do what I like. But I am here to represent my father. I have been wanting to talk to you about this for a long time, but you were always muleheaded about digging."

"Talk."

"I want to form a partnership to make my own money."

David's eyebrows shot up. "With me?"

"Why not? You could combine your work in the shop with buying and selling diamonds. It would give you a good base."

The idea was so overwhelming it took David's breath away. He had long ago realized that *digging* for diamonds was not what he wanted at all. The gems themselves obsessed him; how they were discovered did not.

"Don't say anything now," Peter said. "Think about it." Then he added, "How are you and Hilda?"

"Fine." David's thoughts were far away.

"Does she ever mention von Holzman?"

"No. What happened to him?"

"There's been a gold strike in the eastern Transvaal. He went there."

"He left suddenly."

"Was she upset?"

"I didn't ask her."

"Did she want to marry him?"

"I don't think it had come to that."

"He said he told her he could never marry her because she was a Jewess and his family would not permit it."

"He told you that?" David felt a sudden surge of anger.

"Surely something like that doesn't still upset you!"

"I wasn't thinking of myself! Imagine how Hilda must have felt."

They parted and David went back to the store. As his initial anger cooled, so his concern for Hilda increased. He felt a sympathy for her that was new to him.

During the next few days he made his decision. It did not spring from any dramatic incident, but was rather the culmination of a desire to be rid forever of the merciless work of digging. In a short while he found himself, to his astonishment, a partner in three enterprises: he still shared ownership of the New Chance claim with Jack, but he was also a junior partner in Levinson's Emporium and a full partner in Arendt and Kade, Diamond Merchants. This was a somewhat grandiose title for what he actually was—a *kopje walloper*, a man who walked the diggings with a leather satchel containing money, a loupe and a small pair of scales, and whose job it was to try and smell out recent discoveries and talk the diggers into selling their stones to him, thus freeing them from the long, hot walk into town where the better-known diamond merchants had their offices. This was the way of learning his trade, so to speak. Later, with any luck, he would be a merchant with an office of his own.

But before he signed the partnership papers he went out to see Jack, for his new interests meant that he would not be working the claim. Mr. Levinson had gone to Portuguese Place a few weeks earlier on some pretext, taking with him a basket of fruit for Frans and some coffee and bacon as presents to Susan, and he had told David that things were bad, but even that had not prepared him for the reality. The last time he had been there, cattle and sheep had dotted the scrub desert as far as the eye could see; now the place was derelict. As he drove his hired trap through the main gate he noticed that the nameboard hung askew and that some of the fencing poles were broken and the wire was sagging. He could see the occasional pile of bones which was all that marked the *rinderpest* epidemic of the winter.

Somehow, he had expected at least some outward sign that the money from the auction had been put to use. That had been his idea, and it was one that had worked splendidly. Several times he

had sat with the Levinsons while they discussed ways and means of giving Susan a helping hand, but each time the ideas had come to nothing. "She'd know it's us," Mr. Levinson had said. "She's too proud to take money. I tried. I know." And then they had heard about the auction and David had come up with the idea of allowing Malone and Dan Halkett to bid on their behalf.

"What a brain!" Mr. Levinson had said, patting him on the cheek in delight. "I tell you, the boy's a genius!"

"But . . ." Hilda had begun, and then stopped. They had looked at her. "Nothing. Nothing."

David had organized Malone and Halkett, and even put in some money. At first Mr. Levinson had demurred. "Listen, this is my business. They set me up in the early days. If it weren't for them, there would be no Levinson's Emporium."

"It's my idea," David had said. "Anyway, maybe I could use some good furniture. Who knows, I might need it one day."

And so they had worked it, and Susan had no idea. That was the best part of it. But had it been too late?

The house stood in a kind of wilderness—a man-made wilderness. The view from the stoep, which even to his city eyes had been the most beautiful aspect of Portuguese Place, was now a vista in ruins: bare tree stumps stuck from the ground, interspersed with blackened areas where the light brush had been burnt. The entire area had been scarred and churned up by wagon wheels. The trees had simply vanished and the river no longer looked like a real river, but more like a *donga,* as they called the dry watercourses scoured by erosion. In the distance he could make out a wagon and a Scotch cart coming slowly towards him. At first he thought the drivers must be two hired Hottentots, for they were dressed in men's clothing and wearing battered, sweat-stained hats. But when he drew up with them he found Susan was driving the mule wagon and Marie the Scotch cart. Susan had lost weight and looked like a piece of stringy beef that had been cured in the sun. Marie's complexion had darkened and for the first time he wondered whether Mr. Levinson's remark, which he had dismissed out of hand when first hearing it, was true: could there be some blood in her that was not white?

They pretended, the three of them, that his call was social and that each was about his normal business. It was a pretense which

could not hide the obvious truth, for David realized that what he was looking at were "poor whites," a phrase he had only heard since coming to Africa.

"The crop looks good," he said, pointing to the half-grown maize that covered an area below the house.

"We've had plenty of rain this year, almost too much," Susan said.

They chatted some moments while Marie looked on stonily and then Susan said, "If you're looking for Jack, he's about two miles downstream." David thanked her and drove on down the precarious track.

He found Jack by following the noise of the ax, in a thicket of acacia trees. He was stripped to the waist and his pale body was covered in dust. David had had the foresight to pack a basket with a half a dozen bottles of beer. Jack wiped his mouth with the back of his hand and drank steadily until one of the bottles was empty. He looked like a scarecrow. His trousers were torn and his boots cut, and David felt self-conscious in his new cotton suit with the new white panama on his head. Jack propped the ax against a tree, went down to the river and scooped water over his head and shoulders. It was a burning day.

As he came back he said, "You haven't come all this way to bring me a bottle of beer."

"That's not a welcome, Jack. I came to see how you were. . . ."

"Look at me and you'll know."

"Yes. Things have been hard, I can see that. But you've done a great job." His eyes took in the devastated landscape. "Without you, Portuguese Place would have been finished."

Jack did not reply, but drank from another bottle which David had offered him. The dry tissues of his body soaked it up like blotting paper and immediately sweat broke out on his face and chest and, evaporating, cooled him.

"I never thought you'd stick it," David said, smiling. "You must be a farmer at heart. Me, I'm a townsman."

Jack stared over the top of the bottle at the harsh hills above the river. Why *had* he stayed? It was a question he asked himself regularly. He hated the work. There was tension between himself and Marie. There was old Frans living like an elderly infant in the decaying house. There was Susan working herself to the bone. No one could say it had been fun. But each time he thought of

going back to Kimberley something inside him quailed. He was still bitter about the way Lily had treated him. He sensed now that she had never meant their relationship to be permanent and she had seen Susan's need for him as a way of preparing the ground for breaking it up. It was the first time he had ever revealed himself to a woman and had nearly been destroyed by the experience. He would never do so again. He was learning all the time. First there had been David. He had thought he was his friend but that had gone bad. Now Lily . . .

But the most important factor in Jack's remaining on the farm was part of the central core of his character: it was the fear of humiliation. He had gone from nothing at the diggings to being *someone*. He had knocked out Lothar. He had become the town's boxing wonder and his reward, as he saw it, had been Lily. But now he no longer boxed at the Grand and Lily had left him. He had come crashing down again and was back where he had started. Knowing men as he did, he could see in his mind's eye the smiles behind the hands, the stifled sniggers, the knowing looks.

The farm had been a kind of haven in spite of the fact that Susan had never mentioned the land deal again. Well, when he'd finished the trees he'd confront her. Who knows, there might be diamonds on Portuguese Place after all. Frans had said he'd had the place surveyed and that none had been found; but Frans had not *wanted* any found. Perhaps it had never been properly surveyed. Why shouldn't there be diamonds?

David and Jack sat down near the river and drank beer and talked—or rather, David did the talking, mainly about Kimberley and the Levinsons. Gradually he led the conversation into his own changes of interests. Jack seemed to accept that after his illness David could not work as he had before, and so David pressed on and told him what he was planning.

"What happens to the claim while you go off with your friends?" Jack said.

"That's what I've come about."

"If you're thinking of selling, forget it. I'll never sell. Never."

"I know that. And I've thought of a way. I've talked to Joe Malone and Dan Halkett. Their claim's bottomed out in blue ground. It's hopeless to go on and they can't afford to buy a new one. Joe's been talking about moving on to the Transvaal to look

for gold, but they can't afford that, either. We could let them work the claim and take a share in anything they find. I'd trust Dan with my life."

"I don't like it much," Jack said.

"There's no other way, if you want to keep the claim."

Jack recognized the truth in that. Anyway, he wasn't ready to return to Kimberley yet. The thought of owning a piece of land, any piece, had begun to appeal to him. Land was hard to come by. If he went back to Kimberley now he would have nothing. But if he went back as the owner of a bit of land . . . He picked up the ax and swung it at the base of a tree, using his big, bony body like a machine. "Do it your way," he said.

That was how it was arranged. Malone and Halkett took over New Chance and David began his new life. From an existence in which he had concentrated solely on filling buckets with spoil and then looking through that spoil for tiny chips of crystallized carbon, he widened his experience dramatically. Mr. Levinson had been so grateful for his acquiescence that he put nothing in the way of his separate partnership with Arendt. Even Hilda, from whom he thought he might meet some resistance, foresaw it as a way for him to gain a wider acceptance in Kimberley and become what Arendt had become, a respected Jewish magnate moving in the best cultural circles, something her father, for all the size of his business, had never become.

So David split his day in two. In the morning he learnt how to become a merchant. At first Levinson gave him the benefit of his experience but he and his wife spent much of their time talking about the Cape and planning the house they would have, and when they would leave. It was Hilda who took over David's education.

He had been clever at school and had worked in a bank, so that the bookkeeping at Levinson's was child's play. But that was not the important side of the business. To get the books to show a profit, he had to sell the goods in the shop. Until then he had not considered this angle; his impression had been that people simply came in and bought.

He learnt what to stock and what not to stock. He learnt how to buy large consignments of goods cheaply and to undercut his competitors by a few pence per item. He learnt when to have sales and when not to have sales, that when the diamond market was down he would have to sell cheaply and when it was up to

mark the prices accordingly. He learnt where the best coffee came from, how to tell good Boer tobacco from bad, to buy only enough perishable goods not to have them go bad on him, but whom to sell them to if they did; he learnt what a bill of lading was and how to write letters which began, "Dear sir, In answer to your letter of the fifth . . ." He learnt that white people did not like to be kept waiting while he served blacks, that it was good policy to give children a handful of free boiled sweets and a pat on the head when they were accompanied by their parents. And he also learnt the maxim which Levinson constantly repeated: you can't go broke making a profit. Much of what he did he found distasteful, but what astonished him was the amount of money taken over the counters of the shop. It came in a silver and copper stream, insignificant amounts, tuppences and pennies and even ha'pennies, all adding up to make a bank balance that he realized must be one of the most respectable of any merchant in town.

He also met his rivals and the middlemen, and soon he was wearing the expression of a prosperous burgher.

There was only one thing wrong: he hated the shop, it bored him and sometimes took away his self-respect. So as he served a pound of sugar or a cotton vest or six inches of chewing tobacco to a black man who smelt like the inside of a cold fireplace, he would look forward to the afternoon, when the other half of his life began.

Arendt worked from a wooden shack near Stockdale Street. It had a brass plaque on the wall near the door which stated simply ARENDT AND MEYER, DIAMOND MERCHANTS, BERLIN, KIMBERLEY. Within a week of the setting up of their partnership another brass plate was put up, reading ARENDT AND KADE, DIAMOND MERCHANTS. It looked very new and shiny the first time David saw it and he put out his finger and traced the lettering of his name. Just seeing it there gave him more pleasure than all the money that poured over the counter at Levinson's and all the stones he and Jack had found. But it seemed to lack the romance of the words "Berlin, Kimberley." One day, he thought, it might read "London, Kimberley."

The inside of the shack was simple. It consisted of a desk, three or four plain chairs, a small pair of balances and a safe in one corner. A table with a green baize cloth was set under the

window. "You must have a north light to see the stones at their best," Peter said.

David started his education by being present when Arendt made his deals. When there was no one else in the shack, Arendt would take him through the history and the economic theory of diamonds. The first thing he realized was that the diggers seemed to know very little about their own business. He had listened to a hundred "experts" in the canteens and cosies but when confronted by a real expert their knowledge of their product was sketchy. A man would come in with a stone which he thought was valuable and Peter would weigh it on his balance and examine it by the light of the window. Sometimes he would even take the stone into the street to examine it more closely. All the time the digger would be telling him what a wonderful stone it was. Then Peter would pass the loupe to the digger and say, "You have a look. See the flaw?" And it would be a "black spot" or a "bubble" or a "cloud"—a mass of infinitesimal bubbles too small to be seen individually but which gave the stone a cloudy appearance. The man would either deny it and take the stone elsewhere or else nod hopelessly and say, "What'll you give me for it, then?"

But when a digger brought in a really good stone, Peter would bargain until he finally got it. One day a man produced a stone of about thirty carats. It was a beautiful diamond and the digger wanted three thousand pounds for it. Arendt looked at it carefully and then shook his head. "I'll give you two thousand five hundred." The digger stuck to his price and Arendt suddenly gave in. "All right, three thousand."

He went to his safe in the corner of the room, counted out the notes and handed them to the man.

"Why didn't you bargain?" David said after the digger had left.

"You know who he is?"

"No."

"He a German named Lubbe. He and his three brothers work two good claims. They take out excellent stones. He's never been to me before, but I've offered him more than he has been offered elsewhere."

"How do you know?"

"The stone isn't worth more than two-six, two-seven. I doubt he's been offered two-five. The next time he gets a decent stone, he'll come to me. So will his brothers. You've got to know what's going on, who are the good workers, who are the drinkers, who

have the good claims, who the bad. Most of all, you've got to treat them right. In this business everything is by reputation. There are no written contracts; a man's word is everything. Break your word once and you're finished."

There were long periods when no one came to the office. During these times David learnt about other aspects of the business. He had thought he knew a reasonable amount about diamonds from his reading and from the information he had picked up on the diggings, but it was only now that he realized how superficial his knowledge was.

One afternoon while he ate lunch at his desk Peter began to talk about the birth of a diamond.

"All diamonds come from the earth's mantle," Peter said. "Do you know what that is?"

David shook his head.

Peter reached into the basket containing his lunch and took out a hard-boiled egg. Without peeling it he cut it in half and held up one piece. With the tip of his knife he pointed to the shell. "You could call that the crust of the earth," he said. "It is twenty miles thick and is composed of rock." The knife moved to the white. "You can call the white the mantle. It is eighteen hundred miles thick and also made of rock." He touched the yellow yolk. "The core has a radius of more than two hundred miles and is molten iron. It is in this part," he prodded the white, "in the mantle, that there are huge reservoirs of molten rock and it is thought that diamonds were formed here out of carbon millions of years ago. Then pressure in the mantle forced the molten rock out to the surface of the earth in fissures. We call these fissures 'pipes.' One of the pipes came to the surface here in Kimberley."

He described how the liquid rock in the pipes had cooled and solidified and how over the ages wind, rain, frost and heat had broken it down into the gravel: yellow near the surface where oxygen reached it, blue farther down. The diamonds were found in the yellow ground.

In the years to come, whenever David was describing to others how diamonds were formed he always thought of the hard-boiled egg.

On another occasion Peter took from his waistcoat pocket a silver snuffbox and emptied onto his desk some small brown beans. "Do you know what those are?" he said.

"Some kind of seed?"

"From the carob tree which grows in the East. Look at them. Can you see anything different about them?"

"No, they all look the same to me."

Peter laughed. "You are right, they are the same. In olden times the pearl merchants in the East found that when the seeds were dried each one was almost exactly the same weight as the other. So they used them as measures of weight. You learned Greek at school?"

"And Latin."

"In Greek the work for the carob tree is *keration,* so we get our word 'carat' from it. Of course we have standardized it since then. A carat is a fifth of a gram and there are one hundred forty-two carats in an ounce. But the most important thing for you is that if a stone is flawless, the heavier it is, the more expensive it is. Each carat becomes more expensive. You have seen me buy small stones for a pound a carat. They are nothing. But you saw the man who had the thirty-carat stone. I paid him one hundred pounds a carat."

Often he would talk about the history of diamonds. About the mines in Golconda, India, and in Brazil. As he listened, David was again taken back in time to the security of the big armchair in his grandparents' home, the steaming hot chocolate and his grandfather's stories.

He had been learning his trade for three weeks when he arrived one afternoon to find Peter looking at several articles on his desk. There was a leather satchel, a small pocket balance and a loupe. "It's time Arendt and Kade began to make some money," he said. "All I do here is make money for my father."

Between them they had put up a hundred pounds in capital and now he went to his safe, took out fifty one-pound notes and stuffed them into the satchel. David's spell as a *kopje walloper* was beginning.

He knew about this subculture in the diamond economy for he had been importuned many times by *kopje wallopers* to sell diamonds. He had always refused, never trusting them to give him the best price. Now, as he trudged through the close heat of the afternoon he found himself on the other side of the fence. Being a Jew might have made things difficult for him. The profession was largely dominated by Jews from Whitechapel—he knew that the millionaire Barney Barnato, for instance, had been a *kopje walloper*— many of whom had no money at all and lived on

their wits. But David had one priceless advantage in his relationship with the diggers: he had been one of them. Not only that, but he was a partner of Jack Farson, the man who had fought the greatest fight Kimberley had ever seen.

The idea behind his work as a *kopje walloper* was to drum up trade for the newly formed partnership. Established customers dealt with Peter in his capacity as representative of Arendt and Meyer of Berlin, but new customers, those discovered by David, would legitimately be clients of Arendt and Kade of Kimberley. David had no desire to be a *kopje walloper* for very long, but he knew that until he had built up his contacts he would be bringing nothing to the partnership.

Slowly his reputation as an honest man spread. He followed Arendt's precepts. At first he made many mistakes. He missed carbon spots and other flaws. Sometimes he paid too much; sometimes he missed a good stone by offering too little.

But he tried constantly to expand his clientele and would stop and talk to diggers he had not met before. He did this one afternoon, introducing himself to a man called Ritchie, an Australian.

It was late in the afternoon and David was tired. He asked Ritchie if he had had any luck. The Australian was a tall, mournful-looking man and was seated at his sorting table, listlessly inspecting a pile of gravel. He shook his head, and even that seemed to be an effort. David wondered if he was in that post-fever state of depression which had so recently afflicted him.

"It's going to rain again," he said, to make conversation.

"Too true," Ritchie said. "Some of the claims are waterlogged."

"You been here long?"

"Eight months."

"Found anything decent?"

"No." He wore an air of utter dejection. "I ain't found nothing for nearly a month."

He was starting to sweep the tailings onto a pile next to the table when David's eye was caught by something.

"Stop!" he said.

"What's up?"

"Look!" He pointed at a stone that glinted.

"Christ!" Ritchie picked it up with a pair of tweezers. "Jesus! I almost missed it. Thanks a lot, mate. Canby should give me a few bob for that." He named a diamond buyer in town.

"Wait," David said. "At least give *me* a chance to make an offer."

"That seems fair enough. You spotted it."

David picked up the stone and examined it. Then he weighed it. Then he examined it again. His hands began to shake. It was a beautiful diamond, by far the biggest and the purest he had encountered in his role as buyer.

He calculated what money he had in his satchel, then said, "Two hundred."

The man looked crestfallen. "I could get three in town."

David felt a surge of power and an absolute conviction that the man would not go into town, that the diamond was his.

"Two-fifty," he said. "Take it or leave it."

The man shrugged. "I'll take it."

David counted out the notes and took the stone. "Don't forget," he said. "When you've got something to sell, come to me. The name's Kade."

Later, when he reached the office, Peter spread the afternoon's small haul of diamonds on the baize cloth, then separated Ritchie's. "Where did you get this?"

"From a new contact. An Australian. It's a beauty, isn't it?"

"How much did you pay?"

"Two-fifty. It's worth at least three."

Peter put his hand into his waistcoat pocket, took out a diamond and placed it on the table.

"My God!" David said, and again he felt his body tremble.

"Have a good look at it."

This stone was cut and polished. Light was reflected from one plane to the other. *("What do you see?" his grandfather had asked, and he had said, "Fire and ice.")* He had never seen a stone as good. He was overwhelmed.

"How much do you reckon it's worth?" Arendt asked.

"Thousands. Maybe ten thousand."

"Or maybe ten pounds. It's quartz. Just like the one you bought from the Australian."

David stared at him in horror. "Quartz!"

"Don't worry. It happens to everyone."

"But I *know* quartz!"

"It depends how you look at it. You wanted that stone, didn't you?" David nodded. "You would have gone higher." He nodded again." You wanted it so badly it *became* a diamond. Let me tell

you something, David; don't fall in love with these things. Don't desire a diamond for itself or it will destroy you. They're pieces of crystallized carbon, that's all. You buy them and sell them like anything else. That is your role."

After that David was more careful.

As time passed it was clear that he was becoming someone in the town. Kimberley at that period was a raffish place with a constantly changing population. Everything depended on diamond money and the people who came to dig for the diamonds seldom stayed for long. But the town had to be run. There had to be some kind of firm base and this was formed by merchants and traders who had built up their businesses and who lived in proper houses and gave the place what little air of solidity it had. A club was being built; a library was planned; there was even talk of a town hall.

When a vacancy on the town council occurred an approach was made to David by a delegation of Jewish businessmen. It was led by one of the partners in Milwidsky and Rosenberg, a rival store to Levinson's Emporium. Mr. Rosenberg talked to David in the Levinsons' living room. Mrs. Levinson, overwhelmed, bustled about, shouting at the servants to serve tea, and her husband peered through the door that led from the shop, not quite part of the meeting yet not quite apart either.

Rosenberg was a small man who wore a natty gray suit with a double-breasted waistcoat and a chain over his plump little belly. He was bald, with a fringe of gray hair and liver spots on the top of his skull. "What we're saying to you is this, Mr. Kade," he said. "We, the Jewish community, wish to be represented on the town council. One day we want to build a proper synagogue, and for this one must have power, for there will be strong opposition. In places where we have no representation we always end up in ghettos. Do you know what a ghetto is, Mr. Kade?"

"Yes," David said, remembering his childhood. "I know what a ghetto is."

"A seat has come up and it is in our power to fill it. What do you say?"

"Why me?"

"Your name is well known and respected. Everyone in town trusts you."

"I'll think about it," David said. "I'll let you know tomorrow."

Later that afternoon he went to see Peter Arendt. "Why not?" Peter said. "Diamond merchant. Storekeeper. Councillor. It can only do the business good."

"I wasn't thinking of it that way."

"It ends up that way."

He thought again of what Rosenberg had said: "In places where we have no representation we always end up in ghettos."

The Levinsons circled him like emotional wolves, not wanting to demand a response, but wondering all the time what it was going to be. At supper that evening they ate in silence. He knew they were watching him. What a coup for them it would be. He could just hear Mrs. Levinson: "Such a young man!" That in itself was enough to make him feel like refusing. But what Rosenberg had said was true and there was enough anti-Semitic feeling in Kimberley to bring it about.

That night after the two older Levinsons had gone to bed he sat in the sitting room smoking a cigar while Hilda read the weekly paper.

"They say that the Vaal River is in flood," she said.

He did not reply.

"It's been the wettest year in living memory."

He rose and began to pace up and down the room. She pretended to read the paper, but watched him.

Finally, he opened the window, threw his cigar out and closed it. "I'll do it," he said.

"Oh, David!" She jumped to her feet. "How wonderful!" She put her hands on his shoulders and kissed him on the cheek. "We're all so proud!"

He kissed her, a hungry, passionate kiss. And then he held her and heard himself speak. He was asking her to marry him. It was unplanned, a response to the life he now lived.

He saw she was crying, but they were tears of joy and she ran across the sitting room and down the passage. He could hear her telling her parents. In a few minutes, the three of them entered the room, the old couple in dressing gowns.

"My boy! My boy!" Mr. Levinson said, embracing him.

"Such a person!" Mrs. Levinson said. "Such a young man!"

For a second or two David experienced a sensation of dread. It was as though a door had opened onto a bleak winter landscape, as though something inevitable and irreversible had happened and he suddenly saw the three people in the room with fresh

eyes: the simple and vulgar delight of Mr. Levinson in his rumpled gray dressing gown, "Levinson from Lewisham," as he always said jokingly, which was exactly how he looked. And his wife, gross, treble-chinned, wobbly; the calculating eagerness of Hilda. Was she in love with him, or was he simply a convenience which would enable her to enter the respectability of the married state?

In another flash of insight he saw his own childhood in the house in Kiev: here was no vulgarity, no bad taste. He was a different person from the Levinsons, from a different background, educated, civilized.

But . . . but . . .

By force of will he blotted out such thoughts. In Africa the past meant little; everything was new, untried; a whole pristine world beckoned. You could not go through life looking over your shoulder at the past. In this new life there was the opportunity to be someone, and while he was trying he would have a secure background and base.

The door on the bleak winter landscape began to close and he looked again at the family. Here was love and warmth. He was the center of the world. Soon the two old people would go to the Cape into their retirement. Then, if he wished, he could change things, make a life more suited to his style.

The door through which the scene was so bleak and chill swung slowly to.

14

"The rains have been very heavy this year," Susan wrote. "And the river has been higher than I can ever remember. The wet weather seems to be over for a spell and everything is drying out. But the damage is done." She paused. She was seated at a small table in her bedroom writing in the big Portuguese Bible, using the pages at the back of the book.

It was now well on into the summer and she had been writing for weeks. The need to communicate what had happened in her life had reached a point where she could no longer restrain herself. She had started, not with her childhood, but from the time she had come to Africa. She had described her marriage to the Reverend Parker, their journey north, his murder by the Korannas, her own rape and near murder at the hands of the man called Kaptein, her walk along the river during which she had nearly starved, her meeting with Frans, the slow creation of Portuguese Place, and the happy years when they'd had nothing and when the two of them and their daughter had lived in such harmony. Then the growing realization that Marie might have

Hottentot blood in her; the increase in their flocks and herds and the meeting with Levinson; Marie's time at school at the Cape; the money which came rolling in and was immediately reinvested in cattle and sheep; the growing unhappiness as things moved inevitably out of her control until finally came the *rinderpest* and Frans's stroke. It was all there, every detail of every event recorded as honestly as she could remember.

It was a curious feeling, seeing it all set down in her small, neat handwriting, knowing that no one else would ever read it. It had helped. As she wrote she had felt as though a weight were being lifted from her shoulders. She did not know what was going to happen in the future, but at least she was now less burdened by the past.

She went into the next room to see how Frans was. Now that he had become bedridden she'd had to give up carting the wood into Kimberley. She left it to Marie and Mopedi and spent her days with him. She looked at his head on the pillows with the long white hair and beard and thin pale face. Was this the big, sunburnt hunter who had rescued her when she was on the point of death?

"Is there anything you want?" she said.

His eyes moved to the jug of water on the table by his bed.

"What is it?"

Again he looked at the water and again she pretended not to know what he meant. It was part of trying to keep him alive. Dr. Hibbert had explained that the problem with stroke patients was that they lost the will to live. Making him speak and move his arm was part of the therapy, so she forced him to do both whenever she could. He could speak and move, but would rarely make the effort.

"What, Frans?" she said.

The side of his mouth opened. "Wa . . . ter." The muscles that remained alive around his mouth pulled his lips into a grimace and he said again, "Wa . . . wa . . . ater." She poured a glass and handed it to him, knowing that he would rather she had held it to his lips. He drank shakily and passed it back to her. She pulled up a chair by his bed and said, "Did you have a nice sleep?"

It was as though, having started to speak, he had somehow managed to inject energy into his muscles, for he said, "How is the river?"

"It's come down a lot."

"One day we mu . . . st build a bri . . . dge."

His conversation was still laced with the "one-day" talk of years ago.

"Yes, we'll build a bridge."

The lack of one in the wet weather had hindered them transporting the wood into Kimberley. They had been marooned on the farm for three or four days at a time.

"I wa . . . nt to ta . . . a . . . lk to you," Frans said, his voice no more than a whisper. "When I am gone . . ." He was choosing his words carefully.

"Don't talk like that. Dr. Hibbert says you are making the kind of recovery he hoped for."

But he was beyond this kind of encouragement. "When I'm gone you mu . . . st look after Mopedi."

"Yes." They had been over this several times.

"There is something else." She could see tension in his face, as though he were having to draw courage and strength from the last of his reserves.

She felt a tremor in her heartbeat and knew instinctively what was coming.

"You're tiring yourself," she said.

"It is about Marie. I must tell you that . . ."

The door to the room opened and Mopedi stood on the threshold. "What are you doing here?" Susan said.

"Baas Jack want missus."

"Now?"

"Yes, missus."

"I'll come." She turned to Frans with relief. "I'll be back as soon as I can."

Jack was working so far downstream that she had to take a horse. She rode across the stricken farm, hardly able to bear to look about her. Where once the line of green had softened the landscape and rested the eyes as it twisted and turned with the convolutions of the river, everything was a dun-colored monochrome, churned and cut by wagon wheels. Her maize lands had disappeared, scoured out by the erosion caused by heavy rain on loose soil, so that now the young plants were buried under inches of reddish earth.

She came to Jack at last. He was sitting by the side of the river, the long-handled ax on the ground next to him, smoking his pipe. She noticed how thin he was.

"What is it?" she said, dismounting.

He indicated a pile of logs and said, "That's the end. The last load."

"What do you mean? There must be six or seven miles still to cut."

He led her through a thicket of thorn bush and pointed with the stem of his pipe. The river ran through a gorge. There was no way for a wagon to get along the far bank. On the near one, a track wound between the river and the cliffs, but Susan saw that this was now blocked by a landslide, where part of the cliff had come away. Some of the boulders were as big as a wagon.

"It must have been the last storm that did it," he said.

"What can we do?"

"Nothing. We'd have to carry out each log by hand."

She rode along the cliff top for miles, but there was no way down to the trees that lined the riverbank.

That night after supper they had a conference. They were all tired and depressed and only Marie seemed to have the heart to face the future. It was she who made the suggestion that they sell the farm.

"Who would buy it?" her mother said. "Everyone's afraid of *rinderpest*. This is like a plague spot. People don't come here any-more. Even Uncle Helmut has given up." She had seen him in the town, where he was now working as a blacksmith.

But Marie was not to be put off. "If we sold it, we could get work and live in the wagon."

Susan realized that no matter what the circumstances Marie wanted to leave the farm.

"How can we take your father to live in a wagon?" she said angrily. "It would kill him."

It began to rain again that night, harder than ever, with thunder, lightning and hail. After Jack and Marie had gone to their rooms, Susan went to Frans. For a moment the waxiness of his skin in the soft light of the candle made her think he was dead. But his eyes opened and his mouth began to work.

"What is it, dear?" she said, bending over him.

"Marie!" The word twisted out of the corner of his mouth. "You must look after her."

She nodded, again feeling a cold touch of apprehension. "Of course I'll look after her. *We* will look after her."

"You do . . . do not understand."

"What don't I understand?"

"Sometimes it takes two gener . . . generations for the blood to show," he said. "I can see it in her. That is why you must look af . . . after her."

She did not interrupt. There was nothing she could say.

Then he said, "My father had slaves; so did my grandfather and my great-grandfather. They also had Hottentot servants. Young girls about the hou . . . house. I would have given anything—the fa . . . arm, the stock, anything. I didn't want to tell you. But now you must know because of her future."

She had listened with a growing sense of shock. All these years Frans had kept his thoughts to himself, as she had done. Now she realized that he had assumed it was within his own family, years before, that the act which had put colored blood into his daughter had been committed.

Why had she not told him everything at the beginning, why had she tried to erase it from her own consciousness? It had happened. You could not wish away the past. She felt tears on her eyes. She bent forwards to speak but he had slipped away into that limbo, part sleep, part unconsciousness, in which he spent much of his time.

She sat in his chair hour after hour listening to the rain, waiting for his eyes to open, waiting to tell him that it was not because of him that Marie carried the blood, but because of her.

Jack woke with a start. At first he thought it was thunder that had woken him, but then he became aware that there was someone in his room.

"Jack!" Marie whispered.

He lit the candle. "What's wrong? Is it your father?"

"I want to talk to you."

She was wearing a long white nightdress with a V neck which showed off the milky olive color of her skin to its best advantage. Her black hair hung down to her shoulders. During the months he had been cutting the timber they had hardly seen each other. At first there had been tension between them but slowly this lessened and he realized she must have heard that Lily had gone away. The thought of Lily still caused him more pain than he could ever have imagined. During the early weeks her absence had been like missing an arm or leg, but gradually he had learnt to live with it. He had dulled his mind by work, and living within

a family had also helped to mitigate it.

She was desirable, he realized, looking at her now, and she had changed. She no longer seemed to be an overgrown child; there was a hardness in her which had been absent before.

"Where's your mother?" he asked.

"With Father."

"Why have you come?"

"You'll be leaving the farm now."

He nodded.

"Take me with you."

He thought of the last time she had asked him to do this. It seemed long ago.

"What about your father?"

"Mother can look after him. If I don't get away now, I never will. She'll see to that. I'll spend the rest of my life looking after him and then her."

"But I don't even know what I'm going to do."

"What about the claim?"

"It's leased. Maybe some money will come from it, but I can't work it."

"There are lots of things you can do. You could set up your own boxing booth, you could work for Uncle Helmut—he has more work than he needs. You could mend wagons and sail-cloths. Go to David; he'll give you work."

"No!" he said sharply.

"I would look after you," she said. "We could live in a tent or the wagon. We might even get a little house. I'll look after you better than Lily did. Please."

She lay down beside him and put her hand on his chest. It was as though he were back with Lily. But her smell was different.

What was he going back to now that Lily had gone?

He felt her hair brush his face. "Please," she whispered, and her lips touched his ear.

Because of his relationship with the two older Delports Jack had always been inhibited at Portuguese Place with Marie. Then she kissed him and the inhibitions vanished.

As the thunder rolled around the sky they made sweaty love in his narrow bed, while on the other side of the house a life slipped away.

Susan woke, stiff and sore, in the chair by Frans's bed. He lay

on his back, asleep. She stood at the window watching the hills behind the house turn red as the sun came over the horizon. Frans had asked for this room because it had no view of the denuded river. She let her eyes sweep around in a semicircle, looking at the empty huts that once had housed their servants, and on to the stock kraals that had once been filled with cattle and sheep. One day those kraals would be used again. But who would put the animals there? The thought of doing it herself, of the work and worry involved, made her cringe. The house and farm had been built for a family that had never materialized. She and Frans had wanted children and had managed only one; they had wanted a son-in-law and grandchildren and so far managed none. Had it happened, she would not think twice now about the struggle involved in putting the farm on its feet: the effort would be worth it.

She went to her own room to wash and was about to close the door when she heard a noise in the passage. She opened it partially and saw Marie disappearing towards her own room; she could only have come from Jack's.

She stood where she was for several minutes. She supposed that once such a thing would have shocked her—it would still shock Frans, and she thanked God he need never know—but she had seen so much in her own life that did not conform to the pattern of behavior in which she had been brought up that she did not shock easily.

She returned to Frans's room and sat in his chair. Her decision had been made the night before and now she was waiting for him to wake so that she could set his mind at rest. She had brought the Bible with her and wrote an account of what had just happened. She was finishing when she heard a gurgling noise. She looked up and saw that Frans was in distress. His fingers were gripping the blanket, his back had arched. Suddenly, like the wind going out of a sail, his body relaxed and he sank slowly back onto his bed.

"Frans!" she said. But there was no reply and now there never would be. He lay with his mouth and eyes open and after a moment she pressed his eyelids down and bound up his jaw with a cloth so that his mouth was closed.

Part of her felt an immense and overwhelming sense of grief and loss, yet as she bent to kiss him on the forehead her eyes were dry, for another part of her felt relief, not in any way for herself,

for she would never find anyone like Frans again, nor would ever want to, but for him. It had always been her feeling that if he recovered he would only be a quarter of the man he had been. A quarter would have been enough for her; it would never have been enough for him.

Later that day she sent Marie into town to fetch Dominee Visser, then she laid Frans out while Jack dug the grave. In the afternoon Jack cut part of the sailcloth from the wagon and sewed Frans's body into it. While he was doing this Susan came to watch. It was the last view she would have of her husband. And while she was looking down at him, and while Jack was stitching the sailcloth around him as for a burial at sea, she thought of his last words and the ache inside her grew. "Look after Marie," he had said and then had come his apologia—for that is what it had been. His guilt. His shame. And suddenly, almost as though it were a "leading"—perhaps, she thought, from Frans himself, lingering somewhere still in the house—she knew exactly what to do and heard her voice say, "I have a proposition for you." Jack palmed the big canvas needle through the material without looking up. "I want you to marry Marie."

He stopped. "What?"

"I saw her coming from your room this morning."

His cheeks began to color and she said, "It has nothing to do with that. That only showed me you might be fond of one another. Are you?"

"Yes," Jack said defensively.

"What I have in mind is this: half the farm belongs to Marie now. If you marry her I'll make over another quarter to you and on my death you'll inherit the farm. It may not look much now, but you've seen what it can produce."

"You spoke of land before. You said if I came out to help . . ."

"I know."

"You've never mentioned it since."

"Do you think it hasn't been in my mind?"

He said nothing. After a moment she asked, "Don't you trust me, Jack?"

Of everyone he had encountered since his arrival in Africa the one family he had trusted instinctively was the Delports. But trust had become a dirty word in his lexicon, even in the mouth of Susan.

As though anticipating his thoughts she said, "This time it'll be

done properly, on paper, notarized. I promise."

Again the thought came to him: landowner. There was a ring to it. It would make a difference in Kimberley, a great difference.

"I ain't no farmer," he said, but she could see the temptation begin to grip him.

"I am. I can teach you."

"What about stock? We'd need stock." She noticed the use of the word "we." "That means money."

"We'll find the money."

He turned back and finished sewing Frans into his shroud. "What about Marie? What if she says no?"

"She won't say no. I guess you know that as well as I do."

At Portuguese Place the following day, much to Dominee Visser's surprise, he performed the ceremonies for a wedding as well as a burial. A great storm had gathered in the night and it was still raining at midmorning, when they had thought to bury Frans. As the time wore on and the rain showed no sign of slackening, Marie and Jack were married in the living room. Susan watched them as the old *dominee*, a short Dutchman in black formal clothing, his hair awry from the journey out, performed the ceremony. She had given Marie her own wedding ring. The girl's eyes were ablaze with excitement. Everything had been so unexpected, yet everything, Susan thought, had gone like clockwork. She remembered Frans's body lying in his room as she watched Jack slip the ring onto Marie's finger and she thought: "This may not be exactly what you wanted, but at least she has a strong right arm." If they had children the farm would blossom again—but Frans would not be there to see it.

In a dry spell during the afternoon, and with unseemly haste in case another shower arrived, they buried Frans Delport in his sailcloth. The grave had been dug near the river in a place Frans had loved and where one day the trees would grow again to shade him. There the *dominee* read the Dutch service for the burial of the dead. Besides the *dominee* there were only five people around the grave: Susan, Jack, Marie, Mopedi and Mopedi's wife. Again Susan studied her family, now added to by one. She had said glibly that they would find the money somehow, but she had lied. There was no chance that anyone would lend her money. It would have been hard enough for Frans, but a woman with a derelict farm . . .

As they lowered the body she leant forwards and placed the big Portuguese Bible, wrapped in a new piece of oilskin, on the canvas shroud. It was a gesture to mark the end of a phase in her life. Then she prayed, not for Frans's soul, but for the future of her daughter and son-in-law.

They trooped back towards the house. Water was still running down the hillside and the women lifted their dresses so that they would not become wet. Just then there was a rumbling, grating noise, and a crash. A tide of black mud surged around the corner of the house.

They ran up the slope to the back of the house and stood staring in shocked dismay at the sight which confronted them. The relentless rain of the past weeks had softened the mud bricks of the original part of the house and the walls of a room—the one so recently vacated by Frans's body—had collapsed.

She had planned for Jack and Marie to take the *dominee* back so they could have a night in Kimberley. She had even set aside a small amount of money to pay for their one night's honeymoon. But this was now impossible. She told the *dominee* to take the trap while the rest of them ran for picks and shovels to cut a channel to lead the water round the house and stop other rooms from being undermined.

They worked until late afternoon and by then the clouds had disappeared and the sun shone again.

"That should do it," Jack said.

They were covered in mud. They threw down the tools and were about to make their way to the front of the house when he stopped.

He bent down and as he did so Susan saw something glitter at his feet. He picked it up and rubbed it against his shirt, then he looked at it closely. It was a tiny stone. "Christ! It's a diamond!"

They crowded around him. He held the small, glittering object in the palm of his filthy hand.

"Are you sure?" Susan said.

"I haven't got a loupe, but I know a diamond when I see one. That's a diamond."

"But where did it come from?" Marie said. "Father had experts all over the farm. You've looked yourself. Nothing has ever been found before."

"We were told it wasn't diamondiferous," Susan said.

"I can't help that. It's a diamond, and if there's one, there's more."

He looked back up the slope. The slick of black mud was drying in the sun. Then he said in a voice hardly above a whisper, "The mud! That's where it came from. The mud. The bricks were made of mud. It's been in one of the bricks."

The two women stared at him. It was a guess, an estimation of likelihood, and yet they knew that there was a logic about it. It had to be. There was no other way.

"In the mud!" Marie whispered. "All these years."

"Where did the bricks come from?" Jack asked.

"Frans made them."

"But there's no mud around here. Not that I've seen, anyway." He pointed to the river. "That's sand. And this topsoil is sandy, too."

He bent and scooped up a handful of mud. It was sticky and black. "I've never seen mud like this."

"We dug it from a mudhole," Susan said.

"On the farm?"

"I think so. It's a day's hard riding. I'm not sure exactly where the farm boundaries are. It may be in Hottentot country."

"Could you find it?"

"Could you?" Marie said. "Could you?"

Susan projected her mind back. She saw again the small waterhole and Frans digging out the mud and forming it into bricks and letting them dry in the hot desert sun. "Perhaps. I was only there once. It's in a small valley. One hill is higher than the rest and has red cliffs at the top. When I was feeding Marie I used to watch the rock doves come out from their nesting ledges." She was remembering aloud. "You come through the hills. We were coming east. There's only one entrance. From here we'd have to go northwest." She pointed beyond the first line of hills which reared up behind the empty huts.

"Can you take us there?" Jack said.

"I could try."

They left the following morning on horseback with blanket rolls behind the saddles, spades, a hand sieve and enough food to last four days. Each had a rifle in a saddle scabbard and Jack had brought a shotgun in case they saw bustards or guinea fowl. He was uncomfortable on a horse, having come to the saddle late in life, and did not like going much above a walk. But his horse could tripple and this gait enabled them to cover a great deal of territory without unduly tiring the animals. They rode all day

with the sun on their backs, and soon the sides of his shirt were black with sweat which, drying, left tiny lines of salt. They rode up through the hills behind the house. The scrub bush, usually a dun color, had greened with the rain and the desert floor was covered in tiny flowers. Jack was too uncomfortable and at the same time too intensely preoccupied with what they were doing to pay attention to the shy beauty of the flowering desert. He watched Susan. She was dressed, as was usual now, in male clothing and she wore an old felt hat pulled down over her brow. Seen from the rear she could have been any squat and dumpy male, black or white. Marie, on the other hand, although also wearing trousers and a shirt, invested them with a kind of elegance that drew his mind away from their objective. As she rode he saw her breasts rising and falling and he found himself wanting her. It was not the same feeling he'd had for Lily—when he thought of her his gut still twisted with longing—it was more one of acceptance. He did not regret the marriage; he had done well for himself, and physically she was a pleasure to look at and a pleasure to have in bed. But she was not Lily.

By four o'clock that afternoon he knew Susan had lost her way. She began to ride to the top of every low hill to try and find a landmark.

"I'm sure this is the right direction," she insisted.

"We'd best stop here," Jack said. They had halted on the edge of a small pan of water—they had been passing them all day— and they made their camp.

The following day a wind rose and began to blow the sand across the surface of the desert. Soon they tied handkerchiefs over their mouths as they pushed on into the northwest, their only guide being the sun, a pale yellow ball shining through the driven sand. Again they camped near water and Marie, who had gone to find wood, came back with a piece of iron about eight inches long.

"What is it?" she said.

Jack shook his head. It was so rusted and pitted by age that he could only guess. "Looks like a pistol barrel," he said. "Probably a Hottentot's." He tossed it over his shoulder and got on with making his fire.

The piece of iron *was* a pistol barrel. It had belonged to Bartolomeu Barreto. In his madness he had fired it at the ghost of Father John of the Rosary. It had not been seen or touched

since then, although termites had stripped it of its wood and rust had turned much of the remaining metal to dust.

The next morning they rode on into the wind. About noon Susan reined in her horse and said, "I'll never find it! We must start back before we finish the food."

"She has been lost since we set out!" Marie said, her voice rising. "She just wouldn't admit it."

Susan nodded. "I told you I wasn't sure."

"Let's go on for another three hours," Jack said. "You might see something you recognize."

They plowed on into the wind, but soon he noticed there was less flying sand and by early afternoon the wind was dying and visibility improved.

All at once Susan said, "What's that?"

She was pointing ahead. Jack stared at a hill in the distance. It was higher than the others.

"Are those cliffs near the top?"

They rode on a little farther until he could make out the cliffs of reddish stone.

"That's the hill!" Susan said.

They kicked their tired horses into a canter, Jack hanging on to the pommel with one hand. "Are you sure?" he shouted.

"Yes. Yes, I'm sure."

Low hills barred their way. "There should be a gap to the left," she said.

"It's there!" Marie cried. She was riding slightly ahead of the others.

Jack felt his heart racing. He could see the gap in the hills. It was like a natural road.

"This is where Frans brought the wagon out," Susan said.

The gap was, in fact, also rising ground and when they reached the top they were able to look down into the valley. It was exactly as Susan remembered it: away to the right was the high hill with the red cliffs and the valley itself was a natural basin. But there was one fundamental difference: the floor of the valley was now a single sheet of water. It was a natural pan and the summer rains had filled it. The three of them sat their horses and stared down at the shallow lake. There was no need for comment, each knew that the mudhole was buried somewhere under the water.

After a few moments Jack said, "How long will it take to dry up?"

"Months," Susan said. "Even if it stops raining now."

"Where's the mudhole?"

"In the middle."

"There *must* be something we can do!" Marie said.

"We can go home," Jack said.

He looked down at the slick of mud that had broken away from the back of the house like a river of lava. It was dry now, and cracking. In parts it was three or four inches thick. He supposed that in all there might have been a couple of tons of the stuff.

"What are you going to do?" Marie said, her voice dull with tiredness and depression. They had ridden without stopping from the waterlogged valley and had made the house by early morning, driving the horses in a direct line, flogging them on in their frustration. They'd had only a few hours of sleep. "What are you going to do?" she repeated.

"Pan it," he said. "I'll need help."

She brightened. "Do you think there could be . . . ?"

"Why not? We found one. We'll have to wash all this," he indicated the dry mud. "I'll dig it, you pan it down by the river."

"How will you get it there?"

"Wheelbarrow."

"You'll break your back. Can't we use the pump? If we pumped the water up to the holding tank you wouldn't have so far to go."

"Have you seen the pump? It's been flooded twice. It's almost covered in sand. It'll never work again."

"What do you want me to do?"

They found a large enamel basin in the kitchen and he pushed a load of dried mud down to the river.

"I ain't done much of this myself but I've seen it done. You put the spoil in and scoop up water. Swirl it round like this, letting out water all the time, until anything heavy sinks to the bottom." He looked round for something to act as a sorting table and found a large flat rock. He upturned the basin on it and sorted through the gravel tailings that the mud had left behind. "Nothing," he said. "But that's the way it's done. You think you can do it?"

"You just bring down the mud, Jack. I'll do the rest."

All that day he toiled away like a kaffir. He filled wheelbarrow after wheelbarrow and trundled them down the slope to the river. The distance was about one hundred and fifty yards and in the burning sunshine it was brutal work. At dusk he scooped up

the last of the mud and pushed it down to the river. They had found nothing.

That night they lay in the big double bed where once Susan had lain with Frans. Marie's optimism of the morning had vanished.

"I *can't* stay here!" she said.

"How do you think you'll like living in a tent with no money?"

"Better than here."

"I doubt it."

"All my life I've wanted to get away."

"What if we had money? What if I wanted to farm Portuguese Place?"

"Do you?"

He didn't reply, and lay with his hands behind his head in his characteristic position.

"Are you asleep?" she said.

"No."

"What are you thinking about?"

"Diamonds. There *must* be more. If you find one, there *have* to be more."

"They could be in the bricks," she said.

"If only we could have got to that mudhole. But it can't rain always. It'll dry up eventually and then . . ."

"That could take months. And if it goes on raining, it could be next year." She turned on her side to look at him. A single candle was burning and her skin glowed like honey. He saw that she had fine blond down on her breasts. They were firm and high, good breasts, the nipples and areolas almost black, but even as he looked at them he was seeing Lily, naked: the brilliant white skin, the black hair, the red lips, and he was remembering her breasts, remembering their whiteness and the blue veins that patterned the milky skin.

"What about the bricks?" she said.

"What about them?"

"The mud came from the bricks."

"You'd need to break the house down."

There was a long pause and at last she said, "What if we did?"

"What?"

"Break the house down."

"Don't be so soft. You can't break a house down. Anyway, what about your mother?"

258

"You're the man of the house. You can do anything."

Jack laughed uneasily. In one way she was right, he was the man of the house. But not legally. They had yet to go into Kimberley to draw up the papers. Would Susan *ever* part with her land? Was she another one who'd do him down? She had promised, but what the hell were promises? David, Lily. And now Aunt Susan . . .

Susan picked up a stone and placed it on Frans's grave. It was almost breakfast time and the sun was already hot. She had it in her mind that the burial had been a bad one, perfunctory. There had been rainwater in the grave and she was afraid that now animals might try to dig up the body. She fetched a second and a third stone. When she was satisfied she had enough she began to make her way back to the house. She saw Marie on the stoep. The poor child had hardly had time to know what marriage felt like, she thought, remembering her own early married life which now, in retrospect, was the most precious time she had experienced.

What was to become of them? she wondered. And then she thought, they had the farm and they had the house. They would never starve. As long as they had the land they could rebuild the herds and flocks. Where the money would come from she did not know, only that she would get it somehow. And as long as they had the house they would not only have shelter, they would be a family. This is what she would fight for. Jack and Marie would have children. The farm was their future.

Marie came down the steps of the veranda to meet her. "I want to talk to you," she said.

"It's too hot in the sun. Let's go inside."

"No, here."

"At least let's stand in the shade of the house."

They walked around to the side of the house, which Susan did not like to see now, where the back room had collapsed. It was like a scar on Frans's memory. She remembered him building it with his own hands.

"What is it?" she said.

"Jack thinks there may be more diamonds."

"Diamonds!" Susan was still weary from the long ride to the mudhole. "Can't you think of anything else?" There was anger on Marie's face and she took a pace towards her. "Can't you forget about diamonds? Haven't you seen what happens to people in

Kimberley? Haven't you seen what happened to Jack? Diamonds are an illusion, Marie, the pot of gold at the end of the rainbow. Most people never find them. Look around you; this is a farm, not a mine." She swung her hand to embrace the sunstricken dereliction. "Don't you remember the cattle and the sheep? *This* is your future. We'll build it up again. Listen! You'll have Jack's children. You'll put down roots. You'll live here and so will your children and their children."

"I hate it here!"

"I can understand that. You've been alone too much. There's been no one of your own age. But it'll be different with Jack here."

"And what will we eat?" Marie said.

"When we first came here we had nothing but our rifles and a shotgun—and we lived. We can do that again. Mopedi and Jack can shoot game and I'll teach you how to gather *veldkos* like the Bushmen did—the roots and the plants and the wild onions. That's how we lived when you were a baby."

Jack came to stand by Marie. "We don't want to live like that," she said, turning to him. "Do you want to eat roots and berries? We want people around us. Decent food. We want lights and money, don't we, Jack?"

"We'll get money," Susan said.

"Where? You know no one will lend us money, not after the *rinderpest*."

"If Jack helps . . ." Susan began, but Marie broke in.

"You're always asking Jack! You promised him land and you never did anything. Did she, Jack?"

Jack slowly shook his head.

Susan felt battered. She realized that they must have discussed this between them. She had never seen Marie so angry and even Jack's face was flushed and ugly. "What do you want, then?" she said. "If it is to be diamonds you'll have to wait until the countryside dries out and you can get to the mudhole."

"That could take six months to a year, depending on the rains," Jack said.

"There's enough mud here," Marie said.

"Mud? Here?"

"In the bricks." Marie pointed to the old part of the house, which was in a state of collapse.

Slowly, Susan realized what she meant. "But that . . ."

"Yes."

"But . . ." She turned to Jack. "That means knocking down the house."

"Not the whole house," Jack said. "Only the old part. The part that's been weakened."

"You must be mad! You don't knock down houses in the hope of finding a diamond. Why do you think I've fought to preserve this place? It's for you. For your children. When Frans and I came here, there was nothing. We built this, we created it. And now you want to tear . . ."

"You would preserve *anything*," Marie shouted. She had been whipping herself up into a rage. "You live either in the past or the future. You don't live in the present! We need money now. You say you'll rebuild the farm. How? Why save anything if we can't survive?"

"The old part's unsafe," Jack said. "Maybe we'll find something. Maybe then you'll have the money to rebuild."

Susan's slow anger grew. "I trusted you, Jack."

She could not have said anything worse, and she went on: "How could you think of a thing like that? You meant a lot to Uncle Frans and to me. Right from the very start we . . ."

"Don't listen to her!" Marie said.

". . . we took you in. When you were injured we gave you . . ."

"Stop it!" Marie shouted. "You're always doing this to people. Making them feel guilty. When it's you, *you* who are the guilty one!"

"You must hate this place even more than I thought," Susan said.

"Yes, but not only Portuguese Place."

There was no going back. "What else?"

There was a pause, a kind of stillness. Then Marie said, "You."

"What have I ever done but love and care for you?" Susan already knew the answer.

"You gave me your blood!"

Susan had a flash of memory: Marie examining her breasts and nipples in the long mirror; the half-caste girl in the village of Galilee; the journey home in the trap one day, when it had nearly spilled out.

"I hate you for that!" Marie said.

Susan's anger vanished; instead she felt only love and pity. "Oh, my dear, it's not what you think!" She moved forwards, but the girl backed away.

She knew she could protect her relationship with Marie—such as it was—by telling her what Frans had revealed before he died. But she stopped herself. That would mean the destruction of the memory of her dead husband. There was nothing she could say. Even if Jack had not been there, she could not have described to Marie what had happened in the wagon that night. She had never told a living soul and her secrecy had hardened to a point where she knew she never would. She put out her hand.

"Don't touch me!" Marie said.

Susan felt a shock travel up her body, ringing it like iron. She had never met such implacable hatred before and she felt helpless before it.

She looked to Jack as though for help, but his eyes were glittering with anger, mixed with bewilderment at the scene he had not understood. She turned away and walked down the slope, past Frans's grave and along the river by the Breakfast Pool where they had swum when Marie was a baby. She walked for a long time, and when she returned she saw Jack, a sledgehammer in his hands, smashing down the walls of the room in which Frans had so recently died.

Something inside her seemed to break then and she was never to feel quite the same again. She heard the crash, crash of the hammer and the rumble as bricks tumbled to the ground. And again the crash as Jack broke up the bricks into pieces and trundled them down to the river in the wheelbarrow where Marie was waiting with her basin.

She went to Mopedi and asked him to move the wagon and some furniture into a stand of willow, too young to have been cut, down by the river. She gave him the shotgun and asked him to bring back what birds he could. She took a *riempie* stool which Frans had made and sat on it with her back to the wagon wheel and watched as the walls of the room were smashed to pieces.

The house had been built with love and care. Frans had given it his great hunter's strength. It was a tough house and it took some breaking.

Jack had never worked so hard. He worked from the moment gray dawn enabled him to see what he was doing until darkness overtook the desert. He labored with a kind of dull frenzy, smashing bricks from the wall and then breaking them into small pieces, shoveling the pieces onto the wheelbarrow. With muscles

straining and joints cracking he would trundle the barrow—sometimes weighing nearly two hundredweight—down to the river, upend it on a pile of spoil and begin the slow push back up the hill to the house. All the while, he was aware of Susan's eyes on him. From the moment he started work at dawn she would bring out her *riempie* stool, sit on it and watch. She never spoke as he passed her, but it was like some specter, following every move he made.

The work itself became his cocoon. He worked because he could do nothing else. He believed that there must be more diamonds hidden within the bricks of the house because he could believe nothing else. But he also worked to blot out thought, for he knew that what he was doing was wrong.

Sometimes of an evening, when he and Marie were lying in bed, so tired that they could not even seek solace in each other's bodies, he would express his feelings and she would tell him *their* lives were at stake now and they had to look after themselves, for if they did not, no one else would. It was what he needed to hear and the next day he would go to work with a will—until he saw Susan take her place on the stool to watch him. One day, unable to stand her presence any longer, he went down to her and said, "Don't you see? It's the only way!" But she said nothing, simply looked through him. He felt the welcome anger. "Marie's right!" he burst out. "They're *our* lives!"

He worked for nine days and during that time he smashed down the old part of the house which it had taken Frans, including the time he had spent digging the mud, nearly nine months to build. Each brick was smashed from the wall and in turn smashed into small pieces, loaded into the barrow and wheeled down to the river. He did a good job and he was a neat worker. At the end of nine days there was a hole in the side of the house that looked as if some great animal had taken a clean bite.

Down at the river the pile of spoil grew until he was forced to take a second basin and help Marie wash the mud. The river had gone down since the last rains, and had cleared. But below where they worked the Breakfast Pool, once limpid and pure, was streaked with black.

On the tenth day, soon after breakfast, he heard Marie scream. The sound rose on the hot dry air, flushing doves from the river bush and sending them tearing away in fright. He heard it as he was raising the big sledgehammer to smash into a new part of the

house. His senses were so dulled that for a moment he thought she must have been bitten by a snake. Then he realized that the scream spelled not so much terror as bursting excitement. He dropped the hammer and ran. He ran past the ruined rooms, past the derelict kraals where the cattle and sheep had once been brought, past the patch of scrub willow where his mother-in-law sat, upright and watchful, on her stool. He ran past the bare stumps where the acacia trees had once grown, then been felled, and on down to the river. Marie was running to meet him, her sodden dress flapping with each step. They reached each other and stood, catching their breath: Jack, big, rawboned, red-haired; Marie, dark, smeared with mud; their clothes, once decent, sober garments, torn and stained. One of her breasts was almost visible through the rents in her bodice. She held out her right fist and slowly opened her fingers. Her skin was cracked and ingrained with mud; the nails were torn and blackened. In her palm was an object of irregular but mainly oblong shape about the size of a baby's fist. It was colorless, opaque, and looked like a lump of dirty glass. It was the diamond which Barreto had flung away in his dying moments. Its real life was about to begin.

"Sweet Jesus!" Jack said. He put out a finger to touch it. In spite of the day's heat, the stone felt cold, almost clammy. "Christ and Christ! We're rich!"

She flung her arms around his neck and lifted her feet from the ground. "We can do anything!" she cried.

"Rich!" he shouted. "Oh, by Christ, we're rich!"

Marie broke away from him and ran to her mother. She held her open hand close to Susan's face, forcing her to lean backwards. "I told you!" she shouted. "Father called them stone flowers but they're better than all the sheep and cattle in the world!"

"Don't you see, Aunt Susan?" Jack said. "Now you can build a whole new house if you've a mind to."

But Susan looked away and after a moment Marie said, "Leave her then. If she wants to stay, let her stay."

As they turned Susan spoke. "You'll never have Portuguese Place," she said. "Never."

"Are you drunk?" Marie said, laughing.
"Me? How can I be drunk?" Jack said.
They were a mile or two from Kimberley and he was standing

up in the Scotch cart. As the two big wheels hit potholes and he swayed they laughed boisterously.

"There it is!" he cried, pointing to the dust that hung over the town.

"Wheeee!" Marie shouted, standing up and clinging to him.

This had been their mood all the way to town. It was late in the afternoon and the mules, which had been flogged into a canter, now dragged their feet in the sand and held their heads low.

"What are we going to do first?" she asked.

"We're going to the hotel and we're going to book the best room. . . ."

"The suite. The top-floor suite."

"The suite, then."

"And?"

"Hot water. Buckets of hot water. And a bath big enough for both of us. And champagne for you and whisky for me."

"And then?"

"And then the finest foods in town. What's that stuff the Russians eat?"

"Caviar."

"That's it. Caviar and . . ." His mind groped for examples of fine food, but since he had never had any he was reduced to saying, ". . . and kidney pies and sausages and beefsteak. A good thick beefsteak."

"And fruit," Marie said. "Grapes."

"We'll have bunches of grapes!"

She laughed but the sound was swallowed up in a roll of thunder, for dark clouds hung over the diggings.

"Rain as much as you like!" she cried. "We don't care!" She flung her words into the hot wind that blew across the plains. Jack touched the great diamond which he had wrapped in a hand-kerchief and pinned into his trouser pocket. No, he thought, they didn't care! Not for rain. Or dust. Or heat. Or cold. They need never care about such things again.

The streets were almost deserted as they entered the town and so was the hotel lobby. They booked the top-floor suite. The desk clerk seemed only too pleased to serve them in spite of their dusty, tattered appearance.

"And you can send up a bottle of the best French champagne and a bottle of the best Scotch whisky," Jack said. "We want the

biggest bath you've got. Big enough for a half a dozen. Buckets of hot water. Lashings of it."

The clerk, a young, sandy-haired man, new to the job and unsure of himself, said, "I'm sorry, sir, but we've had trouble with the water tanks."

"You mean you ain't got hot water?"

"We haven't any at all, sir, hot or cold."

"Damn and blast!" Jack said. Then he had an idea. "You've got soda water, haven't you? How many bottles do you think will fill the bath?"

The clerk looked stunned. "I don't know, sir, we've never tried."

"Well, we're going to try now. You send up that bath and go on sending cases of soda water until I tell you to stop. And don't forget the drink."

The suite had been refurnished since the Delports had rented it. The wallpaper was of chintz and the furniture included buttoned chairs and settees in snuff-colored velvet. The bedroom contained an enormous brass bedstead.

"Put it down there," Jack told the two black waiters who had brought the bath. It was a large copper affair with ample room for two. The waiters reentered, each carrying a case of soda water. "Start filling it," he said.

It took the wide-eyed waiters nearly half an hour. They made trip after trip. Jack had no idea how many bottles it took, but when it was about two-thirds full he said, "That's enough." He locked the door after them.

They both stripped and the soda water fizzed as they lowered themselves gently into it. "It tickles," she cried.

He laughed. "Now, where's the champagne and my whisky?"

It was the strangest bath either had ever had. In spite of the fact that it was cold, the day was so muggy and hot that the bursting bubbles felt like tiny prickles on the skin. It cooled and titillated them at the same time. They began to touch each other and before long he scooped her up, dripping wet, flung her onto the bed and had her there, and for the first time it was almost as good as it had been with Lily.

When it was over she said, "Is the bed still here?"

His feet had tangled in the brass struts and one or two of them had bent where he had used them as leverage.

It was dusk by the time they had dressed in clean clothing.

"Now we'll go and have those Russian fish eggs," Jack said, feeling better than he had ever felt in his life.

The lobby was still deserted but when they reached the street they heard the far-off shouting of men's voices and as they went up Stockdale Street Jack saw one or two diggers, running.

He caught one by the shoulder. "What's going on? Is it a fight?"

The man shook off his hand. He shouted something which Jack failed to hear and plunged on up the street.

"What did he say?" Marie asked.

Jack shook his head.

"There's Uncle Helmut. Let's ask him."

Helmut Lessing was working at a forge set back from the street. He was finishing a horseshoe on his anvil. He picked it up with long-handled tongs and dropped it, hissing, into a half barrel filled with water.

"What's happening?" Marie called.

The squat German straightened up. He was wearing a blacksmith's leather apron and holding a three-pound hammer in his right hand.

"Vot is happening? You should know vot is happening! T'ousands und t'ousands of diggers, ja, but now look at them! Nowhere to sell. No one to buy. So they come together like frightened sheep!"

Jack felt his heart jerk. "What do you mean, no one to buy?"

"The buyers are closed."

"But it's not a holiday," Marie said.

"Why are they closed?" Jack said. "For Christ's sake, tell us!"

"They vill not buy more diamonds because of the . . . I do not know the name in English. The star . . ."

"Star?"

"That is falling."

"Jesus!" Jack said.

He ran back to the hotel and found the clerk, who told him the news: how word had arrived the day before that a large meteorite had fallen in a remote part of Mexico. It was said to be the size, according to one report at least, of a hotel. Another said it was the size of a city block. But the important thing for Kimberley was that those who had seen it declared it to be made of solid diamond. Jack did not need to be told the significance, but Marie did.

"This means there's enough diamond to supply the world for a

thousand years," he said savagely. "You won't be able to give the stuff away! Come on!"

They made for the square from which the shouting was coming. There were half a dozen separate meetings going on, with speakers standing on old candle boxes. Crowds were milling around the office of the *Diamond and Vaal Advertiser* and there were more frightened diggers outside the telegraph office, all waiting for the latest news.

Jack had tried desperately not to believe the story but now, as he tugged Marie through the jostling crowds and saw the expressions of panic and despair on the faces and felt the tension in the air, he was finally convinced of the bitter truth. He visited the offices of the established diamond buyers, one after another, and beat on the doors, but they remained uncompromisingly shut.

"What will we do?" Marie said.

He had almost forgotten her. He released her wrist and she rubbed it. What *would* they do? They could not go back to the hotel because they did not have enough money to pay for what they had so lavishly consumed.

As though reading his mind she said, "What about David? Now that the old people have gone, there's room in his house."

"No."

"Why not? He has stayed at Portuguese Place."

"No."

"But . . ."

"I said no."

They stood in the street, with diggers passing on either side, then Jack said, "This way."

"Where to?"

"For Christ's sake, don't bloody ask questions! Do as I tell you."

Her face set in a sullen frown, she followed him along the street.

The old tent was still standing, as he had hoped, but everything in it was damp. He lit the lantern and they inspected the interior. There was mildew on the canvas beds and on the blankets folded away in the chest. Rainwater had come through the sides and the floor was muddy.

"We can't stay here," she said despairingly.

"There's nowhere else."

He took a long time to go to sleep. Each time he thought of the

big diamond he felt sick in the pit of his stomach. Early the following morning, leaving Marie asleep, he dressed and went down into the town to Arendt's house. Although it was not yet breakfast time the streets were filled with little knots of men, most standing silent, puffing at pipes, waiting for news.

The servant let him in and told him that Peter was still in bed.

"Tell him Mr. Farson is here."

Arendt arrived after a few minutes, fastening himself into a long blue satin dressing gown with frogging on the chest. His hair was awry and his plump, soft face pink and creased from the pillows.

"It's very early . . ." he began.

"I want to see you for a minute. It's important."

"Come into the music room."

Jack placed the diamond on a table underneath the window. Arendt approached it on the balls of his feet, like a cat, and stared at it. "My God!" he said, under his breath. He picked it up. The stone had been cleaned of its mud and now its icy interior held an incandescent fire. "Where did you find this?"

"Never mind that. I want to know two things: is it a diamond? I says as how it is, but I want to be sure. The second is, how do I sell it?"

Arendt left the room and came back with a loupe and a pair of balances. He held the stone in the morning light for a long time and looked at it from every angle. At last he put it on the scales and weighed it. Jack could see beads of perspiration on his brow. He opened his mouth to speak, closed it, opened it again, and when he did speak his voice was hoarse.

"It is perfect. A perfect diamond. First water. Do you know what it weighs?" Jack shook his head. "Six hundred and thirty carats. I tell you this: it is the best rough diamond I have ever seen."

"I thought it was. Now what do I do?"

"You know what has happened?"

"Yes."

"Two days ago if you had brought me this diamond you would have been one of the richest men in Kimberley. But today . . ." He held up his hands. "Today I could not give you the price of a new suit. My father has cabled to stop all buying."

"What about the meteorite?" Jack said.

"You know as much as I do."

"Tell me this: is it true?"

"It *could* be. A meteorite fell in Siberia a couple of years back. It was made of nickel-iron and they found diamonds in it. Not many, but some. Another one fell in Arizona and all they found were diamond crystals. Nothing like this new one, if the story is true."

"Do you believe it?"

"It matters not if I believe it. My father does. All the other buyers do."

Jack picked up the diamond, wrapped it carefully and pinned it into his pocket.

"What are you going to do?" Peter said.

"Nothing."

"Believe me, I would give an arm to be able to buy that diamond."

"Yes. Well . . . Tell David I'm at the tent."

"He is in Cape Town buying for the store. I expect him back in a few days."

At the door Jack paused and cleared his throat. "What do you hear of Lily?" he said.

"She does well. A recital at the Queen's Hall. Then she will tour in *Lucia*."

"I don't mean that. I mean, how *is* she?"

Peter stared at him. "Happy," he said. "She says she misses us." There was a slight stress on the word "us." "But she is happy."

So began for Jack the worst time he had ever known, far worse than sailing the Great Southern Ocean in midwinter, worse than digging in the heat of the African sun, worse than cutting down timber along the Green River.

Later that day he walked up to the rim of the great crater mine. It was eerie. No one was working. Many of the claims, including New Chance, were filled with water from the unremitting rains. Pulleys stood idle, the ladders went down to empty claims, the web of cables that crossed the hole swayed in the morning breeze—and that was the only movement. He strolled around the rim, seeing the empty sorting tables, the piles of spoil, the "babies" no longer being rocked to sieve the gravel. It was a catastrophe on a gigantic scale. He sat down on an upturned box and stared at the desolation. It reminded him of Portuguese Place. It did not take much in Africa, it seemed, to wipe out the work of men.

He heard footsteps crunch on the gravel behind him and turned to see Dan Halkett.

"What are you going to do?" Jack said after a moment.

"Wait, like the others," Dan said. "I don't believe everything that's said. If diamonds fell from the sky we'd have known about them before."

"But what if it is true?"

"Joe and me'll make out. There's gold been found in the eastern Transvaal. We'll go there."

"Is there anything owing?" Jack said.

Halkett shook his head. "I wish there was. What with all the rain we haven't been able to dig."

So there was not even a few pounds to come from the lease of New Chance. When you were down, Jack thought, you were really down. He and Marie had nowhere to go, for he knew that after his destruction of Portuguese Place they could never go back there, to face Susan again. He tried not to think about Susan but the figure in the black dress haunted him and he would often have to make a concentrated effort to dispatch it. When he looked back at what he had done he realized that he had destroyed not only part of a house he had known and loved, but a relationship that was important to him, which he had cherished without even being aware of it. Now that it was gone he knew it was something irreversible and something he would miss for the rest of his life. Knowing this was like an ulcer in his mind, sometimes quiescent, at other times inflamed; it was the central core of his wretchedness.

He went into town to try and find a job to earn a few shillings. He tried everything he could think of, including a visit to Helmut Lessing. But the blacksmith said, "I cannot get work for myself. I wish it were otherwise, but times are bad."

Many diggers were spending the last of their money on seats on the coaches going south, but most were walking and lines of men trailed out over the desert to the track that led to the Cape six hundred and more miles away. Many would never get there. Some men sat in their tents and waited. There had been other panics before and they had sat them out. They would sit this one out or go bust trying.

Over the next few days their little supply of money dwindled to nothing. Marie heard that David had returned and pleaded with Jack to go to him for a loan. Finally he shouted at her, "Don't say

it again!" and he raised his right hand to lash her across her face. He stopped just in time and they looked at each other in horror.

And then one afternoon he came back after trying in vain to get a few shillings together to buy bread and found her in the tent in tears. She was sitting on her bed clutching a lump of bloody meat.

"Where did you get that?" he said.

"Uncle He-e-lmut," she said, between sobs. It was half a haunch of venison.

"Well, why the hell are you crying?"

"Because I can't cook it."

"Why not?"

There was no fuel.

It seemed to Jack the final irony. In his pocket was the largest diamond he had ever seen, which he could not sell. In his tent was a luscious, belly-filling lump of meat which they could not cook because they could not afford a few sticks to build a fire.

After a moment he said, "Wait here." He picked up a battered old cake tin.

"Where are you going?" she said.

"To find something to burn."

David Kade and Peter Arendt were in their office. Spread out on the table which was normally used to sort diamonds was a copy of the *Diamond and Vaal Advertiser*. It was a special single-sheet edition devoted entirely to the crisis. Peter had brought it in only a few minutes before and the two men stood reading it. The headline said:

MEXICAN GOVERNMENT DISPATCHES
EXPEDITION TO INVESTIGATE
"DIAMOND" METEORITE

WORLD MARKETS COLLAPSE
KIMBERLEY "COULD BECOME
GHOST TOWN"

Then came the stories. The main one was an account of the scientific expedition hastily organized by the Mexican Government to take samples from the meteorite, which had crashed to earth in the wild Sierra Madre mountains northwest of Durango.

There were reports from Indians that it could be seen shining from thirty miles away when the sun struck it.

"What do you really think?" David said.

Peter shrugged. "In this business you never know. One day you have a piece of desert, the next thousands of people dig it up and find diamonds."

"But a meteorite! It just doesn't seem possible."

"Likely, no, but possible . . . perhaps."

"What a chance," David said thoughtfully.

"What do you mean?"

"If it wasn't true. We could be buying up stones for next to nothing."

"Remember what C. J. Rhodes said at the meeting: if diamonds are allowed to flood the market, the price will end up on the floor."

"Don't you think the Mexican Government knows that?"

"Maybe. Maybe not. That is the problem, we don't know anything. It takes weeks for news to get here. But if I were a speculator there is one stone I would have bought. Have you seen Jack Farson?"

"He was out at Portuguese Place. I heard he had married Marie Delport."

"He's back. They're living in the tent."

"The tent!"

"He's got the best rough diamond I've ever seen. He can't sell it."

David suddenly felt a pang of conscience. His own life had become so bound up with the shop and with the diamond business and generally with making money—he already had a thousand pounds in the safe—that he had forgotten about Jack.

"How did he look?"

"Thin."

That evening he went out to search for Jack. There was no place in his new life for the old quarrel and it seemed a good time to allow it to be forgotten.

There was no one at the tent. He had not slept there for a long time, and it depressed him. He saw the damp patches and smelled the mildew and remembered the early days when he and Jack had thought how lucky they were to have it. As he was leaving, a black man came towards him. It was Mopedi, the servant from Portuguese Place.

"Baas Jack?" Mopedi said, looking past him to the tent.

"He's not there."

"The young missus?"

"She's not there either."

Mopedi shifted from one foot to the other. "Is there anything wrong?" David said.

"The old missus." He pointed towards a wagon stopped on the road. David followed him and, in the back, found Susan lying on a mattress. She was unconscious. There were abrasions on her head and neck and her left arm and hand were swathed in a bedsheet through which blood had seeped. She seemed to be on the point of death.

"What happened?"

"A wall fall on her."

David questioned him and from what he could make out, Susan had been building a wall with stones from the river and it had collapsed.

They took her to Dr. Hibbert's consulting room in the Market Square. He cut away the sleeve and David saw jagged pieces of bone sticking through the flesh.

"Wait outside, please," the doctor said. After a while he came out, polishing his spectacles nervously on a handkerchief, and said, "I've done what I can, but she needs specialist treatment in hospital if she is going to save the arm. It can't be done here. Cape Town's the nearest place."

"I'll take her home with me," David said. "Then I'll find her daughter and son-in-law."

They carried her the few steps to the Emporium and Hilda put her on the bed in her parents' old room.

David drove round Kimberley in the trap. He asked for Jack at several bars, but no one had seen him. It was late in the afternoon and he decided to check the tent again. He took a short cut past the stock pens where Mr. Levinson had once shown him the animals he bought and sold. Wagons were coming in from the outlying farms with wood and water. He kept away from the rutted track and drove the trap over the open veld. In the dusk he saw the figures of the black women following the wagons, waiting for the bullocks to defecate so they could scoop up the dung. He was about fifty yards away from the road when he saw a figure dart forwards to pick up a half-dried turd. At first he thought it was a black man and then, with a sick feeling in his stomach, he stopped the trap and found himself looking down at

Jack's crouching figure. As long as he lived, David would never forget that moment: the big red-haired man, his face thin and bottle-jawed, looking up at him, his hands on the dung. Everything they had ever gone through together seemed to fuse into one solid moment in David's mind. He threw down the reins. "Jack!" he cried, jumping down from the trap. "Jack, for God's sake!"

For a second a look came into Jack's eyes which he had only seen once before, when he had laughed at him for his inability to read and write. But it cleared almost instantly.

"What are you doing?" he heard himself ask fatuously.

"Collecting fuel."

"Yes . . . yes. I know that. But . . . why didn't you come to me? Why?"

Jack stared at him without replying. His hands and forearms were covered in greenish muck. "You'd never ask me for anything, would you?" David said, more to himself than to Jack. "Not if you were starving." Again Jack made no reply. "Well, not even you can fight circumstances all the time." He told him briefly what had happened to Susan.

"Where is she?" There was real distress in his tone.

"At the shop."

Marie was at the tent. While Jack washed she said, "Is she very bad?"

"Very."

By the time they reached the shop, Hilda had bathed Susan's face, neck and legs. Marie looked down at the still figure and David waited for her to do something. But it was Jack who made the move. He went down on his knees. "Aunt Susan!" he said softly.

Marie said to him, "What are we going to do?"

He shifted his weight as a flush slowly suffused his cheeks. "I . . ." he began helplessly.

"The doctor says she'll die if she stays here."

"He didn't put it quite like that," David said.

"But that's what he meant, didn't he?" Hilda said.

Again they waited for Jack, now the head of the family, the breadwinner, to tell them what he proposed.

"I . . ." he began again.

David touched him on the arm and said, "Come into the living room." Jack followed him.

David opened a safe which had been made to look like a cabinet. He rummaged in it and took out a wad of notes, his share so far of both the shop's profits and the diamond operation.

"There's nearly a thousand pounds there. Take it," he said.

Jack stared at the money.

"Take it, Jack. Take it as a loan to be paid back whenever you can. For God's sake, don't be proud! Her life depends on it. You can get her on a special coach tonight. Dr. Hibbert said he'd make up medicines for the journey."

Jack made an effort to speak, but only a strangulated grunt emerged.

"If there's anything left over you can buy stock for the farm. Come on, Jack, forget the past. For once put your pride in your pocket and take what's offered."

Jack fumbled in his pocket and brought out a dirty piece of cloth. He undid a knot. David looked at the object he held in his hand and began to shake. All thoughts that the diamond market might be ruined forever left him. He saw only the most magnificent stone he had ever dreamt of seeing.

"It may not be worth much now, but who knows?" Jack said. David took the stone and looked at it in the lamplight. "It's a genuine, all right," Jack said. "Peter looked it over."

"It's worth ten times . . . more than ten times . . ."

"I won't borrow."

"If that's how you want it." David put the money in a thick manila envelope. "You'd best hurry."

David got to bed late that night and it was nearly dawn before he finally went to sleep. The coach leaving at midnight had been fully booked so Jack had chartered a special for the three of them, with enough room for Susan to lie down. She had been awake and in great pain, and Dr. Hibbert had given her laudanum. But it wasn't so much the activity of seeing them off to the Cape that had overstimulated David's mind. Nor was it the argument he had had with Hilda about having given Jack the money. (He had finally silenced her by saying angrily that it was *his* money and he would do what he liked with it.) No, it was the thought of the diamond. The fact that it might be worthless hardly entered his head; it was worth everything to him. In the early hours he began to plan how it would be cut.

He woke late and by the time he had breakfasted and shaved it was almost midmorning, but it was a Sunday and the shop was closed. He dressed and went to the office he shared with Arendt. Normally at this time on a Sunday morning the streets would have been empty. Instead he saw dozens of diggers, their packs on their backs, striking out for the road to the gold strike in the eastern Transvaal.

The office was empty but there was a telegraph form on Peter's desk and several sheets of paper on which he had been writing. David looked at the telegram. It was from Berlin and the message was in code. He knew that Peter kept the international codes in his desk, but it was locked. He looked more closely at the sheets of paper. Two contained rows of figures which he assumed had to do with Peter's buying and selling, but the third had writing on it. He was about to pick it up when Peter came in.

"I've been looking for you," he said. "I searched for you all over town last night."

David told him about Susan's accident, but he was hardly listening. He put his hand into his pocket and brought out a tobacco tin. He opened it and poured a shining, glittering stream of diamonds onto the green baize table. "Look at that!" he said.

"My God, where did you get those?" They represented, in normal times, thousands upon thousands of pounds.

"I bought them. For next to nothing."

David looked at him, wondering if he had taken leave of his senses.

Peter picked up the sheet of paper from his desk. "This came late yesterday from my father. It says: 'Our Mexican representative says Mexican Government about to deny meteorite rumors stop buy buy buy stop.' So I bought only the best. I could have had ten times as many. But there is one I wanted above all these. Have you seen Jack?"

David touched the diamond in his pocket. It was bigger and better than anything Arendt had bought. He was about to tell him what had happened when there was a noise of shouting from the street outside. Peter flung open the door and they went out into the hot sunshine. The shouting turned into cheers. Men were running from the direction of the square. One gave a whoop and kicked his legs in the air. In a few moments the streets were filled with raucous shouting and singing; some diggers were even dancing. Peter and David walked swiftly to the square.

"What's happening?" David asked a man who was solemnly dancing a little jig.

"All lies," the man said. "All damned lies! All bloody damned Mexican lies!" He danced into the milling crowd.

Later that morning the *Diamond and Vaal Advertiser* put out another special single-sheet edition. METEOR A FAKE, screamed the single heavy headline. Underneath there were only half a dozen lines which had reached Kimberley by telegraph. The meteorite was said to have entered the atmosphere at such a high temperature that where it landed it had fused the sand into glass; glass, but not diamond. It was glass which had been seen glinting in the Mexican sunshine. That day everyone in Kimberley who had a shilling or two to spare spent it in a bar or cosie. By afternoon it was almost impossible to fight your way to the counter for a drink. Madame Delatee's French Café, by comparison, was soberly empty.

In keeping with the fluctuating and eccentric nature of the diamond business, famine now became feast. The price of diamonds recovered to the level before the meteorite crisis, and not only recovered, but began to strengthen. The reason was that where there had recently been too many diamonds, there were now too few, since no one in his right mind had been looking for stones for which no buyer would offer. Suddenly all was reversed. Diamonds were in demand as they had never been before. More telegrams began arriving in Kimberley from the great diamond houses of Amsterdam, Antwerp, Paris and London. It was even said that in Asscher's Diamond Works in Amsterdam cutters and polishers were being laid off because there were no stones to cut. So everyone rushed back to the huge crater which the mine at Kimberley had now become, only to find that half of the claims were still flooded and therefore unworkable. It was Dan Halkett who, in his practical way, helped to solve the new crisis and, in doing so, changed many lives.

One day, he and Joe Malone came to see David in his office at the rear of the shop.

"You tell it," Malone said.

"No, Joe," Halkett said. "It was you who first thought of it."

This was a different Joe Malone. The heartbreaking lack of success had taken its toll. He no longer saw riches over the next horizon. David had heard he was drinking again. But the

comradeship between the two men seemed as sound as ever.

"Well, it's like this," Joe said, in his slow drawl. "Me and Dan ain't doing much good digging for diamonds. You'll know that better than anyone. And now there's three feet of water in most of the claims around New Chance. It'll take weeks and weeks before they're fit to mine again—and that's only if we don't get no more rain. So I got thinking. In Colorado once, at a place called Cripple Creek, we was mining for silver when it rained and rained and we got flooded. But we didn't sit on our fannies like they do here. We got pumps working and we cleared that water."

"If we had a pump we could do the same thing," Dan said.

"It would take months to bring—wait a minute . . . !"

"That's it," Joe said. "I remembered that Jack had come with old man Delport to help bring the pump up. We could use that."

"I don't think it's been used for a long time," David said, remembering the derelict farm. "It may not work."

"I think I could get it to work." Dan spoke with quiet conviction.

"Let me get this straight," David said. "You want to go into business with the pump and stop mining altogether. Is that it?"

"If we can buy the pump," Joe said. "There's always work for a pump. We thought of sinking boreholes for drinking water. We could use the pump for that as well. But what we ain't got is cash to buy it with. That's why we've come. . . ."

"You wouldn't have to buy it. Not to start with, anyway. There's no one to buy it *from*." He told them what had happened at Portuguese Place.

Dan looked doubtful. "You mean, we should just take the pump?"

"Why not? It's not doing any good where it is and we could pay Mrs. Delport a percentage."

Two days later, Joe, Dan and David went to Portuguese Place in the trap, having sent a wagon and several black servants out the day before. Once again David was struck by the devastation wrought first by the *rinderpest* and then by Jack with his long-handled ax. They paused at the house. Shutters flapped in the breeze and there was a derelict air about it as it festered in the blinding sunshine. They stared at the broken section. It was clear that someone had been trying to rebuild the original rooms with walls of river stones. David assumed this was where Susan's accident had occurred. One of the walls had simply come

tumbling down. But what had happened to the original rooms? Where had they vanished to? No one could guess. They walked down to the river.

The pump was in a poor way. It had been flooded twice and river sand had got into the boiler and the valves. Driftwood had banged into it and started to pile up beside it. It had a pathetic air, like some mechanical leviathan left to die in a strange and unfamiliar world. Dan brushed sand off the side until the letters "The Invincible, J. A. M. Gwynne, Hammersmith, London," became visible.

"I'll have to take it to pieces," Dan said. "I'll be a few days."

"I'll go back," David said. "Come and see me when you're ready."

He left the two men and the servants to the job of salvaging the pump and walked slowly up to the house. A hot wind was blowing through the Green River valley and something moved on the ground and caught the periphery of his vision. He turned and saw that a piece of cloth was flapping in the breeze. Then he noticed that the cloth was wrapped around a buried object. He went to investigate. A roughly fashioned wooden cross lay on the ground. He bent and picked up the object next to it, which had first attracted his attention. It was Susan's big Portuguese Bible, wrapped in oilskin. He looked at it, frowning. This was Frans's grave then, and the Bible must have been buried with him. Someone or something had been digging under the cross, possibly jackals or hyenas trying to get at the corpse. He reerected the cross and placed more heavy stones on the grave. Then he picked up the Bible, made his way to the trap and drove himself back to town.

Halfway there he touched the diamond in his trouser pocket, and he forgot about the Bible and the pump—in fact, about everything but the stone. It felt almost alive, communicating its energy, almost burning his flesh through the cloth. He took it out to look at it. He set the loupe in his eye and examined it in the afternoon sun and he was taken back once again to the room where his grandfather conducted his business, to the security of the big armchair and the aroma of hot chocolate. "What do you see, *dushka?*" the old man would ask, and always his reply would be the same: "Fire and ice." And now, he thought as he looked into the crystal cave of the diamond, here was the fire and the ice, heat, cold, brilliance—and he *owned* it. After a while he put it

away and let the horses have their heads as they dragged tiredly over the desert floor.

For the next week he was busier than he had ever been, and so was Kimberley. From the depths of its depression it reemerged with even more than its old exuberance. Diamonds were scarce, prices were high. Men who had stones were selling them well. Diggers were flocking back and everyone seemed to be wanting supplies. Hilda was worked off her feet in the shop. David spent the mornings helping her and the afternoons trying to find good diamonds to buy. His own supply of ready cash was small after what he had given to Jack and he was forced to borrow from the bank.

Dan and Joe returned from Portuguese Place and while he did not have the time to go and see them, he heard they were setting up the pump to clear New Chance and that there was a queue of other owners who wanted their claims pumped out. It seemed that at last Joe and Dan were in the money.

At dusk one evening as he was closing the office and was about to return to the shop for his supper, there was a knock at the door and Dan Halkett came in.

"I hear you've got going at last," David said.

Dan sat down in the chair opposite him and David saw that his face was graver than usual.

"There's nothing wrong, is there? Joe's all right?"

"Joe's all right. He's in town somewhere."

"You want me to help you to look for him?"

"Leave him be."

"Is it the pump? I thought it looked pretty bad."

"It's not the pump. That's working a treat. But we've gone through the yellow ground. There couldn't have been more than a few inches left and the pump sucked it up with the water."

So that was it. New Chance was finished. The yellow ground had finally given out. David found he no longer really cared.

"I got into the blue ground this morning. There was still water in the claim, so I went on pumping." He paused.

"You pumped out blue ground?" David said.

Dan nodded. "I wanted to make some adjustments to the valves before I moved the pipes to a new claim. "And . . ." He paused again.

"And . . . ?" David said.

Dan felt in his pocket, pulled out a drawstring tobacco bag, opened the mouth and poured three diamonds onto the desk. They were of mixed size but the smallest, David saw, would go more than twenty carats. As usual when he saw good stones his heart began to race. He stared at them. "I don't understand," he said. "I thought you said you'd pumped the blue ground. These must have come from the yellow."

Dan shook his head. "That's what I came to tell you. These are from the blue ground."

"But that's impossible! Everyone says that there's nothing in the blue ground."

"I know," Dan said simply.

The two men looked at each other. David felt the hair on the back of his neck prickle. "You're sure?"

"Positive."

"Does anyone else know?"

Dan shook his head. "Not even Joe."

David let his breath out in a long whistle. "Do you realize what this means?" he said.

"It means that there are seams in the blue ground holding diamonds."

David sat in Mr. Bulchand's office and waited for the "arrangements" to be made by Niki. Like almost everyone in Kimberley he had heard of Bulchand, but had never seen him. Had he thought about him at all, it would have been with mild unease; at no time could he ever have imagined himself sitting in the straight-backed chair by the plain table in the wood and corrugated-iron shack, waiting for an audience. His palms were sweating and his heart was thumping in his ears. Ever since Dan Halkett had come to him the day before he had been nervous. He had known at once that he was on the brink of something great; something that could make his name as well known as that of C. J. Rhodes or Barnato; something that, handled correctly, could make his fortune and also make him a power, not only in Kimberley, but in the City of London, in Antwerp, in Amsterdam and Paris, even in New York. But more than that, diamonds in southern Africa were fast becoming a political power base. C. J. Rhodes was so powerful now that when he spoke, the British Government listened. His plans, so David had heard, were grandiose: the annexation, no less, of huge tracts of land in south central Africa

in the name of the British Crown. He was also moving into the politics of the Cape Colony and some said he would be prime minister one day. This kind of future might be ahead of David himself. He found himself wanting it with all his heart, but at the same time he was frightened. It was not like running a shop or a small diamond-buying business. What he was contemplating was the launching of an empire of which he would be the emperor. And what frightened him as much as anything was that becoming an emperor would put him into direct conflict with men like C. J. Rhodes and Barnato, the Joels, Beit, Robinson and groups like the French Company. Not one of these magnates wished for additional competition and they would clearly try to break him. In spite of the evening's heat, he shivered.

Bulchand came in with his son. David rose to shake hands and noticed immediately how beautifully his hands were kept. He was dressed, as always, in dove-gray; his hair was gray; the tufts of hair that grew from his ears were gray; only his skin was light brown.

"My father says, how can he help you?" Niki said. David watched as the plump, smooth, oiled young man took his place behind his father's chair.

He had planned exactly what he was going to say but had not realized it would have to be translated. This made him uncertain at first, but gradually he became more confident. He spoke directly to Bulchand and felt that the old man understood far more than he let on. The gist of what he had to say was simple and easily understood: diamonds had never been found in the blue ground before; therefore whoever could buy up claims could mine the blue ground for a totally new source of diamonds. But he would need money to buy up the claims and money for special machinery, for mining would eventually have to follow the seams of blue gravel underground, as coal is mined. It would no longer simply be a case of hacking pieces out of the desert floor.

"My father says, how much do you require?"

David took a deep breath. "Fifty thousand pounds."

Bulchand's eyebrows rose.

"My father says, why you not go to a bank for such a sum?"

"Because people in banks talk. I've got to buy as many claims near New Chance as I can. Once the word gets out the big companies will move in and fifty thousand will not buy a single

claim. I came to Mr. Bulchand because I was told that above all he does not speak of his clients' business."

Bulchand smiled a small, prim smile.

"And another reason is that banks take time," David said. "They want to know everything about you and then they think about it and discuss it and finally, when it is too late, they come to a decision. I must have this money now. If I don't buy the claims within the next few days someone else is going to find diamonds in the blue ground. The only way I can make a success of this is to act fast and in secret."

"My father says this is a gamble. He is not in business to gamble."

"It may be a gamble to him, but I know mining. It is a certainty."

"My father says, what will you put up as security while you gamble?"

David swallowed. "I have a half share in Levinson's Emporium." From a briefcase he took out a contract and put it on the table.

Niki was about to pick it up and read it but his father put a hand on it and pushed it gently aside. "My father says a fifty-percent share in Levinson's Emporium would not cover a quarter of the money you asked for."

"I have a half share in New Chance, where diamonds have already been found in the blue ground."

Again he pulled out a contract and placed it on the table and again Bulchand moved it to one side on top of the other paper.

"My father says this is the gamble-mine. You cannot put up a gamble as security to cover a gamble."

Father and son waited.

"I have nothing else," David said.

The silence grew until finally he knew he was losing them. He felt a surge of desperation. They couldn't leave him now, not when he had worked out exactly how to pull off this coup. Suddenly he thought of something. He put his hand into his pocket and pulled out the big diamond he had bought from Jack. He placed it on the table where the lamplight fell on it. He heard Niki's sudden intake of breath. Bulchand's hand went out, shook slightly and drew back. The great rough diamond sat there in the middle of the table, winking at them, boasting of its purity. "Do you call that a gamble?" David said.

After a moment Niki cleared his throat and spoke rapidly in Turkish to his father.

"My father says, did this diamond come from the New Chance claim?"

A lie rose to David's lips. Then he knew how he could phrase it without lying. "Do you think I would have come to your father for money if I could have bought this stone?"

Bulchand nodded.

"My father says, why did you not sell it to raise the money?"

"Tell your father he knows very well that until a few days ago no one in Kimberley was buying stones. And he also knows that to sell such a stone well I would have to go to Paris or Berlin or London and by that time there would be nothing left of the mine for me to buy."

Bulchand smiled. It was the logic that he liked: simple, elegant. Deep down in him there was a gambler—he had gambled when he had first bought the cartload of pumpkins—but he liked gambling on a certainty and this was as near a certainty as anything in Kimberley was ever likely to be.

But there was another reason why he decided to lend David the money he wanted, a reason that David would never know: Bulchand was one of the wealthiest men in Kimberley. He had a big house, he wore the best suitings, he had a black footman to drive his trap. In Smyrna he would have been a person of singular importance; he would have been a power in the city. Here he was nothing. Those with the power, Englishmen like C. J. Rhodes and Rudd and Robinson, ran the town their way; they had their clubs and their horse racing and their polo and their Freemasonry and their politics; his skin and his nationality barred him from them all. So why not let the young Jew have the money? Why not let him go into competition with them? Maybe he might even hurt them a little.

However, his emotions were not allowed to exert influence when the loan papers were drawn up. The shop contract, the mine contract and the diamond went into Bulchand's safe before David received his money.

The next few days were the most tense David had ever spent in his adult life. He could speak to no one about what he was doing: not Hilda, because he knew she would not understand and would be frightened; not Peter Arendt, because David knew that he had no real interest in diamonds or mining and that once he had put

together a sufficiently big stake he was going to pull out of the business altogether. Dan Halkett did not have any capital, but David had promised him a share if things went well.

He was working virtually alone and his aloneness began to cause aberrational behavior. He had never sleepwalked, but now he would wake to find himself wandering in the shop at three o'clock in the morning. Once he found himself standing in the huge wardrobe in the bedroom. On another occasion Hilda found him in the kitchen standing by the table, fast asleep.

All the time he was buying up claims. One here, one there, never in his own name, always in the name of the "New Chance Mine." His own name was too well known because of his diamond buying and his work on the town council. But no one had ever heard of New Chance; it was simply the name by which David, Jack, Dan Halkett, Joe Malone and one or two others, most of whom had now gone, knew a small patch of earth at the side of the diggings. Sometimes he would get Dan to buy, sometimes Joe, sometimes other friends, but they always bought in the name of New Chance. Within a few days he had bought a series of claims to form a strip about forty yards wide by a hundred yards long.

Sometimes he would tell himself that what he was doing was sheer folly. At others he would be buoyed up on a froth of euphoria, convincing himself that he was going to amount to something at last. And there was always the nervous strain. He couldn't eat. He began to take a whisky or two in the evenings and at lunchtime a gin and lime or a couple of beers. Hilda noticed the change. She spoke to him about it but he shrugged her off. He was no longer in the shop but constantly up on the rim, watching the pump clear the claims of water.

One night she found him crouched by the table in the living room. He had a bread knife in his hand.

"David!" she said. "For God's sake!"

He woke and dropped the knife on the carpet.

Hilda burst into tears. "Whatever you're doing, you've got to stop it! It's ruining you and it's ruining us. You're never here, and I never know where you are." She held on to the table, her shoulders shaking. He knew then that he had to tell her.

He poured her a whisky and gave himself one. He spoke for nearly half an hour and as he did so he could feel the tension leave his muscles. At the end he felt limp and relaxed. He had spoken without interruption and now there was a moment of

silence as she stared at him. She raised the glass and finished it at a gulp, grimacing at the unfamiliar taste. Her hand was trembling.

"You used the shop!" she said. Her voice was not above a whisper.

"I had to."

"It's not *your* shop!"

"Half of it is."

"It's *not* yours! You never earned it! My father worked and worked for it. You got it by marrying me!"

"I don't think you should say any more. You'll say something you don't mean." She was shaking her head. "Hilda, we could hurt each other."

She turned and left him. For a moment, the door to that bleak winter landscape swung open. Was this to be the future? A marriage built on a belief that he had taken advantage of the Levinsons, that he was some kind of adventurer? Or was it Hilda's mentality—a shopkeeper's mentality? And if it was, could she cope with what might happen; could she keep up? He sat in the room as dawn came up, sipping his whisky. In a way she was right: it was old man Levinson's sweat which had built up the shop. But he had taken a gamble, too. He had left a secure job in the Cape and started afresh on the diggings. Everyone David knew was taking a gamble; that was what Kimberley was about.

He stayed in the living room for most of the day, remaining in his nightclothes and drinking endless cups of coffee and smoking one cigar after another. Hilda came to the door twice, but said nothing. Each time he thought of the claims he had bought and of the money invested, his stomach clenched. What cash he had left over would be invested in heavy machinery—that is, if Dan found proof of diamonds in the blue ground of the new claims. There *had* to be: if you found diamonds in one, there had to be diamonds in others—but not necessarily the ones he had bought. What if the diamonds were in small pockets, some here and some there? He had gambled that they would be in the area around New Chance where Dan had found them. What if he was wrong?

But he was not wrong. At four o'clock that afternoon Dan came to tell him that he had tested the blue ground all the way along the block of claims. He had found diamonds—small ones, to be sure, but diamonds nevertheless—in three of his five attempts. Which meant that the block of claims which now made up the

New Chance Mine might be one of the richest blocks in Kimberley, for that matter in the whole world.

David heard the news in a daze. He was unshaven and in his pajamas. He told Hilda and the three of them toasted the new mine. After Dan had left he was still unable to take it in. He was going to be a rich man, a powerful man, and here he sat, half-drunk, in his pajamas, like some debased Levantine.

"David, I'm sorry I said what I did," Hilda said. "It was just seeing you so upset . . ."

"I know."

"What's going to happen now?"

He shrugged. He couldn't contemplate the future; it was too awesome.

"It's a pity about Jack," she said after a moment.

He had forgotten Jack. "How do you mean?"

"I mean, that we have to share." There it was again, he thought. Meanness? Avarice? Or both?

"But we were partners."

"Yes, I know, but the shop had nothing to do with him."

"Listen to me, Hilda, I know you never liked Jack, and for that matter he and I have had our ups and downs. But if it wasn't for Jack we wouldn't be on the verge of—I don't know what. If I'd had my way we'd have sold New Chance a long time ago. It was only Jack who was stubborn. He wouldn't sell. So you can say that if it wasn't for Jack we'd be back where we were: owners of a bloody shop!"

He rose and, without looking at her, went to his bedroom, shaved, dressed and, still half-drunk, walked to the square and asked Dr. Hibbert for the name of the hospital in Cape Town to which he had sent Susan Delport. Then he went to the telegraph office and sent a telegram to Jack. It read simply NEW CHANCE HAS PUT THE FIRE IN THE ICE STOP DAVID.

BOOK TWO

Why do you hate me? I have not helped you.

—CHINESE SAYING

1

Jack Farson lay in that semiconscious state between waking and sleeping. Far off, as though heard in a dream, were the sounds of London in the closing years of the nineteenth century: the clipclopping of delivery drays, the more hurried movements of hansom cabs, the raucous shouts of the street vendors, the hissing of steam and the clanking of engines from nearby Victoria Station. A pale sun entered the windows of the room, making patterns of light on the tomato-colored carpet and the pink satin bedspread on which he was lying; everything was pink and orange and red, even the glowing coals in the grate. It was a room full of what he called "female flummery." It was also a large room, taking up most of the top floor of the house in Eccleston Square. Through its window he had an urban view of Pimlico's smoking chimneys and slate roofs. Below the window was a table holding the remains of luncheon: part of a capon, the shells of

two medium-sized lobsters, two empty bottles of hock. Even as he looked at it he felt burning bile rise from his stomach into his throat and his gut twisted in pain. He had eaten too much and drunk too much. He supposed he should cut down. Dr. Golding in Harley Street had said that the palpitations he sometimes felt came from too much eating and drinking. He was overweight, the doctor had said. Hell, he wasn't forty-five yet, and doctors talked rubbish half the time. He would never have gone to Golding in the first place if Marie and Jewel hadn't nagged him after he'd had that turn last Christmas. Not that he gave a damn what Marie said, but Jewel . . . He thought of his daughter and a sadness came over him. He was becoming increasingly subject to sudden flashes of memory which he could not control and which sometimes took him unawares. Most were of Jewel. His love for her surpassed even that he had felt for Lily and now he remembered how, when she was a little girl, he had carried her on his shoulders so her golden head bobbed above everyone else. In Kimberley people used to wave and she would wave back as though she were royalty. And she *was*, to Jack. "My little princess," he had called her. His shoulders had become her throne. Then he saw her at the children's fancy-dress party on the ship in which they had come to England. She had gone as a fairy, with gossamer wings and a glittering wand. He had never seen anything so beautiful. He and Marie had taken her from their first-class suite to take part in the parade in the second-class lounge. She had won, of course, and been given a prize of a teddy bear. It had been a tiny thing and Jack had bought her a much bigger one. As big as herself. Expensive. The real thing. But she had always taken the little one to bed with her.

She was seventeen now and the pictures continued to be framed by his memory, but in each he saw a second figure: David Kade's son, Michael, like a dark shadow, spoiling the pictures.

There was a light knock at the door and he heard a voice say, "Are you ready?"

A bubble of gas came up from his stomach, corrosive and painful. He felt sick.

The door opened and a woman came in. Dark coloring. Red lips and black hair. Through half-closed eyes, he saw Lily.

"You're peeping! Naughty Jacky for peeping!"

He groaned. She looked like Lily, but when she opened her mouth she was Violet.

She was wearing a filmy peignoir and, with as much artistry as she could muster, she dropped it at her feet and stood revealed in a garment he had never seen before. It was made of black silk and fitted her body closely. Two circles had been cut out, through which her breasts protruded. An embroidered slit crossed her crotch, allowing the pubic hair to show.

"It's French," she said, her nasal South London voice grating on his ears. "Look!" She turned her back and bent over. Her bottom was bare except for a single green feather which stuck out like a horse's tail and jiggled as she moved.

Again the acid juices rose into his throat.

"You don't like it!" she said, pouting. "Jacky doesn't like it."

Suddenly, she looked uncertain and pathetic and he wondered what the hell he had ever seen in her. She was young, not more than twenty, with a sensual body, but a shop girl's face and a shop girl's voice. And why not? That's what she was. He had picked her up in a shop. He had set her up in rooms of her own and they had been playing these games for nearly a year.

He swung his legs over the edge of the bed and tried to stand up, but his head swam. His heart was hammering in his chest, but it seemed to be beating irregularly.

"Jacky, is there something wrong?"

"No. I don't feel like it, that's all. And for Christ's sake, stop calling me Jacky. I've told you before."

She sat beside him. "Do you want to talk, then?"

"Talk?"

"Sometimes you like to talk."

"To you? What about?"

"Jewel?"

"You shut your bloody mouth about Jewel!"

"I'm sorry," she said in a low voice. "I don't mean to upset you."

"Oh, Christ, it's all right. Don't start crying." He poured himself a glass of wine from a bottle by the side of the bed. He was drunk, but the afternoon stretched ahead of him, and perhaps he was not drunk enough. He tossed off the wine and refilled the glass. Her breasts were near his face and he could see the blue veins below the surface of the skin. Lily had veins like those. He wished with all his power that she were here with him now; not even making love; just talking, so that he could tell her about himself, ask her where they had gone wrong.

"I was happy then," he said aloud, but to himself. He drank

again and lay back against the pillows staring at the molded ceiling. "It was simple. There was the desert, there were the bloody stones if you could find them. A pick and a shovel and a sieve. A plate of beans and a piece of beef. A couple of beers on a Saturday night. Simple. Christ, look at it now!"

"There ain't nothing wrong as far as I can see. I mean, most men would give . . ."

His mind swam back to the present. "Oh, shit," he said. "Help me up."

He took out two five-pound notes and placed them on the table.

"Will I see you Friday, then?" She was embarrassed now in the extravagant costume which would have been more suited to a *boîte de nuit* in Paris than the noonday light of Pimlico. She fumbled for her peignoir and slipped it on.

"I'll see."

He picked up his gray hat and his cane and went down the stairs to the street. He flagged a cab going towards the Buckingham Palace Road.

"New Chance House," he said.

"Northumberland Avenue, guv?"

"Yes."

The cold air and the drive revived him and he felt better when he got out on the corner of Northumberland Avenue and Trafalgar Square. He walked fifty yards in the direction of the river, then turned into one of the big soot-grimed buildings. The doorman came to attention and gave a smart salute. "Good afternoon, Mr. Farson, sir." Jack nodded. The foyer was vast and impressive. The walls were lined with pink Carrara marble and one was taken up with a series of brass plaques. He glanced up at them.

NEW CHANCE MINING COMPANY, LTD.

NEW CHANCE HOLDINGS

NEW CHANCE CONSOLIDATED MINES, LTD.

NEW CHANCE DIAMOND MINING CORP., LTD.

NEW CHANCE DIAMOND SELLING ORGANIZATION, LTD.

NEW CHANCE VAAL "A"

NEW CHANCE DIGGINGS, LTD.

The list was a long one and he should have felt a sense of pride and achievement when he read it. Instead, the names meant nothing. They were the creation of financial consultants and he could not have said how many companies and ramifications of companies and how many ramifications of those ramifications were offspring of the original parent company. He stood, swaying, in the foyer, watched by the doorman.

"Is everything all right, sir?"

Jack ignored him. That's where it had all gone wrong: too many bloody experts. He had thought at the start that things would be simple, but they hadn't been. It was all so bloody complicated.

He turned, and on another wall, by itself, was a plaque which said

DAVID KADE, LTD.

DIAMOND MERCHANT

LONDON, KIMBERLEY

Every time he saw it he felt a surge of irritation. He had no share in this company; he was excluded. He stood there a few moments longer, a big, heavy, balding man in his forties, then he went up to his office, letting himself in through a private door by which he could come and go without being seen.

His room was the best in the building—that had been part of the deal he had made—and the furniture was heavy and solid. There were dark green leather chairs and Chesterfields, a big partners' desk with a red leather top, green velvet curtains and a polished wood-block floor. The room was dominated by tall windows that looked out over Trafalgar Square, but it looked as though it was never used, as though the chairs had never been sat in. The desk top was bare except for a pen-and-ink set and a silver handbell. There were no papers on it.

He took off his hat and coat and hung them on a stand in the corner, then he rang the bell.

A middle-aged woman wearing a severely cut dress of dark gray worsted with white celluloid cuffs entered.

"Has the post come, Miss Trimmer?"

"Half an hour ago, sir."

"Anything for me?"

"No, sir."

"Anything I should know about?"

"No, sir, not as far as I know."

"You sure?"

"Yes, sir."

"Have the papers come, then?"

"I'll check, sir."

He stood at the windows, watching the omnibuses and the drays and the cabs fighting to get through the bottleneck into Whitehall and he was swept by a feeling of unease and restlessness. He felt trapped. Sometimes London was claustrophobic, hemming him in on all sides. He wanted to rush down the stairs and get into his carriage and tell his coachman to drive him as far away from London as he could, somewhere where there was space to move and think.

There was a knock on the door behind him and Miss Trimmer came in. "The papers, sir."

"Turn up the gas."

She went round the room, bringing up the gas jets. He found he needed a good light to read these days. He took the papers to his desk, spread them out and began his afternoon's work.

He still read slowly. Sometimes if a sentence grew too elongated, with too many subclauses, he would put his finger under each word as he read, and work it out exactly.

There were the usual London stories about smells and smoke and the possibility that the Thames might flood on the next high tide. There had been a nasty poisoning in Hackney and in Bow an omnibus had been in collision with a brewer's dray; a passenger on the omnibus had been killed and two horses had had to be shot. And then his eye caught a story near the bottom of the page:

NEW TERRITORY
FOR BRITISH CROWN

KADE GAINS CONCESSION
FOR RAILWAY

News has recently reached our correspondent in the Cape Colony of major land concessions to Her Majesty's Government. It is understood that Mr. David Kade, the mining magnate, has successfully negotiated, on behalf of Britain, a treaty with the chief

of Bavendaland for a strip of territory north of the Limpopo River, on which it is proposed to build a railway to the west coast. Talks have already begun with the Portuguese Government through whose territory of Angola the railway will run. This is believed to be part of a grand design for south central Africa and would link the coast with the territory now being created by Mr. Rhodes's Chartered Company.

Mr. Kade, joint founder of New Chance, the mining house, is already being hailed as "a new Rhodes." This is the second occasion on which his services have been used by the British Government to negotiate a treaty in Africa. In both cases the mineral rights are reserved for his company.

Mr. Kade, who was a member of the Cape Parliament for five years, lives in London and is the owner of the famous uncut diamond the "Southern Cross," said to be the best stone yet taken out of the Kimberley mines.

Again Jack felt a stab of irritation. More and more David was becoming a kind of roving negotiator for the British Government while he, Jack, lived out his life in London. "Someone has to mind the shop and make the decisions," David had said to him a year or two back. But all the real decisions were taken by a series of different boards heavily loaded with faceless financial experts. Everything was based on share flotations, dividends, what was happening on the Paris Bourse or the New York and London stock exchanges. Words like "preference," "ordinary," "equity" were the foundations, it seemed, on which a mining empire was built, and Jack not only did not know what half the words meant, but had no interest in them. He knew a diamond, he knew a pick and he knew a shovel, and he understood the functions of all three. But shareholders' meetings and profit-and-loss accounts and the complex network of company ownership cloaked in City jargon left him totally confused. David understood what it was all about. How the hell had he managed it? Jack wondered. Was it Hilda who had pushed him?

It had started when David had become a town councillor in Kimberley; then he had become mayor and then, when he'd bought his wine farm in the Cape and the railway had been completed in 1885 between Cape Town and Kimberley, he had journeyed between the two places. Then he had taken an interest in Cape politics and before Jack realized what was happening, his partner was sitting in Parliament, an M.P. for one of the new districts of Kimberley.

Was that when things had gone wrong? Before that everything had been wonderful, or at least it seemed so in Jack's memory. The early hardship now seemed to him to have a golden tinge. He had forgotten the cold and the heat and the exhaustion. It all seemed part of a more exciting life. His mind touched on that wonderful day in Cape Town when he had read David's telegram. He recalled the words: *"New Chance has put the fire in the ice."*

He had gone to Kimberley, leaving Marie to bring back her mother, who was making slow but steady progress. But nothing had been as he had thought it would. In his mind, mining for diamonds was straightforward: there was the spoil which had to be dug out; the sieves through which it passed; the stones it gave up. But now, in the blue ground, mining was of a different kind. Now one had to follow the hard rocks down into the bowels of the earth as coal was followed. Mines had literally to be dug and propped and great crushers had to be bought, and gigantic sieves, and a huge steam plant to run everything. And that meant that the Cape Government had to build a railway to bring in the coal and to run the steam boilers to power the machinery to raise and lower the lifts so that miners could reach the galleries and dig out the spoil. It was frightening, and the money Mr. Bulchand had advanced was only just enough to buy the claims.

"What the hell are we to do?" Jack had said, dismayed at the complexities.

"Go to the City of London," David had said. "That's where the money is. That's where we'll get our start."

"Borrow?"

"Of course. That's how it's done."

"I don't like to borrow."

"There's no other way."

So David had gone to the City of London, where there was more cash for speculation than in the rest of the world money markets put together. People were interested. C. J. Rhodes was borrowing heavily for the same reason. Financiers smelled a profit, but they were not going to lend money to two unknown miners without some control. To protect their interests, their own nominees went onto the boards of the various companies. The chairman of New Chance was Lord Levering, the banker, and his deputy was Sir Humphrey Lawrence, the financier. They did not

know much about diamonds, but they knew a lot about money.

Other companies were set up: holding companies and subsidiary companies, and companies which bought diamonds from other companies, and companies which sold diamonds, and companies which invested in diamond-cutting works, and in gold and land and office buildings, until Jack grew dizzy. And all the time more experts were brought in, some of them Jews who had worked for C. J. Rhodes and been enticed away. Clever, flashy men who knew how much a pound note was worth.

But Jack had not been too concerned with these matters then for he had found his niche alongside Dan Halkett, creating the mines themselves, dealing with machinery, with miners, with all the practical aspects of setting up a great enterprise. Let the financial experts—the "paper boys," as he called them—deal with figures; he was dealing with facts. These were the good years. By the beginning of the 1890's there were only two mining houses: De Beers and New Chance. De Beers was by far the larger and Rhodes by far the best-known single individual spawned by the diamond rush, but New Chance was big enough for Jack.

He was carried along on the pure excitement of it all. He built a large house in Kimberley and another overlooking False Bay at the Cape. Jewel had been born. Money flowed in. "Lucky Jack" Farson, people called him, and he was happy.

But gradually as the practical problems were overcome and as the mines became established he had less and less to do. Dan Halkett, with a staff of mining engineers, ran the New Chance Mine. They were experts, a different kind from the paper boys, but experts none the less.

Then the paper boys had wanted to move the headquarters of New Chance to London because it was easier to manage from there. David had bought a huge house overlooking Hampstead Heath, and Marie had nagged and nagged to go there, too, always saying it was for Jewel's sake, until finally Jack had given in and sold his properties in southern Africa and bought a house on Park Lane which cost him far more than even he could afford. At first he had wanted to live in the country and had looked at one or two estates in Surrey, but Marie had the bit between her teeth. She was meeting the kind of people she had always dreamed of meeting: minor European royalty, Irish peers, baronets from the shires, most of them without tuppence to rub together, all

looking for Jack to help them with whatever crack-brained schemes they had for making money. Was that when things had finally gone sour: when he had come back to London?

He turned the pages of the newspaper, skimming the columns without much interest. And then his eye caught a second story:

OPERA COMPANY
ON WAY HOME

DIVA'S OUTSTANDING
SUCCESS

The State Opera Company of Austria have finished their tour of southern Africa with a performance of Mozart's *Don Giovanni* at the Opera House in Cape Town, according to news reaching our music correspondent.

The eight-month tour took in Australia and New Zealand as well as Africa. The company have played to packed houses and critical acclaim. In Cape Town the principal soprano, Madame Montadini, was given the freedom of the city. She was born in London as Lily Bartlett and has become greatly sought after in Europe and America. She has lived abroad for many years.

She told a correspondent that her husband and manager, Mr. Peter Arendt, left the tour two months ago to arrange a series of recitals in Britain and on the Continent.

Seeing Lily's name was a shock. From time to time he had heard about her success and her marriage to Arendt—something he could never understand—and there had been scarcely a day when he had not at some point thought of her. She was bound up in the life he longed for, an integral part of it.

"Excuse me, sir."

He had been so deep in thought he had not heard Miss Trimmer enter the room.

"There's a gentleman from the *Morning Post* here. He's asking to see you but I said I thought you would be too busy. Shall I send him down to Mr. Snell?"

Jack wrenched himself back to the present. "Busy? No, I'm not too busy. Show him in."

He was a small, round-faced young man with a snub nose and poor teeth. "Name's Holliday, sir."

"Sit down," Jack said, pointing to a chair. "What can I do for you?"

"It's about Mr. Kade. There's a story in today's papers about land concessions and mineral rights."

"What about them?"

"I thought I'd get your end of the story, sir. The London end."

They spoke for half an hour about diamond mining and the economics of the control of the number of stones allowed onto the market, and then Holliday said, "Can you tell me something about the diamond Mr. Kade owns? The 'Southern Cross'?"

"What about it?"

"Is it true it's more than six hundred carats?"

"Yes."

"They say it's the best diamond to come out of Kimberley."

"Yes."

"They say it was really your diamond. That you found it."

Jack shifted uneasily. He was seeing again the small leather pouch in which David kept the "Southern Cross." It had not been called anything then; the name had come later. But he remembered the leather pouch because David had touched it as though to reassure himself that the stone was still there when Jack had made his offer for it. That had been less than a year after he had come back from Cape Town, finding himself a wealthy man. David had bought the diamond from him for an absurdly low price, but it was a price that could at that moment have been said to be absurdly high, since the markets had been closed down by rumors of the Mexican meteorite. Afterwards, Jack had not given the transaction much thought. It was Marie who had brought it up. "It's really our diamond. Offer him what he gave you for it," she had said. He did not miss her emphasis on the word "our."

"Don't be daft," he had said. "Why would he want to sell it? Anyway, we've got everything we want."

"But it's ours."

"Rubbish. We made a deal. You agreed to it. He'd offered to *give* us the money. And that would have been bloody charity."

But she had not given up and finally he had gone to David and offered him ten times what he had paid for the diamond.

"I'm sorry, Jack," David had said. "I know how you must feel

about it. But . . ." He had touched the stone.

"It's not for me. It's Marie that . . ."

"Ask me for anything else."

He came back to the present and saw the young reporter was staring at him.

"Why are you asking these questions?" he said. "This hasn't anything to do with the negotiations."

"People are interested, sir. And no one really knows the story of the diamond."

"If you want to know that story, you'd better ask Mr. Kade." Jack stood up.

Holliday was not abashed. "People say that you sold it dirt cheap and that Mr. Kade . . ."

His irritation reached a head. "I don't care what they say! I won't have you coming into my office and asking questions about things that are none of your business."

Holliday rose. "I'm only trying to do my job."

"It's not your bloody job to come prying into other people's lives!"

After Miss Trimmer had shown Holliday out he found himself trembling with unexpected anger. "Don't let him come near me again," he shouted. "I don't want him in the building!"

"Very good, sir." She put her lips primly together. It was what she had originally thought.

Jack paced up and down the office, stopping every now and then to stare out over the thickening traffic in Trafalgar Square. Seeing the paragraphs about Lily had unsettled him, and that bloody hack from the *Morning Post* had made it worse with his questions. He felt tense and wound up. He wondered if he should go back to Violet. Instead he put on his hat and coat and said, "I'm off. I'll be at the club if anyone wants me."

He crossed Trafalgar Square, striding out against the northeast wind. He had to dodge between omnibuses and cabs. There was a smell of horse manure and coal fires in the air and, above that, a harsher, more acrid smell. He turned and saw a chestnut vendor roasting the nuts on his charcoal fire. His mind was taken back to his childhood. He was smelling again the New Cut in Lambeth. He saw, in his mind's eye, Mr. Berkis and Mary and his mother. Sometimes such memories would lie in wait for him. They would stalk him among the smells and the sounds of London, memories

he thought had faded in the dry sunlight of Africa. It was another reason he wanted to be rid of London; there were too many memories. He saw again his sister's dress go up in a sheet of flame, he saw the spurting blood from his mother's head, he saw . . . but he shook himself like a dog and forced himself on against the wind and tried to blot out the thoughts.

His club was in Pall Mall. The bar was almost empty at this time in the afternoon. He ordered a double brandy and threw it into the back of his throat. He saw no one he knew so he lit a cigar and wandered into the smoking room. Several of the chairs were occupied by recumbent figures sleeping off luncheon claret. A voice behind him said, "Hello, Farson; fancy a hundred up?"

He looked around to see a man called Brunton, who had come out of the billiards room and was holding a cue.

"All right."

They began to play.

"I see Kade's in the news again." Brunton was a small, fat man with a bald head and wisps of graying hair. He had something to do with the Baltic Exchange and he reminded Jack of Mr. Levinson.

"I take my hat off to him. Done a marvelous job. It'll make all the difference to central Africa."

"Yes."

"Everyone's for Rhodes but I say Kade's worth two of him even though he's a Jew. Don't you agree?"

"Yes."

Jack played on grimly as he listened to the quacking voice going on about David. At the end of the game Brunton said, "Care for another?"

Jack shook his head. "I'm late as it is. What do I owe you?"

"That's another forty quid at a pound a point. Six hundred altogether."

"I'll get my secretary to send you off a check."

He left the club and stood for a moment on the pavement outside. Late for what? He didn't want to go back to New Chance House. Nor did he particularly want to go home.

"Aren't you Mr. Farson from Kimberley, sir?" a voice said.

It belonged to a man of medium height with a thin, foxy face and eyes set close together. He was dressed in khaki trousers and boots, a plaid shirt and a thick tweed jacket, and on his head was a

wide-brimmed hat shaped to go down in front and at the back to shade the neck. He was a vision from the past and Jack's frown turned into a smile. "That's right."

"I thought so. I saw you fight the half-caste. The tattooed johnny. I said to myself, 'That's Jack Farson.' It was a great fight, sir. It's still talked about."

"What's your name?"

"Leask, sir. George Leask."

"When did you get back?"

"Last week."

"From Kimberley?"

"There and the goldfields on the Rand, sir."

He could not have been older than the mid-thirties, and Jack said, "You must have been a young man when you saw that fight."

"My father took me out to Africa when I was a child. He worked in the Post Office out there."

"But not you, eh?"

"No, sir. I did my share of digging. Then when they found gold in the Transvaal I went up there."

His clothes were frayed and the hat was stained and dusty. He was clearly down on his luck. "Forgive me for stopping you, sir. I just wanted to say you're not forgotten. Never will be."

He had tapped a vein of happiness in Jack that had not been opened for years. "There's no need to apologize," he said. "You're the best thing I've seen all day. What do you say to a drink?"

"No, sir, you don't want to waste your . . ."

"Listen to me, Leask, I've got more time now than I've ever had before. Come on."

He turned back into the club. "This is Mr. Leask," he said to the surprised hall porter. "He's just back from Africa."

They sat in the corner of the empty bar and talked the afternoon away. The subject, naturally, was Kimberley. Leask had started as a diamond digger, then moved to the Transvaal after gold had been discovered on the Witwatersrand. He'd had no luck and had returned to Kimberley. "I often used to see Mr. Halkett there," he said. "Do you ever go back, sir?"

"I haven't been back for some years. Have another." They were drinking brandy and Jack went to the bar to recharge the glasses.

"You'd see a lot of changes," Leask said when he returned.

"I suppose I would." He had often made plans to go back but somehow they had always miscarried. The first time there had been a crisis in the stock markets which had kept him in London; the second time Jewel had been ill and the doctors had thought it was diphtheria—he never wanted to live through that time again.

"And sometimes we see Mr. Kade," Leask said. "He's back quite often. He's doing very well, Mr. Kade is."

"Yes."

"I saw something about him in the newspaper only today about how he's . . ."

"Yes," Jack said. "He's doing well."

Leask registered the tone. His nervous, darting eyes rested for a moment on Jack's face, seeing the mottled skin, the red capillaries on the nose.

"I suppose you've heard about the troubles," he said, hastily changing the subject.

"What troubles this time? There're always bloody troubles." Jack was slurring his words.

"I mean in the Transvaal, sir."

Southern Africa had now split into four territories: the Cape Colony and Natal were owned by Britain and effectively ruled from London. The Transvaal and the Orange Free State were independent Boer republics, ruled by an agrarian population, the descendants of the original Dutch and Huguenot settlers who, in the 1830's, had trekked away from British rule only to find it following them wherever they went. These farming people—the word *boer* meant "farmer"—were now lumped under one heading: Afrikaners. When gold had been found on the Witwatersrand (the "Ridge of White Waters") in the Transvaal, it had attracted as big an influx of foreign fortune hunters as diamonds had done years before to Kimberley.

"The Boers in the Transvaal call us Outlanders," Leask said. "They hate us. They won't give us a say in the country. They won't give us a vote. They try to keep everything to themselves."

"Well, you can't blame them," Jack said. "The immigrants outnumber the Boers. They'd be voted out of their own countries and the place would be run by foreigners if they got the franchise. That's why I never went in for gold. You're in the hands of the Boers. You never know what the hell they're

thinking. Kade put money into gold. He wanted me to do the same, but I said to hell with it. Kimberley's in the Cape Colony with the British Government behind it. No one's going to interfere there, or if they do they'll get their fingers burnt."

The bar had been filling up and he saw with a start that the time was seven o'clock. "I must go," he said abruptly, finishing his drink. On the pavement outside he said, "What are your plans, Leask? Going back?"

"I don't know. I'll be looking for a job until I've made up my mind."

Jack fumbled in his wallet and extracted a ten-pound note. "Get yourself a new outfit," he said. "Come and see me at New Chance House tomorrow."

As he walked through the evening crowds he began to plan what he would do for Leask. He'd give him an office next to his own and he could be his general factotum. He would be someone to talk to, someone who understood what Kimberley and the diamond fields were all about, not like the gutless wonders who could tot up a column of figures but who wouldn't know a blue-white from bottle glass.

Number 32 Park Lane was a graceful, four-storied house with a double front and a glass-roofed porte-cochère. On the third floor it had a balcony of cast-iron lacework. When Jewel was a little girl she and her father had often stood there and watched the sun go down over Hyde Park and he would tell her about the blood-red suns of Africa going down into the dust of the desert, and she would question him about Kimberley and the desert, for she had forgotten what it was like.

Marie was in her bedroom. "Is that you, Jack?" she called. She was half-dressed, the tapes of her stays flapping behind her.

"Where have you been?" she said angrily. "You know we've got a dinner party tonight."

He sat down on the edge of a chair and looked at her. Her hair was piled on top of her head in the latest fashion but even though she went to the most expensive coiffeur in London nothing could hide the fact that she had coarsened. A picture flashed into his mind of her standing naked in the river at Portuguese Place, the sun striking her honey-colored body. He had been frightened half out of his wits at the time, but even so he had registered how beautiful she was. Now she seemed to have thickened. Her nose

306

had thickened, her lips had thickened and, altogether, she held little attraction for him.

"Hurry," she said. "I told Cummings to draw your bath. They'll be here in twenty minutes."

"Who?"

"I told you this morning. Don't you ever listen? Sir John Baker, Lord O'Hara . . . Oh, I haven't got time now!" She went back into her bedroom.

"Where's Jewel?" he said.

"She's gone to the opera."

"Does she have to go so often?"

He lit a cigar and she said, "I've asked you before not to smoke in my bedroom."

He ignored her and leant against the doorframe. "Who with?"

"Michael."

"Michael Kade?"

"What other Michael is there?"

Again he felt the irritation build up inside him and again it came to a head in an outburst of anger.

"That's the third time in a fortnight! I don't want her seeing him so often!"

"You stop her, then."

"You're her mother."

He pushed himself away from the door and staggered slightly.

She watched him with distaste, then she said, "I suppose you've seen the papers? The 'new Rhodes'! That's what *you* should be doing. *You* should be negotiating for the British Government. You know as much about diamond concessions as David does." She had followed him into his dressing room. "And every time they mention him, they mention the 'Southern Cross.' He *stole* that diamond, Jack."

"Rubbish."

"He got it for next to nothing."

"You know why."

"Then why doesn't he sell it back to us? You've never been able to stand up to him. And now look at you. While he's out there making a name for himself you sit in the club all afternoon and come home the worse for drink!"

"For God's sake, be quiet!" Jack said.

"That's a fine way to talk to me."

"Well, stop going on about that bloody diamond."

"You don't understand what's happening, do you? David's always had it over you. Right from the very beginning it was you who did the hard work, the kaffir's work."

"Leave it!"

"And it's David who has ended up with the best stone ever taken out of Kimberley."

"I said, leave it!"

She laughed angrily. "I'll leave it, but I want you to think about it."

2

The afternoon sun was dipping towards the horizon but it was still hot enough to make David thankful he was wearing his panama. He was unused to the heat of Portuguese Place after so many years in London.

"That's new, isn't it?" he said, pointing to a cattle pen made of thorn branches. It was a pathetic, makeshift thing of the kind he had seen outside run-down African villages.

"I built it last year," Susan said, and he realized that he had probably seen it before and possibly even remarked on it. He tried to find something new to comment on each time he came to see her.

They moved slowly up from the river towards the house. She walked with a stick now and kept her left hand in the pocket of her apron. He knew that the arm was more or less useless. He was still not quite sure how the accident had happened and had never felt the moment appropriate to ask her. Each time he made the long journey from London to Kimberley on business—perhaps twice a year—he felt it his duty to visit Susan at Portuguese Place

and give her news of the family. He always felt uneasy with her, but had never thought of trying to make an excuse not to come. And each time he went away depressed. The farm was in a state of massive decay; the house was semiderelict and Susan herself was as worn and twisted as an old peach tree.

As they reached the house she said, "Isn't it beautiful?"

He turned and followed her eyes and was struck again by the view. There had been a time, after Jack had cut the trees, when that same view had been like a blow, the treeless river a scar on the land. But now the trees and bushes, with their prolific growth, had thickened and grown and the great green snake once more wound through the desert and away down into the distant hills.

"I've watched it grow up again," she said.

There was something about the way she spoke that touched him. He visualized this indomitable woman living out here in the wilderness through winters and summers, seeing no one but old Mopedi, too old now to do much work, and watching the bush growing back to what it had been. And every evening as the dusk came down, going into the lonely house and waiting for dawn.

"There's been no more *rinderpest?*" he said.

"No. One hears stories, of course, and it'll come again. But I only have a few sheep and they aren't so badly affected."

"You've sold off a lot of the farm."

"The whole of the downriver section. I didn't get much for it, because it's been picked over by prospectors so often everyone knows there's nothing there. But it gave me a few pounds to buy sheep."

Their supper on the stoep was a simple dish of mutton and ground maize called *samp*, which David disliked. There was no coffee, but she gave him a plate of dried apricots as dessert.

The rooms at the back of the house had never been rebuilt and the whole place had an air of abandonment. There was little furniture and she did her own cooking, such as it was, on a small kerosene stove. Her skin had taken on the look of crushed leather from years of work in the powerful sun and her hands were thickened and calloused and ingrained with dirt. As he smoked a cigar after the meal he told her about Marie and Jack and about the fashionable house in Park Lane which she had never seen.

"Jack's built a library," he said.

"A library! I never thought of him as someone who would read much."

"He learned late."

He told her other details: about the new carpet in the drawing room, the glass conservatory, the Constable which Marie had insisted Jack buy, the grand people who came to the dinner table. David was not very good at details but he knew that she was starved of information, since neither Jack nor Marie ever wrote to her. She listened carefully, but he realized she was becoming impatient and finally, when he paused, she said, "Tell me about Jewel."

It was always the same. He could see the anticipation mount in her as he spoke of the family, and knew it was really of Jewel she wanted to hear. They wrote to each other, but letters took a long time. He thought of the child she must last have seen. Then Jewel had been solemn and shy, but recently she had begun to blossom into a beauty. He wondered what Susan would make of her now. There was something in Jewel that eluded him. He had seen almost as much of her as her own parents, yet he could never have said he knew her. He told Susan about her, describing ordinary, day-to-day things: parties, balls, a visit to Scotland she had made, and he watched her soak up the details so that she could call them back to fill the lonely evenings long after he had gone.

They talked until nearly midnight and it was strange to recreate the London he knew, here in the desert. Then he went to bed in the room he always occupied, the room where he had once overheard Marie importuning Jack. It had not been cleaned for a long while and his bare feet made prints in the dust on the floor.

He left the following morning in a trap driven by one of the liveried black servants of the New Chance Mine. Before going, he performed what had by this time become a ritual.

"Mrs. Delport," he said, "isn't there some way—won't you change your mind?"

"No, David, but thank you all the same."

Her eyes seemed to bore into him. It was a look he had seen in Jewel's eyes: frank and disconcerting.

At first it had been Jack who had tried to make her take money, but as the years passed without breaking down her will, he had given up. Latterly, David had tried. He had even sent out wagon-

loads of food and equipment from the mine. They had been returned. She had taken nothing from anyone. He turned once to wave good-bye, seeing her standing there with her stick, the broken house forming a backdrop, then the green of the river and the hills, and he thought how she seemed to have grown out of the landscape like the hills themselves.

The train to Cape Town left at five o'clock in the afternoon. He had finished his business at New Chance the day before; he had seen Dan Halkett and the local directors, and discussed the immediate future. Now he no longer felt like going near the mine. Instead he went to Levinson's Emporium, which he and Hilda still owned, more out of sentiment than for any other reason, since both her parents were now dead.

He had put in a manager, a Mr. Reeves, who lived with his wife on the premises he and Hilda had once occupied. Reeves was tall and very thin, with a cadaverous face and dark-shadowed eyes, and he appeared nervous and confused at the unexpected visit.

"I've only come to find out how things are going," David said.

Mrs. Reeves had emerged from the back. She was the antithesis of her husband, short and red-cheeked, and looked as healthy as he looked unhealthy.

"There is one thing, sir," she said. "It's nothing that we need, just something I've been meaning to bring to your attention. It's a box of odds and ends, and I was wondering if I should send it to the mine."

"Odds and ends?"

"Books and other things that were left here."

She took him through to the living room. Her husband brought in a wooden kerosene box and levered off the top. "We'll leave you to look at them, sir," she said.

He lifted out each object. There were the books about diamonds he had bought when he had worked in the bank in London. There were the simple school readers and exercise books and pencils he'd bought with the last of his money at the village of Victoria when he and Jack had walked to the diggings. Then he pulled out something bigger and heavier and realized that it was the Bible he had found at Frans Delport's grave. He drew it from its oilskin cover. He really should give it back to Susan, he thought, but how could he explain that he'd had it all these years and simply forgotten about it? He opened it at the

early pages and saw again the spidery handwriting. In the poor light he could not make out individual words. It would be a pity if no one ever . . . Then he had an idea. If he could have this translated, he could give her back the Bible and at the same time supply her with the answer to its mystery. There was one man in Kimberley who might be able to do it for him. He looked at his watch. There was time enough. He said his good-byes to the Reeves and made his way in the afternoon heat to the Oporto Café, where he asked for Mr. Pereira, the owner.

He had not been in the café for many years and Pereira was an old man now. "You don't come to buy cheap cheroots no more," he said.

"That's true."

"Now you can afford the best Havanas."

"Well . . ."

The old man seemed pleased at his visit and, like Mr. Reeves, somewhat flustered.

"I want you to look at something," David said. He opened the Bible at the early pages.

"It is in Portuguese," Pereira said.

"It was found near Kimberley, but no one knows how it got there. Perhaps if we could translate the handwriting here—" he pointed to the tops and bottoms of the pages—"we could find out."

"Excuse, please." Pereira pointed to his eyes. He fetched a pair of spectacles, put them on and frowned at the writing. "I do not think . . ." he began. "A moment." He took the Bible to the door and studied it in the bright sunlight, then he said, "But this writing is not in Portuguese."

"Not in Portuguese?" David had never looked closely at the writing before. He had simply taken Susan's word.

"Let me look." But it had faded over the years and defeated his eyes, themselves now in need of spectacles.

"You haven't got a magnifying glass?"

"So sorry, Mr. Kade."

He still had a little time before the train left and he decided he would go to his office and find a magnifying glass. He was crossing the square when he heard men's voices and saw a cloud of dust rising behind one of the parked wagons. He found a dozen or more diggers forming a loose ring while two men went at each other hammer and tongs. He had a sudden memory of

himself when he had first arrived, landing in Cape Town and stepping off the gangway into a fracas. He looked at the brawlers in distaste and a feeling of territorialism came over him: Kimberley was his town and he did not like fighting.

He stepped forwards and caught one of the men by the collar of his shirt and another by his arm. Behind him one of the onlookers said, "Hey, you! Why don't you mind your own fucking . . ."

He was interrupted by another, who said, "Don't you know who that is? It's Mr. Kade!"

The fighters had spent their energy and appeared exhausted. "That's enough," David said.

Their friends took them away in opposite directions and he turned to one of the diggers who remained. "What was that all about?"

"The usual. One of them comes from back home . . ."

"Meaning?"

"Meaning London, sir."

"And the other?"

"He's a Boer. The Boer says he's owed money, sir, for some wood, but that's only an excuse. It's getting worse and worse."

"What is?"

"This fighting between English and Boers. It happens all the time now. They say it's much worse on the goldfields in the Transvaal. There's going to be a showdown. Can't help it. You'll see, sir, it'll come sooner or later."

David walked thoughtfully back to New Chance Building, a large, red brick affair which dominated the Dutoitspan Road. He let himself in at a side door, went up a private staircase to his office and told his secretary to find him a magnifying glass and then he sat down at his desk, staring at the first entry in the book. Pereira was right. The writing was not in Portuguese. Under the magnifying glass the letters became darker and bigger and assumed firmer shapes. The words were in no modern language at all, but in one that David had studied and in which he had been more than proficient. It was Latin. *"Hic Johannis Pater Rosarii Sancti rem narrabo de nave quadam . . ."* He stopped and wrote down on a pad: "I, Father John of the Rosary, set down here the story of . . ." The next word defeated him. He rang again and asked his secretary if they had a Latin dictionary in the building, but she had never heard of one. He stared at the writing, feeling

frustrated and irritated with himself. The Bible had lain in its oilskin cover at the back of Levinson's shop for years and years—God knew how long it had been on Portuguese Place before that—and all the time he, David, could have translated the writing.

"Sir!" His secretary's voice was nervous. "Sir, the train leaves in a few minutes. Shall I ask them to hold it for you?"

He hated using his power in that kind of way. "No, no. I'll hurry. Here, you keep this. And get a Latin dictionary. Have them here for me on my next visit." He picked up his panama and hurried downstairs.

He stood at the rail of the Union Line's steamship *Leviathan* and watched Table Mountain and its consort, Devil's Peak, grow smaller until they seemed to form a self-contained volcanic island not attached to the mainland of Africa at all. This optical illusion of a huge, flat-topped mountain growing taller and narrower the greater the distance the ship traveled from it had always fascinated him. He had made the voyage between Southampton and the Cape twenty-five or thirty times since New Chance had become a great mining house and always, when the ship sailed out of Table Bay, he would station himself at the stern rail to watch the phenomenon. Dusk had come down and the breeze off the sea was chilly. He turned away from the rail and went to his stateroom to bathe and dress for dinner.

There had been several cables to deal with when he had come on board earlier that afternoon and now, as he entered his sitting room, he saw that his steward had left a card propped on the table inviting him to sit at the captain's table. He would have preferred a table of his own to which he could have taken a book and where he could have read throughout his meal, but the shipping company desired to do him honor and it would have been churlish to refuse. He bathed in seawater, rinsed himself in the basin of fresh that the steward had brought and then dressed himself in a wing collar, black tie and dinner jacket and inspected himself in the full-length mirror in his bedroom. He saw a man of medium height, the cap of black hair that hugged his skull turning gray at the temples. Some years before he had grown a moustache and this, too, was gray. Apart from that, the years seemed to have treated him kindly and he was not displeased with what he saw. He was sunburnt from his journey beyond the

Limpopo River and his face, though lined, still gave an impression of health and fitness—which reminded him: he must tell his bedroom steward to arrange a daily appointment in the gymnasium. He was apt to eat more than was good for him in the three weeks it took to go from Cape Town to Southampton. He always entered the deck-games tournament and enjoyed the deck tennis against the officers, but that was not sufficient to keep his waistline slim.

Satisfied, he left the cabin and went down to B deck to the first-class dining room. He had traveled on the *Leviathan* before and considered her to be one of the best of the fleet. He particularly liked the dining room, which was all shiny dark mahogany, polished silver and white linen. It had a minstrels' gallery, supported on slender mahogany pillars, where the ship's five-piece orchestra was now playing the ballet music from *Faust*. It was civilized and urbane, much more like London than Africa. Kimberley had improved enormously in terms of comfort and luxury but still gave the impression of a frontier town and had nothing to compare with this. And certainly after his journey to Bavendaland to negotiate the treaty for the British Government, he felt self-indulgent.

A man in white tropicals with two rows of ribbons on his chest rose and introduced himself. "I'm Captain Harvey," he said. "We're very pleased to have you with us, Mr. Kade. Allow me to introduce Sir George and Lady Carlyle, General Holroyd, her Grace the Duchess of Wigtown and the Honorable Spencer Laird." David made his greetings and sat down opposite the captain. One chair remained vacant. "Mr. Kade is a regular on the *Leviathan*," the captain said, "although this is the first time I have had the pleasure of meeting him."

The menu was a long one, and David studied it carefully. He had reached the entrées when the men at the table rose. He automatically got to his feet, realizing that the last guest must be arriving. He saw a woman coming towards him. Conversation in the dining room ceased as people turned to follow her progress. She was wearing a magnificent, Spanish-style red dress with a black silk shawl over her smooth white shoulders. Her hair gleamed blackly and her lips blazed red. She wore a necklace of pearls and a single emerald on her breast. She swept down the aisle between the tables with all the confidence of a woman who knows she is both beautiful and accomplished.

The captain moved forwards to greet her. "May I have the honor of presenting Madame Montadini?" he said. He presented her to the other diners, then said, "And this is Mr. Kade."

"Hello, Lily." David took her hand.

Her eyes widened. Then she smiled. "Mr. Kade and I are old friends. Hello, David," she said, and bent forwards and kissed him on the cheek.

The night air was cool with a scent of land. David had put on a scarf and Lily had sent her maid to fetch her fur coat. He lit a cigar and they walked slowly around the deck. They had not been able to talk much during dinner. The conversation had been mainly about the unrest and the ill feeling among the Boers and the Outlanders. General Holroyd had said he was certain that one day war would come. "Revenge for Majuba, what?"

As they walked, a silence—not uncomfortable—grew between them. After a while Lily broke it. "Who's going to be first?" she said.

David chuckled. "I was wondering that myself."

"You."

"No, you. You're the great singer. How did it all happen?"

"It will take me hours to tell you everything."

"We have all the time in the world. We must fill it somehow."

"Three weeks. I can't tell you how I've been wishing for this. It's the first holiday I've had in years. Usually I travel with Peter, and his idea of a holiday is half a dozen rehearsals, an opera and three *lieder* recitals. I've been promising myself not to do anything but eat, sleep and read."

"And talk to me. Now, come along! The last time I saw you the Kimberley Music Society, or whatever it was called, was giving you a send-off to Europe."

"That was the night you collapsed. I wanted to come and see you the next day but I was booked on the coach."

"You didn't miss much. I wasn't a pretty sight for a few weeks. But that's *my* story. That'll come later. You're not going to get out of telling me yours."

She shivered slightly and he said, "Let's go in."

The smoking room and the lounge on the promenade deck were filled with passengers getting to know one another.

"If you don't think it forward of me," David said, "I have a comfortable stateroom and we can sit there quietly and have a

bottle of champagne and we won't have to shout at each other."

They went down to his sitting room and he rang for his steward and ordered a bottle of Bollinger. She took a cigarette from a small tortoiseshell case and leant back in the chair.

So began one of the most important periods in their lives. It started quietly, on a note of old friendship, catching up on the events of past years. David had read of her successes, as she had read of his. They were both in the prime of life—he thought she must be only a few years younger than himself, though her white skin looked to be that of a woman in her late twenties. They were both at the top of their respective trees. They were equal and they treated each other with the respect of one equal for another.

Lily's rise to stardom had been as much the work of Peter Arendt as her own and she was the first to acknowledge it. Two years after she had gone to London he sold up in Kimberley, David buying his half share in the diamond business. He took her to the best voice teachers in Europe and worked with her himself and gradually forced her voice up to a point where she was comfortably singing coloratura arias.

She started in the usual humble position with the Royal Opera but then, like so many other successful singers before her, she got lucky. She was asked to take over the role of Lucia in *Lucia di Lammermoor* at short notice when Madame Girodias had fallen ill. The critics were generous, even ecstatic, and from then on her career climbed. Within a few years she was crossing the Atlantic regularly to sing at the Metropolitan or to make extended tours. When she returned it was to bookings in Leipzig, Vienna and Paris. It was during this period that she had married Peter Arendt and they had made their home in Geneva.

David cast his mind back to the plump, soft German whom he had not seen for many years. He had been fond of Peter but had never considered him a likely candidate for Lily's hand. She was too . . . too . . . He searched for the right word but could not find it. She was a strange mixture of the voluptuous and the simple, the exotic and the down-to-earth. He was not surprised that she had fancied Jack years ago—he could understand her being attracted to his masculinity—but not Peter. He was certain that she did not approach music from the intellectual standpoint as Peter did. She was simply the owner of a superb voice, a machine able to deliver pure musical notes.

As the voyage progressed and he came to know her better he

guessed that while she had achieved almost everything an opera star could hope to achieve, it had not been without bitterness and struggle.

Gradually, as they talked more freely to each other he learnt that in fact Lily's life, like David's own, and Jack's, had been an almost continuous struggle upwards. Even as a child she had been aware of the rise and fall of families, not great families where the fall was dramatic, but the wavelets on which humble families rose and fell. Her own family was a good example. Her grandfather on her mother's side had been a grain merchant and seedsman in Alresford, near Winchester, a man who occupied a respectable niche in yeoman society. But when his wife died he became so depressed he drank himself to death, leaving debts that wiped out the business. Lily's father traveled to London looking for work and found a laboring job on the roads, the lowest of all grades of work. He was a countryman at heart, out of place in a city, especially the East End, but times were hard and he had a job and he stuck to it. He, too, was aware of the changes of fortune and put his pennies aside to give Lily whatever small extras he could afford. "I want you to look and act like a lady," he would say. "That's the first step to being one."

But when, exhausted from hard work, he died of cholera, there was no money left and she went to work in the candle factory. The winning of a prize for singing had released her from the drudgery, although whether her father would have approved of the milieu in which she found herself as a traveling artiste would be difficult to say. It was certainly no place for a lady.

Traveling with Meecham's might not have groomed her for a place in society, but it matured her, gave her an insight into the world and a sense of independence that was never to leave her. She became, at sixteen, her own woman, responsible for her own actions and her own future. Traveling in a small group gave her a certain background and feeling of security, but all decisions were ultimately her own and this itself set her apart from most other women of the times. In one sense the group was like a family: it produced a warmth and center for lives constantly in movement. It was also incestuous. The men and women who traveled in companies such as Meecham's were thrown together so much that it was normal to live together. Although they were not legalized, the liaisons were more like marriages than affairs—domestic, comfortable. In a sense, they came about naturally: a

man needed a woman for his bed and to look after him; a woman needed protection, for they played in the roughest places in the world: the goldfields of Australia, the frontier towns of America, the diggings of southern Africa: places where ninety percent of the audiences were men who had not had a woman for weeks or months or even years. That was when a woman needed her own man; that was when Lily needed someone like Lothar.

Until she met Peter Arendt and David Kade, these were the men Lily was used to. Peter was different from them all: kind, ambitious for her. She responded to him in a way that had nothing to do with sexuality or protection. For once, someone was interested in her for different reasons and she saw in this interest the way to struggle upwards again, this time away from the traveling life that had grown stale.

But her new life had its own drawbacks. When she was struggling to become a famous diva she found she was traveling even more than she had done with Meecham's, this time by herself. True, she did not have to be protected from singers and opera house intendants—but sometimes she wished she did. For traveling like this meant one empty hotel bedroom after another, single cabins, single *wagons-lits*. Finally she became worn down to a point where she fell ill.

It was then that Peter took over. He became her manager, negotiated her contracts, booked her rooms, arranged her sailings, received her money, banked it, invested it; in short, he took on himself the worry and the responsibility of her stardom. It was a short step from there to taking over her complete life by marrying her.

Once, when walking around the deck after breakfast—seven circuits equaled one mile—David said, "And living the sort of life you do, there has never been any time for children, I suppose?"

She checked her stride and frowned. Finally she said, "Yes, you could put it like that."

They went on in silence for a while and then, as though the earlier remarks had been turning in her mind, she said, more to herself than to him, "I would have given anything for a child. You don't know how lucky you are."

A few days out from Cape Town the weather grew warmer and canvas air scoops were placed in the open portholes to divert any cooling breeze into the cabins. The passengers still dressed for dinner, but the dining room became a place not to linger in. It

was the Union Line's intention to keep everyone cool by first making them hot, and at both luncheon and dinner they were served peppery mulligatawny soups and curries.

One hot, blue, lazy day followed another. David and Lily developed a routine. After breakfast they would do their constitutional around the deck, then go to their deck chairs, already placed by the steward in a shady spot. They would take their books, but often these would remain unopened as they sat staring at the hazy horizon or watched the flying fishes spurt out from under the ship. There was no embarrassment in the long silences and David did not feel called upon to make conversation as he would have at home with Hilda, who viewed all lacunae with the gravest suspicion.

It was a life of ease and of a total lack of responsibility. Both had been wound tight when they had come aboard. David had been traveling for nearly two months in the hostile center of Africa, experiencing all the nervous tension inherent in bargaining for land with African chiefs who had no conception of treaties and viewed the ownership of land as tribal, not individual. And Lily had come aboard exhausted at the end of her tour. Now, as the days passed, spent in each other's undemanding company, they began to feel less tense.

On previous voyages David had taken part in the life of the ship: the cricket match between passengers and officers; the deck-tennis matches, the fancy-dress ball, clay pigeon shooting. Now he was content to let each day drift away in Lily's company. Except for one evening when she was prevailed upon by the captain to entertain the passengers with a recital of songs from Viennese operettas she, too, eschewed the entertainments. They formed a small, quiet island in the midst of feverish activity.

David told her about the beginnings of the New Chance Mine, about his marriage to Hilda, about the birth of his son, Michael, and his two daughters, Rachel and Margaret, but even as he described them and his house in Hampstead he began to feel a sense of unreality. If he concentrated, he could see Hilda clearly; if he did not, she became an amalgam of herself and her mother. She had put on weight over the years and now he made efforts never to see her naked, never to take her unawares, for her flesh was beginning to tremble like that of Mrs. Levinson. Then there was Margaret, at sixteen a good, unimaginative girl who would embark on a plain but solid life with some plain and solid

businessman; and Rachel, too young yet to have formed a character. And, of course, Michael. He did not know what to make of Michael. Nor, it seemed, did Michael himself. He would be coming down from Oxford in a year or two, and then what? David only knew that the boy did not want to go into the diamond business.

No, it was best to view his family through the haze of distance. Seen too clearly they produced questions to which he had no answers.

One day Lily asked the question for which he had been waiting. They were sitting in their deck chairs when she said, "How's Jack?"

He placed a bookmark between the pages and put the book under the chair. "Fine."

"Just fine?" She smiled at him. "Is that all?"

He told her briefly about Jack's house, his marriage, his child, but all the while his mind was seeing a different image: the big, gross man, living like some pasha on Park Lane, doting on his daughter, indifferent to his wife, being serviced by a succession of mistresses on whom he spent more than was good for him—or for New Chance, for that matter—yet a man who was unhappy, who had found the pot of gold at the end of the rainbow and did not know what to do with it.

Two weeks after leaving Cape Town the *Leviathan* dropped anchor in the crystal-green water under the great basalt cliffs of Madeira. There was no dock at Funchal so they went ashore by lighter. David had been on the island before and would not have gone ashore except that Lily had never seen it. They hired a carriage and drove through the cobbled streets and then out for a short distance on the road to the interior where the Pico Ruivo carried a sprinkling of snow on its volcanic summit. It was cool and pleasant after the heat of the ship and they sat back on the cushions, Lily under a parasol, and let the gentle clip-clop of the horses lull them.

They had luncheon at Reid's Hotel in the garden, high on a cliff overlooking the sea. When they had finished David said, "I want you to taste something."

He went inside and returned a few moments later with a bottle and two glasses. He poured her a glass of amber liquid.

"I've never had anything like it," she said.

"You may never again. This is a 1792 Madeira. Napoleon took a

pipe with him into exile on St. Helena and after he died the hotel bought what remained."

They sat sipping the wine and watching the trees move in the breeze and she said, "I feel as though someone had just unraveled a knot in my brain."

"If that's what one glass does, you'd better have another."

They drove back to the ship late in the afternoon and as they neared the jetty she put her hand on his arm and said, "Thank you, David. I don't know when last I had such a lovely day."

In that moment, their relationship changed. He never knew whether it was the physical contact or whether it was the mood which the day had produced. Whatever the cause, he felt his skin tighten. She had removed her hand from his arm and on an impulse he placed his open palm on her lap. For a second he thought she was going to ignore him, then she did something that both touched and excited him. She was wearing a pair of light fawn gloves and she took one off so that her hand would be naked and she placed her fingers against his.

He felt the flesh of his hand burn. He found himself wanting to say something, but could not think what. As though sensing this and wishing to put him at his ease, she said, "Your hand is cool. You know what they say about that."

"Cold heart?"

"It's the other way around."

A group of passengers was waiting on the jetty for the lighter to take them back to the ship. David felt that he had to say something to her before the enchantment of the day gave way to the routine of the ship.

"Lily, I . . ." he began.

"Don't, David. Don't say anything."

She heard an echo in her mind as though she had spoken the phrase sometime in the past, but she could not remember when.

They went to their separate staterooms to bathe and change for dinner but she did not appear at the table that night, nor was she there for any meal on the following day as they steamed northwards towards the Bay of Biscay. Captain Harvey told his guests merely that she was indisposed, but David knew the real reason: she was trying to avoid him.

He spent a miserable day. Her empty deck chair was like a mute accusation and he spent the morning reading in his sitting room. The afternoon yawned before him. He walked around the

deck but only saw her maid returning to her own berth in steerage, and when he inquired he was told that Lily had caught a slight chill.

In the middle of changing for dinner he thought: what was the point of dressing up if she wasn't going to be there? So he ordered a tray in his cabin and brought out a sheaf of papers which he had promised himself he would study.

He could not concentrate. At ten o'clock he decided to take one more turn round the deck in case she had come out for air. But she had not. He looked in the smoking room and the lounges and on the dance floor but she was nowhere to be seen. He went back to his stateroom and was about to prepare for bed when there was a knock at the door. A steward stood in the companionway. "Note for you, sir," he said.

David tore open the envelope and read the words on the single sheet of ship's notepaper: "Would you think it very forward of me if I invited you for a glass of wine?"

There was no signature, but there was no need for one. He found himself smiling fatuously at the steward.

"Is there any reply, sir?"

"No. No reply."

She was dressed in a flowing garment of cream silk. "Bollinger, wasn't it?" she said, smiling, and pointed to a bottle of champagne in an ice bucket. "I wasn't sure about the year."

He poured them each a glass and said, "How are you feeling?"

"Fine . . . oh, you mean my chill? It seems to have disappeared."

He tried to sip the champagne and found that he was trembling so much he could hardly bring it into contact with his lips.

Her sitting room was much like his own, with a large sofa and two easy chairs. She sat down on the sofa and he thought he had never seen anyone so elegant and so beautiful. Her black hair shone against the whiteness of her skin and the cream silk.

"You must have caught it in the carriage. The breeze was cool."

"Possibly."

"Yes, that was . . . Lily, I want to make love to you."

"I know."

"I've wanted to ever since Madeira."

"Yes."

He gulped his wine and poured another glass, slopping some of it onto the carpet. He noticed her hand was shaking, too.

"I think I'm in love with you," he said.

He sat beside her on the sofa. She put her hand on his arm in the gesture she had used in the carriage.

"It's the ship," she said. "It always happens."

"I've traveled backwards and forwards for years and it's never happened to me before. Has it happened to you?"

She shook her head.

"And not this time either?"

"Why do you think I've been staying in the cabin? I wanted to work things out for myself."

"And?"

"I don't know. I don't want to fall in love with you. . . . I don't want you to fall in love with me. It's too complicated."

"Is that the decision you came to? That things are too complicated? Why did you invite me here, then?"

"I thought I could control the situation."

"And now?"

"I don't know. . . . I don't . . ."

He kissed her, both of them sitting bolt upright on the sofa. Her body was rigid, then suddenly she relaxed. He put his hand on her breast and she said, "Is this what you want?"

"Yes."

"Give me two minutes."

She went into her bedroom and two minutes later he followed. She lay under the sheet with a night-light giving just sufficient glow for him to see her.

He sat on the edge of the bed and kissed her again. This time she wound her arms about his neck and drew him down on top of her. He pulled away the sheet and saw the full white body. "You're beautiful," he said.

She smiled. "You're overdressed."

Nothing like this had happened to him before. His lovemaking with Hilda, which did not often happen, was a sober, matter-of-fact affair, late at night when she was half-asleep; a coupling in the dark without love, only for release. He had never really known anything else, for he had remained faithful to Hilda not only because he equated faithfulness with marriage, but also because he had always considered himself to have mild sexual

appetites. In one night with Lily this was proved false. She was the key which unlocked the passion that had lain dormant inside him for so long.

The ferocity and intensity of his desire at first surprised and then amazed her. From that first night he dismissed everything else from his mind but his wish to be alone with her. Her maid was told to go back to her berth in steerage and stay there. Food and wine were sent to them. At the captain's table their former companions did not even pretend to believe that they were indisposed. If David had known, he would not have cared. There was only one week left of the voyage and he determined to spend a lifetime in seven days and seven nights. He explored her body, sometimes with passion, sometimes with a curiosity that amused her. What heightened the affair and gave it poignancy was the fact that both knew it could not last. And both were gripped by instantaneous nostalgia for something which was not yet in the past.

Sometimes they would sleep away the days and be awake all night; mornings became afternoons and vice versa; meals were taken when they felt hungry; wine was used to heighten their sensuality or when they felt thirsty.

"Why 'Madame Montadini'?" he asked her once.

"It was Peter's idea. He said that no one would cross the road to hear a soprano called Lily Bartlett, that all the most famous singers were either Italian or Russian."

"Montadinaveskaya would have been worse," he said. She lay back, laughing.

Saying, "Stay like that," he left the bed and picked up his coat. From a special pocket high up under the arm—a pocket he had in all his suits—he pulled out a leather pouch from which he drew a piece of black velvet. He took from it the great rough diamond he had bought from Jack and placed it between her breasts. Her skin contracted with the sudden cold.

He reached for her hand mirror and held it so that she could see the diamond nestling in the white flesh.

"Is that . . . ?"

"The 'Southern Cross.'"

"I read about it. It's the biggest ever taken in Kimberley, isn't it?"

"Perhaps. Certainly it's the best."

She lifted it and looked at it more closely. "Why have you never had it cut?"

He had often thought about this. At first he had simply told himself that the expense of having such a stone cut was unwarranted at a time when every penny he had or could borrow was going into the creation of the New Chance Mine. But that had only been an excuse. He knew the real reason was that rough, the diamond was his; cut, it would have to be worn, and therefore shared with someone else. Hilda rightly felt that the diamond should come to her, or be sold. So he had prevaricated; done nothing. He had always felt that the diamond was a link to his past; in a way it represented his own self, and he had never surrendered that self to anyone—until now. As the years passed it had become a growing shadow on his relationship with Hilda. His constant refusal either to have it cut or to sell it had been a factor in the decline of their marriage.

Now he said, "One day I'll have it cut. One day you'll wear it for me."

The ship plowed northwards through the Bay of Biscay and their time together came to its end. On their last afternoon, as the late sun sank into a mass of purple cloud and turned the sea the color of wine, she said suddenly, "Hold me tight." He held her. "I've wanted that so often," she whispered. "Just to be held in a man's arms." He did not understand fully what she meant, nor would he for some time. Instead, he felt a stab of jealousy.

"Any man's?" he said.

"No. The arms of the man I love."

"Do you really love me?" He had asked her a dozen times.

"You know I do."

"Oh, God, Lily, what are we to do? I can't go back."

"You must."

He thought of his wife and children. They could get along without him. He wasn't vital to their welfare or their happiness.

"What if I don't?" he said. "What would you do about Peter?"

"Don't talk," she said. "Hold me."

3

The Farsons and the Kades took Sunday lunch with each other two or three times a year and today the Kades were lunching with the Farsons at Number 32 Park Lane. Both families were fully represented: David, Hilda, Michael, Margaret and Rachel Kade and Jack, Marie and Jewel Farson were all seated round the big table that looked out through the climbing vines in the conservatory to the terrace.

They had eaten well: turtle soup, sole, a baron of beef, grilled poussin for those who preferred it, a syllabub, then nuts. They had drunk hock and Bordeaux and finished off with a Chateau d'Yquem.

A coal fire burned in the ornate grate at the end of the room, for this spring day in 1898 was cold. The room was formal, with dark paneling, but the walls were brightened by oil paintings and watercolors of Africa, including one specially commissioned by Jack showing the winding gear and the slag heaps of the New Chance Mine.

Now the adults sat sipping port and cracking nuts. Jack had

eaten and drunk heavily and his face had a purple tinge. They had been talking, as they always talked now, about the brooding troubles in southern Africa. There was hardly a day when the London newspapers did not carry some story of mounting tension.

Jack gave himself another glass of port and said, "It's a pity Jameson made a mess of it. We'd have had the Transvaal in our pockets now and all the gold as well. As it is . . ."

"Who's Jameson?" Margaret said.

David looked at his daughter. She was a serious, plain girl with pimples on her face. "Don't interrupt," Hilda said, turning her heavy face towards Margaret.

"It's all right," David said. "He's a friend of Mr. Rhodes's. He led a rebellion in the Transvaal a couple of years ago."

"Why?"

"To take it away from the Boers."

"Why?"

"Because . . . well, because the Boers . . ." It was difficult to simplify.

Jack broke in. "Because the Boers don't want us there. That's why."

Michael cracked a nut. "Why should they?" he said. "It's their country." He turned away, coughing.

"There you go again!" his mother said.

"It's the nut. A piece got caught in my throat."

David looked at his son as he wiped his mouth. His mind went back to hot summer days in Kimberley when he used to take him by the hand and walk out towards the mine and show him the machinery. Once or twice he had taken him down in the steam lift and let him walk along the gloomy, clanking galleries.

"Is it all ours?" the boy had said.

"Most of it. Ours and Uncle Jack's."

"And will it be mine one day?"

"A lot of it. Do you want to own a diamond mine?"

"I don't know," he had said.

Then, he had been the image of what David himself had been as a child: short, sturdy, dark-haired, with the sloping shoulders that anticipated strength in the adult. He and David had gone everywhere together then: for picnics at the Vaal River, to the music hall and the theater and the horse races. David had taken him down to the Cape when he had bought the wine farm there

and they had walked on Table Mountain and swum in the sea at St. James. He remembered once taking the boy out to see Susan at Portuguese Place and with the candor of childhood Michael had looked at the house and said, "It's all broken!"

"It fell down," Susan had said, smiling. "We had a great rainstorm and it fell down. You ask your father about the rainstorm. It's something he won't forget."

"Aren't you going to build it up again?"

"One day, perhaps, when someone strong comes out to help me."

Later Michael had said, "I like Aunt Susan. Why don't we go to see her more often?"

"Would you like to?"

"Yes. Tell me about the rainstorm."

David had told him. After that Michael went out to Portuguese Place whenever he could. It was where he got to know Jewel. She would often spend a week at a time with her grandmother and Susan began to invite Michael as company for her. Right from the start there was a special relationship between the two of them. "I love Jewel," he had said once when he was eight years old.

"Like!" Hilda had said sharply. "You don't know what love means."

Hilda had been pregnant with Rachel then and she was bloated and ugly. Michael had stood facing her with a frown and he had said, "But I do love her. She's my friend."

If anything the relationship had become stronger over the years. Now David looked down the table at Jewel sitting next to her mother. She had always been an attractive child, but now she was blossoming into a real beauty. She had Marie's dark hair with her father's fair skin and the effect was dramatic. Occasionally her mother spoke to her and she leant towards her, but David saw that her eyes always returned to Michael. Marie noticed this, too. She didn't like Michael, David thought. In fact, it was doubtful if she liked the Kades as a family. She had never liked David and the relationship between the two families was built on the partnership which Jack and David had forged all those years ago when, as two penniless adventurers, they had met on the road to Kimberley. He assumed Marie's hostility had to do with the diamond. He knew she still nagged Jack about it.

"I'll tell you why the Boers should give the Outlanders the vote," Jack said. "Because they're just farmers. What do they

know about gold or big business? They haven't got the capital or the training to do anything themselves. They need the Outlanders to develop their country for them. . . ."

David examined Jack as he was speaking. Who would recognize the craggy red-haired sailor now? Then he had spoken with the grammar of the gutter, and now his diction had improved beyond measure; Marie had worked on him, David knew. But in other ways he had deteriorated: he was gross and balding and the whites of his eyes were constantly bloodshot.

"You used to take the opposite line," Michael said. "You used to say that if they gave foreigners the vote, they'd lose their country."

Jack looked angrily at him. "If they want war they can have it. That'll sort things out once and for all."

"Liberal opinion is on the side of the Boers," Michael said.

"Liberal opinion!"

"Germany and France say they'll send troops to help the Boers."

"That's all bloody talk!"

Marie, who knew that Michael had an abrasive effect on Jack, broke in. "If everyone's finished, shall we have coffee in the drawing room?"

"Just a quick cup," David said. "I have to go to the office." Jack raised his eyebrows in surprise. "I've got some work to finish." He looked away as he said it.

The drawing room was on the first floor and looked out over the park where the beech trees were coming into leaf. A cold wind was blowing.

After they had been given coffee, David took Jack aside. "I've been wanting to talk to you," he said. "Don't you think you should spread your investments?"

"What?"

"If war does come, diamonds may be hit badly. I've already sold my gold shares. Snell advises buying industrials. They'll pick up in a war."

Jack shook his head. "Not on your life. I've always stuck to diamonds and I always will. Why, if it weren't for me we wouldn't have the mine. You've said that yourself more than a dozen times. It was only because I stuck to what I knew."

"Times change."

"Not that much. You don't think the British Government will let Kimberley go, do you?"

"I think they're underestimating the Boers. Look what happened to Jameson. Look what they did to the British troops at Majuba. Michael's right. They'll get arms from Germany and France. And if anyone here thinks it'll all be over in a week or two they've got another think coming. You know what the country's like out there."

"I still say they'll never touch Kimberley."

David shrugged. "Maybe you're right." Then he said, "Have you been selling shares?"

Jack frowned. "Why?"

"A block of New Chance Mining came onto the market last week. I wondered if they were yours."

Marie broke in and Jack turned away.

"The young people want to go and listen to the band in the park," she said.

Jack nodded reluctantly.

Hilda said, "You wrap up well, Michael. You've had that cold since before Christmas. Sniff and cough, cough and sniff."

As the four young people went to fetch their coats the Farsons' butler, Cummings, came in and said to Jack, "Mr. Leask to see you, sir."

"Well, I'll get along, too," David said.

He did not like Leask. The man had been at New Chance House for more than six months and David still did not know what he did. He did know that Jack and he were often seen together in out-of-the-way clubs and at prizefights and that he monitored all Jack's visitors. He had started off in a small office but it had not been long before he had moved into a bigger one and had managed to put Miss Trimmer's back up to such a point that she resigned. He had hired a new secretary, a small mousy woman with a cold blue nose who hardly saw Jack and who worked, in effect, for Leask himself. What disturbed David was that a few weeks before, Leask had been given Jack's power of attorney to sign checks and letters. When he had gone to see Jack about it Leask had hovered until David had to say bluntly that he wanted to speak to his partner in private.

"It's only to save time," Jack had said. "He's a paper man, is

Leask. I can't be bothered with paperwork—you should know that."

It had not satisfied David but there was not much he could do. It was Jack's business whom he hired and whom he made privy to his personal affairs. The affairs of the company had long since been moved away from him and out of harm's way.

"What's all this I hear about an estate in Sussex?" he had asked. "The rumor is that you're negotiating for Lord Ryle's place near Midhurst."

Jack had smiled at him and David saw that his teeth were stained by cigars. Altogether he was looking seedy; it was said he was drinking too much.

"I'll let you know when I do. Don't worry, I'll let you know."

The band of the Grenadier Guards was playing on the bandstand at the east end of the Serpentine and in spite of the cold wind many of the chairs, set out in rows, were occupied. Michael and Jewel, with Margaret and Rachel, stood at the back listening to a selection of the latest marches by Mr. Sousa. Everywhere there were soldiers in their walking-out dress, some with ladies on their arms, others standing in groups, smoking cigars. Splashes of red, green and blue from their uniforms lit up the gray afternoon. The sight of the soldiers, as well as the uniforms of the band and the military music, gave a martial air to the proceedings and Jewel said, "Do you think there will be a war?"

"Look at that," Michael said, pointing to a Sunday newspaper lying on one of the chairs. The front page headline said

KAISER ACCUSES BRITISH OF SEEKING MILITARY
SOLUTION IN SOUTH AFRICA. KRUGER BUYING
HEAVY GUNS FROM KRUPP'S.

"I had a letter from my grandmother this week," Jewel said.

"What does she say?"

"There's been more trouble. Some Boer wagons bringing food up from the coast were attacked and robbed. The rumor went round Kimberley that English miners had done it and tents were burnt in revenge. Then it was found that the robbers were Hottentots."

"Does she think there'll be trouble?"

"Yes. She says there was the last time, at Majuba, so there will be this time."

"What happened at Majuba?" Margaret asked.

"The British tried to take the Transvaal once before," Michael said. "The Boers beat them at Majuba Hill."

Rachel said, "I'm cold."

"Don't you want to listen to the music?" Jewel said, then, turning to Michael, "Grandmother says that Mopedi is sick. She has brought him into the house."

Michael hazily recalled the old black man.

"I'm cold," Rachel said again. "And Michael's got a cough. I want some hot chocolate."

"You've just finished luncheon," Michael said.

"I want some hot chocolate."

"There's no place to buy it around here."

"There is in Knightsbridge," Margaret said.

"On one condition," Michael said. "That you sit at your own table and leave us alone."

"You want to hold hands!" There was a look of disgust on Rachel's twelve-year-old face.

They crossed Rotten Row and walked to Knightsbridge. Some of the soldiers watched them, envying the fresh beauty of the girl and the dark good looks of the young, well-dressed Jew.

The Kandahar Tearoom and Coffee Lounge was a rather gloomy place filled with ferns, aspidistras and Benares brass. The chairs and tables were green-painted basketwork. At this time in the afternoon it was almost empty. Michael and Jewel took a table in the window and Margaret and Rachel were waved back by Michael into the dim recesses of the long room. An elderly waitress in a black dress and small white apron took their orders. Michael and Jewel sat side by side and looked out at the window-shoppers walking slowly along Knightsbridge.

"Do you think *they* care about a war in Africa?" Michael said, suddenly angry. "Do you think they care what happens to a lot of farmers who can hardly speak English?"

She felt for his hand and held it under the table. "Please, Michael, don't let's talk about war anymore; we haven't much time."

"All right."

They heard Rachel giggle and realized she was watching them, but they did not care.

"Have you decided yet?"

He shook his head. He did not need to ask what she meant for they spoke in a kind of shorthand, each knowing almost exactly what was going through the other's mind.

"Father was talking to me about it again. He says, who's going to carry on the business if I don't? But I don't want to. I don't even want to stay on at Oxford, and yet . . ."

"And yet you don't know what you want to do when you come down."

"That's what worries him . . . and me. Whatever it is, I don't want it to be here. I feel part of me is still in Africa. I want to find it."

They often spoke of Africa when they were together. He could remember it, but Jewel had been too young when she left.

"Will you take me if you go?" she said.

"Of course."

"Promise?"

The waitress set the tea things down. Jewel poured and said again, "Promise!"

"Of course I promise. You're always making me promise."

"Your mother doesn't like me."

"And yours doesn't like me."

"It'll be difficult. But I don't care. I don't want to stay here without you."

He squeezed her hand. "We'll go together."

She looked into the misty distance. "Tell me about Portuguese Place."

"I've told you before."

"I know. Tell me again."

"I can't remember it all, but I remember the trees by the river. Your grandmother had them cut down once but they grew again. And the house itself, the walls so white they hurt your eyes in the sun. And the patterns of shade from the grapevine." Her eyes were on him, watching his lips, identifying with what he was saying. "The inside was dark and cool and shadowy."

"And the river," she said. "I swam there, didn't I?"

"Often."

"I can't remember." She looked out at the bleak afternoon.

"In the Breakfast Pool. It had a sandy bottom. That's where we used to swim."

"Oh, Michael, wouldn't it be wonderful if we were there and we could picnic by the river and walk under the trees . . . ?"

He sipped his tea, and some of it must have gone down the wrong way, for he had a coughing fit. She watched, worried.

When he regained his breath he said bitterly, "We never will."

"Why not? My grandmother is always asking me to come."

"We could only go if we were married."

"But we've always been going to get married." She looked at him as though he had failed to understand the bedrock on which their relationship was founded.

"I know, but they'll never let us."

"Once we're old enough they can't stop us."

"My mother wants me to marry a Jewish girl."

"What about your father?" They had been over and over this ground.

"I don't think he minds. But, anyway, your own parents would never allow it."

"They can't stop me!"

"You'll see."

"Not when I come of age."

Michael was tolerated in the Farson household, much as his father was; he was part of the partnership. But marriage? That was a different question.

Suddenly Jewel said, "I'd run away."

"Don't be silly."

"I would, if you would."

"Where to?"

"Africa. Anywhere. As long as we were together."

"What would we use for money?" That's what it always came down to, the dismal and mundane need for cash. "Love in a garret?" Michael said, smiling. "Is that it?"

"If we loved each other it would be all right."

He sipped his tea and wiped his mouth with the napkin. Suddenly he crumpled it up in his hand and sat staring at it. Then he said, "I love you more than anything else in the world. If you went away I'd die."

The words were precious to her, yet at the same time they chilled her, for she saw a look in his eyes she had never seen before: a mixture of confusion and need.

"I'll never leave you," she said.

4

By the late summer of that year, 1898, the political situation in southern Africa was deteriorating rapidly. Sir Alfred Milner, governor of the Cape Colony and British high commissioner, was already talking about "the final smash" between Briton and Boer. The Afrikaner republics of the Transvaal and Orange Free State were stockpiling arms bought from Germany and France and brought in through the Portuguese territory of Mozambique. Immigrants, mainly from Britain, were still flooding into the Transvaal to try to make their fortunes from gold, and President Kruger was still refusing to give them the vote, out of a need for self-preservation. C. J. Rhodes had leapfrogged the Transvaal and founded British Rhodesia on its northern borders. In effect, apart from one corridor to Mozambique, the Transvaal and Orange Free State were now completely surrounded by British territory. Switzerland have been brought in to mediate between Britain and the republics and had failed, but most people still believed that war could be avoided, that in the end the Boers

would climb down and allow themselves to be swallowed by Britain.

In October, David Kade went to Amsterdam. He had important business at Asscher's Diamond Works, but the major reason for his visit at that particular time was that Lily was singing there and he had not seen her for nearly two months.

Isaac Asscher had founded his firm in the middle of the century and turned it into the most famous diamond-cutting works in the world. Earlier that year he and his two sons, Joseph and Abraham, had visited David in London to discuss the cutting of the "Southern Cross." The decision to have it cut had taken David nearly twenty years to make. The three Dutchmen had studied the diamond with interest; it was already a legend and few people had ever seen it. They took it to Amsterdam to study it further before making up their minds how it should be cut. When they left, David felt as though they were taking part of his body with them.

Now the diamond was ready and he had come to fetch it. He was welcomed like royalty. The room into which he was ushered reminded him of Jack's room at New Chance House, all dark green leather and green velvet curtains. Under one window was a table covered by a green baize cloth.

Isaac Asscher offered him a chair while one of his sons went to fetch the diamond. Too tense to sit, David paced up and down in front of the long windows. Asscher tried to make conversation. He asked, as everyone did now, what David's opinion was about coming events in Africa.

David shook his head. "It's anyone's guess."

After a few more attempts at conversation Asscher said, "Don't worry, Mr. Kade. Believe me, it is the best stone we have ever cut."

Abraham Asscher returned a few moments later and put the diamond on the green baize cloth. Davd walked over to it. It sat in the middle of the table, a completely different object from the one he had last seen in London. Then it had been oblong in shape and, to the naked and untutored eye, dull, almost uninteresting, but to him it had always been the most precious possession he owned; it had become part of him. Now, as though someone had waved a wand, it had been transformed. It lay in a halo of incandescent light. It was pear-shaped and had been cut with fifty-eight facets. The planes reflected each other like

mirrors set at angles so that they repeated themselves into infinity. They flung split spectra of light from one polished surface to another: red and yellow, blue and orange, indigo, violet. Sometimes the diamond seemed to burn with the white-hot fire of the kiln; sometimes with the shattered brilliance of rain falling through sunlight; sometimes with the cold of an ice cave, needlepoints of blue light shooting from one frozen plane to the next. Everything about it was intense: heat, fire, cold, ice, brilliance. David stared at it with an intensity that matched the diamond, so fiercely that he seemed to absorb on his retinas, or through his skin, the carbon from which it was formed. No one spoke. They hardly breathed. The diamond dominated the room. Eventually David let out his breath.

"Isn't it beautiful?" Abraham Asscher said.

"It is the most beautiful stone we have ever cut," his father said. "Come, we must drink to it."

Abraham tipped four more diamonds onto the table and a number of tiny brilliants, pieces of the original stone which had had to be cut away to give it shape. Several were good stones in their own right, but David hardly spared them a glance.

"Three hundred and twelve carats," Isaac Asscher was saying. "An immense diamond."

David hardly heard him, nor did he feel the glass of champagne being pressed into his hand and he was only later aware that it had been recharged. He was once again back in a different world, a different life. His grandfather, Moshe Kadeshinsky, was standing before the little boy who sat in the big leather chair with the steaming cup of chocolate in his hands. "What do you see?"

"Fire and ice," he said aloud in the room in Amsterdam, and came slowly back to reality.

"We shall send them by courier to you in London," Isaac Asscher said.

"No." He took out a small washleather bag.

"You mean you . . . ?" The Asschers looked at him in consternation and then Isaac remembered rumors that Kade often carried the diamond on his person. He hoped not too many other people knew.

As David was collecting his hat, cane and gloves, Isaac returned to the question of southern Africa, pressing him for an opinion on whether a war would come. David had to drag his thoughts away from the diamond, realizing how concerned the Asschers

must be at the thought of anything disrupting their major source of supply.

He gave, as succinctly as he could, his own views, which were that, although the position was serious, Kimberley was the last place the British Government would allow to fall into Boer hands because so much revenue accrued to them from the diamond industry.

Isaac Asscher nodded, then said, "Mr. Kade, I have shares in several big diamond companies, including your own. You do not then advise me to sell?"

"Of course not."

"I only ask because . . ." He paused and then said, "How shall I put it? Are you not selling yourself?"

"Me?" David said, surprised. "Absolutely not. Why?"

"A big parcel of New Chance shares came onto the Paris Bourse yesterday."

David returned to his hotel, disturbed by what Asscher had said. Those shares had to be Jack's. He had asked him before to let him know if he was selling, so that he could buy the shares himself, for he feared—and he had explained this to Jack—that De Beers would buy up any shares coming onto the market and if they were not careful he and Jack might wake up one morning and find that C. J. Rhodes had a controlling interest in New Chance. Jack had pooh-poohed the whole idea and David realized he did not understand much about shares. To Jack they were just so much paper; he failed to realize their power in the wrong hands. And why in Paris? David wondered. It was an odd place for Jack to sell unless he had not wanted David to know. And why would that be?

But such thoughts disappeared once he reached his hotel on the Kaisersgracht. His windows looked out onto the leafy canal with its traffic of flower barges, food barges, barges delivering furniture, barges delivering grain, fodder, fish, meat. . . . The Amsterdamers used small barges as London merchants used delivery drays. He took the diamond out and placed it on a table near the window and then he sat with his chin in his hands and stared at it until the late sun, streaming through his window, turned the diamond into a ball of fire which hurt his eyes.

That evening it was cool and crisp as he strolled along the canals towards the Konservatorium Zaal. He had arranged his trip to coincide with Lily's Amsterdam recital because she had

told him that Arendt would be in Berlin on family business and that she was being accompanied by a Dutch pianist. The great hall was full but he had a seat in the fourth row. He watched Lily come on stage, a tall, striking figure in a flowing red dress, her black hair shining. She sang a mixture of German romantic songs and *lieder* and some she might have chosen for David himself, for they were favorites of his which he had heard her sing before: Schumann's "Widmung" and Schubert's "Im Abendrot" and "An die Musik." Then three by Brahms and two by Liszt which he had not heard before, and she finished with Schumann's "Frauenliebe und Leben."

He went to the stage door, where a crowd waited to cheer her and obtain her autograph. She saw him and waved, but it was more than ten minutes before she was able to get away and join him. He had reserved a carriage and told the driver to take them back to the hotel.

"Lily!" He brought her hand to his lips. "God, how I've missed you!"

He had ordered a cold supper to be laid in his suite and there were several bottles of champagne. A gas fire glowed at one end of the room but the night was not cold.

He indicated the food. "Now or later?"

"Not yet," she said.

He turned down the lights and the room was lit by the lamps along the canal and their reflections in the still, dark water. There was a slightly sweet, damp smell of decay in the air.

They clung to each other in the middle of the room. He said, "Every hour of every day I've thought of you and wanted you."

"So have I," she whispered.

He began to fumble at the laces of her bodice. They undressed by the reflected light from the canal and he noticed how white her skin looked. She was a miracle, he thought. Her body was still tight, her breasts high. He thought of Hilda and the comparison was saddening. It was not enough to say that Lily had never had children: the facts were the facts.

They made love atavistically, then later more tenderly; the first time like barbarians falling on each other, the second like two people in love. In between they drank wine and ate chicken.

"What was Vienna like?" he said.

"Cold."

"Are you sorry you're not going back?"

"No. Anyway, I enjoy recitals more than opera now."

"What does . . . what does Peter think?"

"Oh, it's all part of his grand plan for me. He was the one who forced my voice up, but you know a singer only has a limited number of years. I sang the *ottocento* roles but then as I grew older my voice deepened and I began to sing mezzo again. That's a good register for recitals. Anyway, I'm tired of traveling."

"You mean you'll be staying in London?" His voice rose.

"Some of the time. Peter has been talking about buying a house in Kensington. Of course, there will be some traveling. I am making a last trip to Africa."

"When?"

"Next year. Perhaps to Kimberley, too, a farewell to the people there who gave me my start. Peter will arrange everything." She talked of her husband in a casual way which upset David.

"Why don't you stop? You can't need the money."

"And then . . . ?"

"And then you could leave him."

Her smile was sad and somewhat wistful. "You're always saying that, but you'd never leave your children."

He did not reply.

"We can still have times like this," she said.

"I want you all the time."

"Maybe we would tire of each other."

"Never. How can you say that?"

"It's contrast that makes life interesting."

He lay by her side in silence, then suddenly he blurted out angrily, "I can't bear the thought of him touching you, of him making love to you."

To his amazement, she burst out laughing. "Darling, darling David!"

"What?"

She propped herself up on her elbow and again he was struck by the beauty of her breasts and shoulders. "Sometimes I wondered, but then I thought, of *course* he knows and he's being a gentleman and it's something a gentleman doesn't talk about. But you don't know, do you?"

"Know what?" he said, irritated.

"Peter's never touched me. Never has and never will. We've never made love. Oh, don't think I would have stopped him. He was my husband. I was grateful to him."

"I don't understand."

"Really? You don't know?"

"Of course I don't know."

"You never saw the young men in his house in Kimberley?"

"Young men?"

"He was very discreet, but . . ."

"You mean he . . . ?"

"That's right."

"Christ!" he said, sitting bolt upright. And then: "But how could you have married a man like that!"

"Don't get so excited, my darling," she said. "I told you why I married him. Because I'd come to the end of my tether. I couldn't stand it any longer and he did everything for me. He *made* me. Don't you understand that? If it weren't for him, I'd still be traveling with Meecham's, living in a wagon and wondering where my next meal was coming from."

"So you married him out of gratitude?"

"That and several other reasons that all fit together."

"But you don't love him?"

"How can I love him when I love you?"

He lay back, pondering on this new situation. Then he said, as much to himself as to her, "But you're still not *mine!*"

The weather held fine and they spent the following day together, a day of sunshine and empty hours which they could fill at their own pace. They strolled along the canals behind the Dam in the morning and had their breakfast of boiled eggs and thin slices of cheese at a cafe in the Rembrandtsplein. From there they walked up to the Rijksmuseum, then hired a carriage and went down to the Ijssel and had their lunch in the sunshine eating smoked eel and the new season's oysters from Zeeland and drinking cold hock. They spent the afternoon driving out in the countryside looking at the building of the new polders and came back into the city in the velvety dusk.

It was a day of unalloyed happiness when just to be in each other's company was enough, but what made it even better was the knowledge that the night lay before them; and, sated with sunshine and wine, they made love in the same unhurried, leisurely way, in keeping with the unfolding of the day. Again the dappled lamplight, reflected from the canal, made arabesques on the wall of the bedroom.

It was one of the loveliest days David could recall and like the

one in Madeira this, too, produced an equation which he felt he had to solve. Why were unlimited times like this forbidden him? He was in his middle age now, but looking back on his life he saw a long struggle upwards to find . . . what? He had all the money he would ever need, so that goal had been achieved. What was left? The act of doing business, to create more wealth and to give birth to more business, bored him. Politics had also eventually bored him. There was talk of a knighthood for his negotiations on behalf of the British Government and that did not excite him much. He had enjoyed the negotiations themselves but he did not ultimately believe that a railway would ever be built to the Angolan coast. The British Government wanted the territory for the wealth the diamond concessions would produce—business again.

He thought of the big baroque-style house overlooking West Heath which conferred status rather than pleasure on its owner. He thought of Hilda, presiding among the tea and cream cakes with her friends from the synagogue. He and Hilda no longer needed each other, that was certain. And he could not think of a time they had. He had let the pathetic luxury of the Levinsons' house in Kimberley seduce him. But it could only be acquired by taking on Hilda and the shop. The shop was a state of mind, but Hilda was a different bargain altogether. He remembered the time she had put his hand on her breast and he had smelled the fragrance of her skin. Had he ever been excited by that? He supposed he had. Linking that remote person with the present Hilda, who daily became more and more like her mother, was hardly imaginable. Would she miss him? He doubted it. Nor would Michael. He wanted no part of his father's empire. And Margaret? Stolid, plain and unemotional. She would not miss him. That left Rachel. What, he wondered, would his absence do to her? They hardly saw each other as it was, for he spent much of the year traveling. What *did* he want? The answer was simple and suddenly the influence of the day crystallized into a decision.

"I would," he said, contradicting a statement she had made the night before.

She was drowsy. "Would what?"

"Leave my family."

She turned to face him. "Are you serious?"

"Yes."

"Is that what you've been doing? Lying there, brooding?"

"Not just this evening. I've been thinking about it a lot recently. You're not happy with Arendt. You can't be with a man like that. And I'm not happy with Hilda. She wouldn't miss me, nor would the children."

"Where would we go?"

"Switzerland, the Mediterranean." He was hazy about this, for Africa kept intruding. Sometimes he would long for the hot desert days, the huge blue skies, the dust, the hard labor; life had been so much simpler then. "Do you ever think about it?"

"No," she said, "because I don't take this seriously. I don't think you would leave them. I think it's a dream. Why don't we enjoy what we have?"

"It's not enough," he said. "It's not enough to meet in hotel rooms and hired apartments. I want you with me always. I want you with me at night when I go to sleep and I want you with me when I wake. Not once a month, but every night and every morning."

Suddenly, as though what he had been saying had been the preamble to an even more important decision, he padded into the other room and came back with something in his hand.

"Look," he said. The great pear-shaped diamond lay glittering on his palm.

"My God, David, where did you . . . ? It's not the . . . ?"

"The 'Southern Cross.' I had it cut at last. For you."

"For me?"

"I want you to have it and wear it."

She took his face between her hands and kissed him on the lips. "Thank you, my darling, but I couldn't do that. You know I couldn't."

"But I want you to."

And then she said, smiling, "You can't buy me, you know."

It was like a blow in the face.

She was upset at his reaction. She had spoken lightly but he had taken her seriously. "It was a joke," she said. "Only a joke." But the pleasure seeped out of him like water through sand and he felt chilled.

Early the following morning he caught the train to Flushing and the packet boat to Harwich. The weather had turned gray and the North Sea was choppy. The sky had filled with dark clouds racing in from the southwest; the day reflected his mood. He walked on deck, but the air was cold and finally he went into

the smoking room and sat with a whisky and soda. Perhaps he should finally let Hilda have the stone, or perhaps he should sell it back to Jack. But the thought of it resting on Marie's neck or on the breast of one of Jack's whores disgusted him, and he realized his momentary reflections meant nothing. He would never sell the "Southern Cross." He would never give it to his wife. It had been created for one person only: if she would not wear it, then no one would; no one would even see it. He felt a sudden urge to take it out of its washleather holder and look at it—a thing he often did, as though to reassure himself that he, David Kade, still owned it.

The association of ideas brought back to his mind the question of the shares which Isaac Asscher had mentioned, and when the boat train deposited him at Liverpool Street Station he took a hansom to Number 32 Park Lane.

He learnt from Cummings that neither Jack nor Marie was at home. Jack was in Sussex. Marie was expected in an hour or two from a shopping expedition to Whiteley's. He was about to leave when Jewel came from the drawing room. She was dressed in a flowered print and he thought how fresh and lovely she looked. "Uncle David!" she said.

"I was looking for your father." He followed her into the drawing room.

"How's Michael?"

He looked at her in surprise. "How should he be? I've been away."

"Aunt Hilda sent a note. He was expected at the party."

"Party?"

"My birthday was two days ago." She smiled at him.

"Of course it was!" He felt a surge of remorse. Then a thought struck him. "But I hadn't forgotten it. I was in Amsterdam collecting something for you." He fumbled in the inside pocket of his jacket and took out one of the smaller diamonds cut from the "Southern Cross." "This is from me," he said. "Many, many happy returns and lots of love on your eighteenth birthday." He put the diamond into her hand and kissed her on the cheek. "One day we'll have it set in a ring."

"Oh, Uncle David!"

"My dear, it gives me more pleasure than you can imagine for you to have it."

For most of the way home he felt a glow of affection for her

which came partly from the pleasure of his own generosity. It was only when he was nearing the top of the hill, with the heath dark and windy in the dusk, that he remembered there had been a note about his son.

The house was in a state of quiet tension when he let himself in. Parker, the butler, was in the front hall, where David noticed a strange hat, coat and bag. Two housemaids were on the upper landing, whispering together.

"What's happening?" he asked, feeling a quickening apprehension.

"It's Mister Michael."

"What about him?"

"It's bronchitis, sir. He's been in bed these past two days. The doctor's here now, sir."

He ran up the stairs. Michael's room was at the end of the first landing. Hilda was by the foot of the bed and Dr. Stein was examining a piece of cotton wool by the gaslight.

David was shocked at the sight of his son. He had only been away a few days, but the boy looked thinner than before he left. His face was wan, with a yellowish pallor.

"What's all this, then?" he said.

Hilda turned her plump, once pretty face to him. It was gray and frightened. "Where have you been? We expected you two hours ago."

"I had some business to attend to." He turned to the doctor. "How is he?"

Dr. Stein was a small, thin man with a domed forehead which was out of proportion to the rest of his body and gave him a dwarfish look. He had long black hair but was clean-shaven. He was younger than David but was said to be a sound man and had been their doctor for more than four years.

"I think we will talk outside," he said. "We don't want to tire my patient. I'll see you tomorrow, Michael. Get as much rest as you can. I'll leave something that will help with the cough and make you sleep."

They went down to the huge, ornate drawing room with its ferns and tall green *Ficus.* Everything about the room gave off an air of wealth, from the Persian carpets on the floor to the Venetian mirrors and the great marble fireplace, in which a coal fire burned brightly, to the tapestries and paintings on the walls.

"Well?" David said.

"I saw him two days ago and I thought it was bronchitis."

"And now?"

But the doctor turned to Hilda and said, "How long has he had this cough?"

"Months. I don't know how many."

"And it's never really bothered him?"

"I don't think so. I have asked him often. He said he used to cough in the mornings but not much during the day."

"And yesterday was the first time he coughed blood?"

"Blood!" David said.

"Don't jump to conclusions," Dr. Stein said. "It's possible that with a cough like this a small blood vessel could have burst. Anyway, I would like a second opinion."

"Get the best man," David said. "I don't care where you have to get him from."

The domed head nodded. "There's no need to go outside London. I shall send a note to Lord Cowley tonight. He's the best chest man in the country."

"You don't think . . ." Hilda began as Parker helped the doctor on with his coat.

"I don't think anything at this stage. Tomorrow we will make up our minds."

They saw him off and went up to Michael's room. The young man was lying back against the pillows.

"Well, old chap, you've given us a bit of a scare."

"What did he say?" Michael's eyes were worried. "Is it consumption?"

The word had not been mentioned but it had been in everyone's mind. David heard Hilda's sharp intake of breath and her half-strangled sob.

"Of course it isn't," he said. "He thinks it might be a broken blood vessel brought on by the cough."

A look of hope and relief crossed his son's face and he felt his heart wrenched by love.

"What have you been doing?" Michael said.

David thought of Lily and himself in Amsterdam while his son was lying in bed coughing blood and he felt a bitter twisting of guilt.

"Business, old chap," he said. "Boring business. Not your kind of thing at all." He turned to Hilda. "Has he had any supper?"

She came to herself with a jerk. "No. And I know exactly what to give him!"

"Mother's panacea for all ills," Michael said. "Chicken soup."

"Like your grandmother," David said. "Your mother and I came to be married, you might say, through chicken soup."

"Tell him about it," Hilda said. "I'll go and see to the food."

David told his son of the fever he had had and how the Levinsons had pressed on him chicken soup day after day and how Hilda had shooed them out and rescued him and read to him and let him smoke cigars in his bedroom.

They sat with Michael through the evening and at nine o'clock mixed the powder Dr. Stein had left and gave it to him. Soon afterwards he fell asleep.

"You go to bed," David said to Hilda.

"No, I'll sit with him."

"Don't be silly."

"You must be tired after your journey."

"Go to bed. It's you who've had the strain."

She was sitting on a low, spoon-backed chair and suddenly she put her hands up to her face. "Come now," he said, and put his arms about her. It was something he had not done for a long time. He felt an old familiar feeling, not love, but a shared sadness. "Don't cry," he whispered. "He'll be all right. We'll look after him."

There was a sofa in Michael's room and he stretched out on it. Sometimes he dozed, but for long periods he lay awake. He tried to read, but could not concentrate. His mind kept going back into the past, back to the time Michael was a little boy: walking along the sands of False Bay hand in hand, reading to him, Michael sitting on his knee. Then the picture changed and the boy was no longer Michael but David himself and the hand he held was his grandfather's.

He thought of their return to England and Michael's departure to boarding school. Before that they had kissed each other as naturally as it was possible to imagine. But when the boy had come back after his first term he had held out his hand and David had known a stage was over. They no longer walked hand in hand and Michael no longer sat on his knee. A lump came to his throat and he told himself that you could not stop people from growing up; everyone grew up.

Michael woke once in the night and coughed, groping for one of the pads of cotton wool which Dr. Stein had left. David rose and held him and wiped his mouth and saw the bright crimson streaks of blood in the sputum.

Lord Cowley arrived with Dr. Stein at ten o'clock the following morning. He was as big and bluff and genial as Dr. Stein was small and dark and reserved. In his heavy shoes and tweed suit and his gray muttonchop whiskers, he looked, David thought, like a Norfolk farmer on his way to spend a day among the pheasants.

"Well, my dear sir," he said, shaking hands. "There's winter in the air. Yes, it won't be far off now."

Hilda and David led the way up the stairs. As David opened the door of his son's room, Lord Cowley said, "If you please, just Dr. Stein and myself."

Waiting in the drawing room, he and Hilda did not speak. She sat staring at the fire and he stood at the window looking out at the leaves fluttering down from the beech trees on the Heath.

Half an hour later they heard steps in the hall and Lord Cowley came in, followed by Dr. Stein.

"Well?" David said.

"No doubt about it at all," Lord Cowley said breezily. "A classic case."

"You mean . . . ?" Hilda began.

"I'm afraid so."

She gave a cry and half fell onto the sofa.

"Fortunately it's in an early stage." Cowley paused. "Mr. Kade, has anyone in your family had consumption?"

"No."

"Do you know anything about the disease?"

"Very little."

"You are going to find out a great deal. Let me give you one statistic: what has happened to your son happens to one-seventh of the entire human race. That may just give you a crumb of comfort. And remember, they are not all carried off, sir, not by a long chalk, not while we're here to fight. Which is what we are going to do. I'm not going to bore you with what causes the disease; it's the cure that we're after. Lots of rest, good food. Those are two factors. But in Britain we have a climate with sudden changes of temperature, and here in London we have

foul, filthy, smoky, nasty, foggy air. No one's going to get well in that, Mr. Kade. There are sanatoria in Switzerland and Germany, up in the Alps where the air's like crystal. And I know of some in America, in California and Arizona. Same thing."

"We'll send him anywhere."

"Happily there is one place, which you should be familiar with, that is just as good as the others."

David frowned. "Where . . . ?"

"The Cape of Good Hope. What do you call that semidesert that runs up from the Cape?"

"The Karoo."

"That's it. The Karoo. You can't beat it. Even better than Switzerland. Dry air. Clean as a whistle. Exactly the stuff he needs."

David tried to conceive of anywhere in the Karoo he could take his son. "What about nursing?" he said. "And doctors?"

"A few years ago that would have been a problem, but there is a place with a sanatorium and a doctor—Dr. Versveld, very sound man. I've sent several patients out there with great success."

"Where is it?" Hilda said eagerly.

"A town called Victoria."

"I know it," David said. "Or at least, I did when it was a village."

"There you are, then. With your resources out there and your organization nothing could be simpler. You can get your people to meet the ship and take him . . ."

"That won't be necessary," David said flatly. "I'll take him myself."

Six weeks later, when Michael had recovered some of his strength, they went together up the gangway of the S.S. *Cawdor Castle,* sailing from Southampton.

It was more than twenty years since David had made his first journey to the Cape.

5

The train stopped in the middle of nowhere. On either side of the track the small brown Karoo bushes stretched away to the far horizon. There was no station, not even a siding, nothing to mark the fact that David and Michael had almost come to the end of the journey of more than six thousand miles, except a white board with

VICTORIA HALT

lettered on it in black. This and a single-horse trap which stood in the shade of a mimosa tree were the only signs of civilization. It was a day in the late southern summer of the year 1899 and the heat was fierce. David helped his son onto the trackside and their boxes were passed down from the luggage van. The train whistled twice and slowly gathered speed until all that was left of it was the acrid smell of gases from its smokestack.

The trap, driven by a gray-haired old Colored man, met all the trains that stopped at Victoria Halt to pick up the mail bags and any passengers for Victoria, and they were soon rattling over the veld on a dusty track.

"I'd forgotten how lonely it was," Michael said, staring at the vast and silent Karoo.

"Victoria is lively enough," David said. "The last time I was there you couldn't get a room for love or money and you had to queue for a meal." He put his hand on his son's shoulder as though to reassure him. But he needed the reassurance himself. He had not expected to be put down in this lonely place. He had to keep telling himself that once they reached the sanatorium everything would be all right.

All the love he'd had for Michael as a child had come surging back on the voyage out. The first few days had been filled with anguish, for Michael had seemed so weak that David had wondered if he was not slipping away. But the ship's doctor had been confident. The illness, he had said, was known for its peaks and troughs, and he had been right, for during the second week Michael had rallied to the extent of David's being able to take him for walks around the deck. They had spent most of the time in their stateroom and David had taken all his meals there. He had arranged for a private nurse to accompany them on the voyage and she had taken some of the strain, but he had spent all his time with his son. When Michael's eyes had grown tired from reading David had taken over and he had read aloud hour after hour.

They had spent three weeks on David's wine farm in the Drakenstein Valley thirty miles from Cape Town while telegrams flew to and from Victoria.

It was then that Michael had, for the first time, mentioned Jewel. One day on the farm, when his bed had been carried out into the cool of the late afternoon and placed under one of the great oak trees, he had looked at the white walls of the house and the big red-flagstoned veranda—an old Colonial Dutch house with curving gables built at the end of the eighteenth century—and had said, "Jewel would love this house. It would remind her of Portuguese Place."

David had been sitting in a deck chair looking at a day-old copy of the *Cape Times*. "But she was only a baby when she went to Portuguese Place," he said. "I'm surprised she can remember it."

"I don't think she can. But we talk about it. She remembers the river—or she thinks she does."

"I used to take you there when you were a boy."

"I know. I often think of the pool. I wish I could swim there now."

"You will one day, old chap. One day soon. I promise you."

But now, as the trap breasted the rise and came down onto the plain where Victoria lay, he no longer felt the same confidence.

He had assumed that, like Kimberley, the village he had once known would have grown into a town. Instead, it looked exactly as he recalled: there the white turrets of the Lord Somerset Hotel with the Union Jack drooping on the flagpole, there the tiny bank, there the shop, the single street, the line of pepper trees and the little river. All was the same except for one thing: nothing moved. There were no wagons, no coaches, not even a horse tied to a hitching rail. It lay dead in the afternoon sun. The railway had killed it. No coaches ran now and no wagons made the long journey hauling freight; everything went north by train, missing Victoria by five miles.

He looked from side to side, vainly searching for a building that might be the sanatorium. When the trap stopped outside a house on the outskirts of the village he made no move to get down. The old Colored man turned to him and David said unbelievingly, "Is that it?"

"Ja, baas."

He found himself looking at a stone-built Colonial bungalow set behind a dusty, ragged hedge of myrtle. Large brown shutters were fastened back from the windows and the roof was corrugated iron, painted green. Was this the place they had come so many thousands of miles to find? Was this the place which Lord Cowley, in his bluff and genial way, had described as a sanatorium as good as any in Europe or America? He bitterly regretted not having brought out his own medical staff, bitterly regretted having believed Lord Cowley. In that instant he made a decision. They would spend one or two nights at the hotel, only long enough for Michael to rest, and then they would go back to the Cape by train and take the next ship to Europe. If all went well he could have the boy in a Swiss sanatorium within a month.

As these thoughts were going through his mind the door of the house opened and a middle-aged man in old, dusty farm clothes came down the steps. He was a white man, as far as David could

see, but burnt brown by the sun. He had a straggly gray beard and wore an old felt hat with a sweat-stained band. He held a filthy meerschaum pipe in his mouth.

David assumed that he had come to fetch the luggage and was about to tell the driver to go to the hotel when the man said in heavily accented English, "You must be Mr. Kade and Michael. I am Dr. Versveld."

David stared at him, speechless.

"I hope you had a good journey. Now, young man, can you walk?"

He smiled up at Michael. It was an engaging smile. His thin, solemn, bearded face turned puckish and David noticed that his teeth were badly stained by tobacco. But there was friendliness and warmth in the eyes.

"Yes, I can," Michael said.

"Right, then, climb down."

"Wait," David said. "I've brought my son all the way from London. He's very ill. We were supposed to find a sanatorium."

"Ja, that's right," the doctor said, moving his head in the direction of the house behind him.

"You call this a sanatorium? We're going to the hotel to let my son rest for a few days. Then I shall take him back."

The doctor turned to Michael. "What do you say?"

Michael tried to reply but he was racked by a coughing spasm and David put his arm around his shoulders.

Dr. Versveld kept his eyes on Michael. "How do you feel about it? Do you feel like giving it a try here? You've come so far."

There was something in his eyes, in the frankness of his gaze that reminded both men of Jewel. "All right," Michael said.

"No!" David said loudly. "We'll return to Europe. I can't think why we came to this godforsaken village in the first place." He turned to the driver. "Take us to the hotel."

"Let him at least stay until he has recovered his strength," the doctor said. "We can look after him better here and the food is wholesome."

Michael was already standing on the road. David followed him unwillingly. "All right. But just until he has rested."

"Come in and have some tea, Michael." Dr. Versveld took his arm and led him into the house as though they had been friends for a long time.

There were no wards inside the house. All the beds were on the

verandas running round three sides. There was a males' veranda, a females' veranda and a children's veranda. The center of the house consisted of Dr. Versveld's rooms and the quarters of the nursing staff, as well as a common room where ambulatory patients could meet and talk and play cards. It was a large bungalow and had clearly been built to Dr. Versveld's design.

He took them now into the common room, which was furnished with comfortable, shabby sofas and armchairs. It was a welcoming room, cool and shadowy behind the half-closed shutters. The doctor went off to order tea and Michael and David were, for the first time since leaving London, embarrassed in each other's company.

David, realizing that his concern for his son had caused him to speak more angrily than he had meant, was conciliatory.

"It's better than I thought from the outside," he said.

His eye fell on two large portraits hanging on the wall. One was a photograph of a bearded man in a black frock coat. Underneath on a little brass plate was the name of Dr. Jacobus Versveld. The next was a painting, showing another bearded man of stern and forbidding countenance, this time wearing a tall hat. Underneath he read the name Dr. Marthinus Versveld.

On the opposite wall were two vellum scrolls framed and glazed. He crossed but could not read them, for they were in High Dutch, though he could see that they were honors of some sort, granted by the Universities of Leiden and Utrecht. He turned away as Dr. Versveld returned.

"Are those members of your family?" he asked, indicating the portraits.

"My father and grandfather."

"So you've been doctors for three generations. And those?"

"I'm afraid that is conceit. What was it your poet Shakespeare said in *As You Like It*? 'My pride fell with my fortunes'? With me it is the other way round. I have no fortune, so I must keep my pride where I can see it."

By the time they had finished tea David's resolve to remove Michael as soon as he could had already begun to weaken. In a few days it had disappeared completely. In spite of himself he had placed his trust in this strange, dedicated man.

David was to spend weeks and months in Dr. Versveld's

company and yet he never truly could say he knew him. He soon realized that his habit of dressing like a laboring man was only partly affectation. One of the keys to his character was his deep, almost passionate love for this dry, dusty country and for the people who inhabited it and with whom he so closely identified. His own family had emigrated from Holland in the eighteenth century and had become farmers and pastoralists and it was only when his grandfather had gone to the University of Groningen and taken a degree in medicine that the rural tradition had been breached. His father had continued the academic line, while his five uncles, like Frans Delport, became hunters or farmers or both. So that by the time Pieter Versveld, the present owner of the Victoria Sanatorium, grew up, the dichotomy was clear: doctor or farmer. In microcosm, this was the dichotomy of his race. He had chosen to be both. He had done brilliantly at university and during all his time in Holland had longed for the semidesert. Once returned he had become a farmer, only to pine for the academic life. His present situation was a compromise. On the outskirts of Victoria he owned a small farm of a thousand *morgen* and on it he grew vegetables and raised a few sheep, cattle and hens. He was able to feed his patients fresh food, and whatever was left over he sold to the hotel.

The reason he had chosen Victoria in which to live sprang from tragedy. He had married in his late twenties and within a year his wife had contracted consumption. He had taken her to Switzerland for treatment on borrowed money, but in the expensive sanatorium in the Alps she had shown no progress and slowly had become weaker. He had taken her home to die. Instead, in the dry air of the Karoo she had rallied and become well again. Then had come tragic irony. She had become pregnant and died of childbed fever in a Cape Town hospital.

Now there were three patients in the sanatorium: Michael, the only man, and two women. The children's veranda was mercifully empty. The two ladies were Dutch and could speak no English. They would nod and smile at the Kades, until one died and was buried in the small, dusty cemetery on the far side of the village where the mica chips glared balefully in the blinding sunshine.

Normally there would have been half a dozen or more patients escaping the damp climate of the Cape but Victoria, though in

the Cape Colony and therefore under British rule, was remote enough to make people apprehensive about going there in the present unrest.

The months spent at Victoria with his son formed a strange hiatus in David's life. For the first time in many years he had nothing to do. The New Chance Mine ran itself under the direction of Dan Halkett. The financial side was looked after in London by a group of highly qualified directors. It was curious, he thought, that he did not feel worried at being left out. He knew that other men in his position would hate to be away from the center of things, would fear the undermining of their position by envious subordinates, or even suffer from a simple need to continue working, to make business create business for its own sake. None of these things applied to him. Removed from the world of business, removed almost from the world itself in this strangely isolated community, one day drifted into another. He had taken a suite of rooms at the hotel. After breakfast he would walk a mile or two into the veld while he smoked a cigar, then take up the duties of the day. This meant being with Michael, reading to him, talking to him, doing crossword puzzles with him in two-day-old copies of the *Cape Times* and the *Cape Argus*. He took his luncheon at the sanatorium and would doze in an armchair which had been put out on the veranda by Michael's bed. Then more reading, more talking, writing and reading letters, back to the hotel to bathe and change. He would have his dinner there, usually roast Karoo mutton, and then he would walk back to the sanatorium. He might play a game of chess with Dr. Versveld or drink a glass of brandy with him while they talked.

The two of them argued endlessly about the troubled times. It was the doctor's view that South Africa should have been left alone to find its own destiny as an agricultural community. It was David's that such a philosophy, while the world was pushing on into the industrial age, would leave the country a backwater, at the mercy of any major power. It was Dr. Versveld's contention that it was Britain's greed for gold which had brought about the present crisis and that the lack of franchise for the Outlanders in the Transvaal was simply being used as an excuse for invasion. It was David's that Britain was in competition with other industrial powers and that the resources of Africa were needed to maintain her position in the world.

These conversations, more or less heated, went round and round as they were going round and round in almost every small town and household in southern Africa. Families were becoming split in their loyalties. Some Boers who lived in the Cape Colony supported the British Government, some the two republics. It looked as if the country was heading for a partial civil war. David was concerned, though not surprised, that in all his arguments, Michael took the side of Dr. Versveld.

The common room contained shelves of books, but few were in English and so David telegraphed his secretary in Kimberley to send him what she could find. A week later two boxes arrived. She had done well. There were some of the more recent novels published in England and there were also a few of the books that David himself had read in Kimberley. There was Mr. Trollope's account of his visit to the diamond fields and there was also his favorite, *Barchester Towers*. For the first time in weeks he was able to make Michael smile by reading him the account of the Proudies' inauguration party, when Mrs. Proudie had lost her skirt. There were several novels by Dickens and a complete set of Gibbon, which David had always meant to read. But the most important of all, still wrapped in oilskin, was the old Portuguese Bible which he had put in his desk the last time he had been in Kimberley. By its side was the Latin dictionary he had asked for.

It was just the kind of mental challenge he needed in the circumstances and he soon added to his routine an hour at the text before breakfast while his mind was fresh. As the autumn days drew in he found himself looking forward more and more to this particular task. He began to get up at half past six, when he would ring for a pot of coffee and ask the waiter to make up the fire in his sitting room. Then, with his Latin dictionary, the Bible and a school exercise book he would settle down at the table in front of the fire and begin to work.

The translation went slowly, for the writing had faded so much over the years that even working with a large magnifying glass it was often impossible to make out words. So he bought some tracing paper and traced the outlines of difficult words. Then he would write down what they looked like; he might find several that resembled each other and he would try each in the sentence to see if it made sense.

Slowly and with infinite patience he began to fill the pages of his notebook. Some looked like mosaics, with large gaps in the

sentences. He would return to these and experiment until he found the correct word. It was like doing a literary jigsaw. And one morning he sat back to read the first two pages and the same excitement he had felt at the discovery of a diamond came over him.

"*Hic Johannis Pater Rosarii Sancti rem narrabo de nave quadam nomine* Nossa Senhora da Coimbra *naufragata in oris Africae inter occasum solis et meridiem anno Domini* MDLXXVIII. . . ."

"I, Father John of the Rosary," he read, "set down here the story of the wreck of the ship *Nossa Senhora de Coimbra* on the southwestern coast of the country of Africa in the year of our Lord 1578.

"We had set sail from Goa in the Indies in November of the previous year. Our number was one hundred and fifty-three passengers and crew and one hundred and ninety-four black slaves, thereby making a total of three hundred and forty-seven souls. . . ."

He read the description of the wrecking of the vessel, of the loss of life as crew and passengers came ashore, of the encampment on the beach, and of the sale of foodstuffs by the sailor Barreto to those who could afford to buy.

He entered a new and unexpected world. It was at once fabulous and yet probably true, for when Father John described the country and animals David recognized the accuracy of the writing. He knew there had been Portuguese wrecks on the east coast of Africa, for they were documented, but this was the first time he had heard of one on the southwest coast.

His fascination with his task became so intense that many an evening, after seeing that Michael was settled for the night, he would give up the opportunity of arguing or playing chess with Dr. Versveld and return to the hotel to continue his work.

Slowly the picture of those tragic sixteenth-century wanderers began to emerge. One after another, and then by fives and tens, they dropped away in death until fewer and fewer struggled along the river. The description of the death of the former captain of the dockyard in Goa, the gross man in the brocade coat with the large cut-glass buttons, he found particularly affecting, for Father John had stolen back along the track after Barreto had entered the camp wearing the coat, to give the dying man

extreme unction, only to find the body already half-eaten by animals. He had prayed over it and made a small cairn of stones to mark the place.

It was this work of translation that saved David from declining into secret melancholia, for his son did not seem to be getting any better. The sanatorium was run on Spartan lines and this, according to the doctor, was part of the cure. The food was simple, nourishing and wholesome, the nursing adequate, but the one thing he could not understand was the doctor's obsession with fresh air. He recalled Lord Cowley's talk of clean air; Dr. Versveld had taken this a step further. His patients lived on the verandas, sleeping out there as well, and now that autumn had given way to winter the nights were bitter. The weather was much the same as David had become used to in Kimberley: still, warm, golden winter days with frosty nights. The doctor assured him that this was a vital part of the cure. "We have to make his lungs strong," he explained. "His own body must fight the disease. There is nothing wrong with cold air; damp air, yes, but cold, dry air is like a tonic."

David began to grow used to the convolutions of Michael's disease. Sometimes the boy would be gripped by a kind of euphoria and his cheeks would become quite pink as though with health; at others he would lapse into depression. Sometimes he coughed blood; then for days, perhaps even weeks, there would be no sign of it and David would tell himself that he was on the road to recovery.

The postal service had improved greatly and there was a regular supply of letters from England. Hilda wrote to him on family business, formal letters without warmth, and there was, of course, much official correspondence from London and Kimberley. Michael, too, received letters from his mother, curiously stiff and filled with admonishments; and also letters from Jewel. David began to notice that when he received one from her it was like an injection of life-force. He would be buoyed up for a day, perhaps even two or three, before the disease pulled him down again.

On his good days he talked a great deal with Dr. Versveld and it was through these talks they became acquainted with the doctor's past. Michael would question him about farming and medicine, always gently encouraged by Dr. Versveld himself.

Towards the end of June, Dan Halkett wrote asking David to

come to Kimberley on urgent business. A conference had been held earlier that month in Bloemfontein between representatives of the two Boer republics and Great Britain, in an attempt to resolve the franchise problem in the Transvaal. It had begun with high hopes, but had come to nothing, and now Dan wrote that he feared war might break out either that year or the next and he was making contingency plans for the protection of the mine.

David traveled up by train and was away for a fortnight. During that time he was closeted with Dan in the building in the Dutoitspan Road, discussing what supplies they needed. Their most immediate problem was coal, for all the machinery of the mine, including the lifts which took the thousands of black miners down into the galleries and brought them back to the surface again, was run by steam. If the railway line was damaged, coal supplies would be cut off.

Dan had bought up thousands of yards of barbed wire and thousands of grain bags which he was having filled with sand. It was typical of him, David thought, to plan for the future. He was one in a million. Steady. Rock solid. Reliable. But for him, David might never even have known there were diamonds in the blue ground. He owed a great debt to Dan, which was why he had brought him into the company and given him stock.

Dan's face had aged and become weather-beaten, but the eyes were still young and as steady as they had ever been. David thought it was a pity he had never married. He would have made a good husband and a good father. He lived now in a big house in Beaconsfield, one of the Kimberley suburbs, all by himself with a few servants, and read mining and engineering journals in the evenings. The mine was his life; it was all he had had after Joe Malone had died.

Perhaps Joe was the reason he had never married. He had taken a long time to die. First it had been his liver and then his kidneys. Dan had looked after him month after month in their big house; had hired the best medical attention, even brought up a renal specialist from Cape Town. When Joe died he seemed to become even quieter, something of a recluse, and the mine became his life and his hobby.

Discussing his preparations, David said, "You've certainly thought of everything, Dan, though they don't seem to agree with you in the town." He had found, wherever he had gone, that

people were dismissing the idea of Kimberley's being in any sort of danger.

Dan was sitting behind his desk and now he looked down at his square, competent hands and said, "We're only a few miles from the Orange Free State border. I know for a fact that the Boers have spent more than a million pounds with Creusot in France and Krupp's in Germany. They've got the latest field guns, some of them huge affairs, and the best machine guns. When I was in Johannesburg they told me trainloads of Mausers had been brought in and there's not a rifle in the world to beat a Mauser. They've ordered tents and food. I'm told there's even a German commando training in the Transvaal. On the British side, there are rumors that they're bringing over three regiments from India. There's talk of reinforcing Mafeking and Kimberley. The thing has its own momentum, David. It's like starting to push a boulder down a hill. It takes a lot to overcome the inertia but once it moves, who can stop it?"

It was a long speech for Dan, and he wasn't finished, for he paused and then said, "There's something I want to ask you. Have you been selling shares?"

"Me? No."

"Someone has. I know De Beers have bought a lot of New Chance shares recently."

David's mind went back to his conversation with Isaac Asscher in Amsterdam.

"What about Jack?" Dan asked.

"Maybe. He's spending money like water: gambling, prizefight wagers, tarts. It crossed my mind at the beginning that he should take a salary and stock like the rest of us. But no. I remember him saying, 'What? Pay myself wages? No bloody fear, what I want is stock.' He's bought an estate in Sussex and he's turning it into a kind of animal park. Spending a fortune on it."

"I heard about it," Dan said. "Well, the three of us are the main stockholders. If you haven't sold and I haven't, that only leaves Jack."

"I asked him and he denied it."

"I heard he has a man called Leask working for him."

"I've never liked the man. Do you know him?"

"Of him. His father used to work in the Post Office. He came out here as a kid. Digger for a while. Tried his hand on the

goldfields, then came back. People say he's been mixed up in several shady deals but no one has been able to prove anything."

"I'll write to Jack, though I'm not sure it'll do much good. I'm never even sure where he is. I'd best write to him in Sussex and send a copy to London. I know Leask has his power of attorney. Snell told me Jack had asked him to draw it up. I'll write to Snell, too."

"We don't want to wake up one morning and find we're owned body and soul by C. J. Rhodes," Dan said.

It was while David was in Kimberley that he read in the local newspaper of the planned visit later that year of Madame Montadini.

There had not been a single day since he had been with Lily in Amsterdam that he had not thought of her with longing and with guilt. He remembered how they had wandered like children through the city, unworried and unhurried. He thought of their naked bodies on the bed. He had not attempted to get in touch with her after his return to London. Now, wherever he went in Kimberley there were reminders of her; places where he had seen her, heard her, spoken to her.

When he returned to the sanatorium he found Michael much worse. He had lost weight. His dark eyes were sunk into his skull; his hands on the coverlet were thin and bony, skeleton's hands.

They talked for an hour or so. David told him about his journey, then he asked how things had been going in Victoria. A new patient—an elderly woman—had arrived from the Cape; one of Dr. Versveld's cows had died; one of the nurses had left; the Union Jack which flew from the flagpole on the Lord Somerset Hotel had been stolen one night and the following morning the village had awakened to see the Vierkleur, the Transvaal flag, snapping at the masthead. So diminished had David's world become that these events seemed more interesting and more important to him than anything in Kimberley.

Michael was visibly tired by talking and David sat with him while he dozed. A little later Dr. Versveld came onto the veranda and said, "Walk with me."

They walked out into the veld on the cart track, the doctor puffing at his pipe, looking for all the world like a laborer talking to his employer.

"He seems worse," David said.

"That's what I wanted to talk to you about. He should be showing signs of improvement by now."

"What can be done?"

"It's difficult to know. He's a strong young man, physically and mentally. But it is as though . . ." The guttural voice paused. "How can I put this about someone so young and with so much to look forward to? It is as though he had lost the will to fight. Do you understand what I mean?"

"Yes."

"And you *have* to fight this disease. Is there anything you can think of that would restore his will?"

"I don't know. He and his mother are not very close, otherwise we could ask her to come to him."

"While you were away we talked. He told me of a young lady. The daughter of your partner."

"Jewel. They've been friends since childhood."

"Friends? It sounded more than a friendship."

"They're very young."

"You don't believe that young people feel strongly?"

"I know his mother doesn't. I've never given it much thought."

"Begin to give it some now, Mr. Kade."

"I don't see that . . . You mean you think their separation is why he's lost the will to fight?"

"It could be. It is part of our adult philosophy to reserve some emotions for ourselves. One of them is strength of feeling."

"What can we do?"

"I think if we want to save him we must make a plan." He put his hand into his brown velveteen jacket and pulled out a piece of paper. "This came while you were away. It is a letter from her. It was after he received it that he began to fail. I am not ashamed to say I took it and read it. Now you must read it. Not here. In the hotel."

David took it to his sitting room and shut himself in.

Dearest,

There is no way. I have tried everything. Father is only interested in Rylands [David knew this to be the estate in Sussex] and will not think of going to Africa, much less taking me with him. Mother shops and takes tea with *ladies* in Knightsbridge. She says she will never go to Africa again. They will not allow me to visit Grandmother by myself. The only way is for you to get well and come back. I pray for you every morning and evening.

I live for your letters. When one comes I take it to my room and look at it for a long while before I open it. Then I only read it bit by bit. Sometimes I can make it last a whole day.

Oh, Michael, what can we do? Often I think we shall never see each other again. You say in your letters that you can think of dying without fear. I feel that, too. If you were to go I would not wish to stay.

I haven't meant to write such a gloomy letter, but it is *hard* to be cheerful sometimes.

[David felt his eyes blur.]

If there was any way I could come to you I would. You are so *far* away. If you were in Switzerland my thoughts would reach you. But Africa . . .

Perhaps I won't post this. I tell myself I must *not* be gloomy. But perhaps I will, because it says how much I miss you.

Good-bye, dearest. I love you so much.

Jewel

David sat for a long while with the letter in his hands; then slowly he folded it and put it in his pocket.

6

In that part of the Sussex Downs which lies between Midhurst and the sea there are valleys hemmed in by wooded hills which are cut off from the rest of the country, secretive, isolated places which can only be reached by rough tracks. Jack Farson owned one such valley. It was called the Rylands Estate after old Lord Ryle from whom he had bought it, and it covered an area of more than five thousand acres. The house was large and built of knapped Sussex flint interspersed with yellow Cotswold stone, with a red-tiled roof and leaded lights.

On a blazing summer morning three heavy closed wagons were drawn up in line on the track that led to the house. They were surrounded by a group of about two dozen people, half of whom were estate workers, the rest Jack Farson and his family and guests. Jewel was there and so was Marie, who stood on the outskirts of the group.

"All right?" Jack shouted.

"Right, sir," his foreman answered.

There was a thud and banging from the first wagon, then the back door was partly opened and the onlookers could see the ends of several trailing ropes. These were quickly grasped by the estate servants, the door was fully opened and out into the sunshine burst a gray and white shape with long curving horns. A gasp went up and then a ripple of applause.

"What is it, Jack?" a man called.

"Oryx. What we used to call a *gemsbok* out in Africa."

The antelope, with its beautiful, masked face, kicked and twisted, but the ropes held and it was finally put through a narrow gate in a high fence and released to go springing and kicking on the lush green turf. They unloaded a second oryx and transferred it safely. Then the wagons moved along the track to a second gate and a pair of black sable antelope were unloaded. The last wagon contained a male and a female ostrich and these, too, were released.

"We'll have to call you Noah!" a voice called, and Jack laughed.

Marie watched him with a stony expression on her face. He was in his element, bustling backwards and forwards, seeing to everything. She wished she had not come—she hated Rylands—but the idea of Jack being host to Lord and Lady Vinnell and Sir Hugh Barber without her was unthinkable. The guests were a mixture of her friends and his and she had come down to guard her interests, so to speak. It was as well she had, for Jack's friends included some from the fringes of the prize ring and a young woman called Violet who was certainly his latest tart.

"Come on, now," he said. "I'll show you round."

He was like a child, she thought, a gross, purple-faced child with a new toy. He was even dressed for the part: khaki trousers, boots, canvas puttees, a plaid shirt and a neckerchief. But it was all a charade, for the clothes were new. His boots had been handmade at Lobb's and there were stiff creases in his new shirt. He was playing at being in Africa, trying to turn the clock back. It might amuse the English, but it did not amuse Marie.

She followed the group with Jewel at her side as Jack took them for a tour of the estate. He had turned the valley into a kind of Africa-in-Sussex. There were large fenced enclosures which contained African antelope: springbok, eland, roan, oribi, harte-beest and half a dozen more species. There were ostriches, a pair

of warthogs, a troop of a dozen baboons and a cage of leopards. But the centerpiece was the lion enclosure, a small rocky knoll with caves in it, a moat in front and a stout fence behind it. The caves were passageways into cages at the rear. All the boulders making up the knoll had had to be brought by wagon but they now managed to convey an impression of naturalness, and the six lions lying about in the noon sun appeared to have lived all their lives in Sussex.

"That must have cost a fortune," a voice said, and Marie mentally agreed. The importation of the animals alone must have cost thousands and when added to the creation of an animal park the sum was astronomical. She had mentioned this to Jack once and he had shrugged it off, saying, "There's plenty where that comes from." Well, she did not care what he did with his money as long as he did not keep her short or interfere with Number 32 Park Lane; he could buy up every animal in the world if he so wished. She'd heard talk of his selling shares, but she did not understand the workings of the share market.

Jewel was walking ahead of her with Sir Hugh Barber. He was a dry, thin-faced widower in his forties, eldest son of a Midlands brewer. He would be worth a considerable fortune when his old father died. Marie knew this because she had checked up on him, as she did all bachelors and widowers who were under the age of fifty and who dined regularly at Number 32. Sir Hugh was not, perhaps, an ideal match for Jewel—she would have preferred someone younger—but at least he was a baronet, and with Michael Kade ill in Africa anything might be achieved. As they stopped to look at yet more antelope her eyes dwelt on her daughter. Her face was thinner and some of the freshness had gone out of it. The hair had lost its shine, the eyes their sparkle. She was mooning after Michael, of course. Marie was sorry about his illness, but in many ways it had come as a blessing; it had broken at last the years of uninterrupted friendship. She remembered Jewel's despair after David had taken Michael away, and the days when she and Jack had thought Jewel herself was ill. Then later there had been her continuous nagging to go out to Africa. They had weathered both phases. She would forget him eventually; young people always did when they were separated. Michael was not for Jewel. Marie had not the least intention of allowing such a match. And nor, she knew, had Jack.

The sun was falling directly onto her daughter's face and she

was able to inspect it closely without being seen. Every now and then she caught herself doing this, but really there was no longer any need. There was not the slightest hint about the lips or the nose or the hair, and her skin was as white as Sir Hugh's. There was nothing to suggest any irregularity in her ancestry. That worry had disappeared from Marie's mind when she had left Africa. She had suspected that this might be the case and she had nagged Jack until he had agreed to move to England. But she had determined then never to have another child; and if that meant refusing Jack his conjugal rights, that was simply unfortunate for him. Marrying him as a means of escape had been her object, nothing more. In the safety of England she had decided that if she could marry Jewel off to one of the aristocrats who came to her house and if she, Marie, never set foot again in Africa, there was no possible way anyone could discover her past.

Luncheon was another attempt to push back the years, with a sheep roasted on a spit and the guests eating with their fingers. She heard phrases like "alfresco" and words like "novel" and "amusing" and she thought that for these people it might be amusing, but the smell of mutton fat flaring on an open fire took her back to Portuguese Place and the blinding heat of the desert. She had no wish to be reminded. So she drank her champagne and kept her eyes on Jewel and saw that she in turn looked after Sir Hugh.

A great deal of champagne was consumed in a short time and after the meal was over coffee was served in the shade of a spreading beech.

"Come on, now, digger," one of Jack's raffish friends called out. "I know they call you Lucky Jack Farson. What's the secret?"

"Tell us how you did it, so we can do it, too."

Jack sat in the middle of the group, his face blood-red from the champagne and the sun.

"Easy," he said. "All you got to do is bend down and pick up the diamonds."

"Upon my word," Sir Hugh said, "you make it sound *too* simple."

"I did pick up a diamond, and that's God's truth."

Marie looked at him sharply. He never spoke about the diamond. "I thought I was a rich man when I found that stone."

"So you were," a voice said.

"Oh, no," Jack said. "Not then. Listen, I'll tell you what

happened. Here's me with the best stone ever found in Kimberley and you know what happens? God sent a thunderbolt."

Someone laughed.

"I mean it."

Marie looked at him with distaste. He had drunk too much champagne too quickly and now he stood in front of his guests, swaying slightly.

"You could call a meteorite a thunderbolt." He told them the story of the Mexican disaster and how the prices of diamonds had fallen to the floor. He told them about the accident to Susan and how he had sold the diamond to David to pay for her medical treatment. And how the meteorite story had been denied almost immediately. Marie noticed Leask was watching him, a thoughtful look on his foxy face.

"But the real story only comes now," Jack said. "This is rich, this is." He told them how David had taken the stone and let Bulchand believe it had come out of New Chance. "He didn't lie, though. My partner's an upright man." He was slurring his words. "Very upright. Wouldn't lie. He just let old Bulchand put two and two together and make five." There was laughter. "That's how the whole thing started."

"Where *did* you find it?" Sir Hugh asked.

"That'd be telling." He drank, and said, "My wife's never forgiven me for selling that stone, have you, my dear?" She smiled as best she could. "But I say, don't worry about it. Let it go. I don't like diamonds, anyway." There was a burst of disbelieving laughter and he smiled. "This is what I like. A few drinks with good friends."

He caught sight of Jewel, stepped to her side and put his arm around her waist. "Man's got to have friends," he said. "This is Jewel. You all know Jewel." His speech was thick and he was mumbling. "My bes' friend. When Jewel was a little girl used to carry her up here." He indicated his shoulders. "Her throne. Called her my little princess. . . ."

"Jack!" Marie said.

"Sat up here and waved, like royalty. Jus' like a princess. . . ."

Marie cut across him. "Jack, I think some people have to catch early trains."

The party began to break up and when the last carriage had gone she said, bitterly, "Well, that was a fine speech! Humiliating me and embarrassing Jewel in front of everyone."

Jewel was standing a few paces away. "It's all right, Papa."

"It's not all right," Marie said. "It was disgusting." She turned and said to her daughter, "Get ready, please; we're going up to town." The girl's eyes brightened momentarily and she knew it was at the thought that there might be a letter awaiting her from Michael. "Your manners leave a lot to be desired, too," she said sharply. "Sir Hugh paid special attention to you today and you ignored him."

"I don't like him, Mama."

"You don't like any of my friends."

"I can't help it." Jewel's lips tightened in a stubborn line, a facial expression she had inherited from her grandmother.

"We'll have to change that," Marie said, and herded her into the house.

One of the servants was coming along the corridor, holding an envelope.

"What is it?" Marie said.

"Telegram for the master. It's just come."

"I'll take it." She turned back to Jewel. "Hurry, please."

She went up to her room to prepare for the journey. The envelope she held was open. Telegrams were unusual at Rylands. She pulled out the sheet of paper and saw that it had been sent from Victoria, Cape Colony, and routed via Cape Town, Durban and Aden.

DEAR JACK,

MICHAEL DESPERATELY ILL AND SINKING STOP DOCTOR HERE BELIEVES PRESENCE OF JEWEL WILL MAKE VITAL DIFFERENCE STOP BEG YOU ALLOW JEWEL COME TO VICTORIA STOP PLEASE DO NOT REPEAT DO NOT TELL HILDA YET STOP I WILL WRITE TO HER STOP SNELL WILL MAKE ALL ARRANGEMENTS FOR JEWEL STOP DOCTOR SAYS IT IS MICHAELS ONLY CHANCE STOP DO NOT FAIL US STOP

DAVID.

She sat for some moments digesting the words, feeling confused and angry. Then she heard Jewel's step on the landing outside and made up her mind. She put the crumpled telegram into the fireplace and set it alight.

"Are you ready, Mama?" Jewel called.

"In a minute." She watched the paper burn to black ash.

*   *   *

Two days later Jewel stood at the windows of the conservatory in London watching rain run down the glass. It was midmorning and the house was silent. Her father was still at Rylands, her mother at her dressmaker's in South Molton Street. The first post had come without a letter from Michael, and now she awaited the second. There had been no word from him for more than a month; usually she received at least one letter a week and sometimes two. She told herself that anything might have happened—a ship might have sunk or been held up in some way, the growing tension in Africa might have caused a delay (she could not think how, but it was possible) or any of a dozen other things: a letter might simply have been lost, one heard of such things happening. There were two contingencies she rigorously excluded from her thoughts: one was that for some reason Michael did not *choose* to write to her any longer and the second was that he was *unable* to write because his illness had grown worse. Whenever these thoughts obtruded she would switch to a fantasy which seemed more and more real the greater her need became: Michael had not written because he had made a miraculous recovery, had left Victoria, had boarded a ship and was even at this very moment alighting from the boat train at Waterloo and hailing a hansom cab to come to her. Each time she indulged in the fantasy her ears would become especially sensitive to the sounds of wheels on the gravel outside. Often she would go to the upstairs balcony and watch the stream of hansoms coming up from Piccadilly as though she could recognize the one bringing Michael. It might have made things better if she had had some one to confide in, but there was no one. All she had ever had—ever wanted as far back as she could remember—was Michael. Her entire childhood had been lived in his shadow. Sometimes, as though in a fading dream, her mind would throw up brief pictures: a house with broken walls, a deep still pool, sheep trailing down to a river in single file to drink. She knew these memories must be of Portuguese Place but she had no memory of her grandmother at that time and place, yet Michael was there in each picture. She remembered when he had been sent away to school and how she had cried and wanted to go with him. She had always thought that particular parting had been the worst experience of her life, but it had been nothing compared with his present absence. She had gone down to Southampton to say good-bye to him. Some troops were also sailing and there had

been streamers and a band playing. Michael had held one end of a pink streamer and she the other and the tugs had moved the liner into Southampton Water and Michael had looked so small standing by the rail on the upper deck and then the streamer had snapped and she had felt that something inside her had broken, too.

Her ears, attuned to the mythical cab, heard a sound of footsteps on the gravel and her heart gave a sudden lurch. Was she dreaming or could it . . . ? It was too early for the second post. She ran across the front hall and flung open the big door, but it was not Michael standing there.

"Mr. Snell!"

"Good morning, Jewel; may I come in for a moment?"

She took him through to the drawing room. She liked Mr. Snell. He was small, with a round red face. He could be choleric, but she knew that both her father and Uncle David thought highly of him. He was a lawyer, and one of the most important figures in New Chance.

"No one at home, then?"

"Except me."

He had a habit of extending his lower lip when he was thinking and he did this now. Then he said, "Well, since it concerns you, perhaps you can advise me. We have arrangements to make."

"Arrangements?"

"Travel bookings, finding a chaperone, packing. A whole host of things. And time is of the essence."

"Mr. Snell, I don't understand anything you've said. Not a word."

His lower lip was pushed out, then drawn back. "Didn't your father . . . ? I suppose you *are* going?"

"Going where?"

"The cable. Didn't your father get a cable from your Uncle David?" He began to search through his pockets.

Suddenly she was frightened. She remembered the servant at Rylands with the telegram, remembered her mother taking it, remembered a smell of burning. "No, he didn't," she said.

"This is a duplicate," Mr. Snell said, handing it to her. "He had it sent to me as a precaution. You can see how serious the matter is."

Jewel read the cable. Fear turned to terror. She began to shake.

"It must have gone astray," she said, and heard her voice as though from a distance. The fear came in waves, gripping her stomach and making it difficult to breathe.

"We have to act quickly," he said. "Michael is obviously in a bad way."

"Yes."

"Perhaps I should go ahead and make a booking? The ships are said to be full of troops and it may take some time."

"Yes." Her mind was racing ahead, testing plans, rejecting them, thinking of others, testing those, finally adopting one.

"I'm sorry to bring you such bad news, but I must say you've taken it with courage," he said. "Just as I would have expected from Jack Farson's daughter."

"Thank you."

"I'll be in touch with your father."

After he had gone she went up to her room and stood staring out at the rooftops. She thought of the telegram arriving at Rylands, of her mother reading it in her bedroom and deciding to sacrifice Michael. A dry sob racked her body and she put her hands up to her face. But there were no tears. She had no time for tears. She was in the grip of a cold rage: she would never forgive her mother for what she had tried to do. But for the moment she pushed all such thoughts aside. She had made a plan, somewhat sketchy, but it was the best she could think of. She put it into action.

First she packed a small suitcase with necessities. She knew she could not take much, or that would look suspicious. Then she took a hatbox from the top of her wardrobe. Under the hats and under the tissue paper she came to a pile of Michael's letters tied with a ribbon. She packed them. Then, from a jar of potpourri on her dressing table, she extracted something that glittered in the morning light. It was the diamond Uncle David had brought her back from Amsterdam. She put it in her purse, put on her hat and coat and rang for Cummings.

"Please tell my mother I'm going to spend a couple of days with Miss Margaret Kade," she said.

"Very good, miss. Shall I get you a cab?"

He saw her into the hansom and, while she settled back against the leather seat, gave the driver the Kades' address in Hampstead. She let the cab get almost to Marble Arch before she said, "I've changed my mind; take me to Hatton Garden."

From Hatton Garden, where she sold the diamond, she went to the offices of the Union Steamship Line, in Fenchurch Street in the City. They had a vessel, the *Scot*, sailing for the Cape of Good Hope the following day. The only place available was in a women's twelve-berth dormitory cabin in steerage. She did not hesitate. The clerk made out her ticket and told her the boat train left the following morning at ten. She thanked him and took a cab to Waterloo. She caught a train to Southampton and asked the stationmaster for the name of a decent hotel. By midafternoon she was in her own upstairs room with a view of the docks. A dozen ships lay at anchor in Southampton Water; a dozen more were tied up alongside the quays, loading or unloading. She had found out which was the *Scot* and now she pulled a chair to the window and sat staring at the busy, smoke-laden scene. She was hardly aware of her surroundings. She was, for all intents and purposes, already in Africa.

"Christ almighty!" Jack said. "Did you really think you could keep something like this to yourself?" It was two days later. He and Marie were in the drawing room.

"I thought it was for the best," she said.

"The best! Who are you to judge what's best and what isn't best for my daughter?" He waved the duplicate cable in her face. "It's me who makes decisions in this family!"

"Did you want her to marry him?"

"Of course I don't want her to marry a Jew!" he shouted.

"Well, that's what'll happen now if we're not careful."

"We could have talked about it. Sent her away somewhere, anything. Instead you've forced her to take things into her own hands."

"What are you going to do? Should we tell the police?"

"Of course not. Not yet, anyway. We can guess what she's going to do."

Leask came in with Snell.

"Well?" Jack said.

"She sailed yesterday. The *Scot*. Union Line."

"Are you sure?"

"Her name's on the passenger list. Steerage."

"Steerage!" Marie said.

Jack ignored her. "Can we stop the ship?"

"It's too late."

"Where does she call?"

"Madeira and Freetown."

"Can we cable the British consul to hold her?" he asked Snell.

"The ship?"

"No, Jewel."

"They've got no power to take her off."

Jack paced the room like one of his caged leopards at Rylands.

"There must be some bloody way!" he shouted. His face was blotched with purple and red patches. He rubbed his jaw. After a moment he said to Leask, "Get Mrs. Farson and me a passage on the first ship. And one for yourself. Don't let them tell you they're booked up. Buy the bloody ship if you have to."

"I'm not going," Marie said.

"You'll damn well come," Jack said. "It's all your doing, anyway."

"I'm not coming, Jack," she said softly. "No matter what you say or do, I'm not coming."

7

The countryside around Victoria was farmed by people of Dutch extraction. Most were Boer sympathizers.

"We may be in the Cape Colony," Dr. Versveld said to David, "but our hearts are in the Transvaal."

There were only six resident English in the village: the postmaster, the bank manager, the owner of the tearoom, the owner of the hotel, and a husband and wife who ran a small school. They had all been accepted and integrated into the village and were as much a part of it as the Boers or their brown servants. And even as political events became more and more unstable, the people of Victoria remained on good terms. Then something happened to change that: a story appeared in one of the Cape papers which reached Victoria two days later of a particularly brutal crime in Johannesburg. A private boarding house owned and run by an Afrikaner family had burnt down, killing the owners and five guests: a total of eight people, including the owners' seven-year-old son. It was thought that the

wooden-built structure had been set alight by a group of drunken British Outlanders—which later proved not to have been the case. The reason Victoria was affected was that one of the dead was the sister of the local banker. When the news reached the village a group of young farmers were drinking in the hotel bar. Above them, like a taunt, flew the Union Jack. When they had had enough to drink they pulled down the flag, burnt it in front of the hotel and then went home. The following morning a new Union Jack was flying in its place. Word got about. That night it was pulled down and set alight but not completely burnt. Mr. Benson, the hotelkeeper, a short, grizzled old man with an explosive temper, managed to get it up the flagpole and there, charred and marked by fire, it hung. Then he put a sign up in the bar which said:

IMPORTANT NOTICE:
ANYONE TOUCHING THE FLAG
WILL BE SHOT

Later he was seen sitting on the veranda of the hotel with a shotgun on his lap. On his chest he was wearing a medal which people said he had won in the Crimean War. No one took him seriously, for he was nearly eighty. Later that night another attempt was made to remove the flag and he shot a man from the upstairs window. No great damage was done, for the lead pellets had been removed from the cartridge and replaced by pieces of rock salt. By the time David, who had been wakened by the noise, came downstairs, the young men had fled, including the one who had been hit and who was later treated by Dr. Versveld for a sore and lacerated bottom. That shot was the start of hostilities in Victoria.

The two communities—the small Boer one and the tiny English one—regarded each other with growing suspicion which turned into dislike and eventually hatred. A series of incidents occurred. The bank manager had a white bull terrier of which he was inordinately proud and which had for years been the terror of the local dogs. One afternoon, soon after the burning of the flag, the dog was found dead in the yard behind the bank. It had bled badly from the mouth and rectum and when Dr. Versveld opened the animal at the request of the local policeman it was discovered that someone had mixed glass with its food.

Then came the withdrawal of children from the school. Most

of them were the sons and daughters of local farmers and one day they did not appear at school. The two teachers, seeing that their future was bleak, if not downright dangerous, closed the school and left for the peace of Cape Town.

The tearoom—the John Bull Café—which was the focus for farmers and their families when they came to the village, found itself boycotted and within a few weeks it, too, closed for good.

"If Michael were stronger I would suggest you made arrangements to have him moved," Dr. Versveld said to David. "When people start this sort of thing there's no telling where it will stop. Have you any news?"

David shook his head. "No, not a word," he said bitterly.

"Maybe the Army is delaying civilian cables."

"Maybe."

In the outside world, a world which David read about in the newspapers which reached them from Cape Town, a world becoming more and more remote the longer he remained in Victoria, things were also getting worse. Shares had fallen on the London Stock Exchange: dispatches from the British high commissioner were published in which he stated to the British Government: "The spectacle of thousands of British subjects kept permanently in the position of helots, constantly chafing under undoubted grievances and calling vainly to Her Majesty's Government for redress, does steadily undermine the influence and reputation of Great Britain within the Queen's dominions." Mercenaries smelling a profitable war were beginning to arrive from every country in Europe.

One evening in July, about three weeks after he had sent the cable to Jack, David said good night to Michael, whose bed had been moved now into the glassed-in section of the veranda, and went into the common room, where Dr. Versveld was reading a medical journal.

"He seems weaker," David said.

The doctor put down the journal. "You've heard nothing?"

"No. I'm not sure it would help now, anyway."

"You mustn't give up hope. It is astounding how the disease can change if the will is there. You know, Mr. Kade, we're only just learning about the part the mind plays in these matters. Out here kaffirs die for no reason that we doctors understand. If they believe they are going to die because an evil spirit has entered

their bodies they turn to the wall and die. It is all in the mind. And if the mind can kill you, it can also make you well. I have seen miraculous 'cures' just because a patient *believed* he would get well. That is the problem—belief, will, call it what you like."

At that moment they heard the noise of a galloping horse. It was an unusual sound at that time of night when Victoria was as still as the grave. A stone came crashing through the window. Slivers of glass spattered the room. Both men leapt to their feet.

"Are you all right?" Dr. Versveld said.

"Yes." David brushed glass fragments from his waistcoat then bent to pick up the stone. It was wrapped in white paper on which there was writing, but it was in Dutch. He passed it to the doctor, who read it, then crumpled it up and threw it in the fire.

"What does it say?"

"I think you can probably guess."

"But why you? You're one of the most respected men in the district." And then he knew why. "It's us, isn't it? It's because we're here."

Later David walked thoughtfully to the hotel. Dr. Versveld had wanted to accompany him, but he had been firm: he was not really frightened and anyway the doctor was needed by his patients. The dirt road was silent; frost glittered on the grass that grew near the river. His footsteps rang like iron. He walked past the John Bull Café, its door padlocked, one of its shutters hanging open drunkenly, and turned into the hotel. An old Hottentot waiter lay sleeping on a pile of sacks behind the desk. David stretched over the desk and took his key.

He made up the fire in his room and stood by it, warming himself. He pulled his writing table towards the heat and began to work on his translation of the old Portuguese Bible. Again the epic march along the Orange River all those hundreds of years before forced his thoughts away from worry about his son and the bitterness he now felt towards Jack Farson. He worked until nearly midnight and then went to bed.

He woke in the small hours. He lay in the icy bedroom, gripped by a sense of unease. Perhaps it was his imagination, perhaps his feeling of worry had been heightened by what had happened earlier. He turned on his side and closed his eyes. Almost immediately they snapped open. There *was* something wrong. He sniffed. That was it. He was smelling smoke. He ran to the window, but all he could make out were the shapes of the pepper

trees across the road. His sitting room had a window which overlooked the rear garden of the hotel. It also overlooked the back of the John Bull Café. Smoke was pouring from the café and he could see flames beginning to lick up the walls. Others were awake now, for he heard shouts and running footsteps. The flames and the smoke brought back an old, forgotten terror. He was smelling again the smoke, hearing again the shouts, feeling again the terror of the pogrom in Kiev. He never knew how long he stood at the window in a state of suspended animation, but when he returned to the present he saw flames beginning to envelop the wooden wall of the hotel. Panic caught him. He ran to the door and was about to dash down the corridor when he remembered his belongings. He grabbed a suitcase and threw into it his personal papers, the Bible, his translation, the dictionary and the clothes in the wardrobe. Then, somewhat calmer, he made his way down into the lobby and out into the road, which was filled with other guests and folk from the village. Some had started a bucket chain from the river nearby but at this time of the year there was almost no water in it. In any case, the fire had too firm a grip and soon the hotel was burning like a torch. But the villagers did not give in. They fought the blaze throughout the night and into the morning. It seemed as though everyone, including some of the neighboring farmers, had come to help. David joined the chain and passed on the heavy wooden buckets until he thought his arms would pull out of their sockets. Eventually, as dawn came, the water supply dwindled and the buckets finally stopped moving. The crowd stood in silence and watched the old building destroy itself.

He found himself next to Dr. Versveld. His face was streaked with dirt and his beard was covered in gray ash. They stood with the silent crowd until finally the doctor said, "Come, you'll stay with me now."

David was too tired to argue. He lifted his suitcase and walked to the sanatorium. Dr. Versveld said, "They're ashamed. They know what they've done. There'll be no more trouble." But David took no comfort from the words, for while he had been watching the hotel burn down a question had entered his mind: had the hotel been burnt down because of old Mr. Benson and the flag, or had it been because he, David Kade, was living there, and if that was so, was it because he himself was an Outlander who had become wealthy, or was it because he was English, or because he

was a Jew? Or was it a combination of them all? He knew one thing: he had to get Michael away, for he knew that this had been, in a sense, a pogrom, and with his experience and knowledge he had no faith that it had ended. But how could he take Michael away when the very act of removing him from danger might kill him?

As they reached the gate of the sanatorium, he noticed that the early mail cart was coming across the veld from the direction of Victoria Halt. He wondered if there would be any letters for Michael. There had been nothing from Jewel for weeks. He paused at the gate, debating whether to go straight to the post office just in case. Then he noticed that the cart was heading in their direction and that there was a passenger seated next to the old Colored driver.

"I think you have another patient," he said.

"No one's expected."

The passenger waved. David sensed rather than saw who it was. He dropped his suitcase and ran onto the veranda. Michael was lying on his side, staring at nothing. "What was all the noise?" he said.

David said, "You have a visitor." He handed Michael his hairbrush.

"Who is it?"

"Who, above everyone, would you want?"

They heard the gate creak and then the driver calling to the horses and the crack of his whip.

"You're lying!" Michael said. "It couldn't be!"

A door slammed and suddenly Jewel was on the veranda.

"I came as quickly as I could," she said.

8

It was early October and spring at Portuguese Place was well advanced. The mimosa trees were putting out new yellow-green leaves and tender thorns, soft and pliable in their infancy. The desert was covered with flowers: yellow daisies, purple everlastings and the hot pinks and mauves of mesembryanthemums. Susan had picked a posy of veld flowers and had walked down to the river with Michael and Jewel.

"You two go on," she said.

"Grandfather's grave?" Jewel said.

"Yes. Now don't tire ..." She laughed. "Listen to me! I shouldn't be giving advice to the nurse."

She turned off the path and went to the grave, or at least the area where they had buried Frans. She no longer knew exactly where the grave was, for in the times she now thought of as her "lost days," wind, rain and animals had obliterated all traces of it.

But she knew more or less where it had been and she found the jam jar which she used as a vase, threw away the flowers she had placed in it a few days before, filled it at the river and arranged the posy, then returned it to the pile of stones which kept it upright and secure. She stood with head bowed, said a short prayer and walked back to the house.

Susan was now in her seventies, her short, square body had lost weight and she stooped slightly. Her left arm had never recovered from the fall of rock when she had tried to rebuild the rooms Jack had destroyed and she walked stiffly because both hip joints were painful. Her skin had become even more like the skins of Bushmen and Hottentot women, but there was still a resemblance to the Susan of the early days: the clear, steady eyes, the firm line of the mouth. She had endured.

But it had not always been so. Earlier that year Mopedi had become ill with fever and she brought him into the house to nurse him. The old man was almost blind and talked continuously about the early days when he had been Frans Delport's "boy" and they had hunted the veld together. She nursed him for more than a month in blinding heat, one of the hottest spells ever known in the area, and so dry that the river had almost ceased flowing. The heat and the heavy work and the lack of food brought on a kind of breakdown. Her mind seemed to become slower and slower until it had stopped. She remembered "waking up," if that was the phrase, one day down by the river with Hans Lessing, old Helmut's eldest boy, standing over her. He had taken over the Lessing farm and had come to tell her that he had found some of her sheep straying through the broken fences onto his land. She knew she must have presented a strange, almost frightening sight for she saw herself in a mirror soon afterwards: gray hair awry, dress torn and stained, eyes wild. He carried her up to the house and found Mopedi's dead body. He must have died a day or two earlier. Hans buried the old Basuto, then hitched up the cart and wanted to take Susan into town, but she resisted.

"I'm all right now," she said. "It must have been the heat."

What worried her was the thought that it might not have been the first time she had had a blank spell, and this was confirmed on the next occasion she went down to Frans's grave. The cross had been knocked down, perhaps by sheep, and then floodwater had carried it away. She knew this must have happened in a "lost"

period, for she had no memory of a storm. She was alone on the farm except for a herdboy who looked after the sheep and the thought of such things happening to her mind terrified her. She remembered the look in Hans Lessing's eyes when he had found her. Did he think her demented? Or was it that he considered she had become a poor white? Or both? He was a good boy. Although he was now in his late thirties she still thought of him as a boy. From the day he had found her wandering down by the river he had made it a special duty to come over to Portuguese Place at least once a week to find out if she was all right. He took the opportunity to bring with him a bag of potatoes or a haunch of venison, some coffee perhaps, or green vegetables—something for her table.

Old Helmut Lessing was dead these five years, kicked to death by a horse that had gone berserk in his smithy, but sometimes when Hans called she seemed to see the old man again, the square, powerful body and the bearded face, and would remember the days when the Lessings and the Jordaans had first come to the Green River valley.

"I've come to feed you up, Aunt Susan," Hans would say, unslinging the bag of groceries, or whatever it was, and carrying it into the house. This was all she would accept from him. He had tried to persuade her to "borrow" a few of his servants, but she was adamant. Nor would she sell up and move into town as he wanted her to.

"Don't you think you've worked hard enough?" he would say. "Don't you think it's time to rest?"

But what if she sold Portuguese Place and Jewel came back? She remembered the child so clearly she could almost reach out and touch her. She remembered taking her down to the Breakfast Pool and letting her play in the sand and make splashes in the water. She remembered walking with her along the river looking for wild honey. She remembered bathing her at night in the old zinc bath and tucking her into bed and reading to her by the lamplight. Jewel was everywhere: in the house, on the veranda, down by the river. When her granddaughter was a baby she had begun to rekindle the plans she had formed for Marie, which had been smashed so badly. In her imagination it was Jewel and her husband who would give back life to Portuguese Place.

As the years passed, as Mopedi grew weaker, as she began to experience her "lost days," she still clung to her great dream, the

dream she had always had, of continuity, of a family at Portuguese Place, of children again. But at last the dream, starved of anything but hope, began to die and so had Susan. She started to deteriorate, physically and mentally.

Then the miracle happened. She was sitting in her chair on the stoep in the warm sunshine when she woke suddenly and there, standing in front of her, was Jewel. For a dreadful moment she thought she might be hallucinating; then her granddaughter stepped forwards and took her hands and kissed her on her cheek and there was nothing of the ghost about her.

"I've brought Michael," Jewel said. "He's very ill."

From that moment, Susan's life changed. She rose stiffly and followed Jewel to the back of the house and there she saw Michael and David; she would never have recognized Michael, he was so thin. His eyes were buried in his head, surrounded by purple smudges. What was it Frans had said that time Jack had come to convalesce? "He's as thin as a winter lamb." Michael was even thinner and shivered in the heat as she looked at him.

She reached the house and climbed up the steps onto the stoep. Now look at him! She could see them walking through the trees by the river. That was the second miracle, Michael's recovery. It had only been four, five weeks, and he was a completely different person. And so was Susan. It was ironic, she thought, that Michael's illness had done her good. It had forced her to take a grip on herself, forced her out of the apathy into which she had fallen.

She felt a blush of shame now as she thought of the day they had arrived, for she had read in their faces, especially in David's, something akin to disgust. She had realized that her clothes were not as clean as they might have been. And then, when she took them into the house, she saw through their eyes the dust and the dirt, the broken windows, the spiders' webs. "I don't go into these rooms," she said defensively.

But when they went into the one room in the house that she did occupy, where she lived and slept and ate, it was worse than the others. The bed was unmade, her clothes were strewn about and some of the food had gone bad. It was then she realized how far down the scale of civilized living she had sunk.

She felt David was about to take Michael back to Kimberley and she said hastily, "I'll soon get this cleaned up."

"I'll help you," Jewel said.

That is how it had started. Jewel worked and she worked and even David took off his jacket and by the following day the house was clean, and if it did not resemble its former self, at least it was neat. As she worked, as she was forced to think ahead, her mind became clearer. She had always been a good organizer and now she found the talent returning to her. She harnessed up the trap and went into Kimberley for supplies for the first time in six months. She found that the town was very different from the last time she had seen it. She knew from Hans Lessing that there was trouble between the Boer republics and the British Government but she had been so cut off physically and mentally from the mainstream of life that she had hardly taken in the news. Now, seeing the sandbags and the barbed wire, the lookout towers, the strutting soldiers, she realized that things must have become a great deal worse than she had imagined. But again her own affairs held her interest and she knew that whatever happened she would be safe enough. Her neighbors were Afrikaners and in sympathy with the Boer cause—so was she, for that matter—but she had lived on the farm most of her life and they were her friends. In any case, she was an American. Nor did she fear the British side, for being an English speaker and an old woman, she assumed she would be totally ignored. They could have their war, if that was what they wanted; she had Jewel and Michael, and Portuguese Place was remote enough for them not to have to bother. No one, in any case, was going to harm a young girl and a sick young man.

David had stayed on the farm for nearly three weeks while Michael started making his dramatic recovery. He told her about Dr. Versveld and how he had said this was possible and how he had not really believed him. "I wish he could be here now," he said to Susan. "I wish he could see what we're seeing."

Each day Michael seemed to gain in strength. It was noticeable that his eyes lost the dark smudges and no longer seemed so far back in his skull. He coughed less. Days passed and there was no blood. He began to eat well, and Hans Lessing brought over a cow so that he should have fresh milk.

Michael and Hans had formed a friendship and Susan watched it grow with approval. At first Hans was shy with Michael, who came from a big city and who had an education far in advance of a simple farmer's. But slowly the barriers broke down and Hans began to talk of taking Michael fishing and hunting when he

grew better. Susan was reminded of the days when her husband had taken Hans along with him. As his strength increased, Michael began to ask Hans about farming and the two would have long discussions about dipping sheep and growing maize; the possibility of cultivating cotton in the valley; new breeds of cattle suitable to the dry conditions.

"He used to talk like this to Dr. Versveld," David said. "Maybe this is what he wants." Secretly, Susan prayed that it was.

Within a fortnight of arriving Michael was beginning to take short walks along the stoep. It was like watching a tree that one had thought dead suddenly putting out buds and breaking into new leaf.

Jewel had made the difference. For the first two weeks she hardly left Michael's side. She would sit with him hour after hour, holding his hand or reading to him. Susan wondered if there was some form of electricity or life-force, some power in her aura which she was transmitting to him, for there was no other explanation.

Now she went into the house and prepared the tea things, for it was nearly four o'clock and David sometimes came out on Thursdays. She liked that; it added one more to the family.

Sometimes late at night before she went to sleep, she thought how lucky she was having a family again. Even if she died tomorrow she would have had that. It was not the family she had planned, but God had granted her a different way of finding her dream and she was more than content.

She returned to the stoep. Michael and Jewel had turned away from the river and were walking towards the house. To her right, lines of sheep were going down to drink. It was a peaceful sight, and even as she looked out over the farm as Frans had liked to do she saw, away to her left, a small cloud of dust that indicated David's trap. He stopped to open the Home Camp gate, took the trap through, closed it again and came on.

She waited for him and he joined her on the stoep. "Look at them," she said, pointing with her stick towards Jewel and Michael.

"I never thought I'd see it." But his face was drawn and his eyes were worried. Then he said, "Jack left Cape Town last night."

They had been waiting for him. He cast a long shadow and it had lain over them, tempering in some degree the happiness they were all experiencing. She knew that David had been in touch

with him by letter and cable both from Victoria and then from Kimberley, telling him that Jewel was now with her grandmother at Portuguese Place and that he need not worry about her. There had been no reply to any of these communications, but they had known he was on his way because Mr. Snell in London was in constant touch with Kimberley. Sometimes David's face wore a worried frown, as it did now, and Susan had known what he was thinking. So had Jewel, for she had said one evening, "I'll never leave Michael No one can make me."

David had smiled at her, but Susan knew what was going on in his mind: if a father wished to take custody of his eighteen-year-old daughter, who could stop him?

9

Clickety-clack . . . clickety-clack . . .The train labored up the gradient. Jack Farson sat sweating in his first-class compartment. Opposite him Leask was packing his nightclothes and closing the suitcase. They were due in Kimberley in an hour but since they were already two hours late there was no telling when they might arrive. In spite of the direct October sunlight which made the compartment even hotter, Jack kept the window open and the blind up. He sat staring at the harsh semidesert through bloodshot eyes. The countryside was familiar; he could see the hills through which he and David had walked all those years before on their way to the diggings. He thought he could smell the faint herby smell of the Karoo bush and feel the desert grit between his teeth. He expected, round every bend, to see Portuguese Place, yet he knew that the railway line passed nowhere near it. He would have to go there tomorrow, perhaps

even this afternoon. He would be seeing it for the first time for nearly twenty years, since he and Marie had ridden away and abandoned Susan on the derelict farm. The memory of that day had never left him—one picture in particular: the old woman sitting in her chair watching him smash down the walls of the house, silent, implacable, accusing. He had never rid himself of it. It burnt away inside him like acid. Deep down in his psyche where only he ever penetrated—and that very seldom—he realized that in Aunt Susan he had found that rare being, someone he could love and respect and trust, but because of what and who he was he had ruined the relationship: because of his inability to trust he had abused her. Sometimes when these thoughts emerged he would find himself as weak and vulnerable as a small boy and with the same desperate feelings of a child who gradually learns that there are some things that can't be changed, some occasions when no second chance is offered, when you have to live with your actions. In spite of the heat, he shivered.

But he had found a way of overcoming these thoughts by unloosing another emotion: anger. Now, with relief, he allowed it to flood his mind. He had been angry from the moment he knew what Jewel had done. He saw her defection as a revolt against him personally. And for what reason? He was her father, he had given her everything and he loved her as he loved no one else. Why had she done such a thing to him? It was a question that had haunted him for the past two months—months of frustration which had started when Leask had been unable to obtain berths on any of the Union or Castle ships because of the pressure of military needs. Not even Jack's powerful commercial position cut much ice with the War Office, which had commandeered several ships to take troops to southern Africa. He had been forced to travel to Bremen and sail in the Norddeutscher Lloyd's ship *König*. She was due to call briefly in at Walfisch Bay in German South-West Africa, but had developed engine trouble and was there for a week before continuing to the Cape. It was a terrible week, with nothing to do except stare at the burning sands of the Namib Desert until eyes became inflamed. Leask spent most of the time panting on his bunk but Jack roamed the deck, unable to sit still even in the heat. He had tried to knock himself out with whisky and *schnapps,* but instead of sending him to sleep the liquor had brought on the pains in his gut.

It had taken a week to reach the Cape once the engines had

been patched up and he had spent a further two weeks there trying to get a seat on the train going north. Again the talk of war had caused a scarcity of rolling stock for passengers. But at last he had managed it.

And now for two seemingly endless days they had been traveling slowly across the Karoo desert. Here were the open spaces, the huge blue skies, the harsh sunlight, the violent extremes he had longed for in the smoky streets of a London winter, yet he was unable to enjoy them. In the dry heat, his cigars became like brittle paper and tasted foul, and he could not eat with any enjoyment because of the wind pains in his stomach which followed each meal, so there was only whisky. To be sure, that aggravated his condition, but provided he drank enough he found he could endure it.

In spite of the fact that it was barely midmorning, he had already had several whiskies and now he poured himself another. Leask heard the clink of the bottle on the glass and turned.

"Want one?" Jack said.

"It's a bit early for me."

"Never too early for a digger. But never mind. You're more of a paper boy, anyway."

He drank and stared out of the window. The whisky calmed him. This was characteristic of the journey as a whole: anger had alternated with periods of calm during which he acknowledged to himself that it was not David's fault, nor Michael's fault, that Jewel had left home. He knew that if their positions had been reversed he would have gone down on his knees to David. When Jewel had been ill with diphtheria he would have made any sacrifice to save her.

There was a rattle at the door and it was pulled back. The conductor, a portly, red-faced, self-important man, stood in the corridor. "Good morning, Mr. Farson, sir. We'll be in Kimberley in half an hour. I'm sorry about the delay, but I hope everything else has been to your satisfaction, sir."

"No complaints. Leask."

Leask opened his wallet, took out a five-pound note and gave it to the conductor. "That's very generous, sir. Very generous indeed. Thank you."

"What's the news?" Jack said.

"News?"

"About the war."

"Oh, there won't be any war, sir. The Boers have given the British an ultimatum. Imagine that, sir. Why, the British Government . . ."

"I know about the ultimatum. Has there been any reply?"

"I don't know, sir, but they say that the Boers in the Orange Free State aren't going to fight. They've left the Transvaal isolated. They say old President Kruger is the only one there who wants war. They say ten thousand British troops have been landed in Natal."

"Who are *they*?"

"People in the know, sir."

Jack looked away. Rumors, that's all one heard these days. The war could come or not, he didn't give a damn; he had his own problems.

There was no one at the station to meet him. "Are you sure you sent a telegram, Leask?" he said angrily.

"Yes, sir, but we're two hours late."

"That's no bloody reason. I'm going to the Grand. You see about the baggage."

He walked across town in the noonday heat. Away to his left a group of townspeople were drilling on the square, each carrying a sporting rifle. He was aware that there were barbed-wire barricades and that some of the shops were sandbagged, but otherwise Kimberley did not seem to think war was imminent.

He took the top suite of the Grand Hotel, the suite he and Marie had taken all those years before when they had bathed in soda water. Now the suite had a proper bathroom and he decided to use it before doing anything else. He gave himself a drink and sipped it while he lay back in the warm water. The bastards might have checked the train time, he thought. His mind was fuddled with whisky, but he began to try and work out some kind of plan. First of all, he'd go to see David. No, why the bloody hell should he go anywhere. Let David come to him. "Leask!" he shouted. There was no reply. He finished bathing and went back into his sitting room. Leask was taking a hell of a time with the luggage. He finished drying himself and went to the window to see if Leask was in view: he wanted a change of clothing. He could see up and down the street, but there was no sign of Leask. He was turning back into the room when he saw two figures turn the corner below him and walk past the hotel on the opposite side in front of Madame Delatee's French Café. It was David, and some

woman. Then he gasped and pressed his face to the glass. "Christ!" he said aloud. He hammered on the glass but they did not hear him. He tried to open the window but the frame was warped and it stuck. He grabbed his clothes and dressed quickly, then he ran down the stairs. But by the time he reached the street they had gone.

"You all right, sir?" the desk clerk said, for his face had become blotchy and he was panting.

"Yes, I'm all right." Slowly, he climbed the stairs to his suite.

Lily, he thought. God, what a wonderful surprise! He wondered how long she had been in Kimberley, how long she was staying. From what he had seen of her she looked just as lovely as he could remember. Lily . . . !

Leask came in and he decided what he would do: he would fetch Jewel now, today, and get that settled, and then . . . his mind leapt into the future. Lily in Kimberley! It would be like the old days!

"Go out and get a trap," he told Leask. "Not from the mine. Get it at a livery stables. I don't want a groom; I'll handle it myself."

The afternoon sun was high in the sky and beat down on him as the trap moved slowly across the desert. He was wearing a light cotton suit but even so the heat was oppressive and he could feel the sweat running down his neck and softening his collar. Again the thought of Portuguese Place made him apprehensive and he touched the flask of whisky at his feet as though its presence gave him confidence. He tried to think of Lily but each time he did so she was replaced in his imagination by Jewel, who in turn was replaced by the implacable figure of Susan.

This had once been a journey of pleasure and anticipation for him. Ever since he had helped Frans Delport with the pump, the farm and the Delports had been special to him in a way which no other place or family had been. He had ruined that relationship just as he seemed to ruin everything he touched. He was caught by a spasm of self-pity. If only Lily had not left; if only they had stayed together, everything would have been different now. Was it too late to start again? To take up where they had left off? He had never stopped loving her and he knew that she loved him. You could not live with someone as they had lived and do all the things that they had done without loving the person. He

remembered the Sunday mornings in her shack when she had taught him to read and write and he had watched her going about her household chores. It had been as though they were man and wife then. It had been a wonderful time; the best of times. Everything had been so simple then. But now . . . he thought of the office overlooking Trafalgar Square, the estate in Sussex, the house in Park Lane; of Marie and her circle, and David and Jewel and Michael and Violet. Everything was so complex now. He had not meant life to become like this. You dug up a diamond, you sold it, you got the money, you spent the money. It was a straight, uncluttered line. How had it all become . . .

He heard the bullet strike before he heard the sound of the shot. It struck the road in front of the horse, causing it to rear and jerk. Then came the crack and the whine of the ricochet in one. The horse stopped dead, its ears flat against its head. Jack looked from side to side, but the desert was empty. Nothing moved in the shimmering afternoon heat. And then, as though a mirage, a line of horsemen rode out from behind a rocky knoll. For a second he thought of whipping up the horse, but each rider carried a gun and he could see the bandoliers of bullets glinting in the sunlight.

There were a dozen or fifteen of them and they stopped in a semicircle around the trap. They were of different ages, ranging between seventeen and fifty. Most wore beards, and even the youngsters had fluff on their chins. One or two faces were familiar. They wore a variety of soft felt hats, many with feathers in the hatbands. Some wore double bandoliers, some single, slung from the left shoulder, coming down under the right arm, leaving the right shoulder free for the rifle butt.

They looked tough and hard, and the rifles they held were new Mausers.

Who were they? Rebel Boers? A raiding party? A criminal gang?

They sat their horses in a silence broken only by a creaking of saddle leather and the jingle of bridles as the animals sawed at the reins. Jack looked closely at the leader.

"You're Helmut Lessing's son, aren't you?" he said.

"Yes." The bearded man sat loosely in the saddle, his feet in long stirrups, the rifle balanced easily on the pommel. "You're Mr. Farson."

"If you know me, why did you fire?"

"To stop you."

"What the hell do you mean by that? You've no right to stop anyone!" The anger came again on a gust of acid wind. "I don't know what you're playing at, but I'm going through."

He raised the whip and was about to cut the horse when the riders closed up, not menacing, but simply making it impossible for the trap to move. "My daughter is at Portuguese Place," Jack said. "I'm going to fetch her."

"Your daughter is safe with Aunt Susan. Nothing will happen to her."

"How the hell do I know that?"

"I am telling you."

"And who are you to tell me? What is this, some criminal gang sent out to frighten travelers?"

Lessing shrugged, spoke a few sentences in Dutch to the men at his side and then said, "Get down. Follow me."

The two of them walked across the burning desert, watched by the other men, Lessing leading his horse, Jack walking behind. They climbed to the top of the rocky knoll. They could see for miles. Lessing handed Jack a pair of new German prismatic glasses. "There!"

Jack focused. Immediately what had been invisible on the rough surface of the desert became clear. He saw field guns and horses, men standing to arms; and, when told to look in another direction, tents, more guns, more horses, more riders. "Jesus!" he said.

Lessing led his horse back down the hillock. He turned the trap around.

"The war you people wanted has started," he said. "Kimberley is cut off. One day soon we will come in and blow up your damned mines. Meantime, stay in town. If we see you on the road again, we will shoot you."

He lashed at the horse's quarter and Jack had only time to grab the reins before he found himself racing back along the track in the direction of Kimberley.

10

David Kade lay on his stomach on a pile of sandbags which formed one of the walls of a redoubt on the Kimberley perimeter, and stared through his prismatic glasses into the shimmering heat haze of the desert. He saw before him a flat plain, broken up by low hills, the surface of which was reddish sand. The only vegetation consisted of small Karoo bushes, each one growing a yard or two from its neighbor, which gave the landscape the appearance of smallpox. It was a sunstricken, cruel picture, and as though to add to that dimension, half a dozen vultures planed across the deep blue sky, landed awkwardly and began to feed on the carcass of a dead horse.

The siege of Kimberley had lasted almost two months; it was mid-December, 1899, and the hottest time of the year. David raised the glasses past the dead horse and focused on a *donga*, a dry watercourse, about two miles away. Occasionally he had seen

movements there. He swept in a semicircle, but nothing moved now, everything seemed dead, as though the besieging Boers had decamped in the night, leaving the town to its own devices. But he knew that this was not so, for when the Boers chose to be, they were invisible. They could fade into a landscape as well as any antelope. They were out there, and as though to confirm this, he heard the sudden boom of a gun, then some seconds later the whiz of the shell. He put his head down and covered it with his arms. The shell exploded somewhere in the town behind him. He looked at his watch; it was three o'clock and the afternoon shelling had begun.

The Boers had ringed the entire town with their new fifteen-pounders, excellent weapons bought in Europe and manned by crews of German and French mercenaries. Over the past weeks a pattern had developed. On six days a week they shelled the town for two hours in the morning and two hours in the afternoon, usually from three to five. But on Sundays the Boer generals, being devout Calvinists, would allow no shelling, so Kimberley had a peaceful day.

David heard a gun crash just below him. The Kimberley artillery had opened up in reply. It was a useless exercise, for the town weapons were only seven-pounders and did not have the range of the Boer guns; all their shells dropped short. It was more a gesture of defiance than anything else.

He saw a movement away to his right, close to another of the sandbag forts placed on the perimeter of the town, and a party of horsemen came riding by. He had no need to look through the glasses; they were close enough to be seen clearly. There were ten or a dozen, well mounted and well armed, wearing the flat-sided hats of the colonial police, light fawn shirts, brown jodhpurs and shining leather riding boots. At their head, with a yellow scarf knotted round his throat, rode Jack Farson.

These were the Kimberley Blazers, a motley collection of ex-diggers and old pals whom Jack had formed, at his own expense, into a private cavalry unit, supplying them with horses, uniforms and rifles in the same way that C. J. Rhodes had formed the Kimberley Light Horse. But where Rhodes's unit had been created for self-aggrandizement, Jack's had come about as a result of his attempts to get through the Boer lines and bring back his daughter. At first he had assumed that the regular army would help him, but when they had refused to be dragged into a

personal problem, even when the problem concerned so important a figure as Farson, he had rounded on them, called them
cowards, harried them and generally made a nuisance of himself
until Colonel Kekewich, the garrison commander and now, since
martial law had been proclaimed, the most powerful figure in
Kimberley, had threatened to have him imprisoned for sedition.

Jack had then hired a few men and tried to force his way
through the lines, only to be driven back by Boer sharpshooters.
He had decided he needed more men, and these were easily
recruited because he was offering good money. When he had
gathered a force of twenty he tried again. This time he had lost
two men and had a horse shot out from under him. He had been
arrested by Colonel Kekewich, held for twenty-four hours, then
released with the warning that if he continued to try to fight his
personal battles in the midst of the siege, he would be court-
martialed and shot. So he had given up for the moment, but had
used his energies to build up a force that he believed would
eventually be big enough to be beyond the power of garrison
control. His official excuse was that it would augment the regular
troops defending Kimberley.

The Blazers actually contributed little to the military presence,
David thought, spending much of their time in the cosies and
canteens, getting drunk and boasting about what they would do if
the Boers ever mounted an attack on the town. But in one way he
was thankful for them, for they gave Jack an interest and
something to do. Ever since he had arrived there had been
tension between the two men.

They had met soon after Jack arrived, in Dan Halkett's
house—neutral territory—to discuss what was to be done about
Jewel and Michael. The conference was, considering the circumstances, surprisingly calm. Each man had some understanding of
the other's point of view. David was able to put himself in the
position of a father with an eighteen-year-old daughter, and Jack
realized David's concern for his son, because he had gone
through a similar experience when Jewel had diphtheria. But
that was as much as mutual compassion allowed. Jewel had run
away from home to follow Michael, and this Jack could not
countenance. But as it turned out, events had overtaken them.
Neither man could influence a war, and their inability to solve
their problems in the midst of the larger one had led to an
artificial situation. They felt embarrassed in each other's com-

pany so, after the first meeting, they avoided each other. Kimberley was a big enough town by now to make this possible. David had moved into Halkett's house; Jack remained at his hotel and they kept out of each other's way.

Now, from his position on the walls of the redoubt, David watched the Kimberley Blazers canter past and disappear from sight, just one more aberration of the strange siege.

Kimberley had changed almost out of recognition since it had first started up as a mining camp in the late sixties and early seventies. After Cape Town, it was now the second largest town in the Cape Colony, with a population of forty-five thousand. Of these twenty-five thousand were white—a good proportion being Boer sympathizers—and the remainder were black mine workers and half-castes who worked as waiters, cleaners, servants and ostlers and at all the other jobs which white men would not perform.

The tin shacks and clapboard dwellings had given way to good brick-built public buildings and solid bourgeois houses. There was an "Old" Kimberley now around the Big Hole, and a "New" Kimberley, comprising a group of suburbs with such names as Beaconsfield and Kenilworth.

But it was still a mining town. Most of it was owned by C. J. Rhodes, whose three mines, the Kimberley, the De Beers and the Wesselton, dominated world diamond production; the rest was owned by New Chance. It lay six hundred and forty miles from Cape Town and four hundred and eighty-five miles from Port Elizabeth and less than ten from the border of the Boer republic of the Orange Free State. A railway line ran north from Cape Town and passed through Kimberley on its way to Bulawayo in newly named Rhodesia. This, too, ran close to Boer territory and had been blown up within the first few days of hostilities. So had the telegraph. Kimberley was isolated, cut off, remote. But it was also the world's biggest diamond producer and the British Government needed it. A relief column under Lieutenant General Lord Methuen had started northwards soon after the war began and should have been in Kimberley weeks ago, having swept the Boers before it. But the painful fact was that it hadn't.

The "siege" was something of a joke. There was no shortage of food or drink; business went on as usual. The Boer shelling killed very few people and did little damage to property: there were ten to fifteen seconds in which to take cover after the bang of the gun

was heard. In one week, more than seven hundred shells were fired into the town and only one black woman was killed. Pieces of the shells were highly prized and readily sold as souvenirs. Unexploded shells fetched five pounds each.

There were six hundred regular troops—mixtures of mounted police and gunners—in Kimberley, plus the Kimberley Light Horse and the Kimberley Blazers, as well as a Town Guard to which David, like all able-bodied men, belonged. Occasionally a mounted attack was made on the Boer positions, but these were discontinued after heavy casualties.

It had not taken the town long to become used to the conditions of the siege. At first there was a water shortage and people filled their baths and watered their gardens with shaving water and washing-up water. But then Rhodes arranged for an underground stream in one of his mines to be pumped into the town and there was as much free water as anyone needed.

If there had to be a siege, people said, then this was how they liked it.

Another shell went whizzing over David's head; again he ducked, pulling his panama hat over his face. He turned and saw it explode somewhere near the hospital and his thoughts turned to Lily who was nursing there. Although the casualties were light, the Boer guns were firing at the town in general and nothing in particular. Lily had as much chance of being a casualty as anyone else.

It was a strange time, he thought. A war brought happiness to some and disaster to others, and there was no doubt it had brought happiness to him. If Michael had only been inside the perimeter. As it was, David occasionally had news of Portuguese Place from black servants who penetrated the lines, or from Boer sympathizers living in Kimberley, who moved with greater freedom than anyone else. Nothing he heard gave him cause to worry. The farm, he supposed, was as safe for a noncombatant as anywhere else, and Michael was said to be making the same good progress.

So he had been able to allay his fears about his son and allow Lily to become the center of his thoughts. She had arrived in Kimberley just before the siege began, to give her promised farewell recitals. Peter Arendt had been due to follow a few days later, but by that time the railway line was cut and the town encircled and she was in the trap.

David no longer questioned the morality of his position. Michael was recovering and he, David, had not sought Lily out. The guilt he had felt after returning to London from Amsterdam had vanished.

She had taken a suite at the Prince Albert Hotel and that was where he spent much of his time, though as far as the town was concerned, he was staying in Dan Halkett's big house in the suburb of Beaconsfield.

As the sun dipped down towards the western hills his tour of duty came to an end and he began to walk across town towards the New Chance Mine to see Halkett, as he did every day. The heat was still severe and he jumped onto a horse-drawn tram. People seemed cheerful, although some of the women looked worn. They were city people, he thought, people who took trams and cabs and lived in brick houses. It was a far cry from the early days.

Dan's office was on the sunny side of the mine building and the shutters were closed against the last of the day's heat, making the big room shadowy and soothing to the eyes after the harsh light into which David had been staring. It was a Spartan, functional room, the only ornaments being models of some of the best diamonds to come out of the New Chance Mine. Against one wall was a glass cabinet in which was part of the pump which Frans Delport had brought up from the coast all those years ago and which had been the real start of New Chance. It still bore the name "The Invincible, G. A. Gwynne, Hammersmith, London" on a shining brass plate.

The two men took up the day-to-day business of the mine. The first problem was coal. Their stocks had dwindled to almost nothing.

"We've got to keep enough to run the lifts," Dan said. "Otherwise we can't get into the shafts for maintenance work."

"We could shut down completely."

"We're practically shut down already. It can't be long before we're relieved and then the railway will be open again."

"How are we off for food?" David was thinking of the hundreds of black miners in the compound who needed to be fed whether they were working or not.

"I laid in a big stock," Dan said, "but I think we're going to have to start slaughtering the horses."

"Will they eat horse?"

"We'll all be eating it soon."

David pulled a face and Dan said, "I've eaten it when times were rough. In stew you'd hardly know the difference. It's only the English who make a fuss."

"I still don't like the idea."

"There's something else. The military wants us to move the dynamite."

"We've already moved it once." It was now kept in a stone-built store impervious to fifteen-pound shells.

"They're still not happy."

"Where will it go?"

"Number one shaft."

"By the time we get it down there the column will have arrived. Any news of it?"

They referred to the relief column every day. Dan shook his head. "Rhodes has been trying to signal to them with a search-light at night. But no one knows if the messages get through. We did have a runner in, though."

"From the column?"

"Yes. They're pinned down by the Boers on the Modder River."

"They thought they'd just come marching up. As if the Boers were going to sit back and let them. They say Methuen has never been in battle before."

"Anyway, we got some post. A letter from Snell." He drew a sheet of notepaper towards him, looking slightly embarrassed.

"Is anything wrong?"

"You read it."

David read the two-page letter. Marie Farson had asked Snell for money and when he had questioned her about the dividends she should be getting from New Chance shares she had professed to know nothing about Jack's financial affairs: he gave her an allowance, that was all. Snell had begun his own investigation and found that Jack was almost bankrupt. Huge sums had been spent on the Sussex estate, the house in Park Lane and various gambling debts.

"He's been spending money like water," Dan said. "And he's running around with his own private cavalry. That's costing him a fortune, too."

"I know."

"What are we going to do?"

David paused, then said, "Don't do anything yet. Let him have what he wants out of my account. I'll think about it later."

He left Dan about seven and walked two blocks to the Prince Albert Hotel. Because of his wish to avoid gossip on Lily's behalf he always went through the charade of asking the desk clerk to send a servant up to announce him. She was standing by the window in her room, wearing a lacy gown which moved slightly in the evening breeze. As always, he was struck by her beauty: the expressive face, the black shining hair, the red lips and the soft roundness of her body under the filmy gown. She kissed him, then inspected him at arm's length. "You look tired."

"It's the heat. I'm not used to it anymore."

"Any news of the column?"

"Still the same. The Boers have them pinned down. What have you heard at the hospital?"

"There's a rumor that there have been talks between the military and the Boers. One of the doctors said he'd heard that if Kimberley fell all the English men would be shot and the women given to the kaffirs."

"That's just propaganda."

"I hope so."

"What would you like to do? I'm told you can still get a decent meal at the Great Northern."

"It's too hot to eat out. I was going to have a bath."

The Prince Albert was a new hotel and Lily's suite had its own bathroom.

"I'll scrub your back," he said.

"No, thank you. Ladies don't look their best hunched up in baths."

"Leave the door open so we can talk. I'll have something brought up."

"And a bottle of cold wine," she said. "I need it after today."

He sat near the window, loosened his tie and removed his jacket. He should have been content, but wasn't. He had begged her to live with him in Dan's house but she had been adamant and, grudgingly, he supposed she was right. She was loved in Kimberley, that had been plain from the moment she arrived. There had been a crowd at the station to meet her and a crowd outside the hotel when she moved in. The first two concerts had been packed, with people standing at the rear of the hall. He could understand she would not want anything to mar this.

What had really made the town her slave was that within a week of knowing she would not be able to leave until the siege was over, she offered her services as a nurse. Since then she had done everything from washing bedpans to helping the surgeons cut off gangrenous limbs. In spite of the fact that the siege was relatively mild, diseases like enteric fever, typhoid and dysentery were beginning to be seen, and it was not only British casualties with which the hospital dealt. Most of the doctors on the Boer side were Americans, Germans and French. If a Boer was badly in need of surgery he would be brought in under a white flag and operated on in Kimberley.

"Are you still there?" Lily called.

"Yes, I'm still here."

"You're very quiet."

"I was thinking."

"About what?"

He was going to say, "Us," but that was something they talked about endlessly, with no solution. Instead, he said, "There's trouble with Jack."

"What sort of trouble?"

He told her the gist of Snell's letter. She was silent for a while, then she said, "I should be surprised, but I'm not. He was never a man to keep a pound note in his pocket."

David remembered what had happened to the first good diamond they had found.

"Is he still coming to see you at the hospital?" he asked.

She nodded. "Almost every day. It's embarrassing, in front of the doctors. They think there's . . . there's something between us. And, of course, there are still people who remember us in the old days."

A shadow seemed to fall between them and he was silent. She emerged from the bathroom, wearing the same filmy gown, which now stuck damply to her body.

"We were different people then," David said at last. "Why don't we let him know about *us*? That would stop him."

"I don't think it would. He seems so strange. He's drinking heavily. In an odd way, I'm frightened of him. At first he talked a lot about Jewel, but now . . ."

There was a knock at the door.

Lily glanced at David and called, "Who's there?"

Jack's voice answered, "It's me." It was very loud.

"What is it?"

"Let me in."

"I've told you . . ."

"Have you got someone there?" The words would be echoing down the corridors.

"Of course not!" She indicated the bedroom, and David went in, leaving the door slightly ajar, which enabled him to see most of the other room.

Lily opened the outer door.

"I thought someone was with you," Jack said.

"I was having a bath."

He looked around suspiciously, then he noticed the damp patches on her gown and David saw him eye her hungrily. She drew the edges of the garment closer together.

"I asked you not to come here," she said.

"I know, but what harm is there?"

"I don't like it."

"We're old friends. More than friends!"

"That's enough, Jack."

David felt himself flushing with embarrassment and jealousy. He hated hiding like some music-hall lover, yet he respected Lily's wish for their affair to remain private—or as private as was possible in a place the size of Kimberley.

"Aren't you going to invite me to sit down?"

"No, Jack, I . . ."

"We could have a bottle sent up. What about dinner?"

"Don't you understand! I don't want you to visit me here!" She moved to the door. "And you're coming to the hospital too often."

"You said I could visit you there."

"But not every day."

"Lily, you don't understand. . . ."

"No, I don't. You listen to me. . . ."

He held up a hand. "All right, Lily! Anything you say. We'll do it your way." With that, he was gone.

Lily went to David in the bedroom. "I'm sorry," she said, taking his hand.

"This sort of thing makes me feel dirty."

"I know."

He left early that night, taking a horse cab through the

barricaded streets, having to show his identification pass every few hundred yards.

Dan was nowhere in sight when he reached home and he assumed he was in bed, for Dan retired early and was up early. The house was large and double-storied, set back in an arbor of fruit trees and vines. The servants let David in and he went up to his room. He sat on the bed for a long while. Sooner or later Jack would have to know about him and Lily, and that would provoke whatever must eventually happen between them. The icy coldness that had existed between them since Jack's arrival could not last forever. Jack never came into the office, never discussed business, spent his time riding awkwardly around the town with his cronies, visiting one canteen after another. Lily was right: he had changed; there was something alarming about him.

David went to a small office safe he kept in his room, and opened it. The "Southern Cross" lay on its bed of black velvet. It was set as a single pendant on a gold chain and looked more beautiful than ever. To hold it and gaze at it gave him intense pleasure. He always marveled at the loveliness of the stone that seemed, paradoxically, to combine cold and heat. But now he found its beauty was no longer sufficient. It needed pale skin to frame it. It needed to be worn. It needed Lily, just as he did.

A few days later he was in Dan Halkett's office discussing what was to be done about water seepage and whether they had enough coal to run the big steam pumps, when Jack burst in. He was dressed in his cavalry uniform, holding a riding crop in one hand and swaying slightly. His face was congested and his eyes were red. Before he opened his mouth David could smell whisky.

"Well, this is cozy," he said. "What is it, a meeting of the management? You forgot me."

"It's nothing like that," David said. "There's water in number two shaft. We're discussing pumping it out."

"That's a bloody big decision," Jack said with heavy irony. "That'll stop the Boers and end the siege. I've got news for you: there's something being done that *will* help to end it."

"What's that?" Dan said coldly.

"C. J. Rhodes is building a gun."

"Building a gun?" Dan said.

"Labram's making it." George Labram was Rhodes's mining

engineer, an American who, like Dan Halkett, could turn his hand to anything.

"What sort of gun?"

"A bloody great gun, a thirty-pounder. Not like these damn popguns we've got. Something to plaster the Boers with."

They looked at him in silence; then David said, "Well, good luck to them."

"Is that all you can say? Christ, all you're doing is lying up on those sandbags all day *watching* Johnnie Boer! At least Rhodes is doing something. And so am I, with the Blazers! You're like an old woman! Where would we have got in the old days if you'd been like this?" He flung out of the office and they could hear his booted feet crashing on the stairs down to the street.

11

David was not the only one to whom the war had brought solace; Susan was finding happiness as deep as she had ever known. The farm was isolated from events in Kimberley. There were no more "lost days," for now she was kept busy helping Jewel. Her granddaughter had taken over the running of the house. Michael's health had improved to a point where she could hardly recall the gaunt, hollow-eyed figure who had arrived from Victoria. He ate well and slept well and his coughing had almost stopped.

With Susan's active help he was taking an increasing interest in the farm. He had read some of the old books on farming which Frans had collected during his lifetime, and would often question her on things he did not understand. One day, when she had not seen him for several hours, she found him near the gate in the Home Camp, mending a fence. He was pulling on a strand of

wire, straining it to the fence post, and the sweat was running off his face. For a moment she was alarmed, but he looked so natural and strong that finally she said, "There are a lot of fences in need of mending."

"I know. I'm only starting."

On another occasion, after some of Lessing's cattle had broken down a fence and come onto Portuguese Place she found Michael repairing the damage with Hans at his side, helping him. She thought what a strange war this was, when a man could come home to mend a fence or milk a cow or bring in the harvest, and then go back to take up the fighting where he had left off; but it was apparently happening all over the country, as a peasant army fought close to its roots.

They saw little of the war, but occasionally they would hear what was happening from their neighbors and from Hans. Part of the time he was with his Boer commando on the Kimberley perimeter, part of the time on the farm doing jobs that neither his wife nor his young child could manage.

"One good push and it would all be over," he said of the siege.

"What then?" Michael said, thinking of his father, a picture rising in his mind of medieval sieges in which the townsfolk were put to the sword after the invaders had come through the walls.

"Nothing," Hans said. "All we want is to close the mines. We've got nothing against the people."

"You know they're saying that you're going to shoot the English men and give the women to the kaffirs," Susan said.

Hans looked at her. "Do you believe that, Aunt Susan?"

"Of course not."

"The English don't fight fair. Have you heard what they do to the waterholes?"

"No."

"Some of them have been poisoned. That's bad for us. We have to use them for our stock and our horses; we can't travel in the desert without waterholes. Now we have to leave men to guard them and we can't spare the men. Remember that when they talk about giving white women to the kaffirs."

She watched the two men. They got on so well, and yet she supposed they were enemies because their races made them so. It was symbolic of what was happening all over the country.

One day this question came abruptly into the open. Hans rode in by himself. He was dusty and sweat-stained and there was a

bitter look in his eyes that had not been there before. Susan gave him coffee and Jewel brought a plate of rusks. Michael, who had been milking, came onto the stoep with a bucket of fresh milk.

"Aunt Susan, will you look after Suzette and the children when the time comes?" Hans said abruptly. Suzette was his wife.

"When the time comes? She's not . . . ?"

"No. But they're taking women and children to camps."

"Who?"

"The English." He glanced at Michael under his heavy brows.

"Are you sure?"

"They say the camps are crowded. People are dying like flies."

Michael said, "There are always rumors in war. We'd never do that."

"We?" Lessing said.

"I mean . . ."

"Is that how you feel?"

"Of course not. It slipped out. It isn't that way at all. Except . . ."

"What?"

Michael shook his head. "I was born here, like you."

"But you wouldn't fight for us."

Michael hesitated. "I've thought about this. It's not that I wouldn't fight *for* you. It's that I wouldn't fight *against* them. They're my people, too." It was a dichotomy that was to overtake many in the years to come.

"You can't have one foot here and the other in England," Lessing said, and turned to leave.

Susan walked with him to his horse. "Don't worry about Suzette and the children," she said. "Tell her to come as soon as she likes."

"We can't hold the British Army forever," he said. "When they break through they'll round up the women and children and burn the farms. You'll see."

"Perhaps the stories about the camps are only rumors. Perhaps Michael's right," she said, and saw a shadow pass across his face. "Remember, his father is trapped in Kimberley. He could be killed at any time."

As the summer deepened and the heat grew more intense, the land dried up and the river dropped away to a trickle. But the big pools held their levels and Susan would go down with Michael

and Jewel in the late afternoons and sit in the shade by the Breakfast Pool. "This is what we sometimes talked about in London," Jewel said. "I could never believe it would happen."

Seeing the two young people together gave her more pleasure than anything else. Sometimes when she stood on the stoep and watched Michael walk up from the river or along from the Home Camp, it was as though she were seeing Frans coming in from a day's work; as though the years had fallen away.

But the idyll could not last. The country was at war and war finally came to Portuguese Place.

Susan was dreaming a dream one night, a dream she had not had for a long while. Once, when the memories on which it was based were fresh, she had dreamt it frequently. She was enveloped in something white, amorphous, like a cloud, and then the blurred image cleared and she was in the wagon and the whiteness was the canvas sailcloth. She was looking through the opening at the back and horses were there jingling their bridles and stamping their hooves and the Hottentots were there and one of them was choking Mr. Parker. Another was coming towards her wagon. She could see the greasy locks, the ring in the ear. She had a shotgun in her hands but when she pulled the trigger nothing happened. The Hottentot came on, laughing at her. . . .

She woke, sweating and rigid—and then came the even worse nightmare of reality. She could *hear* the sounds from her dream: horses' hooves, the clattering of harnesses and something heavy grating over rocky ground. She rose, put on a gown and took the shotgun from its place above the living room door. She went quietly past Michael's room and Jewel's room and made sure their doors were closed. She went out of the house and saw flaring torches down by the old cattle kraal. It was bright moonlight and she stood in the dark shadow of the house. She could hear voices and again a jingling of harness. The sounds were coming from her right, from the track that ran above the old servants' quarters. A team of mules came into view, pulling a gun so big that it dwarfed the animals and the men who walked beside it. They began to maneuver it on its great wheels into the kraal, pulling away part of the walls, which were of cut thorn bush.

"Halt!" a voice cried, and for a moment the flickering torches were still.

Susan had moved closer and by the torchlight was able to see the lettering on the gun barrel: "Schneider-Creusot et Cie. Saône et Loire, France."

She looked at the men closely. There were five of them. Four were dressed in formal military uniforms, although of differing kinds. The fifth was a Boer in his farming clothes, carrying his bandolier of bullets.

One of the gunners—for she assumed the uniformed men to be artillerymen—was a sandy-haired giant in a dark uniform and knee-length black leather boots. He directed the operations in English but with a heavy accent which Susan could not place.

The men began to cover the gun with the old dead thorn branches. The big man turned to the Boer and said, "Are you sure this place is deserted?"

"Ja. That is our information." Susan knew the Boer's accent was that of someone who spoke Dutch as his home language. "She was an old mad woman. She died."

They piled the thorn branches around the gun until it was camouflaged, then the sandy-haired man said, "We will eat and then we will sleep in the house."

She knew there was no question of hiding any longer. She stepped into the light of the torches, holding the gun loosely in her hand.

"What do you want on my farm?" she said, letting her voice rise.

Everything stopped. The big gunner turned and moved towards her, taking off his cap. "Madame!" he said.

"Who are you?"

"We thought this was an empty place."

He looked up at the Boer, seated on his horse, and Susan saw anger on his face.

"It is not empty," she said.

"Now I can see that."

She was aware of the other gunners moving behind the big man. "I asked who you were and what you wanted."

"A thousand pardons," he said. "Bengtson. Captain in the Royal Swedish Artillery." He brought his heels together and bowed. "These are my men." The torches had been brought forwards and she could see him more clearly.

He had a large flat face with light eyebrows and light lashes. His tunic was unbuttoned at the neck and she could see fair skin

covered with a sheen of sweat, for the night was hot. His three men closed in behind him. They were very different. Whereas the Swede carried an air of authority and the manners of an officer, these looked like savages. Their hair was matted, their uniforms were torn and they were streaked with grease and dirt. The Boer dismounted and said, "My name is Smit."

"I asked you what you wanted."

The Swedish captain said, "You are English?"

"American."

"So. It is strange for an American to be here, yes?"

"No stranger than a Swede. You still haven't told me what you want."

"You saw what we were doing?"

"Of course."

"We must rest here two days, perhaps three."

"Here?"

"We were told it was deserted."

"You were told wrong."

"It happens in war."

"You cannot stay."

"I understand how you feel, madame, but . . ."

"There are no buts. I am an old woman alone here, but I can use this." She lifted the shotgun. "I have farmed here for more than thirty years. I say who stays on my farm and who goes."

"You force me to ignore you, madame." He put his cap back on his head and said, "We have come a long way on this mission. We are tired and we are hungry. Perhaps you have food." He had already walked past her and was making for the house, followed by his men. She lowered the gun, unable to use it.

"You must be proud of what you're doing," she said bitterly to the Boer, who looked unhappy and truculent.

"We have orders."

Susan hurried after them. Somehow they had to be stopped from discovering Michael and Jewel. "I have food," she called.

Bengtson paused, nodded. "Good. We will eat whatever you have."

"You can't sleep in the house. It's . . . There is only my room. The others are broken down and filthy."

"Cannot?" Bengtson said. There was a coldness in his tone that frightened her. "First let us eat. Then we will discuss what happens next."

He was about to go into the house when she said, "It's cooler here," indicating the stoep. They sat on the benches and chairs around the heavy table which Frans had made.

"Do you have wine?" one of the gunners said.

She looked at him. He was small and dark, with a shaven head which showed a scar running above his left ear. His accent, she thought, was French. "No," she said.

"Cognac?"

"I have no ardent spirits."

She heard a noise from inside the house. She froze. She tried to block the doorway with her body, but it was too late. Michael, rubbing the sleep from his eyes, was standing in the living room. "What's happening?" he said.

With one fluid movement, the big Swedish gunner was on his feet and had drawn a heavy revolver from the buttoned holster he wore on his belt.

"Come out!" he said. "Come out of there!"

"Who are you?" Michael said.

Bengtson turned to Susan, mimicking her. "I am an old woman alone here . . ." He said to the small man with the shaven head, "Serge, you and Manuel search the house."

"Wait," Susan said. "It's not what you think. I wasn't trying to lie. This is my grandson, Michael. He is an invalid. He has consumption."

The word as applied to Michael seemed ludicrous. He stood in the lamplight, the very picture of rustic health.

"I have seen cases of consumption," Bengtson said.

"He's recovering."

"But from what? From a journey, perhaps?"

"Journey?" Michael said. "Where would I be traveling to?"

"Are you an American?" Bengtson said.

"No."

"English?"

"He's my grandson," Susan said. "An Afrikaner."

"I think you are English," Bengtson said. "And I think you have come from the relief column to spy out the land. Now, madame, is there anyone else in the house?"

Susan stepped back into the doorway and loudly said, "There are only the two of us in the house. Myself and my grandson."

Bengtson smiled. "Serge. Manuel." The two darted past her like whippets.

She turned to Smit. "For God's sake! My name is Susan Delport. My husband was Frans Delport, a good Boer. Have you not heard of him?"

"No."

"And the Lessings and the Jordaans. They're my neighbors. They can tell you who I am. Don't you know Lessing?"

He looked confused. "I know of a Lessing. . . ."

"Hans Lessing."

"Ja. Hans Lessing."

"He's our neighbor. Our friend. Ask him about us!"

She heard a scuffle behind her and the two artillerymen came into the living room with Jewel. She was dressed only in her nightgown and, with the lamplight behind her, her young body was plainly visible.

"You pigs!" Susan said. She pushed past, went to Jewel's room and brought her a robe.

"Well, this is a great pleasure," Bengtson said.

Jewel seemed to realize immediately what was happening. She stood calmly between Susan and Michael, tying the robe and lifting her hair from the collar.

"This is my granddaughter," Susan said. "You had no right to go to her room."

"Ah, the granddaughter," Bengtson said, the disbelief obvious in his tone. "First the grandson, then the granddaughter!" He turned to Jewel. "Is it mademoiselle or madame?"

"It's miss," she said firmly.

Just then the third gunner, a thin German called Hoffman, came out with two bottles of brandy. Susan was genuinely surprised. They were part of a stock which Frans had bought and she had forgotten. Bengtson pulled the cork from one and drank deeply before passing it on. "Smit?" he said, but the Boer shook his head. "Smit is not a drinker, are you, my dear Smit?" Then he said, "This is very interesting, madame. You have told me three things only and they have all been lies. Why, I ask myself. Unless you are enemies."

Susan said nothing, for there was nothing to say. She had put the shotgun down in the living room and wondered how long it would take her to reach it.

"And now we have a problem," he went on. "You have seen what we have been doing." His eyes shifted to Jewel. All four men were looking at her. Only Smit kept his eyes to the ground.

Bengtson looked back at Susan. "You said you had food. Please fetch it."

Susan stood her ground.

"Now, madame!"

"I'll need help. Jewel will come with me."

"Jewel? This is an unusual name. Jewel. But I think not. No, Jewel will not help you, nor will your grandson. I would like him to stay where I can see him. Hoffman can help. He is a good German boy."

Hoffman said, "I found the brandy, Captain."

"That's true. You go then, Smit. You don't drink."

Susan went into the small room at the back which she and Jewel had made into a kitchen and storeroom. Her body was shaking. The nightmare had returned, only this time it would happen to Jewel. The damage would be more to her. She was eighteen: Susan had been in her thirties when she had met the Korannas. Jewel came from the protected atmosphere of London; Susan had come from a country not too dissimilar to the one in which she now lived.

Smit came in behind her. "What is happening here?" she hissed.

He wore the same confused, unhappy expression on his face. He was about twenty, a large, overgrown boy.

"What are you doing here?" she said again, this time in Dutch.

His expression changed to one of surprise. He was young enough to be her grandchild and Boers were respectful to their elders. "We'll use the gun to make Kimberley flat," he said.

"But why bring it here?"

"The ammunition wagons have broken down. We must wait for them two or three days. Meantime, there is no one to guard the gun. If the English knew, they would bring men out and blow it up."

"And you think we could get a message to them?" she said scornfully.

"That's what *they* think, Aunt."

She clinked plates and banged cups to cover their conversation, but her eyes bored into his and she said, "Do you know what is going to happen?"

He shifted his feet, without speaking.

"If those men spend two or three days here, what do you think

will be left of us?" She paused. "They will rape my granddaughter. Be certain of that."

He flinched as though she had struck him.

"And then they will kill us so no one will be left alive to tell what happened. And you are going to see it all. You are going to see them hold her down. Perhaps tie her legs apart."

"For God's sake, Aunt!"

"That's how a woman is raped. They either hold her legs or tie them. Sometimes they threaten her with a knife or choke her. Then they bite her breasts, sometimes they cut them."

"Please! For God's sake!"

"Sometimes they hit her in the face and she loses teeth, sometimes they smash her nose."

His lips were trembling and he was swallowing.

"That's what you'll see, Smit. And if you see it and you do nothing, then you're part of it. Do you think I'm lying?"

He shook his head. "No, Aunt." Tears came into his eyes. "They did it to a Hottentot woman two days ago. Just what you said. They got drunk. They found her by the track. A young girl, fourteen or fifteen. They did it and they left her. They're uncontrollable. They're not like us, they're fighting here for the money. We don't want people like that."

"What are you going to do, Smit?" Her voice was low, but cut like a flail.

There was a gust of laughter from the stoep and he swung round.

"It's beginning," Susan said.

Suddenly he made up his mind. "Have you got horses?"

"In the kraal past the one with the gun."

"Can you ride bareback?"

"Maybe."

"If I can get bridles on three, where can I take them?"

"Below the house is the river. Take them there."

He nodded. "Be ready. You'll know when to go. But don't stay in this valley or go towards Kimberley. They'll hunt you down. I know them."

They carried coffee and rusks to the stoep and she saw that it really *was* beginning—something more violent than just the laughter, for Michael was on the floor, dabbing at his mouth where he had been cut, she assumed, by a blow, and Jewel was

wedged between the Swede and the man with the scarred head.

Bengtson was laughing. He held out his hand and opened it. He was holding the gold chain which Jewel always wore around her neck. The girl's face was flushed.

"You can have it if you can take it," he said.

"Please . . ."

"Let her alone!" Michael was trying to struggle to his feet. One of the men caught him by the shirt and pulled him down again.

"Can't you see she's frightened?" Susan said.

They had a little—not much—respect left for Susan. Perhaps it was the look in her eyes that the Koranna, Kaptein, had once seen, that held them in check. Bengtson dropped the chain in his pocket. "I will put it back personally later."

Smit went down the steps into the darkness. "Where are you going?" Bengtson said.

"To relieve myself."

"Don't do it near the house. You Boers stink."

Susan poured the coffee into enamel mugs and each man laced his with brandy.

"Is that all you've got?" the Swede said. "You people eat badly in this country. Have you no meat?"

She shook her head. Savages were all alike, she thought. She remembered Kaptein and the other Korannas grilling the goat over the fire and drinking brandy before Kaptein took her to the wagon. These men were the same: first the brandy, then the need for meat, then the need for women.

"Here you are, Hoffman, this is your sort of food, isn't it? Zwieback."

The thin German dipped a rusk in his coffee and tried it. "Not so good as zwieback."

Bengtson turned back to Jewel. "A pretty girl like you shouldn't be stuck away here. You should come with us. Maybe you will. We have two or three days to get to know each other." He opened his hand. The gold chain lay in his palm once more. But Jewel sat still. "Never mind, there are other games. Let me put it back. You have a beautiful throat."

She tried to move away, but could not. As his hands went up to her throat, one cupped her breast.

"Don't!" she said, and shivered.

Susan knew that whatever was going to happen, it would be

soon. The gun was lying in the living room. "I'll fetch more coffee," she said.

"Stay where you are!" Bengtson said. "We haven't finished this yet." She felt totally helpless. An old, helpless woman.

At that moment, a shot rang out. It came from the direction of the cattle kraal.

Bengtson leapt to his feet. "Smit!" he shouted. There was another shot.

"Over there!" came Smit's voice. "Behind the huts!"

"What?"

"Six or seven riders!" There was a third shot.

Bengtson ran down the steps, fumbling for his revolver. The other three grabbed their rifles and followed him.

"There are horses down by the river," Susan said. "Quickly!"

They made their way down the far side of the house. Susan stopped once and heard the crackle of rifle fire. She wondered what they would do to Smit when they discovered the riders were only in his imagination; nothing to what they would have done to Jewel. She heard a horse whicker and found three tied where the old pump had been.

In the intense darkness she had lost touch with Michael and Jewel. Now she heard Jewel call Michael's name softly. There was no reply.

"Aunt Susan, is Michael with you?" She could hear the anxiety in the girl's voice.

"No." She tried to remember their movements. They had entered the belt of trees together.

"He was here!" Jewel said. "Michael!"

In the silence they could hear the crackle of rifle fire as Smit acted out his charade.

Suddenly, a tongue of flame shot into the air. It came from the direction of the old cattle kraal. The firing stopped and Susan heard shouts. The fire blazed up, silhouetting the gun. She realized that the old thorn branches used to camouflage the gun had been set alight. They were dry as tinder from the summer heat.

They saw a figure running towards them, brilliantly lit by the flames. "It's Michael!" Jewel hissed.

The firing was resumed, but this time the bullets came cracking

into the trees. The men were aiming at Michael. Just then he tripped and fell.

Jewel screamed. She started forwards, but he scrambled up and came on towards them. The fire was frightening the horses and Susan fought to control them. There was a crashing noise to her right. She saw the artillery mules rush through the trees and vanish upstream. Then Michael was with them and they were struggling to mount the saddleless horses. The crackle of gunfire was almost continuous and the bullets were striking trees all around them. In a moment they were splashing across the river and a little later were riding across the desert on the far bank.

They rode fast for the first hour, hunched against the night sky, expecting to hear the crack of a rifle at any moment. But no one was following. At dawn they stopped at a waterhole and Susan said, "If it's been poisoned, there should be dead animals."

They looked carefully, but could not see any bodies. They drank, and let the horses drink.

"What happened?" Jewel said to Michael. "We were frightened."

"I set the thorn alight. I don't know that I did much damage, but the wheels were wooden. They'll have to be replaced. It'll slow them down." He turned to Susan. "Where are we heading?"

"A village called Galilee." Then she said, "It's dangerous taking sides."

"I know. But my father did. When I was ill, he took my side. If it wasn't for him, I would have died."

"You can't stop the siege."

"But I might have stopped the gun for a while, at least."

She looked at him more closely. His face was very pale and his eyes were framed by dark smudges. The effort had cost him dear in strength, she thought.

As they spoke, two Boers materialized from an outcrop of rock on the far side of the waterhole. They held their rifles with casual alertness, interested but hardly surprised to see three civilians in their nightclothes. The war had produced many more dramatic incidents than this.

"Who are you?" one asked.

Susan explained briefly that soldiers had invaded her house and that they were making for Galilee. The Boer shook his head. "I have orders to bring in stragglers. Come with us," he said.

They rode for most of the morning. To the casual eye the

desert appeared to be empty, but on closer inspection there was evidence of much movement. It was crisscrossed by horses' hooves and iron-shod wheels. Guns, wagons and armies had passed this way.

In the early afternoon they were picked up by a commando of a dozen Boers and escorted to an encampment at the base of a jumble of flat-topped mountains. As they rode into the camp a horseman detached himself from a group.

"My God!" he said. "Aunt Susan!" It was Hans Lessing. Susan had never been so pleased to see the familiar square, bearded figure.

Leaving out Michael's attempt to destroy the gun she told him what had happened. He nodded angrily. "What can I say? We don't like these people, but we need them. They know how to use the big guns. Come, you must be hungry and thirsty. Let me get you something, then we must go to the general."

"Where are we?" Susan asked.

"These are the Magersfontein hills. Look over there. Do you see the smoke? That's the British relief column."

General Cronje was too busy to see them. Susan caught a glimpse of him, a burly, bearded figure in a wide-brimmed hat and a long dustcoat that came down to his ankles, reminding her of pictures she had seen of American road agents. They were seen instead by a vice-commandant who hardly listened to what Lessing had to say. He was a thin-lipped man, clean-shaven, which was unusual in the *laager*. After a few moments he cut Lessing short. "Take them to the family *laager* and tell them to stay there."

The family *laager* was a camp within the big encampment itself and was made up of wives, children, mothers, even grandmothers who had chosen to be with their men. There were nearly a hundred women and children, some of British stock, local farmers who had come to the *laager* for food and shelter, their sympathies with the Boer Army rather than with the British forces.

Susan, who had been only on the periphery of the war, now found herself at its very heart. They were fed and given a tent and when they had rested she talked with other women, some her own age, and discovered that the British relief column had suffered severely at Boer hands in crossing the Modder River a week before but that they were expected to attack the present

Boer positions at any moment in their drive to relieve Kimberley.

Lessing came for them towards evening and they walked over the *laager*. It was sited below Magersfontein Hill, a large flat-topped hill shaped like the prow of a ship. They came to a rise.

"Look down there," he said. At the base of the hill, facing the British lines, Susan made out a line of trenches. They had been so cunningly concealed by acacia branches and Karoo bush that they were almost impossible to see.

"There are fifteen miles of them," Hans said. "We have put barbed wire in front. The British expect us to be up there. . . ." He pointed to the top of the Magersfontein ridge. "They always fight in the same way. First they will use their artillery, then they will attack. You'll see when the bombardment comes."

It came that night, a night of rain and high wind, with lyddite shells bursting on the cliffs above them, lighting up the night sky. The bombardment went on hour after hour until, just after midnight, it stopped. The wind died and the rain passed away. The prowlike hill was etched against the sky. All night the Boers had been moving into the trenches and as the first hint of dawn began to seep across the veld Susan could see their heads and shoulders as dark patches against the lighter background. Then, as the light strengthened, she saw a sight she would never forget: coming towards them across the open veld, shoulder to shoulder, nine ranks deep, was the Highland Brigade. It appeared to be engaged in a formal ceremonial drill, for she could hear faintly on the morning breeze the commands "Close up! Close up! Dressing! Watch your dressing!"

A thousand yards. Five hundred yards. Still this solid mass of marching men came towards the Boer trenches. There was no hurry; everything was calmly paced. Sometimes a man stumbled over a bush or turned his ankle in a *muishond* hole, and a voice would shout, "Dressing! Keep your dressing!"

"My God! What *can* they be doing?" Michael said.

The Boers in their trenches were equally astonished. Their general had promised to set a trap for the British but they had never expected them to walk into it quite so easily.

"Close up! Close up!" The voices came crisply across the veld. The light was shading from dark blue to gray and Susan's eyes could make out the kilts and sporrans of the leading ranks. Then someone in the Boer trenches, perhaps by arrangement, perhaps with a trigger finger tautened by tension, let off a shot. Imme-

diately the Boers began the engagement. Flashes from the Mauser barrels in the half-light rippled along the trenches like a display of fireworks.

The impact of the steel-jacketed bullets, which fired from the new high-velocity rifles could penetrate three men, one behind the other, was appalling. The front rank of the Black Watch disappeared from view as though it had walked into a hole.

Even the poorest shot, and there were no poor shots among these farmers who used a rifle every day of their lives, could not have missed, for the Highland Brigade had done the unforgivable: it had marched in close order on trenches it did not know were there, into a hail of bullets.

"Gather round, Black Watch! Gather round!" came a voice.

Another was shouting, "Charge!"

A third: "Retire!"

Over all this came the skirl of the pipes and the beat of the drums.

No one knew what to do. The Black Watch, in the lead, began to move backwards and collided with the Seaforths. Men of different regiments found themselves stumbling into each other, running past each other, dying in each other's arms. Behind the Seaforths were the Highland Light Infantry. When they saw the Black Watch and the Seaforths come past them towards the rear they, too, turned, trampling down their own colonel. Soon thousands of men were stampeding wildly across the open veld.

Dawn and a blazing sun showed what had happened. The ground in front of the Boer trenches was littered with fallen British soldiers: some were dead, some were dying, some were calling for water, some were pulling themselves along on their elbows, trying to get to the rear. These were picked off by the Boers at their leisure. There were mounds of abandoned equipment: rifles, bayonets, water bottles; and on the barbed wire—totally unexpected, totally unlike anything the British had ever imagined—hung dozens of bodies.

The storm of the night before had passed and the day grew hot, for it was midsummer. In the sunlight the movement of a bayonet, or a flask, or a cap badge or button gave a telltale flash which brought a volley from the Boer trenches. Men were hiding everywhere on the stony, scrub-covered plain: behind bushes and rocks, under blankets, behind dead bodies. There they had to remain as the sun climbed into the sky, grilled by the heat. Some

became delirious and began to crawl towards the Boer trenches. They were killed before they had moved a yard or two. But hundreds endured until the Boers counterattacked at noon, then they fled. It was the worst catastrophe in the history of the Scottish regiments.

As dusk came down, water carts and medical staff came onto the field from both sides. There were few Boer casualties and their doctors went out to help the British. So did many of the women from the *laager*. All that night Susan and Jewel bandaged wounds and set splintered limbs and it was not until the following day that they could rest.

They stayed in the *laager* for nearly a week before they were allowed to leave. Galilee had been burnt down in the British advance, so they could not continue their journey. There was nowhere to go but Portuguese Place.

They reached the Green River in early afternoon and took cover in the trees on the far bank. Michael went forwards, leaving the two women. He crossed the water and stopped in the trees on the home bank. Everything was still in the blazing heat. There was no smoke, no movement. The old cattle kraal was a black scar on the red earth. The gun was gone. Slowly he rode towards the house. A shutter flapped in the hot wind but there was no sign of life. He beckoned the women forwards and they crossed the river to join him.

"The gun's gone," he said.

"I'm sorry," Jewel said.

He shrugged. "It was worth a try. They must have got new wheels. Perhaps the ammunition carts arrived."

He looked at Susan. She was exhausted. "I'll go first," he said, and rode ahead of them to the house.

Apart from the banging shutter, nothing moved. Now was the time they would kill him, he thought. They could shoot him from the house and he'd never even hear the shot. But if the gun was gone, they were gone. It made no sense otherwise.

He dismounted and climbed onto the stoep. The mugs they had used for coffee were still on the table. He felt again the rage that had left him weak and trembling when they had touched Jewel. The front door stood open. The house was empty.

"Come up," he said. "It's all right."

But it was not all right. As they went in they saw a sight none

was ever likely to forget. In revenge for the attack on their gun the artillerymen had left the house a ruin. Furniture had been smashed; cups, plates, pots lay strewn about, some encrusted with food. Susan's bed had been used, the bathroom was a fetid midden. One of the rooms had been used as a lavatory and the floor was caked with excrement.

Something inside Susan seemed to wither. She stood, looking at her ruined home, unable to cope with the thought of what they had to do. There had been too many beginnings.

Michael seemed to sense what was going on in her mind. "Don't give up," he said. "We'll get it right. No one is going to destroy Portuguese Place while we're here."

A scream echoed down the passage. Jewel was standing at the window of her room, which looked out onto the part of the house which Jack had destroyed. A body was hanging from an old beam. It was Smit, or what was left of him. Crows had eaten away his face and his hands and he hung there, a rope tied around his chest, turning in the wind, first one way and then the other.

"Don't let Grandma see!" Jewel said.

They put Susan in a chair on the stoep. She thought she heard a scraping noise and then the sound of a pick and shovel, but she could not be sure. She could not move, not even when she heard them go to work on the house.

For the first time in her life, she felt defeated. Not even when she had been taken in by the Bushmen women, nor when she had been alone on the banks of the Great River, nor when the *rinderpest* had wiped out the farm, nor when Frans had lain in his room half-paralyzed—not even at those times had she felt totally defeated as she did now. It was as though her own body had been smeared with the excrement.

She was half-aware of Michael and Jewel bringing in buckets of water, finding brushes and cloths and brooms; half-aware of the sounds of cleaning; half-aware that they came out every once in a while to see she was all right. Her mind wandered back through her life, back to her childhood in Georgia, and finally she fell asleep.

When she woke she was no longer on the stoep but in her own bed between her own rough sheets. She could see her clock on the wall and the picture of Frans which she kept at her bedside. It was just after dawn. She could not recall having been taken to bed. She did not even know which day it was and for a second she

was terrified she had gone through one of her "lost" periods; she knew that her mind had become fogged by exhaustion and by what she had seen at Magersfontein.

But she felt better now, as though something in her brain had unraveled during the hours of unconsciousness. She got up and saw that her room shone with cleanliness. She went into the living room. Apart from one or two gaps where furniture was missing, it was as it had been when they left it. She tiptoed down the passage and looked in at Jewel and Michael. Both were asleep. The other rooms were empty.

They had worked miracles. The house had been set to rights. She walked out onto the stoep and stood in the shade of the grapevine which Frans had planted. The sun was shining. Everything was peaceful. A ring-necked dove sitting on the roof of the house was calling in lulling tones: "My f-a-a-ther, my f-a-a-ther, work h-a-a-rder, work h-a-a-rder. . . ."

There had been a moment on the stoep, she remembered, when she had nearly given in. She had felt that she wanted to close her eyes and keep them closed forever. But that had passed, thank God. She walked down to Frans's grave and changed the flowers in the little jar and then came back, skirting the old cattle kraal. For a moment she expected to see the great barrel of the gun, but there were only the black scar and the tracks in the soft sand to show where it had been. The farm was hers again. Not hers alone, but Jewel's and Michael's, too. She recalled his words: *"No one is going to destroy Portuguese Place while we're here."* A new day was beginning. The gun had been only a bad dream.

But the gun was not a bad dream in Kimberley. Its presence there was changing everything.

12

It was a hot, dark night, with low clouds hanging over Kimberley. Abruptly, from the edge of the town, a thin pencil of light shot up into the sky. The searchlight wavered nervously from side to side, fixed itself in one position, illuminating the base of one of the clouds, and began to flicker on and off in a series of dots and dashes:

S-I-T-U-A-T-I-O-N G-R-A-V-E

F-O-O-D S-H-O-R-T

S-I-C-K-N-E-S-S I-N-C-R-E-A-S-I-N-G

C-A-N-N-O-T H-O-L-D O-U-T M-U-C-H L-O-N-G-E-R . . .

S-I-T-U-A-T-I-O-N G-R-A-V-E

F-O-O-D . . .

The message was repeated over and over for nearly half an hour, a pathetic, lost voice in the immensity of the African night;

then the light went out. On the sandbagged tower which held the searchlight, a group of men strained their eyes into the darkness, looking south.

"See anything?" one asked.

"Nothing."

"You think they've seen us?"

"God knows."

Jack Farson was standing at the base of the tower. He turned to a major in the Kimberley Light Horse and said, "They never bloody see us!"

"Try again, Corporal," a voice on the tower said.

Again the pencil of light flickered on and off.

S-I-T-U-A-T-I-O-N G-R-A-V-E F-O-O-D S-H . . .

This time the signaler was only halfway through the message when there was a boom like distant thunder. Everyone ducked down. After what seemed like minutes, but was only fifteen seconds, there was a screeching noise above them, followed by a great explosion in the town.

The light was killed, but even as the order to abandon signaling was given, another shell screamed overhead.

Jack picked himself up and dusted his clothes. "It's bloody stupid!" he said angrily. "We should have taken that gun when it first arrived."

Another shell came whistling overhead and a siren began to wail. There was a movement of people in the street, some running, some walking.

Jack mounted his horse and rode towards the New Chance Mine. There was already a large crowd at the minehead and the lift was being prepared.

"Steady!" he shouted. "If you rush, there's going to be an accident!"

About five hundred people were milling about in the dust, half of them black.

Jack saw Dan Halkett, and went over to him. "Have we got pressure in the boilers?"

"Yes."

"I'll get them moving, then."

Jack stayed at number one shaft, Dan went to number two about a mile away and they began to lower the townspeople into the mine. This had become standard procedure since the great

gun called Long Tom had begun to send death and destruction into the Kimberley streets.

In the past weeks there had been a distinct change in the siege. The mock bravado of the early days, when the small Boer guns had been things to jeer at, had vanished under a trio of pressures: food was scarce, disease was rife and the third and most frightening was the gun.

From the beginning of the siege, when shopkeepers had tried to force prices up because of their goods' scarcity value, only to be answered by a military edict making this a crime, it had been apparent that if the siege went on food was going to be a problem. However, no one had envisaged its lasting that long. Wasn't the relief column coming up from the south?

Now, in many people's minds, the relief column was something to be execrated. Only twenty miles separated it from Kimberley, yet it was immobile. Time had spun out, weeks had passed and food was scarce.

Hardship had come with the New Year. The meat ration, mainly horse, was cut to four ounces for adults and two ounces for children. The vegetable ration for three days was five carrots, four small parsnips, nine beetroots and one radish. Eggs, almost unobtainable, cost a pound a dozen. Even horse became scarce and donkeys were eaten instead. Blacks were so hungry they were roaming the streets in search of domestic pets. Kittens were being sold for five shillings and sixpence each and fully grown cats for twelve shillings and sixpence. There was almost no fresh milk and what milk powder existed was kept for the children.

Many more people suffered from disease than from war wounds, the most common being dysentery, typhoid and scurvy. Hundreds died each month, weakened by malnutrition and unable to withstand infection. Worst of all was the infant mortality rate. Among the blacks, it reached more than ninety percent.

But although disease was claiming so many victims, it was the gun which caused the real terror. "Long Cecil," the cannon which Rhodes had had built in his workshops, had given the town a sense of pride and confidence, but that was all it had given. After the first few shells had exploded among the Boers they had simply taken cover and it had fired harmlessly into the desert. Many people were later to say that it was expressly in an-

swer to Long Cecil that the Boers had brought up Long Tom.

This was one of four great siege guns which the Boers had bought from the Schneider-Creusot armament works in France. At one hundred and fifty-five millimeters it was bigger than anything that had previously fired on Kimberley and its ninety-pound shells caused panic. It had been used at the siege of Ladysmith in Natal and had been brought in secret to Kimberley by way of Pretoria. It was, as Susan had seen, a massive weapon, with a thirty-foot barrel, that dwarfed its human gunners. It had begun to fire on Kimberley in the early part of February, 1900, and immediately the inhabitants knew that the quality of the siege had changed. Within a few hours fires were raging in the center of town. People were at first bewildered; they wanted to hide but knew of nowhere to go. Many rushed into the streets; some were killed there by the shrapnel.

After the initial confusion they began to build shelters as fast as they could. They dug holes in their gardens and strengthened them with sandbags; they burrowed under their houses, into walls; they made forts for themselves out of corrugated iron or old railway sleepers. Some even bought bags of coarse salt and built hiding places with them.

Within twenty-four hours a warning system had been developed. Each time the gun emitted a puff of smoke a signaler on one of the watch towers waved a flag. A bugler sounded the alarm and people knew they had between fifteen and twenty seconds to take cover. Even so, many women and children were killed. Ironically, there were no military casualties, and this angered the townsfolk, who felt that war should be waged between soldiers.

The days when the Boers fired their guns for two hours in the morning and two in the afternoon, with a rest day on Sundays, were over. Long Tom fired at any time of the day or night. People started seeking places where they could sleep in safety, and the mines were obvious refuges. Women, children and men not in uniform began queuing at the cages from late afternoon. They carried blankets, mattresses and valuables. The lifts started working at 5:30 P.M., but so many wished to take shelter that it was often after midnight before the last group reached safety.

Blacks and whites were jammed together in the airless galleries, which soon grew fetid because of a lack of latrines, and people would take it in turns to stand at the bottom of the narrow lift

shaft for a breather. What made things more cramped was the fact that hundreds of picks and shovels, boxes of dynamite, ropes, trolleys—all the underground stores—had been piled there for safekeeping. Once they were moved to the entrances conditions improved slightly.

Long Tom was still firing when Jack ushered the last of the women and children into the cage about ten o'clock.

"That's it," Dan said. He had sent his own group down earlier.

"Half of them want to stay down there permanently," Jack said. "Or at least until we're relieved. They keep on asking me when it will be, and I tell them never."

"You'll panic them," Dan said. "They're worried enough as it is."

Just then they heard the boom of the gun and seconds later the explosion and a weird, whirring noise as shrapnel spun against corrugated-iron and wooden walls. Even though the mine was on the outskirts of the town, shells did land there occasionally, and both men had dropped to the ground.

"Bloody thing!" Jack said as they picked themselves up. "We should have taken it right at the start."

"The relief column can't be long now that Bobs has taken over," Dan said.

News had come in the past few days by heliograph that General Methuen had been relieved of his command and Field Marshal Lord Roberts, or Bobs as he was known affectionately, had taken command. He had fought with great success in India. There were pictures of him all over town and there was something reassuring about the elderly face with its white moustache and little goatee beard. He looked like everyone's kindly old uncle.

"He'll do no better," Jack said. He began to walk to his horse.

"Can I have a word with you before you go, Jack?"

"Now?"

"It's important."

But Jack had already decided what he was going to do. He had not seen Lily for days. He knew she did not like his going to the hotel, but his need for her was more than he could stand.

"It'll have to wait," he said. "I've an appointment."

In spite of the shelling, the Prince Albert Hotel bar was busy and he saw half a dozen of his own Kimberley Blazers with their feet on the rail as he passed through the lobby.

"Jack! Come and take a glass," one of them called.

"Maybe later."

He went up the stairs to Lily's suite and knocked on the door. There was no answer. He tried the handle, but it was locked. Frowning, he came down again and spoke to the desk clerk.

"Miss Bartlett's no longer here, sir."

"What do you mean?"

"She left, sir."

"When?"

He consulted the register. "Two days ago."

"Where did she go?"

"I don't know, sir. She just left."

Jack stared at him. "She must have left some address."

"The manager might know."

"Where is he?"

"Helping in the bar."

Jack went into the bar. "Come on, Jack, up the Blazers!" a man called. "Name your poison."

"Just a moment." Jack saw the manager, a short, roly-poly Yorkshireman, and called him over.

"Evening, Mr. Farson, sir," the little man said, sweat pouring down his cheeks. He was in awe of Jack, as were most people in Kimberley, at least to his face. "What can I do you for?"

"Where's Miss Bartlett?"

The manager cupped his ear against the noise.

"Miss Bartlett," Jack said, more loudly.

One of the Blazers heard him and smiled.

"She left two days ago, sir."

"I know that. Where did she go?"

The manager swallowed. There was a sudden lull in the conversation. "Well, sir . . ."

"Do you know, or don't you?"

"With Mr. Kade, sir."

Jack heard someone snigger. "Where did she go?"

A voice behind him said, "Excuse me, sir, could I see you for a moment?" He turned and looked into Leask's foxy face.

"What do you want?"

"I think it would be better if we talked out there, sir. . . ."

Jack followed him into the lobby. There was a gust of laughter in the bar.

"What is it?"

"About Lil . . . About Miss Bartlett, sir."

"Well?"

"It's true, sir, she did go with Mr. Kade."

"You mean . . . ?" A thought suddenly struck him that was so outlandish he could not credit it. "Let me get one thing straight, Leask: she left with Mr. Kade. Are you telling me that she's gone away with him?"

"Yes, sir."

He felt anger rise through him like mercury in a tube, then he rationalized his thought. "You mean she's staying in Mr. Halkett's house?"

Leask said brutally, "I mean she's living with Kade."

Jack caught him by the front of his uniform. *"What* did you say?"

"Everyone knows, sir."

They were hissing at each other like a pair of geese. The desk clerk, pretending to be filling in the register, was craning to hear.

"Living with him? You mean . . . ?"

"They've been lovers for years. In London and here."

Jack stared at him. "And you've known all this time? Everyone's known?" He felt sick as the humiliation grew in him. "Go away!" he said.

"But, sir . . ."

"Fuck off, Leask!"

13

David stood at the window of Dan Halkett's drawing room and watched the flash of an exploding shell near the center of the town.

"How many does that make?" Lily said.

"Twenty-two since the searchlight started signaling."

"Don't you think you should come away from the window?"

"We're safe here."

She was lying on the sofa, reading the new pages of his Latin translation by the soft light of an oil lamp. She was dressed in the colors that suited her best, a red dress edged with black. The room was comfortably, if plainly, furnished, as befitted a bachelor, and Lily seemed more exotic than ever in its setting. It was curious, David thought, that in the midst of war he had never felt so much at peace. It had all happened in the past few days. He had been urging her to leave the Prince Albert Hotel and come to

live with him, but it was only when the hotel dining room took a direct hit that she finally agreed. By that time Dan had moved to a flat in the mine building to be closer in the event of fire and Lily and David had the house to themselves.

In David's fantasy, this was their house and they lived here always, a married couple. Although she had only been with him a few days, it seemed almost a lifetime. It was like the ship over again. He hardly left her. They spent their days and their nights together and, most important to him, she was there when he woke in the morning. It was the domestic life he had always wanted with her.

Sometimes he would allow his thoughts to drift into the future and sometimes he would even open his mouth to speak about it, but then he checked himself. Peter Arendt was in Cape Town; Hilda, Margaret and Rachel were in London. He knew that if he so much as mentioned the future the spell might break. He wanted the siege to go on forever.

"Isn't this sad about the captain of the dockyard?" she said, tapping the page she was holding. He came to the sofa and leant over her. Until recently, he had not looked at his translation for months. Then he had talked to Lily about it and she had become interested enough to want to read it. Now he read Father John's account over her shoulder: "After praying for the soul of the departed I returned to our camp. Later that night the sailor Barreto entered, wearing the brocade coat with the big glass buttons. No one accosted him on this subject for all were afraid. . . ."

He had returned to his work on the old Bible during the past few days and while he translated she wrote a fair copy of the work he had already completed. Her handwriting, though childish, was clearer than his.

"Where did you get to today?" she said, picking up the last page.

"I'll read it to you. You remember Father John was describing the food. He says: 'The water in the river is low. Sometimes we try to catch the baby'—I suppose he means 'small'— 'the small fish with our hands, but they are too swift.'"

"What are you going to do with this when you've finished it?"

"I don't know. Talk to Mrs. Delport about it."

She put up a hand and touched his face and he took it and kissed it.

"It's history. I think you're very clever to have done all this."

"So do I."

She smiled and put down the sheet of manuscript. "I saw the mayor today. He wants me to give a concert."

"In the middle of all this?" He swept his arm around to encompass the siege and the gun and the danger. "Where does he propose you should sing? Down the mine?"

"It's to be a proper concert. He says the town needs something to boost its morale."

"What did you say?"

"I said I'd be delighted. After all, that's what I originally came to do."

"That was before Long Tom arrived. It's dangerous to have a lot of people crammed into one hall. The Boers hear about meetings like that, you know. What if it was hit?"

She ignored him. "It'll be the biggest concert ever given here. The money's to go to orphans and bereaved families. You wouldn't want me to say no, would you?"

He sat on the sofa by her side. "I'll let you do it on one condition."

"What's that?"

He had spoken lightly, but there was an edge to her question.

"Wear the diamond, Lily. Wear the 'Southern Cross.' It's never been round your neck. Anyone's neck, for that matter." She hesitated. "Please! For my sake."

Finally she said, "If it'll make you happy."

He felt a surge of excitement. "Nothing would make me happier."

He stood up and began to pace the floor.

"You don't think it'll upset Jack?" she said.

"I don't know. I don't care. Do you?"

"He still comes to the hospital."

"I thought you said you wouldn't see him."

"I haven't. I get one of the doctors to turn him away. It's difficult, though. There's something about him that makes me . . . He isn't like the Jack I—we used to know." David nodded. "It's as though big business and wealth have been too much for him. I think he was happier just being a digger."

They were silent for a few moments, then he said, "Bed?"

"I couldn't sleep. I'm going to do a few pages of fair copy. You go up if you like."

"I couldn't sleep either. While you're doing that I'll go over to the mine to make sure everything's all right."

"Be careful."

"The shelling's stopped."

She heard him close the front door behind him. She leant back against the cushions, relaxing completely. The house was very still. They had let the servants go. David had wanted her to himself, and she was flattered. But sometimes she worried at the intensity of his feelings, for she did not know what was going to happen to them. The siege had created an artificial world and an artificial life. It was not possible to make plans nor even think of making plans, since no one knew what the future held. They lived from hour to hour, day to day.

Now, as though to lift her thoughts from her own problems, she turned back to the manuscript on which David had been working. He did his translation with so much care, she thought, so much love. Perhaps he should have been an academic. He was too clever to be wasted on the business life. She worked for an hour or more until her eyes grew weary, then decided to stop, gathered up the papers and rose to put them away. In doing so, she banged into the small table at which she had been sitting. It canted alarmingly and the Bible slipped off onto the floor and fell open. She bent to pick it up, marveling once more at the spidery writing of Father John of the Rosary and how it had lasted all these years with such clarity. David had told her how he had assumed it to be Portuguese until he had taken it to Mr. Pereira. Well, *she* would never have recognized it as Latin—or as Portuguese. Sometimes in David's presence—and in Peter's too, for that matter—she felt her lack of education deeply. It wasn't enough to say that she had made up for it in other ways. The lack was always there, like a missing limb. That David could translate some of these words without a dictionary amazed her even more. She did not know what a single sentence meant, not even a single word. . . . She frowned and looked at the book more closely. Then she held it near the lamp. This handwriting was not in Latin at all! She *could* make out words. And not only words, but whole sentences. "The man asked for meat," she read. "Mr. Parker replied that we had no meat, but had other food, and told the servants to prepare a meal. . . ."

She examined the writing. It was different from Father John's: small, neat and written with a modern pen. No wonder it was so

legible. She realized that the Bible had fallen open near the back. She turned to the front and came upon the faint Latin text on which David was working. Then she paged forwards, riffling through the thin paper. Father John's journal occupied the tops and bottoms of the pages in the first quarter of the book. About three-quarters of the way through the new writing began. It started off simply: "Susan Delport's Story, written at Portuguese Place, Cape Colony, 1879." She took the Bible to the sofa and turned up the light. "I, Susan Delport (née Binns), was born in the town of Centerville, in Hannah County, Georgia, and came to southern Africa with my first husband, the Reverend Matthew Parker, in the year 1857. We spent several months in Cape Town before beginning our long journey to the southern fringes of the Kalahari Desert where Mr. Parker was to take up his evangelical work for the Royal Missionary Society of London. We left the Cape of Good Hope in September of that year and reached the banks of the Great River. . . ."

Lily heard the front door open and close softly.

"David!" she called. "David, I've found something."

She went on reading. "Mr. Parker decided to make camp here for a few days to rest the . . ."

"David!"

There was a sound at the door of the room and she looked over her shoulder. "I've found the most . . ." She stopped. "Jack!" she said.

His face was white, with blotchy patches, and his eyes seemed to stare out of his skull.

"Jack," she said again. "I didn't expect you."

He came slowly into the room. "Where is he?"

"Who?"

"You know who."

"If you mean David, he's gone to the mine."

He stopped in the middle of the room and towered above her. He looked ill, she thought. Ill and not altogether sane.

"Why, Lily?" he said.

"Why what?"

"Why have you done this to me?"

"I haven't done anything to you, Jack." She looked past him, wondering when David was coming back.

"You're living with him."

"That's true."

"You never told me."

"I thought you knew."

"You've been . . . been . . ." He could not phrase what he meant and finally said, "You've been doing it in London as well."

She flushed. "Jack, I've told you before, what I do is my business."

He didn't seem to hear her. "It's bloody filthy!"

She was angry now and rose to face him. "It wasn't filthy when you were doing it! It was all right then. 'Marry me, Lily,' you said. 'We'll have a little house with books in it,' you said. I taught you to read and write, remember. There was nothing filthy then."

"You've made me a bloody laughing stock. Everybody knew except me."

"That's not my fault."

"If you do it with him, you'll do it with me."

"That's not so! I'm not doing it with you."

"Yes, you bloody are. You used to say I was the best. I'm still the best."

Her anger was replaced by apprehension. She changed her tack. "Yes, you were the best, Jack. You'll always be the best."

"I want you, Lily."

"I'm not available. Don't you understand?"

"Bugger that!"

"And if I said I didn't want to? You wouldn't want me against my will, would you? Why don't I get you something to drink? Let's have a whisky." She turned away and as she did so, he grabbed her. She felt his hands on her shoulders and smelled the sour breath as his mouth came down towards her own. She remembered another time, in her caravan, only then she *had* wanted him. She felt his hands pull down her dress and take her breasts, and she stood quite still. He forced her against the arm of the sofa but she retained her balance. She stood stiffly, letting him maul her. He kissed her and she kept her mouth closed, a thin hard line. His hands were all over her. She felt his fingers in her crotch. She stood, without reaction. Suddenly, he gave a cry and stepped back and she saw a dark wet patch appear at the front of his trousers. He looked down in utter disbelief.

"You'd better go to the bathroom," she said icily.

He came back a few minutes later and she handed him a whisky. She felt sorry for him. He drained the glass and took another.

"Drink up, Jack," she said. "You'd better be off."

"Lily . . . Lily, I didn't mean . . . I'm . . . I'm . . ."

She knew he was trying to say he was sorry but she could never remember him uttering the word. "It's all right. Nothing happened. Just get hold of yourself and go."

"I didn't mean . . . God knows, I didn't!"

She knew what the effort had cost him.

"I know you didn't."

He looked down at his glass. She wanted him to go before David returned. He was humiliated and anything might happen. When he had visited her at the hospital she had been aware that beneath the superficial talk there was a volcano of feeling waiting to spill out, which was why she had put an end to their meetings.

"It's never been the same, Lily."

"What hasn't?"

"Anything. Not since the early days. Not since I was a digger. Not since you and I . . . I mean, it should be wonderful, but it isn't. It's gone wrong. I don't know how or why, but it has."

He was mumbling and she realized he must have had a good deal to drink before he came. She stared at him, remembering the craggy, red-haired man she had known. Life had been all before him then and he had chased it with both hands. Now it seemed behind him. As if to echo her thoughts, he said, "What's happened, Lily? What's happened to us?"

"We grew up, Jack. People do."

"But we loved each other." He said it with an air of bewilderment. "Didn't we?"

"Of course we did." She was talking to him as though he were a child.

"We should have stayed together. We should have got married. Then everything would have been different."

"I wonder."

"It's not too late."

"Jack, it's finished. It was finished a long time ago."

"No." He shook his head stubbornly. "It's what we should have done years ago. You think I'm a failure, don't you?"

"Don't talk like that. You're a big man, Jack."

He turned to look at her. "They think they can treat me like dirt! Well, they bloody can't!"

"No one's treating you like dirt."

He rose. He was breathing more heavily and she could see the sweat on his face.

"I'd leave Marie," he said. "There's nothing left between us. And Jewel's out here, anyway. I'd sell up in London. I've never liked it. This is where we want to be, you and I. Here or down at the Cape."

"Steady, Jack!"

"You've got to admit I haven't rushed you."

"What do you mean?"

"I always did what you wanted. You said not to come and see you late at night, so I didn't. I came during the day to the hospital. I respected you, Lily."

"Are you trying to tell me that this has been in your mind . . . ?"

"Ever since I knew you were here. From the very first day. I said to myself, 'Things have changed. It's not just Lily Bartlett in Meecham's caravan now and I'm not just Jack Farson the digger. She's a famous singer and has to be treated like that.'" He was staring into her eyes and she saw the glint of wildness that had been there before. "'Gently does it,' I said. 'Get to know each other again. That's the way.'"

"Jack! Jack! It's not like that at all. We're just two old friends."

"It's fate that's brought us together and it's fate that's kept us here. Don't you see? This is where we were happiest. Don't you remember those mornings when I would be at the books and you'd be making coffee? We could do it all again, only better. And you could do your singing."

She smiled. "Where? Here? Aren't you forgetting something?"

"What's that?"

"I already have a husband."

"Leave him. You don't love him or you wouldn't be doing what you're doing."

"That's true enough. But there's someone else, isn't there?"

"Who?"

"David."

She saw him flush again. "I'm talking about getting married! Living together. I'm not talking about having a bit of fun."

"I don't like your choice of words."

"All right, but what I mean is this: you wouldn't want to *marry* David, would you?"

"The question doesn't arise. I'm married already."

"But even if you weren't."

"What makes you so sure?"

He looked at her in genuine bewilderment. "He's a Jew!"

"I married a Jew, remember. Jack, you'd better . . ."

"I mean people like you and me, we may have our differences, but we're the same under the skin. But Jews, well . . . I mean, you just wouldn't, Lily."

She felt hot and tugged at the neck of her gown. "I think you'd better go."

"Wait a bit. I haven't finished yet. I'm not saying David isn't . . ."

"For God's sake, shut up about David! I don't want to hear his name in your filthy mouth! You come in here with your dirty hands and your dirty mind and talk to me about David. Let me tell you something, he's worth ten of you. Not ten, a hundred!"

"He's a bloody Jew!"

"He may be a Jew, but he made you. You couldn't have done a single thing without David. If it wasn't for him you'd still be a digger with callouses on your hands."

"Who was it found the diamond? Without that there would have been no start, nothing. Ask him! Ask him how much he gave for it!"

"I know exactly how much he gave for it and you were glad to take it. He's told me everything about that. There isn't a thing I don't know. But let me tell you something *you* don't know. He's still looking after you!"

"That's a bloody lie!"

"You go and ask Dan Halkett whose money you've been spending on your stupid little army. Go on, ask him! And then you'll find out who's been paying the bills."

"*What?*"

"David's been paying them! Don't you understand, you silly man, you're bankrupt! You haven't a penny. Even your wife's been after David for money."

"It's not true!"

"David has known for weeks. It's *his* money you've been using."

He stared at her, then slowly his head began to nod. At first she thought he was agreeing but then she saw that it was an involuntary action.

"Jack? Are you all right?"

He made a gurgling noise in his throat and held on to the sofa for a moment. His face had returned to the blotchy pattern of purple and dead white.

"Jack?"

He seemed to recover himself and stood without support, then he picked up his hat and walked unsteadily to the door. She was about to go after him, but instead she thought: "If he drops down dead now it might be better for all of us."

She could not settle; sleep was an impossibility. She sat at the window of the room, waiting. David came in shortly before midnight.

"Is everything all right?" he said.

"Yes." She saw him looking at the empty whisky glass. "I couldn't sleep so I had a drink and waited for you." Suddenly she went to him. "Hold me," she said. He put his arms around her. "Tighter!"

"Is something wrong?"

"Of course not. I missed you, that's all." But it was as though he sensed another presence. In a moment he would put a direct question to her and she would have to lie.

She saw the Bible and seized on it as an excuse to change the subject. "I found something extraordinary." She paged to the beginning of Susan's story and passed it to him. He read the first few lines and frowned. "I've never seen this."

"Of course you haven't. You've never looked at the back."

"Should we read it?"

"Of course. It's history, too, and may be valuable. I'll get you a drink. Read it aloud."

He sat on the sofa and began to read. "Susan Delport's Story, written at Portuguese Place, Cape Colony, 1879. . . ." He read the account of how she had traveled north with the Reverend Parker, how they camped on the bank of the Great River, the two meetings with the Koranna Hottentots, the murder of her husband, her experience at the hands of Kaptein and then the long, solitary trek along the river until she met Frans Delport.

He paused and sipped at his drink and they looked at each other in silence.

"Go on," she said.

He read Susan's description of how she had wanted to live with Frans Delport in case she had conceived a child by Kaptein, and it

became progressively clear as the narrative continued that she *had* conceived by the Hottentot. With pauses every now and then to wet his throat, David read for more than two hours and when he finished, Susan's life, until the time of Frans's death, was laid out before them. Gently he closed the Bible and put it on the table, and then he said, "Do you realize what this means?"

"That Marie is the Hottentot's child."

He rose and went to stare from the window. "Long ago old Levinson passed a remark about her. He said there were people in town who thought she was two coffee, one milk. I'd never heard the expression before. I didn't believe it. I was angry with him for saying so."

"Do you think she knows?" Lily said. "Do you think she read this?"

He shook his head. "I think Susan wanted to get this off her chest. It was a secret she could share with no one, so she wrote it in the Bible and when Frans died she buried it with him. Then I came along one day after the jackals had been trying to dig up his body, and found it."

He sat down and in the lamplight she could see how drawn his face was. Two lines of worry were cut into his brow. "But I think Marie must have guessed," he said. "I think that's why she nagged Jack to get her away from Africa and why she wouldn't come back, not even when Jewel ran away." He finished his drink and handed her his glass.

"Another?"

"Please."

She was surprised. Apart from wine, he did not drink much.

"You know what else this means," he said.

"I think so."

"I'm talking about Jewel."

"Yes. I suppose she's an octoroon."

"I don't know what you'd call her, but she's part Hottentot."

He rose and walked to the table, touched the Bible, went to the window, looked out, returned to the center of the room. She was reminded that only a couple of hours before Jack had been pacing the carpet, and the reasons were not too dissimilar.

"You know they want to get married—Michael and Jewel," he said. "Each time I went out there they spoke of it. It always seemed the natural thing to me. It was as if they had been born for each other. They were inseparable right from the beginning.

But I don't think it seemed natural to the others. I know Hilda never wanted it. She wanted Michael to marry one of the daughters of her own circle and I don't think Marie thought Michael was good enough."

"And Jack?" She felt a sudden sense of despair, for what she had just heard from Jack in a different context she was now hearing, or about to hear, from David. She did not care about Jack or what he thought, but this was David and she did care.

"No, not Jack either."

"Why do you think that?" she pressed, hoping that he might discover the analogy for himself. But he did not reply.

"Now you find that you don't like the idea of their marriage either," she said remorselessly.

"I'm his father. What do you expect me to do?"

"To mind your own business."

"His happiness is my business."

"How old is he?"

"Oh, I won't be able to stop him that way, I couldn't refuse."

"What *would* you do?"

"Tell him."

"David! David!"

"It's easy for you, you have no children." She felt as though she had been slapped. "What do you think their future would be in a country like this?"

"Why does anyone have to know?" she said. "You know. I know. Susan knows. That's all. Marie may have guessed, but if she has, she won't be saying anything."

"You've heard the old saying 'Blood will out.' Well, it can happen. Even after a couple of generations. Say Michael and Jewel got married and they had children and one of the children was brown."

"In this country that's a gamble that a lot of people take. And things will change here. I sang in Rio several times and blacks and whites are getting together. Instead of coal-black and pure white a lot of people are brown. Soon there won't be any differences."

"It may work there, it'll never happen here. If anything, it's getting more clearly defined. People are people, Lily, races are races. They don't change."

She felt the despair grow and she also felt an ineffable weariness. "Don't do anything yet, David."

"There's nothing I can do."

"Promise me you won't do anything without thinking about it a lot more, not without talking about it."

He paused, and finally said, "All right."

They were having breakfast the following morning when Dan Halkett arrived. His face was grave and David thought he looked much older. He brushed aside the offer of coffee. "I haven't time," he said.

"What is it?"

He looked uncomfortable and Lily said, "I'll leave you two together."

"It's about Jack," Dan said after she had gone. "He came to see me late last night, wanting to know his financial position."

David raised his eyebrows. "That was an odd time."

"The whole thing's odd. It's as though he knew. You didn't tell him?"

"Me?"

"No, of course you wouldn't."

"What about Leask?"

Dan shook his head. "Couldn't have been. There was a runner through from the column yesterday with a batch of letters—some for you, they're at the office. One was from Snell. We were right about Leask. He's been selling Jack's shares and buying property for himself in the East End of London."

David nodded slowly. "It had to be."

"But it wasn't only Leask. Jack's been spending like a drunken sailor. He's spent more than a million on that estate in Sussex alone. Anyway, when he asked me, I had to tell him."

"About me?"

"There was no way I could avoid it."

"How did he react?"

"That's the odd thing, he didn't. He seemed to know already, or to have guessed. He was angry, though."

"I'm not surprised."

"He was pretty drunk and I didn't like his color much. Then, apparently, he went off in search of Leask."

David suddenly felt cold. "My God, don't tell me!"

"I don't know what he was going to do, but it was too late. By the time he found Leask he was already dead."

"Dead!"

"Leask and half a dozen of those bloody fools, the Kimberley

Blazers—Jack's private army—had been drinking in the canteens and then had gone on to someone's house for more. The house was hit and started to burn and two of the men were suffocated by smoke. Leask was one."

There was a pause and then David said, "What do we do now?"

"We'd better think of something, because Jack's acting strangely. I don't think he's been to bed. I'm told he's been drinking all night and the last I heard he was offering to fight all comers."

David put on his jacket. "We'd better go and find him."

It was barely ten o'clock in the morning and many of the bars were closed, for stocks of liquor were running down. Long Tom had not yet begun to fire and people were hurrying to pick up rations and queue for horsemeat and siege soup while it was still safe to do so. David and Dan went through the hot dusty streets, dodging between the horse trams. There were official boards on the corners of some streets with the latest proclamations by the military authorities, and on each there was a notice of the grand gala concert to be given by Madame Montadini.

They began to comb the canteens and the cosies in Old Kimberley and soon got onto Jack's trail.

"This takes me back," David said.

"Aye, we've done this before."

"The night the Batavian Giant nearly killed him. Remember?"

"That was the night he and Joe Malone went to a whorehouse and sold that diamond. Things were never the same between you and Jack after that."

They found him in the Kimberley Arms, a canteen designed like an English public house with mock Tudor beams and leaded lights. They could hear his voice while they were still out in the street.

"Yellow!" he was shouting. "You're a bunch of yellow bastards!"

They stood inside the doorway. The canteen was kept artificially gloomy. There was sawdust on the floor and the ripe smell of yesterday's ale and last night's vomit.

"That's the spirit, Jack!" a voice shouted. "You give 'em hell!"

He was drinking with two or three of the Kimberley Blazers and now he addressed the canteen at large, urging them to come with him and capture Long Tom.

"We should have done it at the beginning," he said. "The soldiers are too bloody yellow and so're the Kimberley Light

Horse. I say we go out there and take it now!"

"Have another drink, Jack," one of the Blazers said. "Let's all have a drink."

"You yellow bastards! I'll fight anyone in the bar. Come on, now! Who's going to be first? Fifty quid if you can lay a finger on me. A hundred if you can put me on the floor."

He half turned and saw David and Dan. He stood blinking at them, a great, swaying, gross figure in an unbuttoned uniform, hat askew. "Christ! It's Kade," he said. "Come here, you . . ." His knees buckled and he pitched forwards onto his face. David and Dan ran to him.

"Get a doctor!" David said to one of the Blazers.

"He's all right. Old Jack's all right."

"I said get a doctor!" There was something in David's tone that stopped the conversation.

The man put down his glass. "There's one just round the corner."

Between them, David and Dan lifted Jack up onto the bar top. His face was a vermilion color and his breathing was stertorous. Foamy saliva was coming from one side of his mouth and his eyelids kept flickering.

"I don't like the look of him," Dan said, loosening his collar.

The doctor, a young Afrikaner with a solemn, square face and prematurely thinning hair, looked into his eyes and listened to his heart. Then he said, "I think it would be better if he was in bed."

They carrried him to his suite of rooms at the Grand Hotel and there the doctor examined him again. "It could have been exhaustion or drink or heat or all three," he said. "Does he suffer from indigestion?"

"He was always complaining about wind," David said.

"That could cause the irregular heartbeat. I'll look in later."

David sat with him for three hours, but Jack seemed to be resting comfortably. In the early afternoon he left, telling the hotel manager that if there were any problems he would be at home and that they could send a message there. But no message came and he heard later that the doctor had examined Jack about six and found him much better. Jack seemed to think so too, for he had spent the evening drinking in the bar of the Grand, offering to fight anyone who cared to, urging everyone to follow him out of Kimberley to capture the gun.

*   *   *

"It's nearly half past seven," David called through the bathroom door.

"I'm coming," Lily said.

He stood in front of the long pier glass and tied his white tie. He was wearing evening dress, for it was a special occasion: a gala concert to raise the spirits of Kimberley; but also, although she had not said it, he knew this was the last time she would sing here.

The bathroom door opened and in the mirror he watched her come into the room. She walked with the long-legged, confident stride which had carried her onto stages throughout the world. She was wearing only a thin peignoir which billowed out behind her and through which he could see her body. He marveled at the high, firm breasts, the narrow waist, the full, rounded thighs. Just to look at her was a delight; to feel her was as close as he had ever got to paradise.

"You'll have to help me dress," she said. "It starts at eight-thirty."

"I know it does. I told *you*, remember?" She patted him on the cheek and made a soothing noise. David was obsessive about punctuality, while Lily employed a relaxed attitude about arrivals, departures and appointments generally, which often made him nervous.

He began to help her dress. He loved these moments, loved the intimacy, the domesticity of the scene.

"Breathe in," he said.

"I am breathing in. Not too tight. I have to sing, remember."

"You're getting plump."

"That's what happiness does."

He caught her wrist and kissed her palm. "Are you really happy?"

"Of course not! That's why I live here."

She finished dressing and did her hair and face and then he said, "Let me look at you."

She was wearing a dress of dark red satin edged with black lace. The dress matched her lips, the lace her hair; and her light blue eyes heightened the dramatic contrast.

"Lovely," he said. "Just one more thing."

"What's that?"

"Did you forget?" He slipped his hand into his pocket and drew out the "Southern Cross." Its cut facets shot out spearpoints of light as in a sunburst. He saw her hesitate and a shadow

crossed her face. "Don't say no, Lily. Not now. I'll never see it in a more beautiful setting."

Her face cleared and she kissed him on the forehead. He clasped the gold chain behind her neck. Slowly, she turned to him. The stone lay against the rounded white flesh of her bosom. It seemed to pick up light not only from the lamp, but from her skin as well, and to reflect this up into her face and eyes so that for a moment, he thought, she looked almost incandescent.

"Perfect!" he said. "Perfect." It was the moment he had been waiting for.

On the way to the concert hall in the trap her mood became somber and, as though the diamond had reminded her, she said, "Will Jack be there?"

"I shouldn't think so. From all accounts, he's hardly been seen in the past few days—except in the canteens."

"He's killing himself," she said, fingering the diamond.

They were almost at the hall and they could see crowds in the streets. She was holding his hand and he could feel the pressure of her fingers. People saw them and began to cheer. He drove to the back of the hall and helped her down. "Good luck, my darling; you look wonderful."

Abruptly she said, "I love you. I wanted you to know that." She turned away and went into the hall, leaving him standing there in the hot desert night.

The Freemasons' Hall, which lay on the edge of Old Kimberley, within a few hundred yards of the New Chance Mine, was packed to overflowing when he took his seat. The audience was composed mainly of professional people, but there was a good leavening of working folk. The concert had been defiantly organized by the Kimberley and District Music Society as though there were no hardship in the town at all. The hall was dressed in Union Jacks; people had lent their potted plants and these were ranged along the apron of the stage; half the audience were in either evening dress or uniform.

The accompanist came onto the stage and took his place at the piano, then there she was, the red dress flowing, the youthful stride. She stopped, placed one hand on the piano and bowed deeply. There was cheering and shouting. Then a soldier in the front row rose and went up onto the stage. He spoke to her. She held up her hands and the cheering died down. David recognized the man as Colonel Kekewich, the military commander. He was a

man of middle height, bald, with a fringe of black hair.

"Ladies and gentlemen," he said. "You don't want to hear my voice tonight, but I have something to tell you that will add pleasure to the undeniable pleasure that's in store for you." There was a hush of expectancy. "We have had a message through that the column is on its way. The march to raise the siege has begun! They are expected here tomorrow or the day after. There is no stopping them now."

Again the cheers broke out, and the stamping and shouting. People shook each other's hands, embraced, kissed each other. For a moment things looked as though they might get out of control, and then over the noise the pianist began to play "God Save the Queen." As people in the front rows heard the chords, they rose. It had a ripple effect down the hall. David heard Lily's voice begin the anthem, then the whole hall took up the words. He felt a lump come into his throat and found himself proud to be where he was, part of what was happening. As the anthem died away, people settled down expectantly. Instead of a concert to raise their spirits, the evening had turned into one of celebration. Lily began to sing but had hardly ended the first verse of Brahms's "Ständchen" when there was the sound of a shell exploding nearby.

The gun had been silent for the latter part of the afternoon and, although they had not spoken about it, it had been in David's mind as well as Lily's. On several occasions recently it was as though the Boers, with their excellent lines of communication into the town, had heard about congregations of people. George Labram, the American who had built Rhodes's gun, had been killed by a shell from Long Tom and his funeral, attended by several hundred, had provoked an outburst of shelling.

The electric lights in the hall flickered, there was a barely perceptible pause by the pianist and then Lily went on. She finished her song and the applause was rapturous. She began to sing Schumann's "Der Nüssbaum," when another shell landed in the vicinity, and this time the lights did go out. A woman screamed and a man's voice shouted, "Be calm! Stay in your seats!" Within a minute or two, oil lamps were being lit and the hall was illuminated by their soft glow.

Lily had not moved and now she said, "With your permission, ladies and gentlemen, I'll start that song again."

There was a burst of nervous laughter. As she finished

speaking another shell landed, but farther away. Then there were several smaller explosions. David was frightened and yet in a way exhilarated. It was wonderful to see her like this, dominating the hall, the gun, the shellfire. It was she who was holding them. Without her, the people would have begun to fight for the exits, but as she sang, the hall was silent. He had never heard her sing more beautifully, nor more in control of her voice.

The shelling moved to another part of the town. She sang two popular ballads to ecstatic applause and then began Schubert's "An die Musik," which was David's favorite. She turned slightly and sang directly to him. Again he felt the lump of pride come into his throat. Then something went wrong. She faltered. For a second or two she and the pianist were out of time. She went on. He tried to follow. David saw that she was no longer looking at him, but down the center aisle. There was a scraping noise from the back of the hall and voices were saying, "Sshhh. . . ." David turned, and saw Jack. He was standing in the middle of the aisle near the back, hands on hips, his hat askew. An usher was obviously asking him to move against the wall—there were no longer any vacant seats—and put his hand on Jack's arm. Jack shook him off and he stumbled against a chair, falling with a clatter. Lily stopped. David jumped to his feet, angry and embarrassed, and began to go towards Jack. At that moment a shell seemed to hit the ground outside the hall, for the building trembled. Another landed, and another. Someone shouted that the building next door was on fire. The pianist stopped playing. Lily stood still. Colonel Kekewich jumped onto the stage and said, "Ladies and gentlemen, we must evacuate the hall!" He turned to David. "Is the cage working at New Chance?"

"As far as I know."

"Let's get everyone down into safety until this stops."

Ushers began to lead members of the audience from the exits and David lost sight of Jack in the crowd. Shells were bursting regularly and he jumped on the stage and took Lily by the arm. Smoke was drifting into the doors. They ran outside. Several buildings were on fire and the smoke hung heavily in the streets.

"They must have heard about the column," he said. "They're making one last effort to take the town before it arrives."

He could hear their own guns, the small seven-pounders, answering from the perimeter and knew he would be needed by the town guard if there was an attack. But first he helped Lily

along the dusty, rutted road to where the winding gear loomed up blackly against the starry sky. The cage was already in action. He heard Dan Halkett shouting at the people to form queues.

"Have you seen Jack?" Dan shouted.

"He turned up at the hall, then he disappeared. Here's Lily."

"I'll take my turn," she said.

"Look after her," David told Dan. "I have to go to my post."

He held her, then kissed her and said, "I'll see you later."

"David . . ."

People were climbing into the cage, waiting to be lowered.

"What is it?"

Dan shouted, "Come on, Lily!"

"David, be careful! I don't want to lose you now."

She turned and climbed into the cage and Dan shouted to the donkeyman to lower away.

David heard officers calling for the town guard and the constabulary and he was almost ridden down as members of the Kimberley Light Horse raced by. He wondered where and when the Boer attack would come.

He ran back along the road towards the office where he kept his carbine and helmet. He thought he heard someone shout his name and stopped, but another shell landed and set fire to a building on his left. He ran on. As at Victoria, memories of the Podol assailed him and fear of the pogrom added another layer to the fear he was already suffering. Again he heard, or thought he heard, his name. But an unreasoning fear from his past had gripped him and instead of pausing, he ran on. He came to the building, flung open the door to his staircase and clattered up to his office. He was lighting the lamp when he heard the crash of feet on the wooden stairs. The door was flung open and Jack stood on the threshold. His hair was matted with sweat and dust. His eyes were wild.

"Kade," he said, "I want you!"

"Not now, Jack."

"Yes, now."

"All right." David sat down at his big desk, where he felt he was less at a psychological disadvantage. "What is it? I should be getting to my post."

"Your post? Don't make me bloody laugh! You couldn't hit a barn door with that carbine."

David stared at him in silence. Jack was unshaven, his eyes were

bloodshot and his uniform tunic was half-unbuttoned.

"David bloody Kade!" He was staring from the window and now turned back into the room as flashes of light showed where shells were still falling. "You think yourself somebody, don't you?"

"No," David said.

"Well, you should. I would if I were you."

David wasn't sure what he was driving at and decided it would be best to stay calm.

"Don't you want to know why?"

"All right, Jack, why?"

"I'll bloody tell you why!" He put both hands on David's desk. "Because you've won, that's why!"

"Won?"

"You know what I mean."

"I've been in no competition I'm aware of."

"There you go, talking soft again. Everyone's in competition, man. That's life. It's a bloody race to get your hands on as much as you can before it's over."

"I don't look at it like that."

"You don't look at it like that!" he mimicked. "You're a bloody pious bastard, Kade. You sit there telling me you're different from the rest, but you're wrong. You married Hilda to get your hands on the shop and once you'd got that you wanted more and you got the diamond. . . ."

"Wait a minute, Jack . . ."

"No. You wait. Then you wanted the mine and you got that . . ."

There was an explosion nearby and the blast broke the glass in one of the windows, spraying pieces onto the carpet. Jack took no notice.

". . . and then you wanted Lily and you got her!" His voice was rising and his face had become livid. "You've got the bloody lot! Everything! And you say there's no com . . ."

"Jack, listen to me! Maybe you're right about Hilda. But don't forget I'd been ill. And anyway, you married Marie to get your hands on that farm."

"You leave my family out of it."

There was another explosion and the building shook.

"Everything!" Jack said, striding up and down the room. "Everything!"

456

"For God's sake, don't get worked up any more! I know why you're like this and . . ."

"Of course you know why. You've got everything and not content with that, you want to take a man's pride! What are you, Kade, the devil in disguise?"

David, for the first time, felt his own temper begin to break loose and this caused him to make a mistake. He began to lecture Jack, as he had done so many years before when Jack had sold their diamond in the brothel.

"That's enough!" he shouted, starting up and moving round the desk. "You've been spending money like water. You've let Leask steal you blind. If I hadn't come to the rescue, Marie would have had nothing. You talk of me having everything! The reason is, *you* can't hold on to anything. You haven't the savvy. You never think of tomorrow. You never have. If I hadn't helped, what do . . ."

The last time they had argued like this, Jack had walked out. But this was now, and he gave a roar: "Charity, is it?"

Just then there was a huge explosion, bigger than any they had heard in the siege. It was a roar like an avalanche and a tongue of flame shot into the air. For a moment the world stood still. They looked at each other, deafened by the blast. David said, "That came from the mine!" He made to push past.

"I haven't finished yet," Jack said.

"Well, I have."

Jack gripped him by the lapel of his evening coat. There was a ripping sound as the fabric tore. David looked at it in shocked disbelief and then he flung himself at Jack. It was a moment of catharsis. Tension that had been building up in both men for more than twenty years, since that first day in Cape Town when they had walked off the ship's gangway, was released like an orgasm.

They fought like animals. There was no science. It was a frenzied battle using fists, feet, teeth, anything. David was so angry that he was literally crying with rage. They fell about the room, crashed across the desk trying to throttle each other, trying to gouge eyes, tear off ears. They aimed kicks at each other, bit fingers and hands, did everything possible to injure each other.

But they were middle-aged men and it was over quickly. Jack aimed a blow at David and caught him in the mouth. David felt

his teeth driven into his lips and the warm salty blood pour onto his tongue. But the blow had thrown Jack off balance and he hit back. He caught Jack in the throat and the big man fell against the wall, where he slid down to a sitting position. Both knew that the fight was over, both were spent. They looked at each other, the hatred as fierce as ever. Then Jack said hoarsely, "I'll tell you something you'll never have! Not while I'm alive. Not unless you kill me!"

"What's that?"

"You'll never have Jewel in your family! I'll never let her marry your son. Never! And I'll tell you why. No daughter of mine is going to marry a Jew. Do you hear that, Kade? You may have everything, but you're still a Jew."

Rage unlike any he had experienced before swept through David. His eyes seemed to film over with a red haze; he felt as though his veins were about to burst. He got down on his knees and caught Jack by the front of his jacket. "You fool!" he shouted, flecks of spittle and foam flying from his lips. "Do you think I'd let my son marry Jewel? Do you think that? Don't you know her mother's a . . ."

He felt himself go cold. He was unable to finish the sentence. There was a smell of dampness, of mold and urine. He was looking down, not at Jack but at a bundle of rags on the floor of a jail cell in Kiev. The old, shaven figure was trying to explain what was happening to him, why they were going to murder him. Was this where it started? In the hatred of individuals; with one being cleverer, shrewder, more cultured, stronger, luckier? Was it envy, jealousy, resentment that fired the spark?

He felt suddenly drained. He rose and leant against the desk. Jack got painfully to his feet. David saw him for the first time as someone who had nothing, a pathetic, lonely man. On impulse he said, "I'm sorry, Jack. I shouldn't have done that. There's something I've been thinking about for a long while. I want you to have the diamond. The 'Southern Cross.' I'll . . ."

It was the worst thing he could have said and, had Jack still the strength, he would have finished David. Instead he stood with head bowed like an old bull and said, "I don't want your charity, you fucking Yid! You think I'm finished, don't you? Well, I'm not, not by a long way. I found the 'Southern Cross,' remember, and I can find another. And I will. And when I do, I'll come after you. One day it'll be me who's offering charity."

David looked at him. This was Jack Farson, his partner and sometime friend. He walked to the door.

"You wait, Kade!" Jack shouted. "I'll buy and sell you. You'll see!"

David did not reply. As he stepped onto the dusty pavement he heard a voice shouting for him. It was Dan Halkett. He was a couple of hundred yards up the road.

David started to run.

"What is it?" he shouted.

"It's the mine!" Dan was covered in dust; blood was pouring from a cut in his head. "We got a direct hit."

David remembered the huge explosion he had heard just before the fight started.

"Lily!" He pushed past Dan and ran towards the mine.

Dan kept up with him trying to explain what had happened. A shell from Long Tom had plunged squarely down number one shaft and hit the stored dynamite which had been packed below the cage. It was a one in a million chance.

When David reached the mine he saw that the winding gear above number one shaft was twisted and smashed and the sides of the shaft themselves had broken down. People were being brought up in the cage from number two shaft, having been led through the galleries from number one. He ran on. Someone had got the electric light working. There was dust everywhere in the air. It was like a fog. Huddles of people stood in their evening clothes in the middle of the veld.

"Lily!" he called. "Lily!"

He grabbed a man dressed in a white dickey and tails. "Have you seen Lily? Miss Bartlett?"

"Lily?" The man was in a state of shock. His face was covered in dust, his eyebrows like frosting.

"Madame Montadini!"

The man registered the name. "I saw her before the explosion."

David went on, shouting her name.

A woman said, "I saw her."

"Where?"

"She was helping a little girl."

"When? Before or after the explosion?"

"Before."

The top of number two shaft was more than a mile from

number one, and he had run all the way and Dan had run with him. The cage brought another group of frightened, dusty people up from the mine below. Some of the women were hysterical. He noticed that several wore only petticoats.

"I'm going down," he said.

"I'll come with you."

"You stay here in case something goes wrong."

He went down in the cage, down, down into the darkness lit only fitfully by the new electric lights. At the bottom stood another group of people waiting to come up.

"Has anyone seen Madame Montadini?" he said.

They looked at him dully, too shocked to comprehend what he was saying.

There were half a dozen black mine workers who had led the refugees from number one to number two through the galleries.

"Is this everyone?" David asked one of them, hardly daring to hope for the answer he wanted.

"I don't know, baas."

The gallery disappeared into the gloom and he ran down by the side of the tracks that brought the spoil wagons to the crushers. The air was thick with dust and filled with the noise of falling rocks. He went on and on, hearing his own footsteps clanking and echoing in the grim, empty rock tunnel. Finally he knew he was getting near, because the dust became even denser. He could hardly see anything now. Even naked electric light bulbs were only visible from a few yards away. He stumbled over rock, small pieces at first, then he came to larger slabs and boulders dislodged by the blast and hurled along the tunnel. All around him was the noise of falling rock. His foot trod on something soft. He looked down and saw a hand. It belonged to an elderly man. He was lying on his back, formally and neatly dressed from his neck to his waist, but naked from there down. His shoes were gone, but his socks remained. It was David's first experience of the vagaries of blast. There were other bodies. Some were intact, some in pieces: a torso, an arm wrenched from a shoulder and lying by itself. He must have counted almost a dozen corpses in various stages of completeness before he found Lily. She was lying on her side against the gallery wall. She was quite naked. The blast had stripped her of everything and yet had left her body untouched. She lay as though asleep in the

position he knew so well, legs drawn up so that her knees fitted into the backs of his own.

"Lily?" he said. She looked so natural he assumed she must be unconscious.

"Lily?" he said again, shaking her shoulder.

It was then he realized that she was not asleep, but dead.

"David." It was Dan's voice. "It isn't safe. The whole place could come down."

"Leave me."

"Can't you hear the rockfalls?"

"Leave me." He crouched over her body and did not look up.

"For God's sake, there's nothing you can do!"

"Leave me."

"I won't leave you. I'll stay."

David ignored him. They could hear rocks sliding and falling. Puffs of dust came down the gallery and covered them. David took off his coat and shirt and dressed Lily, moving her arms and legs with great care as though afraid to hurt her.

Finally, when he had covered her nakedness, he bent to lift her. "I'll help you," Dan said.

"Don't touch her!"

Slowly, and with great care, so that he did not stumble and fall, he carried her body along the gallery to the cage that would take them to the surface.

14

Susan first saw the smoke when she was laying the breakfast table on the stoep at Portuguese Place. It came from the direction of Hans Lessing's farm. She stood watching, wondering what was causing it. There was no brush to burn; she knew that Hans burned off his maize lands but only after the harvest had been won. There was no reason—no normal reason, that is—why there should be a fire of such proportions, which meant it had to do with the war.

Ever since the huge gun, Long Tom, with its artillery crew, had come to Portuguese Place, she had been afraid that the war would return—not afraid for herself, but for the two young people. So she had cleaned and oiled her shotgun and placed cartridges at strategic points in the house. They had to live, the farm had to be run; there was little more she could do except pray that in their backwater they would be left alone. But smoke

was a portent of war, and if war had come to the Lessings—she remembered that she had promised Hans to give shelter to his wife if it became necessary—war could return to Portuguese Place.

As she shaded her eyes and looked to the east, she saw a small cart drawn by four donkeys come over the brow of a rise near the house. First she checked that the shotgun was in its place behind the bedroom door and then she went to meet the cart. There were two Hottentot women in it, one elderly, one about Jewel's age. The cart was piled with miscellaneous possessions: a chair, pots and pans, bundles of clothing wrapped in blankets. As it drew close she realized that the older Hottentot woman was Nonna, who had once played with Marie. She was Marie's age, but looked more like seventy, with a shriveled, lined skin that reminded Susan of an elephant's.

"Nonna!" she called.

The Hottentot woman stared dully at her and halted the donkeys. Susan knew that she and her family lived on the Lessing farm, where she was an indoor servant.

"What has happened? Why is there smoke?"

"The soldiers have come, missus."

"What soldiers?"

"The English soldiers. Show her," Nonna said to the girl.

Susan realized that this must be her daughter. She was a pretty thing with a heart-shaped face and skin the color of a burnt almond. But she was a good deal younger than Jewel, probably about thirteen or fourteen. She shook her head.

"Show the old missus," Nonna said, more sternly.

"What is it, Nonna?" Susan said.

"The soldiers opened her."

The girl was wearing a torn dress; now she raised it and Susan saw the dried blood on the insides of her thighs. She had been crying and her nose was running. She wiped it on her sleeve.

"We must go inside," Susan said. "We must wash you."

Nonna said in Dutch, "Go with the old missus. She can't hurt you."

Susan took them into the bathroom and put the girl in the bath. Her injuries were not as bad as she had first thought and she cleaned her up and put zinc ointment on the fingernail scratches on her belly and thighs. Then she found an old dress of Jewel's and gave it to the girl. While she had bathed her she had

learned from Nonna what had happened. English soldiers had come to the house in the night and had taken Hans Lessing's wife and children away to a camp. Nonna did not know where the camp was, only that she had heard that other Boer families had also been taken. There were stories that many people were dying of disease in the camps and Mrs. Lessing had pleaded to be allowed to stay where she was. But the English had taken her away. Then some of the soldiers had set fire to the house and while it was burning three of them had found Nonna's daughter hiding in the servants' quarters. Now the two women were on their way to Nonna's aunt who lived at a Hottentot settlement about sixty miles northwest of Portuguese Place.

Susan fed them and saw them on their way and then she returned to the stoep and beat an old plowshare which served as a gong. Soon Michael and Jewel came up for breakfast. She watched them. They had been fencing a small chicken run beyond one of the kraals, where Jewel wanted to keep Bantams. The difference in both of them was extraordinary. Michael had put on weight. He looked more like his father now, his dark hair lying close to his skull, a man of middle height, with broad, powerful shoulders. And Jewel . . . she looked more beautiful than ever, filling out into a woman, with a golden skin and hair slightly bleached in parts by the sun, which reminded Susan of Frans's hair when she first met him. They sat down and had their breakfast and Susan told them what had happened.

She saw Michael look at Jewel and she knew what he was thinking. "She can't stay here," he said. "Not until the valley's cleared."

Susan nodded. "But how long could that take?"

"The column can't be far from Kimberley now, and if the Boers retreat the British will follow them. Things should return to normal then."

"I want you to leave now," Susan said. "Inspan the bullocks and trek west. Follow the river. Stay away for two weeks or a month. Then try and get word to me."

"You'll come, too."

"No."

"Of course you will," Jewel said. "We won't go without you."

"Yes, you will. You'll inspan now and we'll pack the wagon."

"We can't leave you here," Michael said.

They argued for nearly half an hour, but Susan was adamant.

Someone had to remain at the farm to water the stock and keep the animals alive.

"No one's going to harm an old woman," she said.

It took them two hours to bring the bullocks in from the Home Camp, yoke them and pack the wagon. She gave Michael Frans's rifle and kept the shotgun for herself. By eleven o'clock they were ready.

They said their good-byes and she thought how similar this was to the time years before when she and Frans had drifted across the desert in their wagon, going from waterhole to waterhole as the fancy took them. That had been a test of the love between them and it would also be the test, she thought, of the love between Michael and Jewel. She watched the wagon go down towards the river and move westwards until it was lost in the trees that had grown since Jewel's father had cleared the valley. She watched until the white canvas hood was a faint blob against the brown hills, then went up to the house and stood for a moment in thought. There was not much point in locking doors or closing the wooden shutters. When they came—whoever they were—they would smash the doors and the shutters. Instead, she went to her bedroom, fetched the shotgun, loaded it and sat on the stoep in the shade of Frans's grapevine to wait for them. An hour passed. And another. Still she sat, still she waited. She dozed. She woke and, looking east, saw that the smoke no longer climbed up into the sky. She looked along the track that led past the Lessings' farm as she had that morning and saw another cloud of dust.

She wondered how many would come and she wondered what she would do. But then she saw that there was only one rider. He dismounted, opened the gate of the Home Camp and came on. He was dressed in a uniform and a hat. She wondered if he could be a Boer, but the Boers did not wear uniforms. He came round the side of the house and she heard him dismount. She shifted the shotgun so that it covered the steps leading to the stoep. She heard his boots on the gravel and she pulled back both hammers of the shotgun. He came up the steps and she saw it was Jack. His uniform was stained, dusty and torn in places. His face, under the wide-brimmed hat, was brick-red. His eyes were bloodshot and watery and there was a look in them that Susan had never seen before. He stopped at the top and they stared at each other.

Jack blinked at her. His eyes were playing him tricks. Sometimes he felt so giddy he had to hold on to a chair or a door,

anything that offered support, until the spell passed. Now the effort of climbing the steps had caused his heart to leap and jerk. Things became blurred.

He hardly knew where he was, he was so disoriented. He vaguely recalled a fight with David which had been interrupted by a huge explosion. Then he had gone from bar to bar looking for his men. Because of the gun. They would capture the gun. It was something he *had* to do. He had to show Lily. She thought he was no good, that was the reason why she had been so distant. He had only to *do* something, to *show* her . . . and then things would be different.

But he hadn't been able to find anyone. It was said that a Boer attack was expected. He couldn't find a single one of his men. He'd had a few more drinks in an empty canteen—he remembered that—and then he had found himself riding. Was he going to capture the gun single-handed? He couldn't remember. Just as he couldn't remember why he had fought David. All he could remember was that they *had* fought. His throat was sore. That had happened in the fight.

Everything was quiet. The desert was quiet. It was early in the morning. He had found himself on the road to Portuguese Place. Why? The gun wasn't there. He had come to the place where he had been stopped by Hans Lessing a long time ago, the small knoll from which he had seen the Boer guns and the Boer Army. He saw nothing now except the bare and empty veld. He had ridden on. The sun beat down. He drank from his water bottle and felt better. Away to his left he had seen a column of smoke. He wondered what it was; who was burning what? And then he had remembered the column of flames from the great explosion of the night before. That was when he had been fighting David. But why? Had it been Lily? No. It had been about Jewel. That was it. And that was why he was riding to Portuguese Place. He was riding to see Jewel to tell her that she would never marry David's son. Never. Never.

But there was something else. . . .

And then he had remembered that, too. The humiliation. He felt the blood pump in his ears. That was the worst of all. The shame of David's charity. Well, he'd show him. He had said he'd go after him and he would. He'd be rich again, he'd be powerful, only this time . . . this time . . .

He had ridden on, muttering to himself under his breath, until he came to Portuguese Place.

Now he stood on the stoep and focused on Susan. She was wearing a black dress. She looked old and lined but her eyes were bright.

"Where's Jewel?" he said. His voice sounded hoarse and she thought he looked in pain.

She had not addressed a single word to Jack for more than twenty years and now she felt the saliva dry up in her mouth.

"Where's Jewel?" he repeated.

"She's gone."

"Where to?"

"A place of safety. Your English soldiers are in the valley. No one's safe here now."

"Has she gone with that Jew?"

"If you mean Michael, yes."

"Tell me where."

"I can't tell you where because I don't know myself."

"She's not going to marry him. She's not going to marry a Jew. Not ever."

She shook her head slowly. "I pity this country," she said. "There are too many people like you. Whites don't like blacks. Blacks don't like yellows. Boers hate the British. Christians hate the Jews."

"Save your preaching. When did they go?"

"Yesterday," she lied.

"In the wagon?"

"Yes."

"Which way?"

She only hesitated for a moment. Around her was the desert; it was midsummer. Except for the river, the only water to be found was in holes. She had never knowingly harmed another human being, but now in one split second she made her decision. Later, she would often be troubled by this, but she told herself, with some justification, that she had not done it as an act of revenge, but for Michael's sake and, above all, Jewel's. And yet . . . yet . . . there was always the memory of Jack smashing down the walls of Portuguese Place. . . .

"I'm going to bring her back," Jack said. "And when I do, I'm going to find another diamond like the one I found before."

"Not here, Jack," she said.

"Yes, here. You remember the deal, don't you? The payment for marrying Marie? Well, it's time to settle."

"Not anymore, Jack. Not here."

There was something in the way she said it that caused him to pause. He looked at her and then laughed harshly. "You sound as though you're threatening me." He pointed to the gun. "Are you going to shoot me?"

She put the gun down carefully by the side of her chair. "No, Jack."

"Which way?" he said.

Jewel and Michael could not be more than ten miles away. It was only a few hours since she had seen the wagon move off downstream to the west.

"Which way?" he repeated.

She held their future in her hand and now she raised that hand and pointed to the north. "North," she said. "They're making for Griqua Town."

He mounted and rode round the front of the house. She was still sitting in the chair, a black, shapeless bundle with burning eyes. "I'll be back," he called.

And then she spoke to him for the last time. "Good-bye, Jack," she said.

He rode awkwardly—he had never ridden well—with the afternoon sun in his eyes. A wind, hot and burning, from the Kalahari wastes where no rain had fallen for three years, bore down upon him from the northwest. Soon he felt his lips begin to crack in the dry heat and he drank from the water bottle. His throat, where David had hit him, was eased by the fluid.

The wind picked up all that afternoon until by evening the surface of the semidesert was moving under the horse's hooves and clouds of stinging dust and sand made both horse and rider flinch. He tied a kerchief round his mouth and brought the brim of his hat down to shade his eyes. He felt giddy again and there were moments when he swayed in the saddle and almost fell.

He was riding along a track that wound into the hills, the only track going north from the house. He could not see marks from the wagon wheels, for the wind had obliterated all tracks.

Dusk found him on a wide plain with the wind blowing half a gale. He stopped and looked about him. Through the hurling

sand he could see no shelter, only the dim outline of a range of hills ahead. There would be gullies there and rocks where he could find some place of shelter. This was where the wagon would be, he was certain of that.

He pushed on. Darkness came and still he rode. By now he had lost all sense of direction and almost all sense of purpose. He rode on into the night, clinging to the horse's mane, lying along its neck for support. His throat was painful and he eased it every now and then with sips of water. There were pains in his arms and across his chest and, although he shifted his position in the saddle and sometimes dismounted and walked at the horse's head, there seemed no way of alleviating them. About midnight he came to the shelter of a rocky outcrop. He tied the horse to a bush and lay down, making a pillow of his hat. He slept for a few hours. His dreams were turbulent and portentous. He dreamt of blood and wounds, flames and smoke. When he woke the horse was gone.

He staggered to his feet. The wind had dropped and the desert was still. He looked in disbelief at the place he had tied the animal. He had thought the bush strong; instead it had easily been uprooted.

His mind was fuddled and he was talking to himself. He was ill and giddy and the pains were worse. But one thing he knew: without the horse he was dead. It had broken free after the wind had died and its tracks were plainly visible. He began to follow them.

The midsummer sun which rose from the desert floor was blood-red through the high-flown dust and within an hour the surface of the veld seemed to liquefy in the shimmering heat haze. He battled on. Few of his thoughts were coherent now. He had forgotten that he was searching for Jewel, forgotten his fight with David, forgotten the need to find new wealth, forgotten Lily and his humiliation, forgotten Marie, forgotten London. What he did see, flickering through his mind's eye as on a kaleidoscope, were extensions of his dreams: the scene in Perkin's Rents, the blood from his mother's head, the sheet of flame engulfing Mary, Truman Rutter with his lopsided nose and his battered tall hat.

It was midmorning and he had been walking for nearly six hours when he saw Susan again. She was dressed in black and was sitting in a chair at the side of the track. Her face was a skull, her eyes black holes. He gave a cry and fumbled for the big service

revolver he carried at his waist. He cocked it, held it with both hands and fired. She disappeared. One moment she was there, the next she was gone and he was looking at the whitened skull of an antelope blown into a bush by the wind.

He went on, holding the revolver in his hand. The sun was boiling hot but he felt cold; he was sweating but the sweat was clammy. Pains were shooting up and down his left arm and across his chest. His eyes were red-rimmed and half-closed against the harsh glare and the angry glitter of the mica chips. His mind seemed to close down for long periods and then would clear again and he would see the fresh hoof marks leading him on. He finished the water about two o'clock in the afternoon and flung the water bottle to one side.

He was moving through broken country now, of small *kopjes* and valleys and great boulders the size of houses which were burning hot to the touch. About midafternoon he saw her again. She was sitting on a rock, her old hands folded on her lap, the black dress covering everything but her face. He fired and this time a great black vulture rose from the rock and sailed away to the south on outstretched wings. An hour later he came to the valley.

He breasted a rise and there it was spread out before him, a small valley ringed by hills, one of which was faced by high red cliffs. In the center of the valley something glittered—like water—in the sunshine. Standing in the midst of this glittering patch was his horse. He gave a cry, threw away his revolver and stumbled down the slope. Some last vestige of coherent thought told him that this valley was familiar, that he had been here before. He did not know when, nor why.

For a moment he thought the water might be a mirage and disappear as he grew close. But then his horse bent to drink and when it raised its head, chewing on the bit, he saw droplets of water glisten as they fell.

The pan was little bigger than a tennis court, fringed by small reeds and mud. With the last of his energy he ran forwards and fell on his knees, sipping the water like an animal through parched lips. He drank until he could drink no more, then he lay down, allowing his uniform to become saturated. He turned towards his horse and as he did so his eye caught something glittering in the mud he had disturbed. He knelt and gave a gasp. Although his eyes were not focusing very well, he knew he was

looking at a diamond. He prized it from the mud and washed it. It was huge, about the size of a hen's egg, but flatter. He began to shake. His hands were trembling so much he could hardly hold it. He pushed himself to his feet and turned to tell someone, to share this moment of triumph. But there was no one except the horse.

"I told you!" he shouted, and the horse gave a nervous jump.

"I told you. . . . I told you. . . . I told you. . . ." The echoes were flung back from the cliffs above.

They merged with the crack of a rifle and this, too, echoed and boomed, and Jack fell, half in and half out of the water. He fell forwards onto his face, his arms stretched out, his fist closed on the diamond. That was how they found him.

Two members of a Boer commando had been hidden in the cliffs above, guarding the waterhole against poisoning. One was a youth of seventeen, the other a man of nearly fifty. It was the youth who had fired with his new Mauser rifle and now, as the two came down towards the waterhole there was a sick feeling in his stomach at the thought that he had killed his first human being. The older man, sensing what was going through his mind, said, "That shot may have saved a dozen lives. Anyway, you were only carrying out orders."

They reached Jack's body and turned him over. "I've never seen a uniform like this," the older man said. "Where did you aim?"

"The chest."

The older man examined Jack carefully. "There's not a mark on him. You missed him. But he's dead all right."

"I heard him shout and then I fired."

"I know, but you missed him." He saw the look of relief on the youth's face. "Maybe he died of fright. Maybe his time had come." He bent and wiped the mud off Jack's face and said, "You know, I could swear . . ."

"You've seen him before?"

"He reminds me of a boxer I saw years ago. A big Englishman. *Magtig,* he could fight! I heard he became a famous diamond man, rich and powerful. This couldn't be him."

"What are we going to do with him? We haven't a spade."

"We'll take him over by the cliffs and put stones on him."

So they pulled Jack's body to the foot of the cliffs and began to

pile stones over him so that the animals would not get at him. The youth said, "Look, there's something in his hand." He prized open Jack's fingers.

"What is it?"

"It looks like a glass button. You can see where the wire was. I'll keep it for luck."

When they had finished building Jack's tomb they took his horse and returned to the camp they had made for themselves at the top of the cliffs from which they kept watch on the waterhole.

15

On the day Jack Farson died of a heart attack at the waterhole, the same waterhole at which Barreto had died more than three hundred years before, the relief column finally broke through the Boer lines and raised the siege of Kimberley. The town found itself in something of a dilemma. It had to mourn and bury its dead—those killed in the blast at the New Chance Mine—but it also had to celebrate the arrival of the column. So it compromised. Hundreds went to the cemetery. Fourteen people had died in the mine and they were buried together in a mass grave. All except Lily. David had refused to give up her body. He had her buried separately. Some townsfolk objected and stayed away from her funeral, but others understood that she had been someone special, not only in the world of music, but to David Kade himself, and a good crowd was round the grave when the coffin was finally lowered. David watched, stony-faced and dry-eyed; his grief was too intense for tears.

At five o'clock, when the town had done its duty by the dead, it began to celebrate the living. Every shop with anything left to sell flung open its doors, so did the bars, so did the brothels. It was quite a night.

But while the town celebrated, David searched. He went back to the mine the following day, made his way through the galleries to the ruin of number one shaft and there began to look for the diamond that had been round Lily's neck when she died. It was now his only link with her, something that had been against her skin, something that would have taken on a fraction of her aura. That is what the diamond meant to him now; he no longer saw it as anything else. He searched all that day, until Dan Halkett came down and brought him back to the surface. Early the following morning he was back, sifting through the rubble, moving the stones that could be moved, searching, searching.

The town returned to normal, the war moved away and Kimberley became just one of several sieges that the world heard about, and was soon replaced in people's imaginations by the two more dramatic ones of Ladysmith and Mafeking. The Boers, as they had done so often before, had simply melted away from the Kimberley perimeter and lived to fight another day. British troops began to pour into the Cape Colony in ever greater numbers, and although the Boers fought for every hillock and every stream, for every waterhole and railway siding, for every mountain pass and every road junction, numbers were on the side of the British. Gradually the Boers were worn down. Their farms were burned, their women and children taken into camps, their stock animals driven off, their crops destroyed. Two years later Field Marshal Lord Roberts led his forces into the Boer capital of Pretoria, by which time old President Kruger was already an exile in Europe, and the war came to an end.

David hardly registered what was happening in the world outside. He had rigged himself up a "baby" and had returned to the work he had done when he had first come to Kimberley: he had closed off part of number one shaft and he dug the spoil and sieved it and went through it on a sorting table under a bright electric light. But he never found the "Southern Cross."

It became, like the "Great Mogul" and the "Mirror of Portugal" and the "Sancy," one of the "lost" diamonds which he had told Jack about so many years before. Its story had a tragic piquancy. When people came to write about it later they were touched by

the fact that it had only been worn once, by the famous soprano Montadini, that she had worn it at the last recital she would ever give and had died wearing it.

The real story of the ending of the "Southern Cross" is less romantic and would stain the pristine mythology. Like most stories about diamonds, it is one of venality. The blast which killed Lily left only the diamond on her body and it was wrenched from her neck by a black mine worker called Lukey. He was one of the team of nine "boys" who had led the survivors to safety. At this stage of the siege Lukey and his family were on the point of starvation. The diamond simply meant food. He did what thousands of mine workers had done before and would do after him: he tried to smuggle the stone from the mine. He took it from its setting and swallowed it, aiming to recover it the following day when it passed through his body.

But this was not a stone of one or two carats; it was a diamond which weighed three hundred and twelve. It was too big. It became lodged in the small intestine and within ten days had killed Lukey. His body was buried in the desert beyond the shanties in the black cemetery and there the diamond still lies.

David searched for it in the mine for nearly three months. People began to point at him in the streets and said that the death of Montadini had caused him to become unhinged. But slowly he came to terms with himself and before the end of the year he returned to London.

The diamond was not the only thing that was never found. No one ever discovered Jack Farson's body, and his bones remain under the rough cairn which the two Boers built for him. Of course people talked and wondered. He had been seen riding out of Kimberley in the blue-gray of early dawn and they said that he was going to fight the Boers all by himself. He had been drunk the night before, they said, and had been trying to organize the capture of Long Tom. So they assumed he had been killed by a Boer rifle and that his body was one of thousands rotting all over southern Africa, feeding the jackals and the hyenas and the white-backed vultures. People talked about him when they met and the older ones among them recalled the fight with the Batavian Giant and relived that afternoon when Jack had carried all their hopes and a lot of their money. But no one ever knew what really happened. The two Boers who buried him were killed

a fortnight later, and even Susan could only guess.

She never spoke about him, not even when David came out to the farm for the wedding of Michael and Jewel. She found it difficult to live with what she had done and she prayed for forgiveness down by Frans's grave.

In 1905 Marie Farson died of an overdose of gin and laudanum. She had sold the house in Park Lane and the estate in Sussex and there had been just enough left over after paying Jack's debts, and those incurred on his behalf by Leask, to buy a small house in Maida Vale. She lived there on an allowance given to her by David and tried to retain her grip, however slender, on the life and the people she had known. When she had owned a house in Park Lane and had a husband who was a director of the New Chance Mining Company, aristocrats down on their luck had been glad to feed at her table, but a Marie Farson reduced in circumstances and living in a small house in an unfashionable part of town, and with no influence at all, turned out to be an unattractive proposition. She grew more and more lonely. Sometimes Hilda drove down to see her in her new Daimler-Benz motor, but this made things worse, for Marie was reminded of how much she had lost.

She began to drink, and drinking gave her pains in her stomach, for which she took laudanum. Her mind became hazy. She no longer ate properly. She no longer knew nor cared when weeks began or ended, no longer saw the change of seasons. One November morning, with a yellow pea-souper enveloping London, she could not face another single day of life, and made an end of it.

Hilda Kade outlived her by nearly five years. She had inherited her mother's constitution and she put on weight easily. By the time she was in her early fifties she resembled her mother down to the last quiver of the last chin. This inherited tendency to put on weight masked, for a time, the symptoms of the disease which killed her. She died in 1909 of a dropsical condition brought on by inflammation of the kidneys. In the end, her legs were so swollen by fluid that she could not walk.

The following year the British Government passed the Statute of Westminster in London which brought about the Union of

476

South Africa. The four provinces—Cape Province, Natal, the Orange Free State and the Transvaal—were unified under a central government and became part of the British Commonwealth.

On the death of his wife, David Kade sold the big house overlooking West Heath, bought a ticket on the Orient liner *Hong Kong* and spent the following two years traveling around the world. His two daughters were married and he was a grandfather several times. They no longer needed him. No one needed him.

There was nothing to keep him in England and he had no wish to see Kimberley again, although he dearly wished to see Michael and Jewel and his grandson, John. But the memories there were too painful. He had even withdrawn from New Chance. His problem was that he had nothing to do. He felt, on this journey around the world, like some planet lost in interstellar space, circling the universe forever.

Then one morning he woke up in a hotel bedroom in São Paulo, Brazil, and for a few dreadful seconds he did not know where he was or how he had got there; it was almost as though he did not know his own name. He held out his hands and looked at them and was reassured. They were his hands, David Kade's hands. He looked at himself in the ornate mirror. Yes, the image was one he knew of as David Kade né Kadeshinsky of Kiev, Kimberley, London and . . . where? Was there anywhere he could say he truly belonged? What if he died here in this hotel? Would anyone know who he was? Would anyone care? How would Michael even know? And Jewel? And Susan? Suddenly he saw himself afresh: the image in the mirror was not the David Kadeshinsky who had fled from Russia, nor the David Kade who had dug in the dirt and built up a mining empire; it was some different man who had, in the last years, dried up, grown cold, withdrawn. The result was that he was alone, truly and dreadfully alone. He thought of Jack and Lily, the Levinsons, Lothar, Peter Arendt; he thought of his grandmother and grandfather in Kiev; the fire in the ice. He even thought of his tutor, Mr. Hemlow. They had passed through his life and were gone and now he was in a vacuum. He had lost all contact with people; it was as though his heart had turned to stone.

And he realized something else: he had been running away from his memories, running away from the past. The people who mattered to him were all together, there for the taking, offering

him the love and warmth he needed, if only he could respond.

There had to be more: just to bask like some old man in the sunshine of his family was not enough for a man who had done what he had. But he had lost whatever interest he had once had in money and power. His thoughts turned back to Africa, and he realized that, apart from his family, there *was* something else waiting for him that was both creative and important: the completion of Father John's narrative. It was a part of history, and he knew it would make an exciting addition to man's knowledge. In that instant, he made his decision. He would go back. He still owned a wine farm at the Cape. He would work on the translation; he would make wine; he would cultivate his own backyard; and he would be near enough to see Michael and Jewel occasionally.

Less than two months later he was walking down the gangway of the ship *Inverary Castle*. He wore a neat gray suit and a white panama hat on his head, just as he had when he had first arrived more than forty years before. He stood on the quayside for a few moments sniffing the salty, fish-tainted air, and felt a lift in his spirits he had not experienced since Lily's death.

Susan Delport died in her eighty-first year, three months before her great-grandson, John, was born. She died peacefully, sitting on one of the old *riempie* stools under the grapevine which Frans had planted so many years before. Up to the end she was lucid and in command of her faculties. There had been no more "lost" days.

She lived alone at Portuguese Place for the last five years of her life. Michael and Jewel had built their own house about a mile farther downstream. It was of brick, plastered and painted white, with a good corrugated-iron roof and Dutch gables, so fashionable in the Cape, and big shutters to keep out the desert heat, and wooden floors.

They had asked Susan to come with them, for the old house, which had lasted so well, was beginning to show signs of age. Year after year of storms and baking heat had damaged the walls; worms, beetles and termites had got into the wood. But Susan refused to move. This had been the first home of her own she had ever had and, as she said to them, it would last her out. But they saw each other every day and it could be said that Susan had achieved what she had set out to achieve, the continuance of

Portuguese Place, with herself as an integral part of it. And she was busy up to the last. Although her hearing was fading, her eyes were still good and it had been one of her great pleasures to be of use to Jewel, making the baby's clothes.

They buried her near the river, close to the spot where they thought Frans was buried, and they put up a small, hand-cut granite stone with the two names on it. The house, now that it was empty, deteriorated more rapidly. It was no longer strong enough to be repaired, so it was left to die quietly by itself.

As the years passed, more and more of it collapsed. Cattle sometimes rubbed themselves against its walls, breaking away bricks and smashing joists, each lesion weakening the structure still further.

In February, 1919, there was a cloudburst directly over the farm which swept away the old servants' quarters and most of the remainder of the main house.

Four years later thorn bushes had grown up through the powdery floorboards and a wild fig tree sprouted where once Frans Delport had had his comfortable chair. The wall on which the grapevine was pinned collapsed and the vine itself grew over the ruins like a creeper. Its roots had gone down deep and by chance were near a small spring of underground water. The vine survived and Michael and Jewel made expeditions to pick the grapes when John was a little boy.

Soon the bushes grew so profusely they obliterated all signs that a house had once been there. And had Father John of the Rosary and Captain Manuel da Sa and Bartolomeu Barreto stood in the shade of the trees by the Breakfast Pool and looked up the gentle slope of the hill, they would have seen little change: they might have noted the headstone and the vine, but for the rest the land was much the same as it had been when they had passed that way more than three centuries before.